Matters of Life & Death

A NOVEL

BECKY DOUGHTY

BraveHearts
Press

Matters of Life and Death: A Novel

Copyright 2021 Becky Doughty

Published by BraveHearts Press

All Scripture quotations, unless otherwise indicated, are taken from the New American Standard Bible, Copyright 1960, 1962, 1963, 1968, 1971, 1972, 1973, 1975, 1977, 1995 by The Lockman Foundation. Used by permission. (www.Lockman.org)

Scripture taken from *The Message*. Copyright 1993, 1994, 1995, 1996, 2000, 2001, 2002. Used by permission of NavPress Publishing Group.

Author Info: BeckyDoughty.com

ISBN: 9781953347480

Life ~ Death

It's the dash in the middle that counts.

Ranae

"Our death question of the day comes from listener ConstanceClearwaterRevival69." Dani pauses and narrows her eyes at me. *Is this you?* she mouths.

I shake my head. Sure, we occasionally make up our own questions when listener pickings are slim or when there's a hot topic one of us wants to rant about. This one, however, is totally legitimate, one I pulled from last week's fan mail.

Although I admit that I chose it solely on the merit of the username.

I lean into my microphone. "Well, hey there, Constance. You sound like a girl after my own classic rock heart."

Dani shakes her head frantically and draws a forefinger across her neck in the universal sign to cut, mute, full stop. I pretend I don't understand and keep going. She doesn't like me rabbit-trailing—it usually means more post-production editing—but I'll keep it short. I like the question, and this little morsel of music trivia I'm about to throw out there is both relevant and relatable.

Trust me, I try to communicate to her with only my bright smile. I know she can practically read my mind. *This is how we endear ourselves to our listeners.*

Dani's frown and crossed arms communicate to me that she is washing her hands of me, cutting me loose. *Don't say I didn't warn you.* Her British accent is far more pronounced when I hear her voice in my head.

I continue, undeterred by her disapproval. "Creedence Clearwater Revival's epic song 'Bad Moon Rising' released in 1969, right, Constance?"

Dani sends me a slow blink, the kind that indicates a bone deep desire to hit the backspace button for me. Then she clears her throat. "Actually, ConstanceClearwaterRevival69 is the *nom de guerre* of one Jeff H."

Oh.

Cut. Mute. Full stop. Backspace.

I grimace sheepishly, silently admitting my *faux pas* with a shrug. We'll have to edit all that out. Thank goodness we aren't doing this live.

Even when we make mistakes, we rarely hit the pause button during recording. We cut our teeth on live radio where stopping and starting was not an option, and we find that doing so now, even though our podcast is pre-recorded, interrupts our flow and makes for a disjointed show. Besides, our audience appreciates our bloopers and *faux pas*—admittedly, mostly mine—so after we edit the show down to our usual twenty-five-ish minutes, we tack a blooper reel on the end of each episode. It's a fun way to encourage listeners to stick around.

A midwife and a mortician walk into a bar…

That's been our tag line from the beginning. Our slightly irreverent human-interest blog started as a joke. Not a funny, ha-ha joke. More like one of those tongue-in-cheek, ironic kind that evokes eye rolls and reluctant smirks. But apparently, folks took us far more seriously than we took ourselves, and we got picked up for a column by our local newspaper. It then morphed into a two-year run on a local radio spot before WYNX 83.6 FM went bankrupt. Not because of us, mind you. In fact, our growing number of listeners inspired us to scoot our butts—actually, it was our faces, thank goodness—over to our own YouTube channel. But after only a few months, we accepted the inarguable fact that we were generally better behind a microphone than in front of a camera. So once again, we explored our options and found a home in the world of podcasts. With the support of our followers, and Dani's and my mutual passion for the topics we covered, we jumped in with both feet.

Five years later, our *Matters of Life and Death* podcast is still going strong.

Dani's expression is just a little smug, sure, but she smiles at me in that special way she reserves for people she loves despite themselves, and therefore is forced to tolerate. I don't mind. She's had to endure a lot of my open-mouth-insert-foot moments over the years. "Jeff H. would like to know if anyone has ever requested to be buried on a full moon at Fair Havens, and if so, how do you keep the body fresh if the person dies at the wrong time of the moon's cycle?" She settles back in her chair, then picks up her mug and takes a sip. "Gack," she mutters, her face contorting in distaste.

I chug a swig from my own cup, relishing the kick of the smoky brew. I like it muddy, and since we record *Matters of Life and Death* in the tiny room that was once my grandfather's home office-turned-recording booth, I make the java.

Dani makes faces almost every time she drinks my coffee.

Every once in a while, she makes muffins or cookies, too.

"Hey, Jeff. Forgive me for calling you Constance." I don't meet Dani's eyes lest I get a case of the giggles. "Yes, Fair Havens has received a few requests for full moon and some midnight funerals over the years. However, we don't offer burial services after dark. Our cemetery is a conservation green burial ground, and we take great care to protect both our visiting wildlife—humans—as well as our residential wildlife, the flora and fauna, and the land that sustains us all. We are only open to the public from dawn to dusk."

"What about a full moon service in the middle of the day?" Dani asks, returning her mug to its coaster. She pushes it away from her as though even the smell of it is too vile for her refined senses. "The full moon phase isn't restricted to nights, right?"

As a midwife, she knows all about full moons. Call it science, magic, or the miracle of creation, but without fail, her busiest time of the month is directly linked to the lunar calendar.

"Absolutely," I say. "But I'll be the first to admit that a full moon service during daylight hours kind of lose its flair."

"Right. I can imagine." Dani has already put in her time answering the birth question of the day. It's one that pops up pretty regularly: what do people do with the placenta after a home birth? She always seems to have a new suggestion to offer, though. Today, she talked about placentophagy, which is the practice of ingesting—Dani's nice way of saying *eating*—the placenta. Although she doesn't recommend it herself, she offered some well-researched pros and cons of doing so and discussed the different ways people prepare the organ for consumption.

As unsettling as the topic of eating placentas might be to some, it certainly doesn't warrant the way she slumps uncharacteristically in her chair. Her long hair is pulled up into a messy bun that has been knocked askew by her headphones, and although she wears her standard "natural look" makeup, her usual glow is noticeably dim. She looks wrung out. She must have had a long night with a patient. I'll have to ask her about it when we're finished recording.

I gather my thoughts and continue, but now that I've noticed the state Dani's in, I'm having a hard time staying focused. I glance down at my notes. "Um, so the second part of your question, Jeff, about preserving a body, is a little more subjective. In most circumstances, with appropriate after-death care, of course, there are very few reasons that a body must be buried immediately. It's generally not a problem to wait a few days to hold services." Over the years, I've learned to keep my voice carefully modulated when discussing death and the care of a corpse. I love what I do, and in the early days, I often got a little too amped up while informing folks about their options—and their rights—regarding death and the deceased. I'm pretty sure I scared several potential clients away with my exuberance. In this country, it's typically frowned upon to gush over anything to do with corpses, especially when said corpses are loved by the people you're conversing with.

"A few days, sure," Dani prompts from her semi-reclined slouch. Yep. Exhausted. She doesn't even bother to sit forward, just raises her voice so that her microphone picks up her question. "But if a person dies a few weeks or more before a burial service can be performed, then what happens?"

"Of course, embalming is always an option for long-term preservation," I explain. "But it's not something we offer at Fair Havens. If that's the route you choose to go, I would direct you to a funeral home like Niemeyer Mortuary in Evansville, Indiana, where you and your loved ones will be cared for with the utmost dignity and respect." I plug my father's business every chance I get. We may do things differently, but we totally support each other.

"Our services at Fair Havens, however, are strictly natural or green. Because embalming is not a natural process, we don't do it, nor do we bury embalmed bodies or even cremated remains of embalmed bodies here." I choose my next words carefully. "We do, however, have a refrigeration unit here. It's what we use for preservation if a service needs to be delayed. Within reason, of course," I add. "We simply aren't equipped for long-term storage."

"What's the longest period of time you've, um, kept... uh, *stored* someone?"

I shoot Dani a a quizzical look at her clumsy attempt to ask what should be a straightforward question. One of the goals of our podcast is to normalize the discussion of birth and death, and to host a forum where we can talk openly with our listeners about doing more of both in the comfort of home. Granted, in her line of work, death is not a welcome presence, and when it comes up with her patients, the conversation is usually in hushed, hesitant voices on their part and careful phrasing on hers. So I understand her sensitivity around the topic.

"If a body is fully intact, several weeks is doable. I've heard of some places allowing up to five or even six weeks, although that's not something I would be comfortable offering. The longest we've had a body in refrigeration here at Fair Havens is just over three weeks. That included a few days of significant reconstruction we performed here on site so that the parents of the deceased could participate in a short visitation. We then placed the body in our refrigeration unit to wait until the spouse was able to be here for the funeral."

Dani sends me a silent nod of encouragement. I clear my throat and swallow the lump of emotion the memory of that day stirs up in me. Then I continue in what my daughter calls my 'teacher voice.'

"Decomposition can be significantly slowed down with refrigeration, but it doesn't stop it. After a couple of weeks, a body does begin to deteriorate." I don't mince words about death. But then, without it, I wouldn't have a job. At least not this job. "So when we put a body into refrigeration, it's already shrouded and ready to be buried. Again, it's not something we do very often, nor is it something we recommend. Fair Havens is all about allowing the natural order of things to take place by burying a body, not preserving it in an in-between place."

"An in-between place. That's a good way to look at it." Dani straightens and glances at the old-fashioned clock on the wall. "You don't hold services after dark, Ranae, but you do host a special nighttime event at Fair Havens. We have a minute or two left. Why don't you tell our listeners about your bonfire nights."

My best friend is also my biggest fan, just as I am hers. Dani brainstormed the bonfire nights idea with me, and she loves the event almost as much as I do. I salute her with my mug, the one my daughter, Ruby, gave me last Christmas. It says *Folks are just dying to meet me...* in ghoulish lettering.

"Sure. On the third Friday of every month, we host what we have dubbed our "Live and Let Die Bonfire Night" at Fair Havens. It's primarily geared toward folks who have loved ones buried in our cemetery, but it's also a bit like an open house. It's a great opportunity to come and remember and grieve and share and commiserate, and of course, celebrate. But it's also a great time to ask questions about us and the services we offer."

"More often than not," Dani interjects in her refined—albeit rather Americanized—British accent. "The family and friends who attend are always ready and willing to answer questions and share their personal experiences."

A lump forms in my throat as it always does when I talk about the event. "Sometimes my work world can be pretty heavy," I readily acknowledge. "Hearing folks share about the positive impact we've had on their lives is truly a boon to my soul."

Dani leans closer to her microphone. "Those nights are pretty special, listeners. Like most people, I'm admittedly not good with death. In fact, in my work world, I do everything I can to prevent it. But Ranae's bonfire nights, held out under the stars at the edge of the woods, help me put death in its rightful place, which is right here in the middle of all this life around us." She holds my gaze across the desk. "I'm not the only one moved by your Live and Let Die Bonfire Nights, my friend. So many people have told me they feel the same way."

And now there are tears in her eyes. Dani isn't a tears-in-her-eyes kind of girl. I frown at her, but she glances away.

"Thank you, Dani," I say, more than a little embarrassed over the effusive praise. I know she thinks the bonfire nights are one of my better ideas, but she rarely gets this demonstrative toward me, at least not publicly. Sure, at the moment, we are closed up in our little padded booth, but if even half our subscribers listen to this episode, that makes her gushing pretty public.

She presses a hand over her heart and says, "It's always a wonderful and healing event. Everyone leaves feeling lighter. Lifted up, somehow."

That stupid lump still there, I swallow hard and speak around it. "So if you're in our neck of the woods on the third Friday of the month, listeners, come visit Fair Havens after dusk. Everything is well-lit, and there's plenty of parking. For safety reasons, the trails are closed, but the chapel is open if you want to spend time in there. We serve coffee, tea, and lemonade—"

"And sometimes hot chocolate," Dani chimes in with a sing-song lilt.

"Yes, indeed. During the colder months, absolutely. No alcohol, please, but feel free to bring your own food. Your leashed pet is also welcome. All we ask is that you clean up after yourselves."

"It'll change your life," Dani states, then with a soft chuckle, adds, "It may change your death, too."

"Touché!" I toast her with my mug again, then check the clock. "And I think that's about all the time we have." It isn't a smooth segue by any means, but I want to get off the air so I can find out what's going on with Dani. While she queues up the end-of-the-show bumper music, I give a shout-out to our sponsors, thank listeners for their positive reviews and menagerie of questions, ask folks to share

Matters of Life and Death with their friends and loved ones, and invite everyone back for another episode next week.

"And that's a wrap," Dani declares, lifting a finger and swirling it in the air above her head.

I push my chair back and roll my shoulders to loosen up. I love our show, but I'm always tense by the end of our sessions. It doesn't help that we record in such close quarters. I'm not claustrophobic, but I've never been great with sitting still for long periods of time, especially indoors.

I crack open the door a few inches to get the air in the tiny room moving. A whiff of something delicious drifts in, but whatever Gran is cooking up out in the kitchen will have to wait. "So tell me what's going on with you," I say, pulling one arm across my body and holding the stretch as I eye my friend.

Dani remains slouched in her chair, her head resting against the high seat back as she watches me unwind. She opens her mouth, then closes it and swallows, shaking her head.

Forgetting all about my trivial discomfort, I drop to my knees in front of her chair, my heart racing. "What is it? What's wrong?"

Her unshed tears reflect the rainbow hues of the image on the computer monitor. It's a picture of Dani and me taken at Ruby's sixteenth birthday party a little over a year ago, standing beneath my favorite Redbud tree in the back yard. Festooned with streamers, paper lanterns, and twinkle lights, the tree is bursting with blooms in the shot, making it look especially festive and fanciful.

Ruby's parties are always a big hit with her peers. A birthday bash next door to a cemetery? They come in hordes.

"I think—" Dani swallows audibly, takes a deep breath, and starts again.

I grab her hands and hold them tight.

"I think Adam is going to leave." She blinks, and then, as though I need clarification, she adds, "Me. Leave me."

Before I can respond, I hear, "Mom? Are you here?"

It's Ruby, and the distress in her voice has both of us turning toward the sound.

Our Irish Wolfhound, Blimey, whimpers for my daughter's attention, but she dismisses him with a firm, "I love you, Blimers, but I don't want to play right now." Then louder, she calls, "Mom?"

Dani

"WE'RE NOT FINISHED." RANAE squeezes my hands as she rises from her crouched position in front of me. "You sit tight, and I'll go find out why Ruby is home from school already."

I nod and spin my chair so I'm facing away from the door, just in case the teenager is close enough to see my expression. If I look even half as off-balance as I feel, the intuitive girl will pick up on it.

I am, in fact, surprised Ranae didn't notice my dark mood sooner. Granted, I didn't give her much of an opportunity, purposefully rushing in at the last moment before we were scheduled to record. I'm still not sure I'm ready to talk about Adam, not even with my best friend.

But when I opened my mouth to insist that I was only tired, the words lodged somewhere in my esophagus, and what came out instead was the truth.

Something about Ranae, her sincerity, her tender heart, makes it difficult for me to withhold information from her. Her mother learned long ago not to include me in on any kind of surprise gift or party plans because I'm helpless to resist when Ranae looks at me with those enormous, puppy-dog eyes.

If there is anyone I can trust with my heart, however, it's Ranae Niemeyer.

I am the only child of two obstetrics and gynecology practitioners who adopted me as a newborn after more than a decade of trying unsuccessfully to conceive on their own. My parents, Michael and Francis Nelson, met through Doctors Without Borders in Beira, Mozambique. They fell in love as they worked together to provide medical care to pregnant women, sex workers, and sexually violated victims, while waging an even deadlier war against the dual epidemic of HIV and tuberculosis. When their mission ended, my mother returned to work at Queen Charlotte's and Chelsea Hospital in London, my father to St. Vincent Hospital in southern Indiana. Six months later, Francis accepted Michael's proposal. They were married in a quiet courthouse ceremony in Evansville, just in time to head back on another mission to Mozambique as newlyweds.

They both insist that it was the honeymoon of their dreams.

My parents were almost forty when we became a family, and shortly after, my mother was offered a highly coveted teaching position back at Queen Charlotte's and Chelsea in London. My father landed a job at St. Mary's Hospital in Paddington, so we moved to a flat in Kensington near Holland Park for the first several years of my life.

Fetal Dopplers, gestational diabetes, Apgar scores, and postpartum depression were common topics discussed in our home, and when I asked my curious questions, my mother and father answered in simple, straightforward explanations, never presuming I was too young to learn about the miracle of birth. I used the medical terms for belly buttons and girl parts long before I could pronounce the words correctly. My only cousin on my mother's side, Auggie, used to goad me into saying "bagina" every chance he got, then he'd laugh uproariously while I demanded he explain why he thought female reproductive organs were so funny. When I was five, however, Aunt Adele happened to overhear him teasing me, and to my utter delight, Auggie had to eat soap as a consequence. Of course, when I learned that I'd been saying it wrong, I forgave my cousin for laughing at me, agreeing that it did make me sound rather silly.

Cousin Auggie has redeemed himself by growing up to be quite respectable. He's a happily married man with two daughters of his own, and I know he'd do serious damage to any boy who pulled such shenanigans on his girls.

As a child, I believed my parents had the best job in the history of jobs. They helped bring new life into the world. They were the first to see and be seen by each baby expelled from the womb, the first hands to touch an infant's skin, the first set of eyes to evaluate the condition of a newborn. They determined in an instant if a babe needed immediate medical attention, or if he or she could be handed to an awestruck father or laid against a tearful mummy's breast. They had the task—nay, the privilege—of severing the umbilical cord, that last physical tether between mother and child, in a final and permanent separation of identities.

From as early as I could remember, I wanted to be just like them, to make a living delivering babies.

Not everyone applauded my devotion to—or obsession with, depending on who you asked—the world of birth and babies back then. I was reprimanded repeatedly for discussing things not appropriate for classroom conversation.

It wasn't my peers' fault that my interests were so different from theirs, but I did often wonder if there was something wrong with me. I found it difficult to relate to children who couldn't resolve simple problems in a sensible, objective manner. If I skinned my knee, I washed it with warm water, slathered it with antiseptic cream, and covered it with a plaster. If my loose tooth was ready to come out, I counted to three, and pulled hard as I breathed out. It usually bled fiercely, certainly, but then I'd shove a piece of gauze in the gap until it stopped.

And if a boy picked on me, I ignored him until he assaulted me physically. When Ernest Hampton-Rawlings back at my posh London school pushed me off the swing and made me bite my tongue so hard it bled, I got up, wiped the dribble from my chin and the sand from my knees, and kicked him soundly in the groin. After which, I calmly told the teacher what had happened, thereby both emasculating the bully and eliminating the threat of being tattled on. Of course, I was disciplined and sent home from school the one time I did so, but my father put his arm around my shoulders that night and told me he was proud of me for sticking up for myself.

"That horrible boy got what he deserved," my mother said in her lyrical voice.

It remains one of my fondest childhood memories.

It was after the trouble with Ernest Hampton-Rawlings that I met someone who looked like me, who spoke like me, who understood me. We shared a name, too: Danielle. I went by Dani, she was Elle.

Elle wasn't imaginary back then.

Being adopted was something that made me feel unique, special, even if no one else knew I was. I don't remember ever *not* knowing that I'd been born to a woman who couldn't or wouldn't take care of me. Nor do I remember ever feeling less fortunate, or less loved because of it.

"You were the baby meant for us. It didn't matter what birth canal you came through to get to us, Danielle," my father used to tell me. "The moment we held your slippery little body in our hands, you were ours." He and Mum got to deliver me themselves.

"You were always ours," my mother would echo. "Before you were even born, you were meant to be ours."

Cool, calm, collected, and a little reserved, that's what my parents have always been. Sure, they often responded with clinical analysis and intellectual reasoning to times when other parents might offer hugs and sympathetic noises, but I never doubted their love for me.

I was often lonely, though, and it wasn't until Elle and I found each other that I discovered the difference between being lonely and being alone. I didn't mind being alone as long as Elle was alone with me.

By the time we moved back to America, shortly after I turned nine, I was a bit of a solitary bird. Because of Elle, I didn't really mind the ostracizing that happened as a byproduct of my lack of age-appropriate social skills. In fact, it bothered me far more when my new Evansville schoolmates accused me of faking my somewhat Americanized British accent. Most of them believed I was aloof and stuck up, but that was far from the truth. I felt like I walked on thin ice every time I stepped foot on the school campus.

Elle tried to soothe my ruffled feathers, told me I sounded lovely when I spoke, and reminded me that I was the best friend she'd ever had. For the first time, I found that I didn't believe her, and when I stopped believing her, I stopped believing *in* her. One morning I woke up to find her gone, my hand resting on the empty spot on my pillow where she'd been when I'd drifted off to sleep the night before.

I was left to face the world alone... and lonely once more.

How I longed for a connection with someone *real* besides my parents, anyone with whom I could be myself around. Someone who thought that the way I viewed the world we inhabited was important. But I was afraid to speak my mind, worried I'd inadvertently say something that would make others uncomfortable. So, like a giant sponge, I absorbed information voraciously, learning not to give in to my predisposed compulsion to share everything I knew with those around me. By the time I started high school, I was well-practiced at behaving just like my parents. Cool as a cucumber, totally unfazed by the roller coaster of hormone-driven teenage transformation.

At least on the outside.

I learned who Ranae Niemeyer was our first year of high school. *Everyone* knew who she was, or at least who her family was. They owned a multi-generational family funeral home in town, Niemeyer Mortuary, a fact that either fascinated people or gave them the willies.

Ranae was as much my opposite in personality as she was in appearance. She was friends with the whole school, or at least it seemed so to me. She was always surrounded by people, swept up in the middle of things, her laughter ringing out bright and lively, her eyes dancing with a sparkle that drove people mad to know what was going on inside her head. Queen of the Populars, I labeled her, writing her off my short list of important people.

But one lunch period, while watching an especially boisterous group she was a part of, I saw something that made me sit up straight. Ranae did none of the things so many of her peers did to try to fit in. She didn't throw herself at boys. She didn't cling to other girls. She didn't behave differently with different people. She was just *being*. It was everyone else who reached for her. Others intentionally engaged her. They pulled her in, as though they couldn't help themselves. She was like a magnetic force field, and guys, girls, even teachers leaned into the smiling, effervescent Ranae Niemeyer. She wore her uniqueness like a ray of golden sunshine, and everyone around her seemed desperate to bask in the genuine warmth she exuded without even trying.

She had somehow sorted out how to be in with the in-crowd without having to actually *be* the in-crowd. I couldn't decide if I loved her or loathed her.

I still remember the way my stomach clenched at how *easy* it was for her.

Then in tenth grade biology, our alphabetical seat assignments had us sharing a lab table, and my life changed irrevocably. By the end of the first week of class, it was as though someone had opened the floodgates between us. I was fascinated by her stories of growing up in a home where death and grief were discussed as commonly as labor and delivery were in mine. And to my delight, she was just as intrigued by my own upbringing. I felt like I'd stored up more than a decade of conversation that was suddenly clamoring to be set free, and when I apologized one day for talking too much, she grabbed my shoulders and shook me, declaring, "What are you talking about? I'm blown away by the things you say, by the way you talk about birth and babies and our crazy reproductive systems, the way you examine and analyze everything about... well, about *life*."

"And I love the way you talk about corpses and cremation," I told her, the last vestiges of my fear of rejection flying out the window. "About *death*."

"Seriously? I mean, because people usually think I'm way too casual about death, you know? With you, though, I feel like I can just be me without worrying you're going to think I'm some kind of freaky morgue girl." She had embraced me then, and whispered creepily in my ear, "I see dead people, and I like it."

"You are kind of a freaky morgue girl, you know," I teased her, awkwardly squeezing her back.

It was the first time I'd ever been hugged by a friend.

I was fifteen.

I experienced a lot of firsts once Ranae entered my life.

Ranae had a voluptuous figure that would have made Marilyn Monroe jealous, and big green eyes that contrasted with her dark, chin-length curls. I was nearly half a foot taller than she, all knobby arms and legs, and catastrophically flat-chested for far too many of my teenage years. I finally grew into a padded B-cup bra the summer before our senior year. I once drew a picture of a stick insect and a ladybug, labeled it *Friendship*, and hung it on my bathroom mirror. I didn't think of myself as pretty or ugly, just average, with naturally straight teeth, light gray eyes, and a dimple on my left cheek that showed when I smiled. My ash-blond hair, however, was my secret pride and joy. It fell sleek and long down my back, and Ranae complimented me on it the first day we sat together. She said I reminded her of Gwyneth Paltrow, but with better hair.

One thing we did have in common: we were both adopted. She, too, had been birthed by a woman who had opted out of being her mother. That's where the similarities ended, though.

I would never have guessed that Ranae was adopted. Her two older brothers had the same bold coloring and ready smiles as she did, and by every appearance, they looked genetically matched.

"I know," she said when I told her she looked so much like the rest of her family. "No one ever believes me," she continued. "My mom says that people who live together sometimes start to look like each other, so maybe that's why."

I didn't look anything like my parents, so I wasn't convinced of that explanation. I behaved like them, to be certain, but my gangly gerenuk stature and flaxen coloring made it clear I had different origins than those of my mother or father. They were both of average height, brown-haired, brown-eyed, clean-cut doctors who were more comfortable in hospital scrubs and Dansko clogs than pedestrian clothes, while I leaned toward long skirts and blousy peasant tops that camouflaged my skinny limbs and bony joints.

When I started spending time with Ranae and her family, however, I began to wonder if she wasn't right, if it was possible that somehow, the five of them had melded together, their DNA mingling and redistributing, until the whole family had become a cohesive, undivided unit. In her home, creativity and individuality were celebrated and encouraged, even expected. Every single one of them had large personalities that didn't feel bloated or puffed up, but rather genuine. Her mum, Noralee Niemeyer, was a makeup artist who liked red lipstick and big hair, high heels and the latest fashions. She was Jamie Lee Curtis right out of that *My Girl* movie, and I was her biggest fan back then.

"Noralee," Carl Niemeyer, Ranae's father liked to say. "I thank the good Lord every day that he gave me such a drop-dead gorgeous wife." He'd always emphasize the 'drop dead' as if none of us would catch the joke. "You keep our little family business flourishing." He'd laugh heartily at his own terrible humor—he had the biggest laugh I'd ever heard on a man, quite the opposite of what one might expect from a funeral director. Then he'd grab his wife around the waist and pull her up against him, kissing her thoroughly, right in front of all of us. Finally, Noralee would push him away, more than a little breathless, and scold him for messing up her lipstick. The boys would hoot suggestively, and Ranae would pretend to cover her eyes in embarrassment, before Carl and Noralee turned their attention to their children, pouring out their exuberant love on each of them in turn.

If I was there, I inevitably got swept up in their embraces, as well.

I still do. They are my extended family in all the ways that matter.

Don't misunderstand me. My parents love each other, and they truly adore me. I can't imagine being raised by anyone else but them. However, I've never seen them banter and play together or lavish uncensored affection on each other the way the Niemeyers do. And although I've never wished the two of them to be any different than they are, I'm grateful for Ranae's family who have opened their hearts to me, and in so doing, have opened my eyes to a whole new way of living and loving.

I press my cool hands to my cheeks, frowning at the slight tremble in my fingertips. I can't seem to still them, no matter how hard I try.

Ranae has left the studio door slightly ajar, and I can hear conversation coming from the kitchen. She's speaking in hushed tones to Gran, and I hold my breath to listen, trying to make out the words. I can't tell if something is wrong or not, then Gran bursts out in her rusty cackle, and Ranae futilely attempts to shush her. Before I can give in to my curiosity and go find out what's happening, I hear Ranae's footsteps coming down the hall.

"Dani?" She pokes her head in the tiny room, her face an odd mix of emotions. "Hey, I brought you some of Gran's lemonade," she says, handing me a pale blue Mason jar filled with the delicious, chilled drink. "So, apparently evil Aunt Flo dropped by a little early this month and paid Ruby a surprise visit during American Literature today. Now my poor baby says she's too embarrassed to ever show her face at school again."

"Oh no." We might talk openly about reproductive cycles and the rate of decomposition on our podcast, but I'm not so stuffy that I poo-poo conversational euphemisms, especially when engaging with Ruby. And I could sympathize about Aunt Flo's unwelcome visits. My own menses started when I was only twelve, and although I'd been mentally prepared to celebrate the momentous occasion, its ferocity still took me by surprise. Shockingly heavy and unpredictable for the first few years, I'd often been caught by surprise. Only once, however, had I endured the utter mortification of realizing I'd walked around campus with a telltale spot on my skirt. No one ever made mention of it, though; they were either too disgusted by it, or they simply hadn't cared enough about my existence to notice.

That won't be the case with Ruby. Like her mother before her, the girl has a million friends.

"Honestly, I couldn't see anything on her pants," Ranae whispers, allaying my concern for my favorite teenager. "But she said when she got up to excuse herself to the restroom, she almost fainted in class, and she insists everyone in the hall was staring at her by the time she got to the bathroom." She takes a deep breath, then offers a wry smile. "Poor thing. She has the worst periods. Can you give me a few more minutes? I don't want to leave her alone right now, but you and I need to continue this conversation, too." She waves a finger back and forth between us. Lowering her voice, she adds, "Besides, if I don't get back out there to run interference, things could get weird. Gran is on her phone Googling period euphemisms right now—"

"Hence the cackle?" I ask, grinning.

"Hence the cackle," Ranae confirms, then rolls her eyes as another hoot sounds from the kitchen.

"Miss Scarlet is visiting the plantation. Oh, Ranae, that's clever, isn't it?" Gran's gravelly voice calls out. "Oh! This one is my favorite! Paging Edward Cullen! Paging Edward Cullen!" She moves to stand in our line of vision at the other end of the hall. "That's the cute vampire boy from those movies we love."

Ranae snorts. "*You* love, Gran. Those movies *you* love." Under her breath she mutters, "I swear she binge-watches the series at least once a month. Opa would turn over in his grave if he knew."

"I'm old, girls. Not deaf," Gran shoots back, pointing a bony finger at us. "Opa liked watching anything Audrey Hepburn was in. I like watching anything Edward Cullen is in, and since he's only in five movies, my options are limited."

"Not true. He's in a ton of other movies," Ranae begins, but I can tell by the tone of her voice that it's a conversation they've already had. "And his name is not Edward Cullen. It's—"

"Na na na!" Gran covers her ears and shakes her head. "I don't care about the actor. I just care about Edward Cullen."

"Go, Team Edward." I laugh, then sidle around Ranae and down the hall to greet my favorite octogenarian. "Hello, Gran," I say as I approach her. She wasn't around when I arrived earlier.

She opens her arms and I step into her hearty embrace. There is nothing like a Gran hug on a rough morning, and I wonder if Ruby has gotten one yet.

"You look a little peckish, Dani-girl," Gran says as she steps back. Then she snickers and squints at her phone screen. "Are you... um... oh, here's a good one. Are you staying at the Red Roof Inn this week, too?"

"Geez, Gran. Enough already," Ranae says, draping an arm around the woman's shoulders and pressing a kiss to the gray hair at her temple.

Gran's got panache, that's for certain. "Not me," I assure her. "I'm just tired."

"Well, I've got a pot of beef stew started for dinner; it's just the thing to fix you right up. Will you stay and eat with us?"

Gran is of a mind that every ailment, every worry, every wound or heartache, can be soothed with a home-cooked meal. In the past, her beef stews and pot roasts were the things of legend, but a few years ago, she discovered the wealth of recipes she could access on the world wide web, and she's become something of a daredevil in the kitchen. Her favorite show is "Nailed It." Although Ruby often opts for a ham and cheese sandwich when her great-grandmother experiments, Ranae has never been a picky eater and is always game to try just about anything at least once. She also loves her grandmother and is more than willing to be a guinea pig taste tester, knowing how much joy Gran gets out of puttering around the kitchen. But some of the concoctions Gran puts on the table aren't fit for human consumption, or any other species' consumption for that matter, and I know better than to go in blind.

"Is it your own stew recipe?" I ask. "Because you know I love yours the best." I already know I won't be staying, though. Adam and I need to talk when he gets off work this evening. *If he even bothers to come home, that is.* The thought sobers me, but I do my best to keep my smile in place.

"It's mine, I promise," Gran says with a knowing chuckle. "I woke up this morning wanting comfort food, and now I know why. All three of you could use a hearty pick me up. Did Ranae tell you about the folks that came by first thing this morning?"

"I haven't had the chance yet," Ranae cuts in, giving her a quick squeeze before stepping away. Crossing to the counter, she pulls a heating pad out of the microwave, the scent of jasmine rice and lavender filling the air. "I really need to get back upstairs to check on Ruby and give her this, but you can tell her about them, Gran."

"Go, go." Gran shoos Ranae away with the wave of a hand. "You let Miss Ruby know that I'm brewing a ginger and fennel tea right now. It'll help soothe her stomach." She lifts a scraggly brow at me. "Would you like some, too? It'll put a little color in your cheeks." In spite of her lack of convention, Gran Niemeyer is a nurturer through and through.

I shake my head and hold up the blue mason jar of lemonade. "No, thank you. I'm fine with this. It's lovely, as usual. The perfect balance of sweet and tart." Turning to Ranae, I ask, "Would you like me to come talk to her? I had a similar experience in high school, remember? And look." I hold out my arms. "I'm still alive."

"Would you?" Ranae pauses on the first step and waits for me to catch up. "She thinks you're way cooler than I am."

I chuckle at that. Ranae has always been the cooler of the two of us. In high school, the boys wanted to date her, the girls wanted to be her, and good grades came easy. School was her playground.

People even forgave her for befriending me.

Then Ranae got pregnant during our senior year, and everything changed.

Ranae

MY PORCELAIN-SKINNED DAUGHTER LOOKS like one of those tragic beauties straight out of a 1920's silent movie. Her smudged makeup and tear-spiked lashes make her eyes appear luminous and soulful. Her lips are bruised plums from chewing on them, her expression one of deep suffering and despair. Nudging her legs aside, I sit on the bed next to her and reach over to tug on one of her curls, so like my own, but bleached a white blond, the ends dipped in fuchsia. I thumb away a tear that tracks down her cheek.

Dani stands in the doorway, smiling tenderly. "Hello, Ruby darling."

"Aunt Flo's an evil witch and I hate her," Ruby snarls, the edge in her voice sharp enough to leave a mark. I keep silent and just nod sympathetically. "I'm not old enough to have a baby, so why do I have to endure this torture and... and disgusting humiliation?"

I hadn't believed that I was old enough to have a baby when I was my daughter's age, but ironically, it was my sweet—and at the moment, angry and belligerent—Ruby who turned me into a mother just weeks after I turned eighteen.

"No offense, Mom."

My thoughts, according to those who know and love me, are projected in living color on my face. She bumps my thigh with her knee, then narrows her eyes at Dani. "And don't start with your whole 'glories of womanhood' spiel, Dani. There's nothing glorious about this."

Dani, who knows my daughter well, doesn't take offense at Ruby's accusatory tone. She moves to sit on the other side of the bed and offers my daughter her lemonade as a token of goodwill.

Ruby accepts the glass and guzzles down most of it. I let it slide that she refused one from me a few minutes earlier.

"I mean, it's not like being a teenage girl isn't hard enough already," she bemoans, setting the nearly empty cup on her bedside table and swiping the back of her hand across her mouth. "Lopsided boobs, gigantic butt, thigh dimples, pimples, and stress B.O." She ticks things off on her fingers as she lists them. "We have to shave hair off random body parts, then put hair back on other parts—false eyelashes and extensions, anyone?" she says impatiently when she notices the confused expressions on our faces. "Makeup, jewelry, perfume, great hair, the right clothes, because, you know, we have to be all cute and sexy, right?"

"But not trashy," I interject. It's a fifty-fifty chance she'll accept my comment as a show of solidarity, or she'll glare at me for pulling the mom-card on her.

Solidarity wins out.

"Exactly," she declares. "We're not even allowed to *talk* about farting or burping, no less, let one slip out. But guys? I mean, that's how they mark their territory, their personal air space. It's so gross and unfair at the same time."

I suddenly begin to wonder if this tirade have something to do with a guy she's trying to impress. My heart aches a little more for my girl.

"And then we get periods on top of all that?" She snatches her pillow from behind her head and covers her face with it, flopping back on the bed in misery. "What was God thinking dumping all this on us?" Her voice is a muffled moan, but her words and emotions are perfectly clear.

"I couldn't agree more," Dani says in her best soothing midwife tone, her lovely accent making her sound both exotic and wise. I'd give my left pinkie to talk like her. Sometimes I try to mimic the way she speaks, but I usually end up sounding like my tongue has gone numb and my jaw has locked up. "I'd take a voice crack over menstruation any day," she adds.

"Any day," Ruby echoes. She lifts her hand and Dani high-fives her. "I mean, why couldn't he give boys the stupid curse?"

"Well," Dani says, cocking her head as though seriously considering the idea. "Boys can hardly handle having a cold. Just imagine them trying to survive nine months of being pregnant."

I chuckle at her response; Dani usually isn't one to man-bash.

"The whole human race would die out," Ruby grumbles in agreement. "When does menopause start again? I'm going to start a countdown calendar."

"Careful what you wish for," I chime in. "No period, sure, but hot flashes, unmanageable weight gain, chin hairs, and age spots."

"Seriously? Just kill me now," Ruby wails into her pillow.

Dani slow blinks at me and mouths, "Way to go, Mum."

My phone buzzes with an incoming call, but I ignore it and let it go to voice mail. This, right here, is priority.

"Actually," Dani starts up again. "Do you want to know how I see it, Ruby? It may not be glorious in the way of diamond tiaras and ball gowns, but we are magical creatures in our own rights."

"Yep," I interject. "We're unicorns."

"Think about it, Rubes," Dani continues, pointedly ignoring my contribution. "Our cycles are set by the ebb and flow of the tide—"

"Don't say *flow*," Ruby interrupts from behind her pillow.

Dani bites her lip but doesn't laugh. "Right. My apologies. Women's bodies echo the rhythm of the tide, the swell and pull of the ocean. We are in sync with the cycle of the moon, and at the same time, we're in sync with each other. On top of that, we have the astounding and miraculous capacity to grow another human being inside of us. Which is all well and good and ultra-cool, right? But that's not the real magic. No, no, no!"

I grin at how animated she is. I love it when Dani gets worked up over this stuff, and right now, it's putting a little color back in her cheeks, too.

"Our magic is in the way we get up each morning and face life with dignity and pride, with a smile on our faces, even knowing what lies ahead. I remember when you were anxiously awaiting your first period. We'd told you all about it, but were you scared? No, you were a little warrior, preparing for battle. And I still remember when your mother found out she was pregnant with you, and then when she went into labor."

She reaches over and squeezes my hand. I smile, eternally grateful for her friendship in my life. In *our* lives.

"She was so ready to meet you, Ruby. That was the magic. She knew she faced the—the *rending* of her body in childbirth, but she looked forward to it. She charged into battle; a warrior ready to fight for what she believed in."

I poke my daughter in the ribs. "And you know what? I've never held the rending thing against you, either, Rubes. I rent pretty badly, let me tell ya."

"Yeah, and you never did it again, did you?" Ruby challenges, lifting the pillow so she can breathe easier. She's always wanted a little sister or brother, used to ask for one every Christmas until she was old enough to grasp that it was one gift I wasn't ponying up. But I know her challenge for what it is; she needs to be told she is worth every ounce of pain I've endured in all the seventeen-plus years that she's been mine.

"Hey now." I knuckle her in the ribs again. She flinches and bats my hand away. "That had nothing to do with childbirth or you. I'd have had a dozen of you if I could." I shrug and admit, not for the first time, "It's the whole finding a man who wants to be more than just be a sperm donor; that's the problem. I'm a little gun shy there, you know that, honey. But childbirth? Bring it on. I laugh in the face of rending."

Dani narrows her eyes at me. "Mock my word choice if you must, but my point remains." She pats Ruby's arm. "Our magic is in our tenacity. Our determination, and our ability to not only survive, but to rise up and embrace our power as women. Even warriors grow weary at times, like you are today, my sweetums. But it's in this, right here," she says, circling a hand in the space between the three of us. "We women coming together to empower one another. To have each other's backs. It's in your great grandmother downstairs brewing up a tea for her daughter's daughter's daughter."

"Her son's daughter's daughter," Ruby corrects.

Dani nods. "I know, but you get my point, don't you?"

Ruby plops the pillow back over her face, but her words are still easily discernible. "So we're magical bleeding unicorns? Is that what you're saying?"

My phone buzzes again and I sneak a quick peek at the screen. I grimace at the caller's name, noting what time it is. I am late. I lift one side of the pillow so I can see my daughter's face. "I need to take this call, Rubes. Are you okay if I leave you two unicorns alone for a few minutes?"

"Is it a guy?" She reaches for my phone. "Let me scream in his ear. Maybe then I'll feel better."

"It's Hugo," I tell her. "And you'd feel awful if you yelled at him."

"Yeah, but he's the only guy in the world who might understand." Ruby thinks Hugo is king of all men. Most people who know him share her admiration of him.

Dani takes Ruby's outstretched hand and brings it to her lips for a quick kiss on the knuckles. She's always uncharacteristically demonstrative with my daughter, and I'm certain she'd make some lucky child a fantastic mom. However, I've learned, somewhat painfully, to keep my opinions on the matter to myself.

A little over a year ago, after a quiet dinner at Dani and Adam's place on a night Ruby spent doing girlie stuff with my mom, Dani asked me—no, *told* me—to stop judging them for not wanting to have children. I was shocked by her choice of words. I didn't think of myself as being a judgmental person, but when I opened my mouth to deny it, I found myself momentarily at a loss for how to say so without sounding defensive.

When I remained silent, Dani continued, as though orating a rehearsed speech. "Adam and I aren't ready to start a family, at least not at this point in our lives."

"I want to come home to a sanctuary at the end of the day." Adam picked up where Dani left off. "I don't care if it's a mess or if there isn't anything ready for dinner as long as it's peaceful. After spending all day with other people's children, I honestly believe I wouldn't have much left to give to my own. I'd hate myself, knowing that my son or daughter only got leftovers, the dregs of my day, so to speak. And Dani feels the same way." Adam had his arm draped around the back of his wife's chair, and when he squeezed her shoulder none too gently, I felt a vicious urge to reach over and snap each of his fingers off.

Except that I did understand, at least to a certain extent. Dani's hours as a midwife were irregular and unpredictable at best, and there were times she went from one birth to another, living on green energy drinks and cat naps. Labor and delivery didn't wait for convenience, and a midwife was on call twenty-four hours a day. Adam, an elementary school counselor, worked with children and families all day long. Most of what he did was rewarding, but he sometimes faced overwhelming or even tragic situations where his best efforts weren't enough. School counselors didn't offer long-term therapy, especially in severe cases, and Adam often talked about how discouraging it was to have to refer out the ones who needed the kind of help he wasn't equipped to give.

"Hey, I love leftovers," I countered, trying to find my footing while also attempting to lighten the mood a little. "And do you know what makes mashed potatoes and gravy great? The gravy. Which is made from the meat pan scrapings. The dregs, so to speak," I added, teasing him with his own words.

When he didn't respond, I continued, not exactly oblivious to the hole I was digging, but unable to stop myself in the face of what felt like an attack on my character. "You only get the worm when you get to the bottom of the tequila bottle, Adam. You only get to lick the spoon after the cake goes in the oven, and every kid will tell you that licking the spoon is the best part."

As a child, I'd looked forward to the end of the day when my father came home and swept me up in a big bear hug. I certainly hadn't begrudged his absence while he worked, probably because I knew that he looked forward to coming home to us, too. And he saved the best of him for us. For his family. I knew I was fortunate, that there were many kids who didn't share my childhood experiences, people with "daddy issues" or no daddy at all—my daughter, for one. I knew most kids would take ten minutes of Captain Fantastic over ten hours of Deadbeat Dad.

"Don't rule fatherhood out because you're worried you won't have enough to give. Sometimes the dregs are the best part," I finished with a smile that made my jaw ache.

Adam stared across the table at me, his expression one of condescension and... pity? "You don't have to agree with us, Ranae," he finally said, his voice deceptively droll. "But you do need to respect that this is our decision to make. Not yours," he added unnecessarily.

I averted my gaze first, but only so I could gape at Dani. She flinched uncomfortably when our eyes met.

"Try to understand," she finally said into the leaden silence. "Adam and I love the work we're each doing, and as you well know, having a child would require one or both of us to sacrifice a good portion of what we've invested in our future."

Her reprimanding words stung like slaps. Was that how they—how *she*—saw me? As someone who had sacrificed my future to have my precious Ruby? I wanted to reach across the table and shake her, to ask her if she really meant the words she'd said. If we'd been alone, I might have done just that.

But then, I had a sickening feeling that had we been alone, she wouldn't have drawn such a hard line in the sand.

I sat there with one fist clenched in my lap, the fingers of my other hand casually tracing patterns in the condensation on my water glass. I caught Adam's eye for one brief moment before he looked away, then I turned to my friend and apologized for making her feel judged, explaining that I would never intentionally do so.

I did not apologize to Adam.

I don't hate Adam.

At least I didn't in the beginning.

In the beginning, I thought it was wonderful that he could see past the facade Dani wore. To the world, she was a quiet, swanlike woman, long and lean, head dipped demurely in a way that people sometimes confused for coyness. With me and my family, however, and especially with Ruby, the swan came to life—genuine, frank, and avidly curious about the way we did relationships. That was the Dani I wished the whole world knew, but no matter how much I encouraged her and even pushed her, she'd spent too many of her formative years withdrawing and holding back, sticking to the shadows. She seemed almost content to tag along with me, to just be a part of my world. It was Adam who helped Dani see she had a world of her own to inhabit.

They met when she was still in med school. He was the son of one of her mother's colleagues, and their parents introduced them at a hospital Christmas gala. It hadn't been love at first sight. Adam was still in school himself up in Indianapolis, but they stayed in contact and become friends, and after he graduated and accepted a job in the nearby town of Princeton, they began seeing more of each other. Dani and three other midwife peers were preparing to open Breathe Birthing Center, and she was afraid he'd be a distraction, but he proved to be just the boost she needed. It was the classic slow burn love story, and under the care and nurturing of Adam Granger, Dani seemed to blossom. She became approachable, confident, and courageous, as if a light had been turned on inside of her and she could finally see her way. Adam had somehow cracked her casing and helped her open up in ways I never could.

Although Adam and I never became best pals, I loved seeing Dani come into her own, and if he was the reason for it, I was happy because she was happy.

After their first blissful year of marriage, however, things seemed to shift subtly, in ways I couldn't exactly put a finger on. And for the first time in our friendship, I began to withhold things from Dani.

Little things at first, like the way her new perfume, a gift from Adam, smelled more like him than it did her. Or why she'd started putting a hand to her lips when she smiled, and no longer laughed with her whole body; she had a Julia Roberts laugh, mouth wide open, head back. Or how much I missed that sound.

And then there was the big thing.

When Adam discovered that his wife had never had a surprise party, he approached me and asked me to help him plan one for Dani's thirtieth birthday. Over the course of the next several weeks, he and I ended up spending a lot of time together, and to my surprise, I found myself enjoying his company. I felt like I was finally getting to know the side of him Dani loved. He teased Ruby, Gran, and me about our all-women household, he laughed at himself and his clumsy efforts to 'think pink' as Ruby instructed, and the evening before the party, he came over and worked as hard as any of us at everything from vacuuming and dusting to hanging patio lights and cutting out paper chains.

The night had grown quite late, Gran had gone to bed hours before, and Ruby had conked out on the sofa. Adam and I were putting the finishing touches on everything, and we were both rather proud of what we'd accomplished.

Just inside the back door, I bent over to straighten a rug that had been kicked out of the way, when Adam walked by behind me, brushing his fingertips along the curve of my backside. I straightened and spun around to stare at him, horrified, but he didn't stop or even acknowledge what he'd done, just pushed out the door with a lantern he'd been repairing at the kitchen table. I stood there, frozen with my warring thoughts, trying to convince myself that I'd imagined it. Maybe it wasn't his hand. Maybe it was the lantern. Maybe he didn't even realize he'd done it?

No. It might have been ages since I'd felt a guy's hands on my body, but there was no mistaking it for what it was. Adam had copped a feel. He'd groped me. *Sneaky, slimy snake.*

I couldn't let it go. Not only was he my best friend's husband, but I hadn't given him permission—or in any way, invited him—to touch me that way. Fortunately, Ruby was still sound asleep with her face turned toward the sofa cushions, so I headed out to the back porch where he was up on a ladder with his lantern. I closed the door behind me. I certainly didn't want my daughter waking up to whatever was about to go down. Or Gran, for that matter. He glanced over his shoulder at me, then started down the ladder. I didn't wait for his feet to hit the ground.

"Adam, I've been wracking my brain to come up with a good reason, even a good excuse, for what you just did to me in there. But I have to tell you, none of what I'm coming up with would qualify as *good.*" I made air quotes with my fingers, glad to see they weren't shaking.

If I hadn't been glaring at him, I might have missed it. A momentary pause, a twitch in the shoulders, a lift of the chin. Then he descended the last two steps and turned to me with a look of frighteningly believable confusion.

"I'm sorry?" It was a question, not an apology. Brow furrowed, he met my stare straight on, unflinching, unwavering.

It was all I could do not to look away, my body suddenly awash with doubt. "Right. So you don't know what I'm talking about?"

He ran a hand through his thick blond hair and shook his head, still frowning. "Did I miss something?"

"Oh, no," I shot back, my voice drenched in sarcasm. "You did *not* miss." I crossed my arms and widened my stance. "I think you'd better leave."

"Hey, hey, Ranae. What's all this about?" He took a step toward me, one hand outstretched. Something in my expression must have made him think twice, because he halted and let his arm fall to his side again.

I could think only of Dani and how his behavior would rip her guts out. "Go home, Adam." I pointed at the steps. "We're done for the night."

"Ranae." His tone was urgent, but not desperate or fearful. "I really don't know what you're talking about. I'm not leaving. Not like this."

Was I wrong? Was it possible? "You groped me." It came out as an accusation when it should have been a declaration, and I felt my certainty, my righteous indignation, crack just the tiniest bit.

"No." His answer came out firm. Appalled. Wounded, even. "Ranae, I did not grope you." He held his hands out, as if offering proof that there was no trace of my flesh on his fingertips.

He seemed so sure. So... right. But was it an act?

Maybe I *had* imagined it. Maybe I was making a mountain out of a molehill. Oh, Lord, if I was wrong? I felt another surge of heat, more intense than my anger, as mortification prickled my chest, flushing my cheeks, and tightened its grip around my airway.

"I'm sorry if I inadvertently came in contact with you in any way that seemed inappropriate," he continued. "But you are Dani's best friend. I would never do such a thing to either one of you." He held my gaze a few moments longer, then turned to fold up the ladder. "I'll put this in the shed, then I'll be back for my things."

He'd deposited his messenger bag and jacket on the bench just inside the front door when he'd first arrived.

I watched him maneuver the ladder down the porch steps, careful not to bump the decorations draped along the handrails. What was I going to do now? At a complete loss, I went inside, checked on Ruby, and scooped up his things, wishing

I had a pair of gloves. I felt dirty just touching his stuff. At arm's length, I carried them out onto the back porch just as he was returning across the lawn.

He paused for a moment at the bottom of the steps. "I'm not going to try to defend myself," he said, then started up slowly, but with a self-assurance that made me want to shrink.

No way.

No one was going to intimidate me or make me feel like a victim in my own home.

I straightened my shoulders and kept my gaze fixed on him, doing my best to keep my expression blank so he wouldn't see my inner turmoil. I had nothing more to say to him; I just wanted him gone. *Dani, oh Dani, oh Dani,* my heart cried again and again.

He kept talking. "It's obvious that whatever happened has upset you, and I truly am sorry if I'm responsible." He picked up his jacket from the porch swing where I'd laid his things. He slid his arms into it. "I'm going to leave now, but I'll be back tomorrow with Dani as we planned." He reached a hand up to sweep the hair back from his forehead, then said, "If not for me, then for Dani's sake, I'm asking you to think about what you're accusing me of. Ask yourself if it even makes sense for me to do something that would jeopardize all that we've worked on together to celebrate the person we both love so much." He gestured at all our festive decorations. "She deserves all of this."

He was right on that count, at least. But how I was going to manage pretending nothing was wrong was beyond me. I'd only kept one real secret in my entire life, and there were times I thought it might kill me. "For Dani's sake, not yours," I finally said. "Against my better judgment and for Dani's sake alone, I'm going to pretend nothing happened."

"Nothing did," he interrupted.

I ignored him. "But if you ever, *ever* touch me inappropriately again—"

"There is no *again* here."

I narrowed my eyes. If he cut me off one more time, the gloves were coming off. "Or if I catch a whisper of you touching or even looking inappropriately at a woman—or a man—other than Dani, all hell will break loose on your head."

He nodded. Slowly. After a long pause, he picked up his computer bag and said, "You're a good friend, Ranae. I hope Dani knows how lucky she is that you have her back." Then he walked out into the night without a backward glance.

When my legs felt steady enough to support me, I headed inside and took a long, hot shower. His unshaken composure had me more unsure than ever.

The surprise party went off without a hitch. Adam presented himself as a happily married man in love with his beautiful wife, and graciously thanked me for everything I'd done to make the event so wonderful. He and Dani lingered long after the last guest left, and Adam behaved as though nothing had happened, as if nothing had changed between the three of us. I wanted, more than anything, to pretend right along with him, but there was no undoing something like that.

The next morning, Dani surprised me when she showed up shortly after I'd dropped Ruby off at school. She was armed with a box of my favorite pastries from The Red Mill. "I'm here to help with party cleanup," she said, her words too cheerful, especially for this early in the morning. "But maybe we can start with a cup of coffee and some of these, okay?" She set the box on the small section of the table I'd cleared for Ruby to eat her breakfast, then lifted the lid and leaned close to breathe in the rich, buttery aroma.

"I take it Adam talked to you about what happened between us?" I knew what was going on, but I wasn't going to beat around the bush the way she seemed prepared to do. I'd thought long and hard about the incident, and I'd made up my mind on what I believed happened. Adam had made one of those passes that left no question about what was being offered, the kind that could also be dismissed as a misunderstanding if things didn't go as hoped.

But I hadn't cooperated. Not only had I rejected his advances, but I'd called it what it was and refused to be gaslighted into believing it hadn't happened.

And apparently, Adam decided not to trust me to keep things to myself. So he'd taken matters into his own hands and gone to Dani with his version of the story before I could tell her mine.

"He did," she confirmed. "We don't keep secrets from each other, and he felt awful about not telling me sooner. The only reason he waited until this morning was because he didn't want to spoil the surprise or the afterglow of the party."

I had no doubt his take on things had been vastly different from mine. "So he told you he groped me."

"He didn't grope you, Ranae. Come on." She lifted a caramel and chocolate drizzled croissant from the box and took a bite.

I pressed my lips together. Fine. I'd let her tell me what happened, then.

She chewed and swallowed while I waited in silence, then she said, "He ran a hand across your backside, right?"

I was so surprised to hear the truth that I stammered, "Um, yes. Exactly."

"He does that to me all the time." She turned to pour herself a cup of coffee, then extended the pot in my direction. "Do you need a top off?"

I covered my cup, wishing she'd stop pretending we were having a normal conversation. "You're his wife, Dani. I'm not."

"I know that." Her voice had a defensive undercurrent, but her smile remained calm. "You two have recently spent a whole lot of time together because of me, talking about me, thinking about me, and according to Adam, missing me."

My eyes widened, and I felt my eyebrows disappear under my bangs. "So since your ass wasn't around for him to grab, he grabbed mine instead? Because he was missing you? And you're okay with that?" My voice rose emphatically, and I was glad Gran was out at the grocery store with Mom. She wouldn't have liked the argument or my crude language. I jabbed at my chest as I continued. "Because I am definitely *not* okay with it. His behavior or you excusing it."

"No, no." She peeled off a delicate layer of pastry and popped it in her mouth. Then she sighed. "I'm not okay with it, either; I assure you. But try to understand, Ranae. Adam is a demonstrative guy. He's touchy-feely, you know that. He said he was totally absorbed in thinking about me, about how thrilled I'd be by everything you two had done for me, and it was a subconscious thing. He was so embarrassed that he couldn't look at you—"

"Wait." I held up a hand to stop her. "Let me set the record straight. He *could* look at me. He *did* look at me, Dani. He looked at me the whole time he was lying to me, playing dumb, acting like he had no idea what I was talking about." I could hardly believe we were having this conversation.

"I mean, as soon as he realized he'd done it," she said. "He told me he practically ran outside, and when you didn't follow him, he hoped you hadn't noticed. By the time you came out to call him on it, he'd almost convinced himself it hadn't happened. Then, well, he got defensive when you accused him—"

"Accused him?" I cut her off again. "I didn't accuse him, Dani. I stated facts. He groped me without my permission or invitation, and now you're sitting at my table making excuses for him." I was appalled. Not so much at Adam. My initial shock had morphed into disgust toward him. No, I was appalled at Dani.

Appalled that she apparently believed Adam to have "accidentally" fondled me. Appalled that she was defending him to me—*me*—of all people.

"I'm not making excuses," she shot back, her voice finally beginning to rise as well. "I'm telling you what happened. His version of the facts."

I gaped at her. "How can there be different versions of the facts?"

"Because maybe you misinterpreted his actions—the *fact* that he touched your backside—as intentional, when it wasn't."

I stared at her for several moments, at a loss for what else to say. Finally, she sighed and nudged the pastry box my way.

"I don't want to fight about this, Ranae. I already feel way too vulnerable right now, and the only reason I can swallow my pride and accept his explanation and apology is because I trust you. I know you would never do anything unseemly or inappropriate toward Adam, so his version of things—that he made a stupid, thoughtless mistake—really does make more sense than the notion of him actually making a pass at you without provocation."

Oddly enough, the longer she talked, the more I was starting to see her point of view. Besides, I'd told him I'd let it go. He didn't have to say anything to Dani, but he'd chosen to "come clean"—well, his version of things, at least. Or was it because he knew Dani would sense something was wrong and it would all spill out of me in the end, regardless? I reached into the box and withdrew an enormous bear claw. My friend knew me so well.

"I need you to accept his explanation, too," Dani continued, her voice laced with need, the edges a little tattered by something I thought might be fear. "And his apology. He's so sorry, and he's worried this will cause trouble between us. That's not what any of us wants, right?"

What I wanted was to seriously injure Adam Granger.

I also wanted to take a massive, angry bite of my maple-drenched almond pastry, but I wasn't sure my stomach would let me.

"He said you two had such a great time together planning the party and then executing it, and he's so afraid he's messed things up." She cocked her head. "You *did* have a good time doing all this, didn't you? You and Adam?" The question was so sweet, so hopeful, and I wondered, not for the first time, if my inability to relate to Adam was a result of some deep-seated resentment toward him.

I let out my breath in a long sigh. "I did. It was fun," I grudgingly admitted. When her eyes lit up, I added, "I feel like I got to know the man you love."

"I do love him, Ranae," she whispered. "So much."

"I know." I set down my pastry and circled the table to stand in front of her. "I know you do," I reiterated, taking her hands in mine. "I want you to be happy, Dani. But even more, I want you to be sure. You know Adam far better than I do, and if you believe what happened was a mistake? An accident?" I paused, giving her one last chance to deny it. When she said nothing, I forged on. "Then I'm willing to accept that it was, too."

She nodded, her eyes bright, and tugged me close for a quick hug. When she pulled back, she said, "He said you were the best friend a girl could have, that I was lucky to have you at my back."

Those words didn't bring me any more comfort than they had when he'd said them to me.

Later that day, Adam called to apologize again, taking full responsibility for his bad behavior. I forgave him. I at least tried to, I really did. And then we got on with life. Over time, I found myself starting to believe his version of how things had played out that night, but something happened as a result of me backing down.

My trust was broken.

Not in Adam. I never fully trusted him, even when I agreed to believe him.

Not my trust in Dani, either.

It was my trust in myself, in my own intuition and wisdom, that was broken.

Again.

It had taken me so long to believe in myself after the fiasco of my senior year of high school, to trust my instincts about people, and suddenly, I felt like that teenager again, standing on shaky ground, my footing uncertain at every step.

So, that night a little over a year ago when Dani and Adam sat across the table from me and accused me of being judgmental about their decision to not have children, I couldn't help questioning my own motives, wondering if I was, indeed, judging them, and just too stupid or blind to my own weaknesses to realize that I was.

And once again, I found myself backing down. Closing my mouth.

Because the most important thing was that my friend was happy. If Adam made her happy, then it wasn't my place to stand in the way of that.

However, she certainly wasn't smiling in the recording booth when she told me Adam might be leaving her.

In fact, she hasn't been smiling much at all for months now. Maybe longer.

I think Adam is going to leave.

I study the back of Dani's head as if I can see the words spinning haphazardly through her mind. Her admission, though unexpected in the mundaneness of everyday life, hasn't come as a shock to me. I want to tell her that I saw this coming long ago, back on the night before her big birthday bash when he gave me a glimpse of his true colors. But I hold my thoughts captive, because I think she already knows.

"Go find Hugo," Dani says to me over her shoulder, snapping me out of my reverie. "Bring me some more lemonade first, though. Your child chugged mine."

I point at Dani. "We're not done," I remind her with a beady-eyed look. "Don't leave before I get back."

She smiles and nods, but I have a feeling her previous vulnerability has been packed up and put away for the day, that it will take a crowbar to get it out of her now. She shuttles me off with a flick of her wrist, and I swipe my phone open as I rise, tapping the green button that will redial the missed call.

"Hey, Hugo," I say when he answers with his usual gruff greeting. "I'm on my way. Where are you?"

"Meet me out at the trail head." He always sounds like he's just rolled out of bed, as though I'm the first person he's spoken to all day. I once teased him about it, and he shrugged and said, "Well, other than Chloe, you *are* the first person I've spoken to today."

"I'll be there shortly." I shove the phone back into my jeans pocket and grab Dani's glass to refill it before heading out to meet my grave digger.

Dani

GOT TO RUN - I have a mum in active labor. Ruby fell asleep while I was rubbing her head and telling her all your deepest darkest secrets. Good show today - we'll talk later. D.

I prop the note against a vase of colorful dahlias on the kitchen table where the women of the house can't miss it. The enormous multi-petaled blossoms are most likely from Aileen Niemeyer's garden out back, and although I know Gran wouldn't mind, I resist the temptation to grab the bundle and take them with me. Gran tends her flowerbeds as carefully as she does her vegetables, and she always has something glorious blooming, no matter the season. I peer out the kitchen window toward the garden and spot her yellow, wide-brimmed hat bobbing up and down behind a tall row of plants. She's on her knees digging something up, and I push open the screen door and step out onto the porch to holler at her. "I'm heading out, Gran. I've got a baby to deliver."

"Go get 'em, Dani-girl. I'll be praying for you." That's her way of saying goodbye, her promise to pray. She means it, too, and knowing she's praying for me is a little like getting a virtual hug.

"I left a note for Ranae on the table. Ruby is taking a nap," I call back, hoping our loud conversation doesn't wake the girl.

I look towards the woods, hoping to catch a glimpse of Ranae returning to the house. A quaint footbridge crosses the all-season stream separating the homestead from the cemetery. Across it, a gravel path skirts the bonfire clearing that sits close to the banks, then travels on to the little country chapel where Ranae's great-grandfather, Gerhard Niemeyer, and his father before him led church services for the local farming community.

On one side of the white building lies the 150-year-old graveyard where more than sixty headstones of varying shapes, sizes, and ages mark the places where different congregation and community members have been laid to rest over the years. The Reverend Gerhard Niemeyer was the last man to preach at the little church, and his son, Ranae's grandfather, Opa Alec, is the most recent Niemeyer man to be buried in that little church plot. The graveyard is cordoned off for private family use only now, but it has officially become part of Fair Havens' history, a piece of the past that Ranae has built the cemetery's future around.

Not far from the little chapel stands a one-room schoolhouse Ranae has converted into her office and storage room. The building was in a sad state of neglect when she took over, but she painstakingly salvaged the structure herself, refusing to take the advice of those who thought she was better off leveling it and starting from the ground up.

The chapel only comfortably seats about sixty people, so in the clearing in front of the two buildings, Ranae has constructed an outdoor chapel with benches made from felled trees and local limestone. They are set in rows facing a living bower of redbud and dogwood trees under which stands a lectern carved out of an enormous chunk of the same native limestone. In good weather, it's where they hold most of their funeral services.

A local stonemason spent several weeks on the job, and shortly after the last bench was completed, he asked Ranae out. They'd dated for a few months, but nothing had come of it other than the lovely outdoor cathedral. Phil Dunn. Good old Phil. He had as much of a sense of humor as the rocks he took his chisel to, and although he was a nice enough fellow, there was no way he'd have been able to keep up with Ranae, no less with her precocious daughter and even more precocious grandmother. They'd parted as friends, as Ranae does with all the men she dates.

Not that there have been that many. Besides Phil, there have been three, maybe four others in the seventeen years since high school.

I can see no sign of my friend across the way, but I linger a moment longer, just taking in the beauty that surrounds me. The leaves on the trees are turning, and the cool, late morning breeze sets everything in motion, stirring up a whispering melody that sweeps over me in sighs and swells.

In so many gardens around town, dried corn stalks gossip harshly about the impending winter, and fading pumpkin vines droop wearily. Gran's garden, on the other hand, is splashed with frothy pink and lavender wood anemones, autumn crocuses, cobalt gentian trumpets, and, of course, a rainbow of dahlias. I wave one more time at the woman who has been as much a grandmother to me as she is to Ranae, and duck back inside to grab my things.

Fall has arrived overnight, it seems, but I've been so preoccupied with the state of my marriage that I've missed the subtle harbingers that herald my favorite season. I feel as colorless and prickly as the cut alfalfa fields that I drive past on my way back into town. I roll down my window and let the cool air rush around me. "Snap out of it," I mutter, frustrated at my constant state of despondency. If I am looking for a way to convince Adam to stay, this isn't it. I wouldn't want to hang around me, either.

At home, I change into my yoga pants and a clean tee under a colorful scrub top, my standard uniform for work. I pull my hair back into a clip to keep it out of the way. I keep it long because it softens the lines of my angular face and too-long neck, but it only hangs a few inches past my shoulders these days. Long enough to tie back while I work, but short enough to make me look groomed and grown up the rest of the time. In my spotless kitchen, I grab my emergency energy kit—an organic green juice, two homemade protein bars, and a jar of trail mix made of raw almonds, chunks of dark chocolate, and dried apples and cranberries—then cross to the mudroom where I keep my birthing bag. I am sliding in behind my steering wheel in less than ten minutes. I've honed the skill of getting ready quickly, prepared at all times.

Before pulling out of my driveway, I switch to my Bluetooth earpiece, clip my phone to the holder on my dash, then check in with Cheryl and Pete Thornburgh to let them know I'm on my way.

This is the second baby I've helped them bring into the world, and Cheryl's first labor was long, her progress from stage to stage slow, so I am not too worried about getting there expediently. That said, babies are good at surprises, and when she breathlessly tells me her contractions are already less than five minutes apart, I assure her I'll be there as soon as I can, and I offer to stay on the phone with them if that would make them more comfortable.

"We're fine, really," she starts to say, then chuckles, and amends her statement. "*I'm* fine. But Pete, not so much. He's getting the pool set up, and poor Georgie doesn't understand why he's not allowed to get in it. But my mom is on her way over to pick the little guy up, so it's all good."

As soon as I get off the phone, I call my assistant, Gail, and ask her to swing by Breathe to pick up a few things for me. I've decided to err on the side of precaution and go straight to the Thornburghs' house rather than swinging by my birthing center on the way. "I need a postpartum recovery kit and the good baby scale—I left it there after last week's birth." The one I have in my bag is a backup; it's a bit clumsy and must be re-calibrated a little too often for me to fully trust its accuracy. Gail lives only minutes from Breathe, and she assures me she'll meet me at the Thornburghs' in half an hour.

Cheryl Thornburgh is one of those women who makes motherhood look easy, and that includes pregnancy and childbirth. In spite of her twenty-eight hours of contractions with her firstborn, she kept her head and remained focused on the task at hand throughout the whole event. When it came time to push, she got on her knees in the birthing pool, faced her husband who sat on a low stool close by, wrapped her arms around his neck, and then asked him if he was comfortable. I smiled when Pete had gently chastised her for worrying about him. Then Cheryl kissed his chin, closed her eyes, and pressed her forehead into his chest. For the next fifty-one minutes, she strained and breathed, trembled and prayed softly, and Pete remained bent forward, leaning over the edge of the pool while she clung to him through wave after wave of contractions. I knew the man wasn't even close to comfortable, but he never let on to his hard-working wife. Cheryl didn't cry out until George broke free from her body, his arms flailing gently in the warm water as I reached for him. Pete, too, made a manly sound that could only be called a sob, but it wasn't anything I hadn't heard before.

It's the fathers' reactions that get to me—I choke up every time a daddy cries at the first sight of his newborn son or daughter.

I pull up at the Thornburghs' home just as Cheryl's mother, Trudy, pushes open the front screen door, three-year-old George in tow. I know Trudy—she's been at several of Cheryl's prenatal visits with me, helping with George, and just being an attentive mother to her own child, and I wave at them both as I climb from my Forester and circle around to the back of it to get my gear.

"Things seem to be going quickly in there," Trudy calls out as she approaches, scooping up George so she can walk faster. "I brought food. Cheryl's already digging into the fruit salad, but I made plenty to go around. There are also green beans, a scalloped potato casserole, and sliced ham, Cheryl's favorite meal. I went ahead and put the ham and potatoes in the oven on warm, in case anyone is hungry now, but if you think it's going to be awhile, feel free to pull it out and put it in the fridge instead. I let Pete know about it, and he nodded and thanked me, but I'm not quite sure he even knows we left."

I reach over and pat her arm. "I'll take care of it when I get inside. And my assistant should be here in the next few minutes so she can help, too. Thank you for all you're doing," I add, giving her the "everything is under control" smile I'd mastered when I was too young to appreciate how valuable it would become to me and to my clients.

I turn to the little guy perched on her hip. "You have fun with your grandma, okay, George?" I cup his pudgy round face, the curve of his jawline fitting perfectly in the cradle of my hand. He just stares at me with big, curious eyes, then rests his head against Trudy's shoulder.

"My grandma," he says in a quiet voice. A certainty in a day that must feel a bit chaotic to him.

"My Georgie Porgy." Trudy rests her cheek against his hair. He smiles shyly from under his grandma's chin, and something inside me spasms, a quick, sharp twist, and then it's gone.

"Well, I'd better get in there," I say, dragging my eyes from George's sweet face. "You two have fun. I promise we'll keep you posted." I have Trudy's number if Cheryl and Pete are too preoccupied to call.

In the kitchen, the birthing pool is already aired up and lined with the disposable plastic sheeting. A garden hose connected to the kitchen tap is draped over the side of the pool. I swipe my hand through the water, grimace at how cold it is, and cross to the sink to adjust the temperature. "I'm here!" I call out. They're probably in the bathroom; pressure on the bladder in the last stages of labor can be intense.

"Hi, Dani. Back here." Cheryl's voice is a little strained, but cheerful and welcoming as usual.

"Thank God you're here!" comes Pete's not so congenial response. I head down the hall in the direction of their voices, checking my watch. Gail should arrive any minute now, and she can take care of things in the kitchen, including the food Trudy has left in the oven. I'll be free to help Pete focus on his wife.

"How is everyone doing?" I ask when I come to the open bathroom door. Hunched over, her forearms braced on the counter, Cheryl is taking long, steady breaths in and out as a contraction grips her body. She wears a thigh-length flannel robe, and when she lifts her head and grimaces at my reflection in the vanity mirror, I smile encouragingly back. "Looking good," I tell her.

Pete stands behind her, his big hands splayed across her hips, his thumbs pushing gently against the pressure points at the base of her spine. Deep worry lines crease his forehead above eyes shadowed with a hint of panic. "It's going so fast this time."

"You're looking good, too, Pete. Nice job." I pat his shoulder reassuringly. "How long between contractions?"

"Less than three minutes now," Cheryl pants.

"Stop talking and breathe," Pete leans forward and chides her gently. Then turning to me, he repeats, "Less than three minutes now." He doesn't see Cheryl roll her eyes in the mirror.

"That's great. Things seem to be progressing nicely, hm? I'd like to get a listen to baby when you think you can handle it." I hear the front door open, and Gail calls my name. I step out into the hall and see her standing a little uncertainly in the entryway. "I'm here," I say with a wave. I catch her up to speed, and while she heads to the kitchen, I duck back inside the bathroom.

Cheryl has straightened and is taking a deep, cleansing breath. I grin at the sight of her distended belly protruding from her open robe. "Ugh," she mutters, gazing at her reflection. "I have stretch marks on top of my stretch marks."

"Hey." Pete, having regained a semblance of his composure, slides his arms around her and cups his hands protectively over the curve of her abdomen. "That's my wife you're talking about, and I'm not going to stand around and let you badmouth her, you hear?" He nuzzles her neck, and she leans her head back on his shoulder. "Besides, I think stretch marks are sexy."

Cheryl snorts softly, her eyes closing as she relaxes into his embrace. I step out into the hall again to give them some privacy.

When a quiet moan tells me another contraction is starting, I check my watch. Just over two minutes.

"I think I need to get into the pool," Cheryl manages to say before drawing a deep breath in through her nose.

"As soon as this one is over, we'll get you there," I promise, then hurry to the kitchen to make sure Gail is ready for us.

Gail Sandusky is far and away the best assistant I've ever had, and honestly, there are times I don't know how I managed before she came to work for me. She would have made a wonderful midwife herself, but she insists she doesn't want the responsibility that comes with being in charge. "I love to be a part of the whole thing without having to be responsible if things go wrong. Is that bad? That I only want to take credit for good stuff? Besides, you're the best boss in the world." But then, Gail makes being a boss the easiest job in the world.

So, of course everything is ready. In the five minutes since she's arrived, she has somehow managed to finish filling the pool, has placed a low stool for Pete at one end, a stack of towels close by, and is efficiently unpacking all the things I might possibly need throughout the rest of the birth, laying the items in an organized array on a disposable pad on the table.

"Can we bring Cheryl out yet?" I ask, glancing over the array of implements in front of her. They are the tools of my trade, and the usual calm settles over me as I itemize each one in my head. Everything is there, right down to my shoulder-length sleeve gloves that I wear once my patient climbs into the pool. Thanks to Gail, we are as ready as possible for whatever comes next.

Minutes later, Cheryl is settled in the warm water, and she leans back against the cushy side of the pool, sighing pleasurably. "Oh wow, this feels heavenly."

"Give it two minutes," I tease, because I know she'll appreciate the irony. At least at this point while she still has her sense of humor.

"What a great shot," Gail says from behind me, camera raised to take in the scene. Gail also plays amateur photographer when parents either don't have a friend or family member they're comfortable sharing the experience with, or simply can't afford the often high-priced services of a professional. She uses a quality point-and-click camera I bought her after I'd seen some of her phone photos, nothing fancy, but she has a good eye for capturing tender moments, the unstaged, raw beauty of childbirth.

"You got this, babe," Pete says, settling onto his stool and leaning forward to kiss the top of his wife's head. "I have your water bottle and lip balm right here if you need it," he adds, gesturing at the things he's set at his feet. "And a cold washcloth, too." He's a pro already, even if he doesn't know it.

Before another contraction starts up, I squeeze some warmed gel low on Cheryl's abdomen and slide the Doppler probe in small circular movements along the top of her pubic bone. The baby has been head down for the last several weeks, and it isn't difficult to hone in on that magical swishing sound. "There you are," I say, before glancing up to see Cheryl and Pete beaming adoringly at the sound of their child's heartbeat. I listen for a few moments, instruct Gail to document the readings, then assure the parents that everything sounds great. We wait for another contraction to release its hold, then I perform a quick pelvic exam. "A hundred percent effaced, but not quite fully dilated, so no pushing just yet, okay? A few more contractions like that one ought to do the trick." I'd already checked Cheryl's vitals in the bathroom, so unless Pete keels over, I am fairly confident we will be wrapping up a textbook home birth and meeting the newest Thornburgh family member in another hour or so.

I am wrong. Twenty-seven minutes later, before Cheryl has time to get into her preferred position on her knees, Jewel Esther Thornburgh makes her grand entrance into the world. "You have a daughter," I coo, my own eyes burning with the sting of unshed tears as I bring her up out of the water. Her arms flail reflexively and her squishy little face scrunches up at the shock of it all, hairless brows furrowed in baby rage at being so rudely thrust from her cozy little womb. I verify that she is breathing on her own, then lay her on her stomach against Cheryl's chest, her damp head bobbing up and down as she shows off her impressive newborn neck strength.

Pete drops his forehead to his wife's shoulder and lets out a few overwhelmed sobs, then he lifts his gaze to marvel at his daughter, wiping away a smudge of vernix and blood from the baby's creased brow. "She's so beautiful," he croaks. "Look at her, Cher. Isn't she perfect?" The words of a smitten father.

Gail drapes a soft, pre-warmed hand towel over the baby so she won't get chilled with only the lower half of her body in the water. Jewel's tiny mouth opens and closes, and she makes sweet kitten-like noises as she bobs her head up and down between her mother's swollen breasts, instinctively rooting for a nipple. With one corner of the towel, Cheryl cleans around the baby's mouth and nose, all the while, cooing and sighing in wonder and love for her precious baby.

"She acts like she's ravenous!" Cheryl exclaims, grinning at her daughter's antics. "Can I try nursing her yet?"

"Absolutely," I tell her, relishing in the sense of euphoria filling the room.

Oh!" Cheryl exclaims a moment later, a sure sign that Jewel has found her mark. The first time a newborn latches onto a mother's breast is always a little startling, no matter how many children a mother has. The instinct to nurse is powerful in its execution, tiny jaws and gums and tongue working fiercely to draw from the life source a mother's body offers.

"That's my girl," Pete murmurs, his cheek pressed to Cheryl's as they watch their baby nurse like a pro. I'm not sure which of them he's talking to, but it doesn't matter.

After the cord stops pulsing, I clamp it, then hold out the umbilical scissors to Pete. He'd been too nervous to cut George's cord, but he'd insisted he wanted to do this new baby's. He hesitates a moment, but I'm fairly certain it has more to do with not wanting to take his eyes off the precious faces of his wife and baby girl than anything else.

"You'll regret it if you don't," Cheryl whispers, grimacing as her body continues working to expel the placenta, the oxytocin coursing through her speeding the process along nicely.

Pete grins proudly as Gail snaps a photo of him cutting the cord, then he quickly returns his attention to the two most important women in his life.

With a little helpful massaging from me, Cheryl delivers the placenta several minutes later, and I examine it to make sure it's intact. Gail disappears into the bedroom to ready everything in there, then Pete and I help Cheryl stand in the water, Jewel still clamped to her breast.

"Can I take a quick shower?" Cheryl asks after getting a good look at the murky water in the pool. "Just to hose this stuff off before I get in bed?"

"If that's what you want to do, sure." That is one of the beauties of home birth—a mother's instinct is always given top billing. I take a droopy-eyed Jewel from her, wrap her in a dry blanket, and hand her to Pete. Gail joins me as Cheryl and I head for the hall bathroom that has a shower instead of a bathtub. I don't want her to have to lift her leg over anything else if she doesn't have to. She seems fairly stable, probably because this labor and delivery has been so short, but if she gets lightheaded or dizzy, we need to be able to help her out of the shower with as little effort as possible.

A few minutes later, she's ready for her bed, and I can already see that borderline frantic look of a mother who has been away from her baby too long. After the slightly wobbly mama is settled as comfortably as she can be in bed, I perform a post-delivery exam on her and declare her a champion birth warrior. While Gail helps Cheryl into a pair of disposable mesh underwear lined with an enormous sanitary napkin, I go in search of Daddy and Baby.

In the front room, I pause, pulling out my phone to take a picture before Pete notices me. He stands in a soft beam of light coming through an opening in the blinds, tears glistening on his cheeks as he gazes down at the tiny bundle he holds high against his chest. He runs a fingertip down the line of Jewel's nose, then chuckles softly when she lifts her chin and lets out a little squeak.

"I think Mummy is ready for you," I say, quietly, so as not to startle him. "And I need to do an assessment on Jewel before too much time passes."

Pete swipes at his cheeks with the back of one hand, not a trace of the earlier panic on his face. His smile lights up the room, and I step back to let him pass.

Would that I could carry this feeling of euphoria home with me, that I could make the sensation buoy me up through the storm I know is coming. I square my shoulders and set aside my troubles so I can fully revel in the joy bursting from every corner of the Thornburgh home. When I enter the bedroom, Pete is sitting on the edge of the bed beside Cheryl, holding Jewel out for her mum to smother her face in kisses.

Even though I work quickly, Jewel doesn't like being unwrapped to weigh, or stretched out to measure her length, nor does she appreciate me pressing her tiny feet, one at a time, onto an ink pad, then onto the Welcome certificate I issue to each new baby I help deliver. While Gail holds her, I measure her head, test her reflexes, and check her vitals. When we finally finish poking and prodding the tiny girl, Gail hands her, along with a newborn diaper, to Pete. We all clap softly when he puts it on without a fumble, then lays the baby in Cheryl's outstretched arms.

I watch to make certain all is well, but Cheryl is a natural. She settles Jewel into the crook of her elbow and brings her to her breast, cupping the back of the tiny head for support. Jewel, too, knows exactly what to do, and clearly doesn't mind having a second lunch when it's offered. Pete stretches out on the bed beside them, and Gail and I gather up our things and slip out of the room. I'll whip up an electrolyte-boosting energy mocktail for Cheryl first—coconut water, wild local honey, blueberries, ginger, and pomegranate juice—then Gail and I will make quick work of putting the kitchen back to rights.

"Wow." Gail props one hip against the counter and breathes out a dreamy sigh. Then she cocks her head at me. "You doing all right, boss?"

Ranae

Blimey, our Irish Wolfhound, emerges from the woods, drops to his hindquarters at the head of Wild Rose Trail, and sweeps the ground with his long tail in a happy greeting. I know Hugo isn't far off, likely stomping through the trees nearby, watching me make my way from the farmhouse and over the creek to the woods. I snicker at how creepy that makes him sound, partly because he probably does come across as a little lurker-ish to some folks. He's a big guy, strong in the way of men who perform long hours of manual labor, but he doesn't stomp anywhere, especially not in the woods. He has the rare gift of being able to make his way through the undergrowth almost noiselessly.

"Dude. I think you're the *real* last of the Mohicans," Ruby often tells him.

The other day, she and I were clearing a new grave site when Hugo suddenly appeared on the trail. He startled us both, making us shriek in surprise, and I threatened him with my shovel when I saw the self-satisfied grin on his face.

Ruby said, "You know, if we were to put you in a long black cape with a hood and give you a scythe, people would totally believe you were Death the way you creep around through the woods so quietly." Turning to me, eyes shining with glee, she said, "Mom, we should totally do it! Let's dress Hugo up as Death. People would be so freaked ou—"

"Ruby Noralee Niemeyer!" I interrupted, appalled, while at the same time, trying not to laugh at the horrific scene my mind conjured up. *Laugh!* What was wrong with me? "A funeral is no place to pull a prank like that."

"I wasn't serious, Mom. Geez! What kind of person do you think I am?" She shot one of her famous long-suffering looks at Hugo, the kind that asked, *See what I have to deal with?* Hugo's head was down, his thumbs hooked in the pockets of his jeans, but I saw the corners of his mouth turn up.

"Are you smiling?" I asked, poking him in the chest. "Don't encourage her."

He lifted a brow at my daughter and said drolly, "You are a terrible, terrible child, Miss Ruby."

She grinned, bounced into a quick curtsy, and then slid her arm through his, tugging him along with her so she could show him what we'd gotten done that morning. "Why thank you," I heard her say. "I think that's the nicest thing anyone has said to me in a very long time."

I'm glad they're friends, and I know I can trust the man to treat my daughter as if she were his own.

He is more than just my grave digger. I met Hugo Beckenbauer and his wife, Chloe, through the Indiana Wildlife Federation, an organization whose stamp of approval I'd needed to help me nail down two coveted grants I'd applied for. I'd spent maybe ten minutes with them before I knew I wanted them on my team, sensing in the couple a deep love for the land, and a genuine interest in my unorthodox plan to protect the twenty-five acres entrusted into my care.

The organization, and the Beckenbauers in particular, were a huge help to me, even beyond procuring the grants, during the somewhat arduous task of turning our generations-old family land into a conservation burial ground. They took a personal interest in the project because of their own values, but Hugo and Chloe also took a shine to Ruby, and the couple quickly became like extended family. They lived not quite three miles from Fair Havens, and especially at the beginning, they often showed up unannounced on their own time, offering to help in whatever capacity I needed. I soon discovered that they couldn't have children of their own, and it didn't take a genius to realize that they were here as much to enjoy the company of my young daughter as to help carve eco-friendly trails through the woods or put up split-rail fencing along the property border.

I know without their help that Fair Havens would not be what it is today.

I hurry over the creek and across the bonfire clearing, skirting the tree stump seats and stone benches that form a misshapen circle around the growing mountain of organic debris in the center. Our next Live and Let Die Bonfire Night is in three weeks, and all month long, we will add to the pile as we keep the grounds of Fair Havens visitor friendly.

Hugo's figure appears on the path behind Blimey. I wave, and then let out a startled squawk as I trip on the end of a branch jutting out of the bonfire pile. Lurching forward, I frantically helicopter my arms to keep from falling on my face. Somehow, I manage to stay upright, and when I come to a halt, I press my hand to my chest, and take a deep breath, already beginning to laugh at myself. I straighten my shoulders and lift my chin before I look up at Hugo.

The man hasn't moved. He just stands there, one hand on his hip, the other stroking Blimey's head, as though waiting for me to stop fooling around so we can get on with the business at hand. I can't decide whether to be offended or grateful that he hasn't hurried to my aid. Maybe he doesn't want to further embarrass me by racing to my rescue? But—but still. Even a "You okay?" would be nice.

He waits until I am a little closer. "You okay?"

Well.

I clear my throat and pat my chest again. "Whew! Yes. I'm fine. But that could've gone very differently, you know." So I'm not the most graceful girl in the world. Not by a long shot. Between my natural exuberance and my, uh, generous curves, I tend to misjudge door widths, furniture corners, and other things I have to maneuver around. Or through.

Hugo knows this all too well; he once had to assist me out of a—literally—tight spot one afternoon a few months after we got Blimey. An absolutely mortifying, ridiculous, only-me kind of tight spot.

Ruby and I were playing Follow the Puppy Leader, and Blimey was the leader. My pipsqueak of a daughter went through Blimey's doggy door after him, so I went through after her, good mom/follower puppy/optimist that I was. Only, my hips hadn't read the rules, and halfway through, it occurred to me that since Ruby and I were making this game up as we went, I could have included *No doggy doors!* on the list. At Ruby's encouragement and because I couldn't accept that my rear end was that much bigger than Blimey's—an enormous Irish Wolfhound, remember? Sure, he was still young and gangly at the time, but still—I attempted to force my way through. Bad idea. I only managed to get the frame of the doggy door past the curve of my backside, at which point, I started to panic.

Then Ruby started to panic.

But when I tried to back out, the frame started coming away with me, and I froze. I'd busted my hiney getting that doggy door in. It wasn't the kind that locked in place at the end of a sliding glass door, mind you, because the old farmhouse didn't have sliding glass doors. No, I had to buy a special reciprocating saw to cut a hole in the wall to install this one. Then I had to buy special wood screws and caulking to seal the side where I cut the hole too big. I wasn't about to rip the thing out, not after all the work I'd done putting it in.

Of course, that's when Hugo and Chloe happened by for an impromptu visit, approaching our home from the back yard by way of the cemetery. Ruby, declaring that if they didn't help us, her mommy was doomed to live the rest of her days half in and half out of the mudroom, launched herself into Chloe's arms, weeping inconsolably. Even though they assured her everything would be fine, my daughter, the light of my life, the apple of my eye, the jewel in my crown, begged Chloe to let her live with them if I didn't make it out alive, refusing to let go of the poor woman until she agreed.

Which left only Hugo to help me. And of course, Blimey, standing at the ready, his tail periodically thumping me in the face.

"It could have gone differently, indeed," Hugo says now, bringing me back to the present. Is he thinking about the doggy door incident, I wonder? How could he not be? Every time I see him, I think about it, at least in passing. And Ruby likes to bring it up periodically, too, just to remind me that I am the imperfect mother of a teenager. In case I'd forgotten.

Blimey lumbers to his feet and comes to me, bumping his nose against my waist before collapsing gingerly to the ground and rolling to his side to expose his belly to me. His golden-brown eyes, a little hazy now, peer up at me, his mouth hanging half open, the tip of his ridiculously long tongue resting on the grass. "Rub my belly, woman." I swear the dog is telepathic. I can *hear* his voice inside my head, and he sounds a lot like Richard Harris as Dumbledore in the Harry Potter movies—a series Ruby and I binge-watch on a regular basis. Gran usually joins us; she especially loves the fourth movie in which her beloved "Edward Cullen" tragically guest stars. Blimey isn't huge by Irish Wolfhound standards, but when he and I walk side by side, I can rest my hand comfortably on his back. For most of his adult life, he's hovered right around one hundred and thirty pounds, but he's lost a little weight in the last year. He doesn't look sickly, though, and I figure the lighter load is easier on his poor old hips, too. In fact, other than the gray that streaks his once toffee-colored coat, he still presents a rather formidable sight to those who don't know that the old guy is living on borrowed time. He'll turn nine years old in a few months, well past the average lifespan for the large breed.

My Irish Gran adores Blimey. She grew up with wolfhounds back in the old country before she and her family emigrated from Ireland, and it seems every story she tells about her childhood includes at least one gigantic dog in it. After Opa died and it was just us girls living out at the farmhouse alone, we decided we needed an Irish Wolfhound of our own. I finally tracked down a breeder outside of St. Louis, and Ruby, Gran, and I made the three-hour drive to pick out our puppy. I'd been a bit shocked by the size of the mommy dog, and when the breeder showed me the sire in the yard out back, for just a moment, I had second thoughts. But by then, Ruby was already gushing over the puppy love being lavished on her by six twenty-five pound, four-legged canine toddlers, and Gran assured me I wouldn't be sorry. There was no going home without one.

She'd been right. Blimey is another part of my life I can't imagine being without.

I moved in with my grandparents during the spring of my senior year of high school. Ruby was due right around graduation, and I'd decided to finish school at home, but since my parents both worked, everyone agreed when Gran suggested I move in with her and Opa. With my grandfather working in town with my father, Gran spent much of her days out at the homestead alone, and the thought of having me—and a new baby once mine arrived—hanging around her home all day thrilled her heart. She'd be around if I needed her, and my midwife, Rose Bergmann, was one of her best friends who also lived out in the country, less than ten minutes away.

The 150-year-old farmhouse we live in sits back from Kirchwood Lane in a clearing large enough for an enormous kitchen garden, a small pole barn, and a lawn perfect for family reunions and birthday parties. Separating the acre-and-a-half homestead from the rest of the property is a year-round stream, and on the opposite bank sits the one-room schoolhouse and the quaint country church where Niemeyer men once pastored a ragtag congregation of German farmers and their families.

Which means that the Niemeyer family has been in the funeral business in some form or another for several generations—it was part and parcel to a reverend's job at one time.

But my grandfather broke tradition, determined he wasn't cut out to shepherd a flock. While his father was still preaching hellfire and brimstone in the country, Opa Alec got a job in town working for an undertaker. He saved every penny he made and purchased one of the old, abandoned mansions along the horseshoe of the Ohio River. Over the course of two years, he renovated the place in his spare time, turning the upstairs into living quarters, and converting the main floor into Niemeyer Mortuary. It was where he brought his young Irish bride, where they raised their four children, and where he worked for the next thirty years. By the time my father proposed to my mother, my grandparents had grown weary of the hustle and bustle of city life. So Opa made my dad his partner, then moved with Gran back to the family farmhouse, making way for my parents to move into the upstairs residence. Opa continued to work alongside my parents, and over the years, the father and son team turned Niemeyer Mortuary into one of the most reputable funeral homes in Southern Indiana.

After Opa's father, the good reverend Gerhard Niemeyer, passed away, the little chapel sat empty except for cobwebs and small critters that found their way in through knotholes and warped shiplap wallboards, and the schoolhouse became a storage unit for things that no longer had a place in the farmhouse.

Out of respect for the dead, as children, we weren't allowed to play in the old church graveyard, but while I waited for my baby to arrive, I spent many solitary peaceful hours wandering among the hand-chiseled stone markers, imagining the people whose bodies were laid to rest on my grandparents' land, and coming to terms with the journey of motherhood on which I was embarking.

After Ruby was born, I began working part time at the mortuary so that I could contribute financially to our living expenses. The death industry has always been a way of life for me. I grew up in a home where corpses arrived in various conditions, and time and time again, Opa and my parents worked their magic to all but bring the dead back to life. I knew the tricks and tools of the trade like I knew the contents of my makeup bag: spiky eye caps to hold eyelids closed, gold wires to keep jaws from gaping open, various scalpels and hooks, forceps, needles and suture thread, and I was oddly comforted by the rhythmic whirring of the embalming machine. I watched countless times while my mother acted as beautician to the dead. To my ears, *beautician* was a combination of beauty and magician, and the title suited her. Sometimes, I was even allowed to suit up in a gown, gloves, and a face mask, and act as an assistant, handing tools, carrying trays, opening bottles. I'd never imagined doing anything else.

So when Ruby was out of diapers and old enough to be good for Gran, I went back to school to get my mortuary science degree so that I could be the next generation to work in the Niemeyer family business. Neither of my older brothers had taken up the trade. Jared pastored a large church on the east side of Evansville, and Nolan, a Civil Engineer, taught courses like Structure Analysis,

Hydrologic Design, and Fluid Mechanics, all of which I knew nothing about, at the University of Southern Indiana.

It was while I was at school that I began to question the traditional funeral practices employed in modern America. I understood the motives behind the gut-wrenching desire to preserve a body, to have a loved one laid to rest looking as normal and unchanged as possible—like he or she was only sleeping. But I wondered if our perspective of *normal* wasn't a little skewed. Questions kept playing through my thoughts, month after month, course after course.

We learned about safety precautions, like full body protective wear and proper ventilation, things that were taken far more seriously now than they were when I was a child, or back when my grandfather was just getting started. We knew much more about the long-term effects of the carcinogenic chemicals used in embalming, and the more knowledge I gained, the more unsettled I became. I had countless memories of both my father and grandfather bent over bodies on the embalming table, working without any form of protection except a bib apron and a pair of gloves. My mother, too, wore only a hospital mask over her mouth and nose while she worked, although she didn't have quite the same degree of exposure as Dad and Opa. I'd looked them up myself as the numbers weren't offered in class, but statistics were shockingly high for embalmers with nasopharyngeal and other respiratory tract cancer due to the prolonged exposure to the toxic chemicals plied in the trade.

Sure, I could take all the precautions I'd been taught, and I did really get great satisfaction from all the tasks necessary to prepare a dead body for services. When we installed our crematory, I took over the operation and management of the cremation services we offered. But I was now responsible for someone besides myself. I had a daughter to think of, and I wanted to be around for a very long time to enjoy being her mother.

I had endless conversations about this dilemma with my parents and grandparents, and each of them, in their own ways, encouraged me to challenge the norm and to pursue alternative options, if that's what I wanted to do. By the time I was in my final year of the program, I was aggressively researching green burial practices around the world and wondering why it wasn't a more common practice in our country where recycling and repurposing were common mantras, where biodegradable and organic methods were being implemented in almost every other industry.

It was my grandfather who first suggested I research what it would take to open a green burial cemetery in our part of the country, that he wanted to help me if I did the legwork to find out how to make it happen. I almost fell out of my chair when he told me that he had no desire to be embalmed or buried in a casket. "I want to be wrapped in the sheet from the bed I shared with my beloved wife. I want to be laid to rest right out there next to my father, not in some fancy manicured lawn cared for by strangers." He'd pointed out the back window toward the little church graveyard on the other side of the creek.

A few months later, during an especially blustery winter, my aging grandfather started coughing. He refused to see a doctor, insisting it was just a cold. He had an inside view of the modern medical system and secretly blamed them for more than a few of the deaths that kept his business up and running. When the handkerchief he politely held over his mouth showed spots of blood, Gran and I insisted, but by the time we took him in, the damage was irreversible. My grandfather was diagnosed with acute bacterial pneumonia, but it was the mass they found on his lungs that sealed his fate. He was gone only a few weeks later.

As he'd requested, we buried him next to his father in the graveyard just across the little stream where Gran could still visit with him as often as she liked. Because of the condition of his emaciated body, we decided to forgo a wake, and instead, held a private family burial. Even though it was winter, the ground was not frozen, and as though opening its arms in welcome, the earth gave way easily to our shovels as we dug. We lowered his shrouded and unembalmed body into the grave, mounded the dirt over his resting place, then decorated the place with pine boughs and other winter greenery from the surrounding woods.

My dad and his sisters walked the property until they found a large fieldstone boulder to use as a grave marker; a stonemason would carve an epitaph later.

We all worked together to clean and decorate the little church and to clear the driveway from Kirchwood Lane to the churchyard so folks wouldn't have to come via the house and across the aged footbridge. We invited friends and neighbors to join us the following day in celebrating Opa's life with a small service we planned to hold in the old white chapel.

But more than a hundred people made their way down the gravel lane to pay their respects, so we moved the whole thing outdoors. It was cold, but the sun shone down in brilliant warm beams, a winter blessing on a life well-spent and a man well-loved. After most of the guests had left, my dad and brothers built a small bonfire and we gathered around to warm our hands and faces and to tell more stories about Opa, not quite ready to end the celebration.

We still burn our Live and Let Die bonfires in the same spot.

I'd been surrounded by death culture my whole life, but my grandfather's family burial, and then the memorial service that followed, friends and family gathered under the bare, interlaced branches of the poplars, elms, and maples overhead, had been the most authentic funeral experience of my life.

"I want everyone to have the option of a natural burial and memorial service like Opa's," I said, months later, one night after the family had come out to the farmhouse for Sunday night supper. I'd finally graduated and was in the middle of my yearlong Funeral Director internship under the watchful eye of my father.

Dad, too, had been deeply moved by the whole experience, and he nodded. "I can understand why you would."

My brothers still sat at the table with us, Jordon's wife next to him, while their two little boys and Ruby were sprawled on the floor in the family room watching a Disney movie. Everyone wore the languid expressions of contentment that followed a good meal with good company. Dani and her parents had joined us, too, but Michael and Francis left shortly after the meal as Francis had an early morning start the next day. Gran had gone to bed, too. She hadn't slept well since Opa died, and by eight or nine o'clock at night, she'd usually tuck in.

"It's not something most people would choose, is it?" Mom asked, her brow furrowed in thought. "People want one last look, one last memory, and that's what we give them." She slid her chair close to Dad's and sat curved against his side, a perfect fit. I coveted what they had; I was holding out for someone who would treat me like my father treated my mother, how Opa had cherished Gran.

"I know that," I said. "You and Dad are so good at what you do, Ma. People trust you with their loved ones because you take good care of them." It wasn't just a business to them, but a way to help people through a very difficult time.

Dani spoke up, comfortable in our midst, as if she were one of us. "I do think things are shifting a bit, Noralee. I see it in the OB-GYN industry, too. People are becoming more interested in doing things as naturally as they can, both for themselves, as well as for the environment. There's a heightened awareness of what kind carbon footprints we're leaving, and this concept of green burial falls under that umbrella."

"I agree," my father said. "If a person is looking for an environmentally sound option, green burial is the way to go. No chemicals. No steel caskets or concrete burial vaults that will take a million years to break down. We're receiving more and more questions about green burial these days, so it's certainly an option we need to be educated about."

"People seem less afraid of death these days. Of the natural process, I mean," I said. "And I believe people will be looking for more end-of-life options in the years to come. I'd love to be on the ground floor of that movement, you know?"

"What about cremation?" Nolan asked. I could see the skepticism written all over his face. "Isn't that a better option than a decomposing body in a hole in the ground? Environmentally speaking, I mean?"

"Cremation does, of course, leave a smaller footprint than embalming does," I agreed. "But it has its own environmental issues, like smoke, mercury poisoning from burned dental work, and more." I waved my hands in front of me, not wanting to get into a debate. "Don't misunderstand me, please. I believe there is a place and a purpose for all of these options in the death industry." I pressed a hand flat against my sternum. "I'm just not sure our modern traditions are the best way for *me*, personally, anymore. I don't feel comfortable with what feels like masking the normality of death by trying to make a corpse look alive." I leaned toward my parents in my sincerity. "Again, I'm talking about me and my own direction, not you. But what is wrong with viewing a body that has died naturally? Or if someone, in death, is greatly changed, like in Opa's case, or in the case of someone who dies in an accident, we wouldn't have to have a viewing at all, and thereby preserve the dignity of the dead by allowing people to remember them the way they were when they were alive and well?"

"You've got a valid point there, little sister," Jordon interjected with a chuckle, his arm draped along the back of his wife's chair. "How many kids have been traumatized by the sight of big and brawny Grandpa lying in a casket wearing too much blush and lipstick? Or because they could see the stitches keeping Grandma's eyes and mouth sewn shut? Not that you two would ever be so remiss," he added, nodding in deference to our parents.

"It's more than just whether or not to embalm someone," I said. I knew I sounded like a young upstart, fresh out of school and all geeked up on my own perspective. But these were things I whole-heartedly believed in, and I didn't think I was the only one out there with questions about 'the way things are done.' I sighed and shrugged. "I want to help people get intimate with death."

"You are kind of a freak, Nae," Nolan said with a snort. I kicked him under the table; he threatened to throw a spoon at my head but stopped when Mom gave him the stink eye.

"I know," I acknowledged, not even pausing to gloat. "That's what I'm afraid of. What if I am just a freak? What if no one else thinks going old school is cool?"

"Except I was there," Jordan said, his tone thoughtful. "At Opa's funeral, I mean. I get it. I think you might be surprised at how many people will listen to you, especially folks our age. And people like Opa and Gran who prefer to be laid to rest in their family graveyards. Green burial," he stated. "We were just talking about that at our last church board meeting. Someone's family members live in Maine where green burials are becoming fairly common. More of an FYI topic at our meeting, yet it's interesting timing now that you bring this up, too."

"How do you see this play out, Nae?" Nolan asked, serious again, and I appreciated him asking the question. "Dad and Mom would be all but out of a job if they weren't embalming or selling caskets and urns. No offense, parents."

"None taken," my father said with a chuckle. "Good question."

"I don't exactly know," I admitted. "Opa challenged me to look into what it would take to open a green burial cemetery in our area, and I have to tell you, the more I research, the more I long to do it." I didn't mention to my family my grandfather's offer to help me out if I did the leg work. It seemed callous and self-serving without him there to explain his intentions to the rest of the family. He hadn't really unveiled them fully to me, beyond telling me that he wanted to participate. "It would be a major endeavor, logistically, financially, of course, and certainly not one I'm prepared to undertake on my own. At least not right now." I hesitated, not sure how to present my thoughts to my family without sounding presumptuous. "But maybe it's something we could consider for the future of Niemeyer Mortuary. Maybe a way our company can diversify and keep up with the changing times." We had been approached on multiple occasions by the big funeral companies to sell out, but my parents were determined to keep the Niemeyer name a small, local business. I shrugged, suddenly feeling young and uncertain without Opa there to root for me.

"What about this place?" Gran startled us as she spoke from the hall. No one had heard her come back into the room, but she leaned quietly against the doorframe of the dining room and studied us, her expression thoughtful. I wondered how long she'd been standing there, how much she'd overheard.

"What do you mean, Gran?" Jordon leaned forward to peer around his wife.

"Your grandfather and I often discussed what we should do with all this land. Developers have approach us about selling it a hundred times over the years, and we even considered it a few times, but it never felt right. Once you started talking about your flower-power-woo-woo cemetery, Ranae, Alec suggested—on more than one occasion, mind you," she pointed a gnarled finger at me. "He suggested that your idea might be a wonderful way to honor the legacy of our family. Maybe not all the woods, and certainly not this side of the creek, but the family church and graveyard might be a good place to start."

She came into the room, tightening the belt of her bathrobe around her waist before sitting in the chair Nolan pulled out for her at the table. She thanked him and continued. "Back when that graveyard was in use, folks didn't make the effort to preserve a body the way we do now." She toyed with a cloth napkin on the table in front of her. Her tone was casual, conversational, but that didn't mask the solemnity of what she was saying. "Every one of the bodies buried out there was wrapped in a simple shroud, maybe put in a wooden box made by a family member or in a handwoven basket, and then it was laid in the ground as natural as they come. Just like your grandfather. You probably wouldn't find more than a few half-penny nails out there in most of those graves. The earth took them back. From dust to dust," she finished.

The group around the table had gone quiet, but Dani reached over and squeezed my leg encouragingly. What Gran was suggesting was something I'd secretly thought about for some time, ever since Opa's challenge. My friend was the only person I'd ever shared that dream with, and now I was a little afraid that perhaps I was, indeed, dreaming.

It was land that would eventually go to the next generation, to my father and his three sisters. What if any of them had plans for it after Gran died?

And yet, as long as she was alive, it was hers to do with as she pleased, wasn't it? As if reading my mind, she laid a hand on the table between us and waited for me to place mine in hers. "Sweet girl, I know you believe that you moved in here because you and Ruby needed us. But did you ever think that maybe we also needed you? You have been a comfort and a source of strength to me, since Alec passed, especially, but you two breathed new life into this home the moment you moved in. It's as much yours as it is mine, and if you can put that land, that church and little school to such a noble use, then what are we waiting for?" She cocked her head to one side, then furrowed her brow in bemusement. "Opa wanted to help you; didn't you know that? I thought he told you so."

I was crying. Fat tears spilled from my eyes and dripped off the line of my jaw. "He did say he wanted to help," I managed to get out, a happy smile pulling on the corners of my mouth. "But he never mentioned specifics, and certainly not the property. I would have remembered that."

"Well, he mentioned it to me. Repeatedly." She let go of my hand, pulled a tissue from the pocket of her robe, and gave it to me. "Here you go, sweetie."

"Oh Gran," I murmured as I dabbed at my face. "That would throw the doors wide open on something like this."

I turned to my other family members. "But what about you guys? It's family property, not mine."

"No, it's not," my father countered. "It's your grandmother's land and she can do with it what she likes."

For the next few weeks, we hashed out the pros and cons of diverting so dramatically from the way the Niemeyer Mortuary operated. But when I discovered that the land could be registered as a conservation green burial ground, thereby saving it from ever falling into the hands of developers, there was no turning back.

"I believe in you, Ranae," my father told me one day while he watched me perform facial reconstruction on a man too young to be on a mortician's table. He'd had a heart attack while painting his pole barn and had fallen from near the top of a twenty-foot ladder. "I'm proud of you for knowing what you want in life, and for pursuing it with all you've got." It was high praise coming from him. By taking on this new endeavor, I was essentially leaving the family business without a third generation to take it over.

This would change all of us.

"Thank you, Daddy." Knowing I had his support and approval boosted my faith in myself exponentially.

With the help of many hands, including Hugo and Chloe's, it took more than a year for us to open our doors for business, and it was two more months before we had our first funeral service and green burial at Fair Havens.

It was a breezy mid-May day and the redbud trees had burst into color all around the clearing, the raspberry blooms a vibrant contrast to the fresh white paint of the two restored buildings. We laid Rose Bergmann, mine and Ruby's beloved midwife, and dear friend to Gran and so many others, to rest in a place of honor at the head of the first official nature trail we christened Wild Rose Trail. At the head of her grave, Chloe transplanted a wild Carolina Rose from deeper in the woods, and Ruby picked out a gorgeous chunk of local fieldstone in varying shades of rust, ocher, and umber to use as a marker near the trail.

Now, as I do my best to avoid the indiscernible look in Hugo's eyes, I am reminded how fortunate I am. I couldn't have asked for a better job, or a happier place to live.

And we certainly couldn't have asked for a better dog than Blimey to share this little piece of heaven with.

Behind him, the sight of Rose's headstone makes me smile. I greet the old woman in my heart, then crouch down beside my dog.

"I love you, Blimers," I say in my goofy, reserved-for-Blimey voice. "You're the best boy in the whole world, aren't you?" I scratch his belly like a good human, and Hugo crosses the short distance to stand beside me.

He grins down at me. "Stop goofing around, Ms. Niemeyer. We've got a grave to dig." He offers me his hand and I take it, hating myself for loving the way mine fits so perfectly in his, and I rise as gracefully as I can. I don't miss that he has to shuffle his right foot a little to keep his balance against the drag of my weight, but he just smiles and releases my hand when I'm upright, and I follow him back toward the trail that disappears into the woods.

Blimey remains sprawled in the warm sunshine, abandoning me to walk the woods alone with Hugo Beckenbauer.

Dani

"I think I'm just tired," I say to my assistant. "I haven't been getting enough sleep lately." I sigh and sweep a few stray wisps of hair from my face. "I hope I'm not getting sick."

"Take a breather, then," Gail orders. "I've got this." She indicates the aftermath of the water birth around us. "Take Pete and Cheryl food, check on the baby, then come sit down and eat something. Today was textbook, so clean-up will be a breeze." She grabs three plates from the cupboard and hands them to me, then points at the oven. "That potato casserole looks divine. The ham is in a covered dish in there, too."

Suddenly, the thought of food has me feeling lightheaded and queasy. I put my hand to my mouth and swallow hard.

Gail cocks her head and narrows her eyes. "Did you just turn green on me?" She puts the back of her hand against my cheek. "You sure you're okay?"

When I don't answer right away, she takes the plates from me and sets them on the counter. "Go. Sit." She points at one of the dining room chairs lined up against the wall out of the way of the pool. "Now."

I obey. Lowering myself gingerly to the padded seat, I lean forward and hang my head between my knees. *Please don't be sick, please don't be sick,* I don't want to have to tell the happy couple that I'm not feeling well. What a bummer that would be, especially if I turn out to be contagious.

Gail finds a large cookie sheet in a kitchen cupboard, and on it, she lays out two heaping plates of food, silverware, and two glasses of water, and carries it into the bedroom. I still have my head down when she returns several minutes later. "Not getting any better, huh?" Her tone is heavy with concern.

"I'm okay." The lightheadedness is starting to fade a little, but I don't think I'll be eating anything right now. "I think I'd better stick to my green juice. Can you grab it for me from my cooler?"

When I open the lid on the juice, and the aroma reaches my nostrils, another surge of nausea catches me by surprise. Something is definitely wrong; I usually love the smell of my concoctions. I close my eyes and hold my breath, waiting for it to pass. I was a bit sick to my stomach last night, too, but I assumed it was because of the terrible way the conversation between Adam and me ended.

Who am I kidding? It might have started out as a conversation, but it ended as an argument. Then Adam stormed out of the house, and I haven't seen him since.

I hear Gail rooting around nearby, and I'm grateful for her help. When she touches my shoulder, I look up. She's holding out a small plastic cup and a bottle of test strips she's rummaged out of my midwife supplies bag.

For several seconds I just stare at the items in her hand, uncomprehending. Then suddenly, a wave of a different kind sweeps over me. Shock, momentary denial, and certainty. I lift my gaze to hers, and she starts to withdraw her hand.

"Did I overstep?" she asks. My expression must be fierce.

I shake my head and take the items. My fingers are trembling, and I almost drop the cup. How have I missed the signs? What a stereotype I am! A midwife who doesn't know she's pregnant?

With a shaky breath, I stand. Gail stays close, one hand outstretched, ready to steady me if I should wobble. In spite of the emotional roller coaster I'm on, though, the queasiness seems to have run its course.

Gail steps back to let me pass, but I reach for her and give her a quick hug before heading to the table still covered in the birthing supplies that we didn't use. "Thank you, my friend. But I'll help you get this wiped out first, then head home after I check on the little family one more time."

"Are you sure? I can manage." Her concern is palpable, but she doesn't push. I love her even more in that moment.

I shake my head and flash her the amber plastic bottle of test strips before tucking the items into the side of my bag. "I—I don't want to do this here."

Because I already know what the test will show, and I don't want to be here when I see the inarguable results, not in this home where the miracle of life is being celebrated. As much as I love and appreciate Gail, it isn't fair to ask her to be my support system, even just for the time being, either. I need to be with someone who loves me when I take this test. Someone who will stand by me through thick and thin, through hell and high water, no matter what.

Ranae

Digging a grave with hand tools is an arduous task that requires strong arms, a tireless back, and an eye for detail. It might take one experienced person a good six or seven hours to prepare a burial site, and considerably longer in inclement weather, particularly if the ground is frozen.

A lot of thought and care go into the process in a place like Fair Havens. We strictly regulate the operation of motorized vehicles and equipment on the property, and instead, use shovels, pickaxes, pry bars, rakes, saws, and other manually operated implements whenever we can. First, the surrounding area is cleared of debris while preserving as much of the native flora and fauna as possible. Then we determine the optimal position of the grave and stake out the three by eight-foot rectangle with pegs and twine. We lay out two tarps side by side; they'll hold the soil we remove one shovelful at a time. The first eight to twelve inches of earth is made up of decomposing leaf mulch and loamy topsoil, the next two or three feet is heavier, more compact clay and silt, rich with minerals, but dense and heavy. As part of our conservation practices, we attempt to return the layers of earth in the same order we pull them out.

It's our policy to have at least two people on the grounds when a dig is taking place. It's not so much to help with the actual dig—once a certain depth is reached, having two people in the hole isn't very efficient. The second person is more of a safety precaution. If someone is hurt out in the woods while digging—a back injury, a misjudged shovel thrust, or if a person accidentally stumbles backward into a finished grave....

Yes, it has happened.

To me.

I twisted my ankle badly in the fall, too, and had I been alone, I would have been in a bad way. Fortunately, Dani was hanging out with me that morning, and she was able to help haul me out of the pit I'd just spent all day digging. After much deliberation, she emptied the wheelbarrow I'd used to haul in my digging equipment, then braced it while I clambered into it. We somehow made it back to the house, Dani laughing hysterically the whole way, me with my white-knuckled grip, cry-laughing and begging her not to dump me over, and a much younger and far more energetic Blimey loping along the trail ahead of us. It wasn't long after that incident that Hugo casually informed me he'd be taking over as official grave digger. I could be his assistant if I wanted to participate in the digging.

I don't mind the hard work or getting dirty. It can be rather cathartic at times. But Hugo is admittedly much better at it than I am. In decent weather, I can dig a grave in six or seven hours. I don't work fast, but I'm persistent, and I stay at it until I'm finished. Hugo, on the other hand, has it down to under five hours when he digs alone. Every time. I used to work with him, and together, we could get the task done in less than four. Not because I'd help dig, but because while he worked on the grave, I cleared the site and readied the surrounding area for the pending burial service. We made a good team, I always thought.

Hugo, solitary by nature, likes to work alone, though, and I don't mind the extra hours in my day. We usually head out together to get things started, but then I leave him to it. I check in on him every hour or so, just in case he needs anything. He never does, but I show up anyway, usually armed with a cold or hot drink, depending on the weather, a hearty, if not always healthy, snack of some kind, and an encouraging word.

Besides, I like watching him work. Not in a creepy stalker way, mind you. It's appreciation. Every move he makes is deliberate and thoughtful. Each shovelful of dirt is scooped out and set aside with care and intention.

"There's something... spiritual, I suppose, about preparing the earth to take back one of its own," he'd once told me. "The fact that I get to do this final act for someone's loved one is a privilege I don't take lightly."

Essentially, that is the main reason we dig graves by hand. Conservation doesn't exactly prevent us from using a backhoe; we choose to forgo machines because we strongly believe in the power of human touch in all aspects of this business.

I'm a Funeral Director and Mortician, but I'm also a certified Death Midwife, or Death Doula, a provider of end-of-life care for the dying, and for their loved ones who remain in the land of the living. My job is to make the transition from this world to the next as peaceful and intimate and as positive as it can be. In many ways, I kinda do what Dani does, but at the other end of life. I'm not a grief counselor or a therapist; I simply offer help and support to people preparing to say goodbye.

If possible, I spend time with the person dying, making note of their likes and dislikes, what soothes and relaxes or unsettles them, if they prefer music playing, conversation, or company, or just silence. I help family members organize and understand difficult paperwork and what to expect of the legal process of death in the United States, and I make sure folks eat and drink and sleep. After a person has died, I work with the loved ones to wash and clothe a body in preparation for what comes next. Sometimes my job ends when a body is picked up for transport to a funeral home and the care of the loved ones is handed over to the staff there.

More often than not, however, the clients who request my services are those who have opted to forgo the traditional funeral home route, many of whom will end up at Fair Havens. I help set up in-home wakes or viewings, delegate hostess tasks so the focus can be on paying last respects and not on things like keeping the coffee fresh and the cookie platter full. Then, when the time comes, I help ready the body for burial. If the services are to be held at Fair Havens, I also transport the body in our customized Dodge Caravan, an anonymous donation we received a few years ago.

I especially love the services at Fair Havens for families I've spent time with in my role as an end-of-life care provider. Having walked through such a personal and intimate experience with both the dying and their loved ones, it is impossible not to form lasting relationships. And those same family and friends often make appearances at our Live and Let Die Bonfire Nights, turning the evenings into informal family reunions.

Today's grave, however, is for an elderly woman whose children—the folks Gran mentioned during our brief conversation with Dani—kept insisting their mother would have wanted to "go green" if she'd known about Fair Havens before she passed. After meeting Marcia's lethargic, fifty-something-year-old son, Frank DiSarno, and his Big Gulp-sipping sister, Pam, I suspect their decision to make Fair Havens their mother's final resting place has more to do with our below average plot prices than because of a desire for an eco-friendly funeral. Especially after I had to remind Pam not to leave behind her plastic 64-ounce gas station cup on the side of the trail. Twice. Both times that we stopped so Frank could catch his breath along the short walk from the plot they'd selected back to the schoolhouse where my office is.

Folks sometimes choose Fair Havens because of our reduced costs, not because we are cheap, but because they are cheap. Sure, there are those who really are financially challenged, but I don't think that's the case with these two. Not if Frank's enormous Lincoln Navigator and Pam's champagne-colored Lexus are any indication of their finances. The fact that they didn't see fit to carpool out to our property is more evidence that conservation isn't likely what motivated them to choose us. But dying is expensive, and there is no way around the dying part or the paying part, at least not legally, so I do my best not to judge anyone who comes to us with their loved ones. For all I know, Marcia DiSarno was a monster, and at least her children are fulfilling their obligatory duty in taking care of her remains.

Regardless of their reasons for choosing us, in my mind, they are giving their mother the best of the best.

The main expense our clients have is for the piece of land they purchase in which to lay the body of their loved one, and that cost includes the labor to prepare the grave site for the burial, and then for us to tend it afterward. We stock a few biodegradable coffins of various sizes—untreated pine, woven styles made from bamboo, willow, and seagrass, and a simple heavy-duty earth-friendly cardboard—an option often chosen by families with children because decorating it is a great way to get younger ones involved. We also carry natural fiber shrouds of different styles, but the cost for each of these items is minimal.

Alternately, customers don't have to use any of our products; they are free to construct their own coffin from untreated, biodegradable materials or wrap their loved one's body in a favorite blanket, if that's what they want. I charge a nominal fee if I'm asked to direct a funeral, but I rarely have the opportunity to do so, as most folks have a family member, or their own religious leaders do the honors. I consider myself more of a cemetery steward; my job is to manage the affairs of the little piece of land entrusted to me, and to oversee the comings and goings on it, making sure expectations, comforts, and needs are met to the best of my abilities.

So it doesn't offend me when people like Frank and his sister bluster their way into our sanctuary with questionable motives. By burying their dead at Fair Havens, by not embalming in toxic fluids, by not encasing those bodies in steel and concrete in the ground, I see our services as a way for us to restore balance, to do right by the earth that has sustained those bodies in life.

I also do right by the dead, no matter what reasons or circumstances bring them to us. Tomorrow morning, I will honor Marcia DiSarno with the same care and respect as I do every other body that comes to me, and her funeral, though, according to Pam, might be attended by fewer than half a dozen people, will be lovely. We'll lower her shrouded body into her final resting place—I'll have to hire a few of Ruby's high school friends to come help since Frank informs me that he's the only one fit enough to do any heavy lifting, and I'm not so sure about him, either. Then, per Pam's adamant request, we'll wait until the mourners are gone, then Hugo and I will cover Marcia in a cool, comforting blanket of earth. We'll finish by laying sprays of wildflowers and branches over the bare mound, then we'll set a chunky piece of the local fieldstone at the end of the grave closest to the path as a natural marker.

The siblings have opted to maintain the "green theme" by not having anything engraved. We assured them that wouldn't be a problem, that we use a GPS service to map the graves, so any time they want to come visit, we'll have no trouble showing them where their mother's remains rest.

My heart squeezes with the knowledge that it's unlikely I'll ever see either of them again once their obligations are met.

Other than those in the small churchyard, the small private plot now designated for Niemeyer family members only, the graves at Fair Havens are located on either side of the eco-friendly trails that crisscross through our woods. In the early days, Hugo, Chloe, and I spent countless hours threading through the trees in a method that mimicked animal trails. Our goal was to create paths that caused the least amount of damage or disruption to the ecosystem of the woods, but that would still be traversable by us humans and our old-fashioned wooden pushcart—what we use to transport a body from chapel to grave. We wanted our visitors to have easy access to their loved ones' graves, but also to be able to enjoy the beauty and serenity of the woods without ever having to leave the trails.

I lead the way to the site Frank and Pam purchased during their visit early this morning, but Hugo has already been by, having located it by GPS while waiting for me to finish up recording with Dani. His loaded wheelbarrow is parked just off the trail, and he's already started clearing away some of the underbrush in preparation for digging.

Together we determine the best position for the grave, then mark out the three-by-eight-foot parameters with stakes and twine. While I take a few before pictures of the location, Hugo shucks out of his lightweight jacket and drapes it over one of the handles of the wheelbarrow.

We hardly speak as we go about our normal routine. Hugo takes his time preparing for the task ahead of him, his face a mask of serious contemplation. I give him his space, but I must force myself to keep my eyes averted, to not watch him lay out his tools, to not allow my gaze to linger on his wide shoulders as they strain against the fabric of his shirt. It is an act of will to focus on the way beams of noonday sunshine pierce the canopy overhead and the play of light and shadows on the ground, rather than on the curve of Hugo's back as he bends over to examine the edge of his shovel, the blade of his pickax.

There is something magnetic about the way he moves, fluid and stable at the same time. He is a man rooted by his inner strength, and therefore, able to bend and flex and even give in to the storms that come with living.

Sometimes, on my weakest days, I let my camera drift his way, capturing his image at the edge of a shot, just as I do now. My heart races with the knowledge that I've stolen that moment from him—a moment of his life that he doesn't know I've claimed. I always delete the images or crop him out later. I refuse to allow myself to pine for a man who is not available, and my love for Chloe empowers me to remain strong, to be honorable. To treat them both with the respect they deserve.

No, I don't pine for Chloe's husband.

But I can't deny that I want a Hugo of my own.

Dani

I SIT IN MY car, engine still running, staring at the front of our home. A sense of disquiet wraps itself around me like a scratchy blanket.

I prefer to park in the garage since I keep my trunk stocked with birthing supplies, but the garage door is blocked by Adam's Ford Escape. I shake my head at the irony; my husband purchased the SUV in April, and it seems like he's been trying to escape ever since. Our disagreement yesterday—because we rarely fight, not like those couples in the movies who yell and throw things—was about another purchase he'd made. One, like his car, he did not bother to tell me about until after the fact. More accurately, we disagreed because he hadn't bothered to tell me at all, and I learned of it in a rather unpleasant way.

I found out about the car when I headed out to a birth in the middle of the night and found it parked beside my trusty old Forester. For a moment, I wondered if I was dreaming, but when I peered inside the driver's window, I saw his travel mug in the console and his sunglasses on the dashboard.

Adam had come in from work the evening before, sat across the dinner table from me while we talked about how our days had gone—well, he talked about his day, but we'd finished our meal before I shared about my day. He made love to me in our bed, and then fell asleep with one arm draped around my waist. Yet he hadn't bothered to mention the new car he'd bought.

He'd been gone to work by the time I got home from the birth the next morning, and we hadn't seen each other until that evening. When I finally brought it up over our dinner of sautéed chicken and veg and quinoa, Adam insisted he'd told me he was planning on buying it, and the fact that I was surprised was proof that I never listened to him. He used our ensuing argument as justification for not including me in the actual buying process. "I knew this was how you'd respond, Dani. Maybe that's one of the reasons I don't include you in decisions like this."

The plural form of the word "decision" had me reeling. What else had my husband decided without including me?

We had agreed before we even married that we were a team in every way. We combined resources and shared debts, so making a purchase like this, although not exceptionally extravagant as vehicles go, was certainly something we should have done together. When I asked him about the financing on it, he dodged the question at first, then finally said he'd paid cash for it; cash that came from our joint savings account. And no matter how much he insisted he'd told me about his plans to purchase the car, I knew he hadn't.

"You were exhausted that day, Dani. You'd had two births back-to-back and were running on a few hours of sleep in three days. You probably just don't remember."

"And you thought that was a good time to mention something as important as dropping a chunk of our savings on a new car? While I was sleep-deprived and worn out from work?" I'd shot back, hating how blindsided I felt. "Besides, I wouldn't forget something like that, no matter how exhausted I was. If anything, I'd have asked you to wait to talk to me about it until after I'd gotten some sleep. And you know it."

He only shrugged and said, "Well, it's your word against mine, at this point. Besides, it's done. I'm not going to return the car."

He'd left the house for several hours that night, and I finally gave up waiting for him and went to bed. He came in at some point after midnight, but I hadn't allowed myself to look at the clock.

A few weeks later, we argued over my increased client load. He complained that I was spending too much time away from home and too little time in his bed. Adam had let it slip that he sometimes wondered if I was, in fact, going someplace other than a client's house on my long nights away from home. A lover, perhaps?

I was appalled at his accusation. "And where are you going when you stay late after work?" I asked him, hating the tremor in my voice, suddenly afraid of what his answer might be.

"I see what you did there," he shot back, his tone oozing contempt. "Answering a question with a question. Good evasion tactic, Dani."

Once again, he'd left the house, and for the first time in more than six years of marriage, he didn't come home at all.

I spent the next several hours pouring my anger, frustration, and fear into cleaning our home. He was right about one thing; I'd been too busy to do much more than spot cleaning in quite some time, and although Adam did all right with general upkeep, the deep cleaning was my job. I preferred it that way. I bleached the bathrooms and kitchen, cleaned out the refrigerator and pantry, laundered bed linens, curtains, and throw rugs. I swept, mopped, dusted, and vacuumed, and then, physically drained, I showered and went to bed, where I tossed and turned all night long.

The following evening, Adam glibly said, "Looks good in here." But before I could thank him for acknowledging my efforts, he added, "I swear the only way to get you to clean this house is to make you angry. Works every time."

In the last several months—in fact, now looking back, I realize it's been since he bought that stupid car—Adam has spent several nights somewhere else. But until the argument over my busy schedule, he's always been very open about where and why, usually conferences out of town. He's designed a student screening system that seems to be gaining in popularity in the school system, and he's been invited to speak on a fairly regular basis. At first, the events were local, and when I could, I'd tag along with him. But lately, he's been going farther from home, and since the conferences typically cover his speaking expenses, he often opts for a hotel room rather than a long drive home.

Lately, though, he hasn't said much of anything, sometimes not even bothering to come home for dinner before leaving on one of his trips. And the one time I told him I missed him when he was gone, he didn't bother looking up from the piece of chicken he was slicing, only saying, "Now you know how I feel."

I'd been shut down far too many times as a child to not recognize when a person has no intentions of engaging. I'm not good at games, especially the ugly ones.

It is easier to back down. To stop asking.

Well, I got answers anyway.

Yesterday, while Adam was in the bathroom washing his hands for dinner, his phone, set to vibrate, started buzzing on the counter where he'd set it beside his keys. As a general practice, we don't answer each other's phones, not unless specifically asked to do so, but out of the corner of my eye, I noticed it shimmying closer and closer to the edge of the counter. I lunged for it just in time to catch it before it tumbled to the tile floor. He has a screen protector on his phone, but no case, as he prefers the sleek feel of the slim phone over something with rubber bumpers like mine.

But when I grabbed for the phone, I inadvertently accepted the call, and for a moment, I stared at the screen, watching the timer start racking up seconds. Then a voice said, "Hello? Mr. Granger?" Another short pause, then, "Hello?" It was a woman on the other end of the line, but the fact that she called him Mr. Granger had me at a loss as to whether or not I should answer for him. Presumably, it was something official, and to hang up on her now might make things awkward for Adam. Especially if he had to call her back and explain my part in it.

On the other hand, it could be a sales call, and my husband would be only too happy for me to hang up on her.

Making up my mind, I took the plunge. "This is Dani, Mr. Granger's wife. I apologize for that. I almost dropped the phone."

"Oh! Hello, Mrs. Granger. Not a problem." The woman's voice was warm and friendly, reminding me a little of Noralee Niemeyer. She spoke to me like she knew me. "This is Anna with Design in a Day. I'm calling to schedule an installation date for your window treatments." She proceeded to rattle off some appointment options, but my mind drew a complete blank.

"Window treatments?"

"Yes, and I'm so excited for you to see these. The French Country shutters are absolutely stunning. Just the right look for your lake house. They arrived yesterday, and I've been staring at them all day, jealous as heck that you get to have these hanging in that gorgeous living room. Your bedroom drapes will be here first thing in the morning, too. That fabric you two chose is elegant and lush, and they'll look fantastic on those floor-to-ceiling windows; I just know it. Anyway, I wanted to get you on the calendar right away so you can see them for yourself as soon as possible."

Wow. She was everything a designer ought to be. Bubbly, enthusiastic, gushing. But Designer Anna from Design in a Day was gushing up the wrong tree.

"I'm sorry," I interjected when she paused for a breath. "I think there's been a mistake. We haven't ordered any window treatments...." The words died on my lips. I leaned heavily against the counter, afraid my legs wouldn't hold me up.

We hadn't ordered any French Country shutters for *our* living room, but that didn't mean Adam hadn't. *Our* bedroom didn't have any floor-to-ceiling windows, but that didn't mean Adam hadn't ordered drapes for someone else's bedroom windows.

I shook my head sharply, berating myself for letting my thoughts get away from me. Surely not.

"Oh, but, Mrs. Granger, I'm sure this is the number you wrote down for me," Anna countered, undeterred, her words only adding credence to the direction my mind was tumbling. "Yes, here it is." She rattled off the number to make sure she'd dialed correctly.

It wasn't the number that had my hand shaking so hard that the phone rattled against my hoop earring. I hadn't written down anything for her. I hadn't been with Adam when he ordered shutters and drapes for windows we didn't have. Who was the Mrs. Granger Anna thought she was speaking with?

"H-hold on, please," I managed to get out, then lowered the phone to my chest. I pressed my fingers to my lips as though that would be enough to hold back the odd sounds that were trying to work their way out of me. Every time I opened my mouth to speak, nothing came out but a hitching gulp that sounded a little like I was drowning. In fact, that was exactly how I felt. Like I was drowning.

"Hey," Adam said, skirting the end of the table to get to me, an expression of concern on his face. "Wait. Is that my phone?" He pulled up short before reaching me. His eyes frosted over, and his mouth pressed into a tight line.

I turned it toward him without a word. He snatched it from me and stormed out of the room, his pleasant tone as he addressed Anna a disquieting contrast to the throbbing, pulsing anger that rolled off him in palpable waves.

When he returned, I'd composed myself enough to sit down at the table. My fingers fluttered aimlessly over the place setting in front of me, straightening cutlery, sweeping away invisible lint from the tablecloth, nudging my glass to the right a quarter of an inch, and then back again. I kept my gaze locked on his, my expression blank.

I'm very good at keeping my expression blank.

He'd bought a lake house. "It's an investment property," he explained, not bothering to sit down. He braced his hands on the back of his chair instead; his posture almost aggressive as he loomed over me. "A vacation rental. People pay hundreds of dollars a night to rent places like these. It's a one-bedroom house with a dock and a Jon boat; the perfect little vacation spot on a private lake, Dani, and I got it for a steal. If it's rented even one weekend a month, the place will pay for itself."

"What on earth is a Jon boat?" The question was ridiculous; I could care less what a Jon boat was. My husband had bought a lake house and a boat. Without me.

"A flat-bottom boat with two bench seats. Perfect for a lazy day of fishing on the lake," he explained, then added, "Could be very romantic, too, if that's what our guests want."

He spoke so reasonably, as though every word out of his mouth made perfect sense, and the expression on his face was a cross between a challenge and self-satisfaction. Like he expected me to congratulate him. "I don't understand, Adam. Why would you do something so... so *extravagant* without at least informing me first? This is property we're talking about. I'm almost afraid to ask about the financial part. Did you pull money out of our savings again?" First his car, now this? It felt like my husband was launching a whole new life behind my back.

"I told you I got it for a steal. From Greg Bishop—you remember him, right? Sixth grade teacher? His wife's been riding him for ages to get rid of it. I took a look at it last month. It's dated, and there are some minor signs of neglect, but it's mostly cosmetic. He didn't want to do the cleanup, so I made him a ridiculous offer, and he took it on a handshake. No down-payment required."

The next words popped out of my mouth before I could bite them back. "Sounds like you and the other Mrs. Granger will be very happy vacationing there together."

His shoulders stiffened visibly, but before he could make a rebuttal, I crossed my arms and kept going.

"In fact, it sounds a lot like a secret love shack to me." In for a penny, in for a pound. "For you and your other wife? Is this where you've been going all these nights that you're not coming home?"

Adam tugged viciously on the knot of his tie and yanked the strip of fabric from around his neck. "It's a vacation rental, Dani. An investment property. A bachelor pad for a guys' fishing trip. A romantic getaway for couples." He balled up the tie and shoved it into his pants pocket, then spun on his heel and started toward the hallway. Over his shoulder, he added, "And the Mrs. Granger you're tossing out accusations about is my mother, not some woman masquerading as my wife. She's helping me decorate it because you're always too busy." His tone was so filled with venom, I flinched.

His mother? He'd told her about his little getaway, but not me? I still wasn't completely buying the vacation rental thing.

A few minutes later, he charged back into the dining room, where I still sat unmoving in my chair. "I did this for us, you know," he stated, arms crossed, his chin lifted defiantly. "To replace the money we spent on my car."

I stared at him as my mind frantically tried to connect the dots of his reasoning. *We* spent? For us?

"It was supposed to be a surprise, you know. I was going to get it all ready, then take you there to surprise you." His tone went from angry to petulant. "Thanks a lot. You've ruined it now."

He was blaming me? For discovering he and his mummy were decorating his secret man cave together?

No. Not a man cave in our basement or lad loft over the garage, or even a converted shed at the back of our property. And certainly not a Hawaiian timeshare getaway to surprise his wife with. A vacation rental, my great Aunt Tilly.

He'd bought a bachelor pad.

And not for a guys' fishing trip, either. For a married man.

As I studied his expression, I somehow knew with utter clarity that he'd had no intention of telling me about it. Ever.

Today, I'm no less certain of it. Even now, as I stare at the back of his shiny new car blocking my way into our garage, I replay last night's argument in my mind, and I have no doubt that I have ruined his secret, not his surprise.

Because Adam needs a place of his own where he can get away.

From his wife. From Mrs. Granger. From me.

In his Escape.

I put my car in reverse and swing around in the wide driveway. In my peripheral vision I see the front door open, and Adam steps out onto the porch. He crosses his arms and widens his stance as he watches me, but I refuse to acknowledge him. Shifting into drive, I floor the gas pedal, gratified to hear a short, sharp squeal of my tires. I didn't know my automatic transmission had the audacity to peel out, and by the time I pull out onto the street, I am grinning.

It doesn't last long. At the stop sign, I feel a tingle at the bridge of my nose, a burning in my eyes, as an overwhelming desire to cry rolls over me. I swipe angrily at the few tears that threaten, and I yell instead, loudly, wordlessly, unrestrained in the knowledge that no one is around to witness my tirade.

As if on autopilot, I wind my way out of the suburbs and head toward the country. Fifteen minutes later, I pull into the gravel drive of my friend's farmhouse, weak and shaking in the aftermath of my spent frustrations.

"Stop being so dramatic," I order under my breath, forcing myself to climb out of the car.

Then I bend over and empty the contents of my stomach onto the pebbles at my feet.

"Dani-girl? Oh, sweet child. Goodness gracious." It's Gran, and I just about collapse in relief at the sound of her voice as she hurries off the front porch toward me.

She stands by me, holding loose tendrils of hair away from my face as the waves of nausea continue purging me. When my stomach finally settles, she helps me sit back on the edge of my driver's seat. I reach for my metal water flask in my console, but my hands are shaking so badly I can't get the screw top off.

She takes it and opens it, pulls the dishtowel from where it's draped over her shoulder, wets a good portion of it, then hands both the towel and the bottle to me. "Here you go. Wash your face. Drink. Then let's get you inside, okay?"

Ten minutes later, Gran has turned the hose on the mess I made, and I am inside and feeling significantly better. I've heard on more than one occasion from a pregnant woman that fighting the nausea only prolongs it.

"Better to barf," a young mum, pregnant with her third, assured me after a quick dash to the loo during one of our appointments. "It's always better to barf."

Two months later, she handed me a lapel pin she designed for her Etsy shop. *It's ALWAYS Better to Barf*, it said in elegant gold lettering on black enamel. "It's one of my best-selling items with my pregnant mommy shoppers." It is now pinned proudly to one of the pockets of my birthing bag.

It isn't until now, though, that I fully understand why that pin sells so well.

"The girls headed over to the cemetery a few minutes ago," Gran says as she studies me. "Hugo's been digging all afternoon, so they're checking on him. Took him some lemonade and a cornbread muffin, too." The beef stew she'd started when I was here earlier has simmered on a back burner all day, and the house smells like home. "I can call them up on the radio if you like."

Cell phone reception can be spotty out in the woods. "No, no. It's all right. Perhaps I'll go hunt them down." If I stay inside with Gran, I'll only end up pouring out everything to her. It isn't that I don't want to tell her what's going on; if Ranae had been here with us, I would already be talking. I just don't know that I can bear to say everything twice.

"Are you sure you're up to the walk?"

"I feel much better now, really, I do," I assure her. "A walk in the fresh air will do me some good." I stand, glad my legs hold me, and wait to make sure I don't get lightheaded.

"How about I come with you, then, just to be certain you don't tumble off the footbridge on your way over." She turns off the burner under the pot on the stovetop. "Would you like a muffin for the way?"

I shake my head, not quite ready to test my stomach with something so delicious. The lemonade she plied me with has helped get rid of the taste of sickness in my mouth, but I want to give myself a little more time before I try eating. "I'll wait on food for the moment."

"Well, the invitation for dinner still stands, too, Dani-girl." She dips her head toward the stew. With a wink, she lowers her voice and murmurs, "There's enough there for the both of you."

I gape at her, no blank expression here. "How—I mean, I'm not—" I break off, realizing I am about to try to lie to Gran. Something I learned long ago to be futile. I reflexively rest one hand against my abdomen. "I don't even know for sure myself."

Gran laughs and pats my cheek gently before slipping her arms into a cable knit cardigan. It gives her a slightly misshapen form, but it warms my heart with its familiarity. She's worn that jumper for as long as I can remember. "I'm an Irish grandmother, Dani-girl. An ancient one from the old country," she says, playing up her lilt more than a little. She holds the back door open for me. "We *know* things, we do."

The days linger this time of year, and the sun still shines down warmly on us as we make our way past her lush garden and across the wide expanse of lawn toward the cemetery. The water is little more than a trickle gurgling merrily under the bridge, and I pause to peer over the railing at it. The sound of water in nature always soothes me, and with my emotions in such turmoil, I want to grab up any comfort I can find.

Gran says nothing, just stops beside me and waits, until the sound of Ruby's laughter flutters out of the woods toward us. I glance at the old woman and frown, suddenly not sure about my timing. Ruby's day has been traumatic already, which means Ranae will be bending over backwards to lavish her daughter with extra helpings of love and time. Who am I to intrude with my own worries? I have parents of my own I can go to. My mother will be sympathetic and kind, my father, intellectually angry about Adam's behavior, and they'll both say supportive things if—no, *when*—the pregnancy test shows positive.

And then there's Hugo to consider. I know Ranae is out there with that beautiful, bottomless well of a man. I can't just drag her away from him and the work they're doing.

But I want my friend. I need her. I sat with her and waited for the pink lines to show on her test stick almost eighteen years ago, and now I need her with me while I wait for my own pink lines.

Ranae

"We're going back to the house," Ruby tells us as she and Millie stroll past down the trail, arms linked companionably, giggling over some shared gossip.

It's good to see my daughter's spirits so lifted after this morning's debacle. Millie, a lovely girl who lives close enough to ride her bike over, came to check on Ruby after school. They both have driver's licenses, but no cars, and honestly, I'm not in any hurry to see either of them grow up that fast. They are both barely seventeen and still content to ask for rides when they want to go anywhere. And I am still content to drive them wherever they need to go.

"Oh! And my mom said I could stay for supper," Millie says over her shoulder. "But only if I help with cleanup, too."

"Tell your mom I love her," I declare, then wave them off.

I turn back to Hugo. He stands waist deep in the near-perfect rectangular hole he's dug this afternoon. This is the fourth time I've been by to check on his progress, but he is nearly finished, so I am staying to help wrap things up.

Hugo leans on his shovel, the hair at his temples damp with exertion, crescent-moon curls forming at the back of his neck. It's past time for his monthly haircut, but it isn't my place to remind him. I like it a little shaggy the way it is now, but I know he prefers it short and low maintenance. He watches the girls meander off down the trail, not saying anything, but the half-smile on his face is one of fatherly affection. Ruby has wonderful uncles who are willing to drop everything if she needs them, but with Hugo, the need goes both ways.

Blimey, too, stares after them, debating which of his charges needs him most. I do. I pat my thigh and call his name. He must stay with me and protect me from myself and my wayward heart.

He lopes over, and as usual, misjudges his own size—in that way, he truly is my dog—and rams against my hip as he positions himself beside me, nearly knocking me off my feet. His eyes, however, are still on the retreating backs of the girls.

Irish Wolfhounds are sight hounds. Their keen vision is their claim to fame. At the sight of prey, they are known to charge instinctively, no matter how well-trained the dogs are to heel or come or sit in any other circumstance. As Blimey's sight deteriorates, he seems to spend more time watching the world around him, as though he is memorizing the lines and angles of those he loves before we grow too dim to recognize. I know he's not long for this world; he's painfully slow to get up in the mornings, and he hasn't made much of an effort to chase anything in some time now.

"You're a good dog, Blimers." I crouch and point at the ground beside me. "Lie down, boy. Lie down and I'll rub your belly."

In his younger years, the dog would stand on his hind legs with his front paws on my shoulders for a tummy rub, but these days, his old hips don't work the way they once did, especially when it's cold and damp. Another winter is just around the corner, and I worry about him. Hip dysplasia is common in large breeds, but we've been proactive about prevention from the very beginning. The breeder gave us a whole packet of information on proper care and feeding of Wolfhounds, and we've followed his recommendations to the letter, from the varying amounts and types of exercise and food, depending on Blimey's age and development, to making sure he has the right bedding that provides adequate cushioning under his joints.

Now, he gingerly lowers himself to sprawl on his side for me, and I oblige with a hearty scrub of his undercarriage. He makes a low rumbling sound, almost like a cat's purr, and it always gets a smile out of me. I stroke his head and fondle his velvety ears. Blimey sighs heavily and closes his eyes in appreciation.

When I look up, Hugo is watching me, and the raw emotion in his eyes makes me avert my gaze quickly. I start to rise, but I am awkward in my self-consciousness, and I lose my balance, landing on my backside in the dirt. Blimey lifts his head to check on me, then flops back down again, as I right myself and stand.

When I dare to look Hugo's way again, he is concentrating on tidying the corners of the already flawless grave.

Dappled sunlight winks and shifts through the thinning leaf canopy overhead, and it flickers across the raised pattern of scars that lace one side of his face and neck, disappearing down his back beneath the collar of his Henley shirt. I have no difficulty picturing the puckered skin that sweeps in a wide swath over the expanse between his shoulders, even though I've seen it only twice since it healed over. It makes me think of an angel whose wings have been viciously ripped off.

Hugo Beckenbauer is no fallen angel. He is a man who believes he can no longer dream of flying.

Blimey lifts his head again and cranks his gaze around toward the trail. It's Dani, and I wave, surprised to see her again today.

"Hello, you two," she calls out in greeting. Then she spots the dog. "Hello, you three. Sorry, Blimers," she corrects, using my nickname for the dog.

Relief washes over me. A distraction, a diversion from the thoughts wreaking havoc with my emotions. "Hello, yourself," I say with a hug. "What are you doing here? I thought you had a baby to deliver." I study her carefully when she pulls away quicker than usual. Her face is pale, but her expression gives little away.

Dani waves at Hugo, then shrugs. "I essentially just watched the whole thing. It was a lovely textbook home delivery. A darling little girl with a whole lot to say about being thrust so unceremoniously into this great big world. When I left almost an hour ago, mummy was already up and about, preparing for visitors, and daddy was taking a recovery nap."

Hugo chuckles, a sound that rolls over me. "Shouldn't it be the other way around?" He lays his shovel on the edge of the tarp nearby and hauls himself out of the grave. After dusting his hands off, he takes a long swig of water from his thermos, then douses a bandanna from his pocket and scrubs his face and the back of his neck with it.

Dani grins easily, quelling my concern a bit. "You'd think, wouldn't you? But we women were designed to handle childbirth, Sir Hugo. Men, not so much. A man trying to help a woman he loves go through it?" She shakes her head. "Sometimes I'm not sure God intended for men to be a part of the actual labor and delivery at all. Half the time, they're the ones we practitioners watch the closest. The last thing we need is another patient."

Hugo pours a little water into his hands and runs his fingers through his curls, shoving them away from his face. They spring back rebelliously. Dani insists he has a brooding Henry Cavill look about him, what with his hazel-blue eyes and sun-bronzed coffee curls, the hint of gray at his temples and in his five o-clock shadow at the end of a day. I don't think he looks like anyone but himself. He frowns slightly, cocking his head as though pondering her words. "Really? That surprises me, coming from you."

I, too, shoot her a quizzical look. I usually love Dani's unique perspective on things. She's one of the smartest people I know, and her viewpoint sometimes borders on controversial, but it's not because she intends it that way. She's just gifted with clarity about hot topics. I'm not so sure I agree with her on this point, though.

She must read my expression, because she continues before I can challenge her. "Stop looking at me like that, Ranae. Don't misunderstand me. I'm not saying they shouldn't be there, or that they shouldn't participate. I'm only saying I find that the whole birthing experience can often be more overwhelming for a man who must stand by and witness it play out than it is for the woman who's actually laboring. Not because one is weaker or stronger than the other, but because we were designed for different purposes. One is designed *to* labor, the other is designed to go *through* labor, right? Which makes it utterly exhausting for a man to do so little while the woman he loves is doing so much." She lifts her hands in frustration. "Oh, I'm just making this all sound like nonsense."

"No, you're not," Hugo says in his gentle, gravelly voice. "Speaking as a man, that makes perfect sense."

And there it is. She might be a little flustered right now—my spidey senses are on high alert—but it's this kind of thinking that makes her such a great podcaster. She always offers a slight twist on things, and our listeners love it.

"Thanks, Hugo," she says, but offers no further discourse on the topic. Her shoulders droop a little.

"Did you run into Ruby and Millie?" I ask, changing the subject. "They just left."

"We did. Gran walked out here with me." Dani waves a hand in the direction of the farmhouse. "She went back with them. Said they'd have dinner ready when we got there." It doesn't matter how long she lives in the Midwest, Dani still calls supper dinner, as does her mother.

"You're joining us after all?" I ask, pleased and surprised, both.

Dani religiously shares the evening meal with her husband whenever she can, making it priority to be there when he comes home at the end of his day.

"I suppose it's old-fashioned," she once told me. "But we think it's important that we touch base over a good meal every day, or at least as often as our crazy work schedules allow us."

I applaud her motivation, but I secretly wonder if there's more to it than she's letting on. It isn't Adam's schedule that's crazy. And I have a gut feeling that he makes her feel just the tiniest bit guilty over how often he has to fend for himself for meals.

She nods now and simply says, "I am." An uneasy quiet settles around us. The only sound is the scraping of Hugo's shovel as he scoops up dirt from the tarp to make the pile a little neater.

I wait, sensing that Dani has something she needs to get off her chest, and knowing that if I don't give her the room she needs, she'll lock up. I shoot a quick glance at Hugo, who is now laying two pallets over the open grave, as much a precaution against critters stumbling into the open hole as it is for clumsy humans like me. But he carries on with his task, seemingly unaware that there is turmoil brewing.

Either that, or he's fully aware and is letting it play out. He, I know from personal experience, is really, *really* good at giving people their space.

"Um, how much longer do you think you two will be?" Dani asks, her eyes darting around the little clearing.

"Maybe only a few more minutes," I begin.

"You ladies go on ahead. I'll finish up," Hugo interrupts. To me, he adds, "The grave is covered. I promise I won't fall in." His eyes are alight with humor, even though he doesn't smile.

Dani snorts loudly, then covers her mouth in embarrassment.

"You're a funny guy, Hugo Beckenbauer," I retort, feeling my cheeks warm.

"That's what everyone says." Actually, they don't. No one, other than those of us who know and understand his dry sense of humor, ever accuses Hugo of being funny.

It isn't embarrassment Dani is covering, it seems. She makes a stifled gagging noise, and I glance over at her just in time to watch the color of her skin go slightly green. Then she lurches across the trail and vomits into the undergrowth.

"Whoa!" I hurry to her side and put a hand on her shoulder. She hasn't brought much up, at least not from what I can tell, but she remains bent over, dry heaving periodically. "Dani, what can I do?" I mean, she's the doctor here.

"Wa—water," she gasps, but Hugo is already at her side. He hands her the half-full lid of his thermos. She straightens slowly, washes out her mouth, then hands it back to him empty.

"Come sit," he insists, putting an arm around her and leading her over to the camp chair still folded up in the wheelbarrow. He says he brings it for when he needs to take a break, but the only time I ever see it set up is when he pulls it out for me to use when I come by to check on him. With his free hand, he grabs it and shakes it open, then steadies it while she sinks into it.

I refill the thermos lid and hand it to her. "I know I'm stating the obvious here, but you don't look so good, girlfriend," I tell her.

Hugo steps away and begins quietly gathering his tools and loading them into the wheelbarrow.

"Give me a minute," Dani murmurs, resting her forehead in the palm of one hand. "Hugo, can I use your bandanna?"

"It's dirty," he says hesitantly.

"With what? Your sweat? I was just elbow deep in amniotic fluid, blood, and quite likely a little urine and feces, to boot. Oh, and now you can add vomit to the list, too," she says with an angry gesture at the trail. "Hand it over."

Hugo's brows shoot up in shock—it's probably the first time he's ever witnessed Dani raise her voice at anyone—but he does as she asks. I bite my lip; I doubt either of them would appreciate me laughing right now.

Dani takes the thermos from me and douses the paisley cloth with cold water before pressing the fabric to her neck and chest.

After I'm certain my urge to giggle is under control, I beckon for Hugo to help me cover the dirt piles with more tarps. It isn't likely we'll get rainfall between now and tomorrow morning, but in this part of the country, sudden cloudbursts often occur year-round.

"I'm sorry," Dani finally says, just as we finish anchoring the corners and edges of the two tarps with stones.

"Oh, please," I counter. "Are you apologizing for hurling in my woods? Or for not feeling good?"

"I'm not apologizing to you, Ranae," she says, rolling her eyes at me. "I'm apologizing for being so rude to Hugo." She waves the bandanna, then presses it back to her neck. "Please don't worry," she assures him. "I did wash my hands. More than once. And I seriously doubt I have any of that stuff on me, I promise. I was just being belligerent."

"It's not a problem. I've handled worse," Hugo says with a half-smile.

"Well, I'm sorry anyway. That was completely out of line. I'll wash this and return it to you in a day or two."

Hugo nodded. "Forgiven."

"What's wrong, Dani?" I ask, glad to see she's recovering a little. "You didn't look so hot this morning, either. The flu, you think?" My mind goes to Gran, wondering how much time Dani spent with her before coming out to find us. My grandmother endured a horrific bout of pneumonia last winter that required a short stay in the hospital. We are approaching flu season again, and even though the old gal is pretty hearty, pneumonia has a way of rearing its ugly head when her immune system is taxed.

"I'm not contagious, if that's what you're asking," Dani says flatly. "You don't have to worry about Gran."

Dang, that girl really can read my mind. Or my face, I suppose.

"And yes, I can read your mind," she mutters. "Your thoughts are written all over your face."

Hugo clears his throat. When we both look over at him, he says, "I'm going to take these tools back to the schoolhouse and get the golf cart. I'll be back to pick you two up in a few minutes, okay?"

When he disappears down the trail, Blimey plodding along at his heels, Dani says, "One of these days he's going to catch you staring at him like that." She stays hunched forward over her knees, not bothering to look at me, but I know what she's talking about.

I press my lips together and close my eyes, but I still see Hugo imprinted on the backs of my eyelids, his forearms rippling as he steers the loaded wheelbarrow, his hair flopping boyishly with each step. "I know," I mutter, disgusted with myself.

"Would that be such a bad thing?" she asks, lifting her head to meet my eyes.

"Dani!"

"What? You moon over him like some lovesick schoolgirl." She shakes her head slowly. "I have a hard time believing he doesn't already know, anyway. Why not just confess and get it over with?"

"Don't be ridiculous. I could never do that," I say with a snort. Then I drop to sit cross-legged on the ground near her. I toy with one of my own dark curls, and in a hesitant voice, tell her, "You know, I think he does know. Right before you got here, I was petting Blimey, and I glanced up at him. He was staring at me, and—" I break off, my heart in my throat at the memory of that look. "He looked so sad, so hopeless. Like he was carrying all the pain in the world on his shoulders." My voice drops to a hoarse whisper as I continue haltingly. "But, I mean, he was staring at me like... like... I don't know. Like he thought maybe I could do something about it."

Dani straightens, her brows lifting in interest. "See? That's something, isn't it? What did he say? What did you say?"

I roll my eyes and let my head fall back to peer up into the branches overhead. "Nothing," I admit with a sigh. "I fell on my backside, instead. When I looked up at him again, he was back at work, and the moment had passed."

"Oh, Ranae. My darling girl, you are such a klutz."

"I know, okay? Don't rub it in. But he makes me self-conscious. Uncomfortable. I feel so awkward when I'm around him."

"Ranae."

The way she says my name makes me look at her. "What?"

"He makes you feel self-conscious and awkward? Those aren't good things."

"No, no, no. That's not what I mean." I push to my feet and kick at a clump of dirt before pacing away from her. "At least, not in a bad way. I mean, I'm self-conscious because I want him to notice me. And I'm uncomfortable because I feel so much for him, and I feel awkward because I'm afraid my feelings are written all over my face, as you say, which makes me super self-conscious every time he looks my way. Besides, if I ever come clean, things will change between us; you know they will. And then what if he doesn't feel comfortable working here anymore and decides to quit? What will I do then? And what about Chloe?"

"Whoa, girl!" Dani declares, holding up a hand to stop me. "Rein it in a little, crazy pants."

"Ugh. I know," I moan, lacing my hands together behind my head. I take a few deep breaths, then lower my hands. "Besides, we need to talk about you right now." It's almost painful being pulled in opposite directions at the same time. I know I need to focus on Dani, but a rather desperate part of me wants to race down the path and launch myself at Hugo, tackle him to the ground and declare my feelings for him.

Most of the time, I can keep that part of me in check, thank goodness.

That look, though. Talk about wearing his heart on his sleeve. Except the heart on Hugo's sleeve is battered and broken, a charred pile of a million smoldering pieces. Humpty Dumpty has nothing on Hugo Beckenbauer.

Dani

"So are you going to tell me what's going on? Does this have anything to do with Adam leaving?"

Ranae is standing across the little clearing from me, having paced there in her fretfulness. Her eyes are focused on me, but I can tell it's an act of sheer will. She would much prefer to wallow in the emotions Hugo stirs up in her. I can't say I blame her.

I wonder if perhaps I'm wrong to unload my troubles on her right now.

But then it occurs to me that I've been wondering a lot of things lately. All I do, it seems, is second-guess myself. Should I, or shouldn't I? Will I, or won't I? Do I, or don't I? I know Ranae better than anyone else in my life, even better than my parents, and I know for a fact that she would want me to tell her everything that is going on.

"*Is* he leaving?" Ranae prompts gently.

Before I change my mind, I blurt out, "I think I'm pregnant."

The array of emotions that washes over Ranae's face is rather comical. Her jaw drops open, her eyes widen, then she whoops with excitement and charges at me. But before she reaches me, she jolts to a stop and covers her mouth with both hands, and I can see every thought registering in real time.

"This is good news, right?" she finally asks from behind her hands, standing close enough to touch me, even though she doesn't. "Or is it?"

My heart lurches at the memory of that dreadful night when I put her in her place about Adam and my decision not to have children. I accused her of being judgmental even when I knew there wasn't a judging bone in her body, and I will never forget how she closed her mouth, unable to find the words to defend herself to us. I wonder if she remembers it, too, and if that is why she's so careful with her response to my announcement.

"It's terrible news," I admit. "Because of the timing," I amend. "Not the pregnancy itself."

Ranae frowns and nods slowly, but I can tell she's waiting for me to explain. She's trying so hard not to assume anything.

"If it weren't for my belief that Adam is, indeed, making plans to leave, the timing might not be an issue, either." I reflexively place my hand against my stomach, an act I suddenly recognize as protective. *My baby*. I'm going to be a Mum. Ranae's gaze follows my gesture, and she sighs softly, her eyes suddenly glistening. I know there are words storming the gates of her closed mouth, and her fingers are trembling against her lips.

I can't help it. I smile at her. It's a sad smile, I know, but suddenly, the idea of a baby where there wasn't one only hours ago, sends out a tiny tendril of what can only be hope inside me. Maybe a baby is exactly what Adam and I need right now.

Ranae drops to her knees at my feet, then wraps her arms around my waist, hugging me gently. "Don't barf on me," she says. "And I'm sorry-not-sorry, but I don't give a flying fig about Adam's plans to stay or leave. If he chooses to walk out on you and this baby, he's a bigger fool—" She breaks off and jerks back to look at me, her eyes wide again, this time in a combination of shock and rage. "Is he leaving because you're pregnant?"

"No, Ranae. And if you don't stop squeezing me, it won't be my fault if I do vomit on you. Let go." I push her away, and she releases her hold around my waist, but she stays close, still kneeling in front of me, her hands resting on my knees. "I don't know for certain that he is leaving," I admit. "And I don't know for certain that I am pregnant. So obviously, he doesn't know about it, either."

Ranae frowns. "Wait. You need to back up. So everything you just told me is conjecture? Even the pregnancy?" She flops a hand in the direction of the trail where I purged what was left in my stomach several minutes ago. "Wasn't that morning sickness?"

I take a deep breath and shove the canvas chair back a little. My friend has no concept of personal space. "Right. I know I sound like a crazy woman." I rise and wait to see if my stomach will rebel, but all seems peaceful for the moment. "Listen, I came out here because I thought if I waited for you at the house, I'd only end up spilling my heart out to Gran. I don't mind her knowing what's going on, but it's you I came to see, Ranae. I—I just needed to see you."

Without warning, my breath catches, and then a sob tears through some kind of invisible barrier in my chest. I can actually feel it forcing its way up the back of my throat, rushing over my tongue, and pouring out of my mouth. Then again, maybe I'm just dry-heaving. I'm not exactly sure anymore. I try to speak through it, to mask it with words. "I—I can't—I need—" But there's no use. Tears well quickly and spill over, and I bring my hands up to cover my face, unwilling to give in to what feels like mounting hysteria.

I'm afraid Ranae is going to throw herself on me again, and that if she does, I'll either come completely undone, or worse, I'll lash out at her in my anger over my inability to maintain control. But she surprises me with a gentle brush of her fingers on my shoulder.

"I hear the golf cart, Dani. Here." She's offering me a cup of water from Hugo's thermos again, and I take it with trembling hands, gulping down the cold liquid in between the soundless shudders that pass through me.

"Thank you," I whisper when I can catch my breath. Sure enough, Hugo appears on the trail a moment later. I pour the last of the water onto his bandanna and run the cool, wet cloth over my face again. I don't want him to worry any more than he already is; the fact that he broke Fair Haven's cardinal rule about only using the motorized vehicles in emergencies is evidence of his concern.

We are a quiet lot as we make our way back through the woods. Hugo doesn't take us to the small utility shed behind the schoolhouse where they usually keep the golf cart. Instead, he drives straight out to Kirchwood Lane and delivers us to the front steps of the farmhouse. The teenagers are sitting on the porch with their phones, and Ruby snaps a picture of us as we climb out of the cart, Hugo gallantly hurrying around to offer me his hand. I'm glad I'm one of those lucky few who doesn't turn red and blotchy when I cry. Ranae hates me for it, but it certainly is a benefit when I need to present a composed front.

"I think I'll head on home," Hugo says, remaining at the cart as Ranae and I start toward the porch steps. We both turn as one toward him. "Will you tell Aileen for me?" He's looking at Ranae, but I see the worry for me etched on his face all the same.

"Were you planning on staying for dinner, too, Hugo?" I ask, reaching out like I'm going to touch his arm, but of course, I don't.

"You ladies need this time." It's not an answer to my question.

"No. No, don't do that. Please." In a moment of clarity, I realize I actually want Hugo to stay. I want his steady spirit and solid company. In fact, his presence at the table may help me find my own footing in the middle of the storm that seems to have swept me up in it. Besides, I know Ranae will be slower to react if he's there; he seems to steady her, too, in spite of the emotions he simultaneously stirs up in her. "Please stay," I repeat.

"Are you guys coming in, or what?" Ruby calls from the top step. "We're starving."

"You know Gran will be disappointed if you don't. She's made her stew, one of your faves," Ranae cajoles him, shooting me a questioning look. She's checking to make sure I'm okay with this, and I nod firmly in agreement.

Hugo is silent, weighing his decision carefully.

"I'd like you to stay, too," Ranae says, her voice cracking on the last word. She blushes prettily but doesn't turn away.

The man studies her a moment longer, then to me, he says, "If you're sure."

"Come on, you guys!" Both girls are hollering at us now.

Despite the girls' imploring, dinner is not quite ready when we all pour into the house. So Hugo heads out to return the golf cart to the cemetery, then back to his place just around the other side of the woods for a quick shower first. Ranae and I disappear upstairs to her bedroom with its small adjoining bathroom. I have my test strips and the comfort of another calming hug from Gran. When we return, both of us a little more subdued than before, she hugs us again, me a little longer, then hooks a knuckle under my chin.

"Everything is going to be all right, Dani-girl. You'll see."

About thirty minutes later, we women are gathered around the table waiting for Hugo. Just as Ranae is filling the last of the glasses with sweet tea, the front door opens to let him in.

Ranae sloshes tea into her daughter's empty bowl, and a few drops splatter the front of Ruby's yellow shirt.

"Mom!" The girl shoves her chair back and lifts her arms at her sides in a dramatic posture of disbelief.

"I'm so sorry," Ranae says, grabbing one of the broadcloth napkins off the table and tossing it into the bowl.

Hugo detours to the kitchen, where he pulls a dishtowel from the oven door and brings it with him to the table. In moments, the mess is mopped up, and everyone is settled in their seats again, this time, with Hugo sitting in what was once Opa Alec's chair at the head of the table. We all dutifully bow our heads as Gran leads us in a quick prayer of thanksgiving.

It is there, our heads bent over our waiting bowls, that I realize how much I have to be grateful for. This circle of people is only the first layer of goodness in my life. My parents, Ranae's parents. Her brothers and their families. My mother's family, small, but mighty, in England, and my father's family, even smaller, in West Virginia. My clients. The other midwives who operate Breathe with me. Gail, my assistant—

"We also ask that you watch over our loved ones who can't be with us this evening." Gran's words jerk me out of my thoughts, but not before I realize I have not listed my husband among the people I'm grateful for. A coil of shame snakes through me, and I let it squeeze, until Gran declares "Amen!" and everyone around the table echoes her.

Hugo rises from his chair and offers to serve the stew. I study his long, elegant hands as he ladles out the thick, chunky soup from the cast iron Dutch oven in the middle of the table. His movements are graceful and fluid, deliberate, and he doesn't spill a drop. His are the hands of a concert pianist, or a surgeon's, not a grave digger's, I think to myself, and yet, I get the feeling he wouldn't change careers for the world. He seems to love Fair Havens almost as much as Ranae does, and his sense of purpose in his work there is apparent when he speaks of the cemetery.

He holds out a hand for my bowl, and I catch a glimpse of the pale puckered ridges that mar the flesh on the inside of his forearm. I don't allow my gaze to linger, but Hugo doesn't attempt to hide his scars, either. Even so, I wonder what goes through his mind when he sees them. Do they still distress him? Does he study them in the mirror after a shower? Does he trace the lines with his fingertips, wishing they would disappear? Does he even see them anymore at all, or does he make every effort *not* to see them?

I smile at him as I take my full bowl back, and he meets my gaze with a steady, knowing one. I have the feeling he can tell when people notice his scars, even when they do their best to hide their shock. A sympathetic ache for the man wells in my chest, but I don't allow that to linger, either. Hugo isn't the kind of man who would want to be pitied.

"Gran, this is di-vine." Ruby says each syllable emphatically before lifting another spoonful of the stew to her mouth.

"I wish my grandma cooked like you do," Millie declares. "This is the kind of stuff people write books about."

"Well, aren't you two just the most delightful young ladies," Gran chortles. "Don't let *your* grandmother ever catch wind of such a sentiment, Miss Millie." Millie's grandmother, Judith Kissler, is a dear friend of Gran's. "She'll have your guts for garters; you can count on that."

Ruby makes a face. "That's disgusting."

"All the best sayings are," Gran tells her.

Our dinner conversation meanders through a myriad of topics. We talk about the DiSarno siblings and the small funeral for their mother scheduled for the morning. The girls regale us with stories from their first several weeks back at school, and I let them ask me questions about some of my home birth experiences. Hugo and Ranae have a quiet discussion about an upcoming Indiana Wildlife Federation meeting, and Gran smiles contentedly around her table, inserting her two bits into each conversation in turn.

Finally, the girls ask to be excused, and then, without being told, they clear the table. We adults sit back and beam proudly at the teenagers we've all had a hand in raising. Not so much with Millie, but she's been a constant in Ruby's life long enough to have felt the influence of this household, this family, in her own life.

And yes, I consider myself a part of this family, just as the man at the head of the table does, too.

Tension is building between my shoulders, though, and I know that as soon as the girls dash upstairs, I'll be on the hot seat. I can see the questions in both Ranae and Gran's eyes, although Hugo remains stoic. I take a deep breath and sit back in my chair, satisfied, but not too full. I haven't had any nausea since coming inside, and I'm hoping it's passed, at least for the day, but I'm not going to give my body any excuse to backfire on me. Besides, it would be a terrible waste of Gran's good food.

The four of us talk quietly over trivial matters while the girls finish up in the kitchen. Gran puts on the kettle for tea and brews a pot of coffee when both Hugo and Ranae say they'll have some.

When Ruby and Millie head upstairs, Gran covers my hand with hers. "Okay, Dani-girl. Give us the down-low."

Ranae snorts. "The down-low, Gangsta Gran? Since when did you go street on us?"

I turn to my friend, one eyebrow lifted. "Haven't you heard? They call her Granny from the Graveyard."

If the teenagers were still here, they'd be appalled at our attempts to be funny.

Hugo, good man, grins appreciatively, one side of his mouth curving up, the other pulling down toward the scars at his jawline.

Gran, however, doesn't take the bait. She keeps her gaze fixed on me, and since I don't immediately begin divulging, she dives right in. "Where is Adam tonight?"

Ah, the million dollar question. Beside me, Ranae rests her hand on my back, and I hate the prickle of tears behind my eyes. I glance over at Hugo again.

I'm certain, if asked, he'd rather excuse himself from this churning maelstrom of estrogen and emotions, but he remains, nonetheless. He even seems comfortable in his seat at the head of this table of women; he doesn't fidget, or gaze longingly at the door, or worse, the clock.

Perhaps our Ruby is right. Perhaps Hugo is the king of all men.

"Adam was home last I knew," I finally say. "But I don't think he was planning on being there for long." In fact, I'm sure of it. "His car was in the driveway," I add, as if that explains everything.

It does, though, at least to me. If he'd been home for the day, he would have pulled into the garage.

No one speaks, and I gather my thoughts. I've spent the whole meal pondering where to begin, but I'm still coming up short.

"What makes you think he's leaving?" Ranae finally asks. She's not asking because she's surprised, I notice. Her question is a prompt to get me started.

"Oh, Dani-girl," Gran murmurs, her already wrinkled brow furrowing deeply. "It's that way, is it?"

I tell them about the new car. "An Escape. Not a sports car. It's so odd. You're a man, Hugo. Tell me. What grown man buys an Escape as a midlife crisis car?" I don't wait for him to respond; it's not a fair question, anyway. I acknowledge that I am, indeed, working long hours, and that I have been for months now. "But it's always busiest between May and October; all those cold winter and spring snuggles turn into summer and fall babies." That elicits a snort of appreciation from Gran.

I tell them about last night's phone call and Adam's explanation that he's purchased an investment property. "A vacation rental, he called it, but at one point, he actually referred to it as a bachelor pad. He claims he was going to surprise me with it." As the words come out of my mouth, they sound even more ridiculous than they did when Adam said them. "I'm such a fool," I mutter, rubbing my eyes and shaking my head. "A blind, ignorant fool."

The three of them remain silent for far too long, and my stomach is starting to sit up and speak to me. Not in the language of morning sickness, thank heavens, but with the acid gurgle of stress. "Somebody please say something," I whisper.

Ranae says something, all right. Her words are few, but choice, leaving no doubt of how she feels about Adam at the moment.

"Hush, Ranae," Gran tells her, although she doesn't sound angry at the outburst. To me, she says, "You are not a fool. You are a woman who wants to be able to believe her husband."

"Yeah, and now you're pregnant." It's Ranae who says it, but I happen to be looking at Hugo when she does. He flinches, his eyes widening, and something tragic flashes across his features. I turn back to Gran quickly, not wanting him to know I've seen.

"And now I'm pregnant," I confirm. Gran already knows, of course, but I'm in desperate need of a voice of reason, of wisdom, right now. She just studies me, still holding my hand.

"Does Adam know?" Hugo asks quietly, but when I meet his eyes again, there's something fiercely protective there, an emotion held in check, albeit just barely. And for a moment, I wonder if Adam has ever looked at me that way.

I shake my head. "No. Believe it or not, I just figured it out myself today." Yep. Blind, ignorant fool in so many ways. I make a sound that might have been a laugh had any of this been funny. "I actually thought I was coming down with the flu, or not getting enough sleep."

"Are you going to tell him tonight?" Ranae asks.

"I don't know," I admit. "Right now, I don't ever want to tell him. Right now, I don't know that he even deserves me, no less a baby." I'm aware of how childish I sound, but I actually feel a little like a child, truth be told. I need someone to hold my hand and tell me everything is going to be okay.

I hear Gran's voice in my head, and I can almost feel her arms around me, hugging me fiercely. *Everything is going to be all right, Dani-girl. You'll see.*

Instead, she says, "Well, of course you must tell him." Her tone is firm, even though her eyes are gentle. "As soon as possible. Don't let more time slip by without laying things out on the table between you. Perhaps this baby is just what your Adam needs to remind him of who he is, of who he committed to be when he married you."

"Oh, Gran," Ranae murmurs, a little censoriously. "You're not serious, are you? A baby doesn't solve problems that exist already."

"Yes, I'm serious. And why not? Children are the most precious gifts we can ever hope to receive." Gran darts a look at Hugo, then back to Ranae. "What better reason is there for a couple to try to work things out? Is it so wrong to ask a pair of full-grown adults to set aside their self-pity and self-indulgence, to focus instead on giving their child the best they have to offer?" Her frown deepens, if that's even possible. "I know I'm old-fashioned when it comes to marriage, but whatever happened to sacred vows to love and cherish until death do us part? Why is everyone these days so intent on finding themselves, no matter whose hearts—especially their children's—they tromp on while they're on such a selfish quest?"

"Gran." Ranae is clearly unsettled by her grandmother's rant.

"No, no," she says, holding up a hand. "Let me finish. I'm going to say this only once, but please let me say it."

Ranae sits back in her chair, looking a little chastised, but her eyes spark with a passion of her own. There's a storm brewing inside her, but she's giving Gran the floor for the moment.

I, too, am a little surprised by Gran's vehemence, but not by her sentiment. Marriage and family is everything to her.

Hugo, of course, remains silent, his expression unreadable.

"Listen, Dani-girl," Gran says, leaning forward over the table toward me. "I'm not going to ask you if you *want* to stay married. It doesn't matter what you want, because you made a vow before God that you would. It's that simple in my book. Nor am I going to ask you if you *want* to have this baby. I'm not even going to ask you if you think your husband is making plans to leave you for another life, because if we're all being honest about this, there doesn't seem to be much of a question there." She squeezes my hand hard, and the love in her eyes takes away some of the sting of her words. "Of course, I could be wrong, and the—the *foolish boy* is telling you the truth, as selfish and childish as it may be."

"The foolish boy is a liar," Ranae interjects.

Gran gives her a look that shushes her, and my friend's mouth tightens in rebellion, but stays closed. "I am going to ask you this, though. Are you willing to sacrifice your own happiness, your own wellbeing, for your child's?"

"Gran, that's a trick question," Ranae starts in again.

"Of course it is. But it's a fair and straightforward question, too, at least as far as a child is concerned. Yes, you are willing to sacrifice your own wellbeing for your child's, or no, you are not willing to sacrifice your own wellbeing for your child's. It's that simple." She squeezes my hand again. "I'm not trying to bait, you, Dani-girl. I simply want you to shed all the peripheral baggage you've been carrying around for the past few months and make this choice first. Once you've said yes or no to this question, the rest will sort itself out one way or another." She turns to Ranae. "And just to clarify, I do believe in the sanctity of marriage, but I'm not so naïve or callous as to believe *every* marriage is worth saving. It's obvious, even to me, that Adam is something of a blackguard. But is he violent? Perverted? Abusi—"

"A blackguard, Gran?" Ranae rolls her eyes. "A scoundrel? A rake? He's not a pirate, he's an elementary school therapist."

"Then he, of all people, should know how devastating a broken marriage can be for a child," Gran shoots back.

"Yes," I say, cutting in on their bickering. Then I realize Gran might erroneously think I'm agreeing with what she just said about Adam being influenced by his work.

Because I'm not really sure Adam's job gives him any special insight into his personal affairs. He considers his career as something separate from his private life, and most of the time, he expects me to do the same. When I start talking about an especially eventful birth, he'll remind me that we agreed to "leave work at the office." I've never minded too much; I have Ranae and Ruby and Gran to tell all my juicy stories to. But that's also been his response to any talk of having children of our own. "Let's not bring our work home with us, okay?"

I clarify. "What I mean is yes, I'm willing to sacrifice my own happiness and wellbeing for my baby's."

"Good girl." Gran nods.

It's not like she didn't already know what my answer would be. But I surprise her when I say, "I look at it differently, though, Gran. My willingness to sacrifice for my child is all the more reason to let Adam go without a fight. Why on earth would I put that kind of burden on an innocent baby? Make him or her bear the responsibility of saving our broken marriage? Because, as you pointed out earlier, if we're being honest here, we all know it's broken all the way down to the very foundation."

"Yes! Sacrifice Adam, please," Ranae snips. "Dani isn't the problem here, Gran. She's not the one planning her escape." She turns to me. "Sorry for the pun. Not intentional at all."

"But apropos," I concede. Ranae's anger toward my husband, although justified, is niggling at me. I feel disloyal to him for allowing her to talk about him with such revulsion. At the same time, I feel feeble and gullible for having the desire, although decidedly incremental at the moment, to defend him.

I feel, if I am honest, a little as though I've been conditioned to defend him.

Which makes me both angry and frightened, on top of everything else.

The more I ponder the situation, however, the more certain I become that if Adam is already creating a world apart from me, if he's already planning his escape—as Ranae so bluntly put it—from the life we share, then now is the time to put this baby first.

This baby. *My baby.* The words send a tremor of apprehension through me, adding one more loop to the emotional roller coaster I'm on.

Adam's baby. A baby he's never wanted. A baby he's never wanted to even discuss the possibility of.

"He'll think I got pregnant to coerce him into staying." My words hover in the air over the table, and for several moments, no one says anything. They all recognize them for the truth.

I catch Hugo's eyes; he's studying me, his expression unreadable. "Hugo? Any insight you can offer? As a man?"

After a moment, he clears his throat. "I'm not Adam—"

"Thank God," Ranae mutters. Gran sends her the stink eye again. "Sorry," my friend grumbles.

Hugo continues after barely a pause. "And, in light of Adam's, um, behavior lately, this may make me nothing more than a selfish man."

"Never." I lean forward, anxious to hear what he has to say.

"Speaking as a man, though, I think you should tell your husband about this pregnancy as soon as you possibly can. While there's still hope; maybe not for the marriage, but at least for a relationship between you two. He's the father of your child, and you can't change that by withholding this from him. Again, I'm not privy to Adam's thoughts, but if anything was going to shake me up and set me back on the right track, it would be the knowledge that the woman I love is going to have my child." He swallows hard and continues. "That said, saving a marriage doesn't mean simply tolerating a life together, at least not in my book. Saving a marriage means rescuing and restoring it to what it once was, to what it should be. I suppose I'm kind of old-fashioned, too, but I have to agree with Aileen. In my opinion, a child might be the best reason there is to fight for restoring a marriage."

It may be the largest number of words I've ever heard Hugo string together. From the look on Ranae's face, she's thinking the same thing.

He's right, of course. I need to tell Adam immediately. Shame flutters inside me at the realization that I'm sitting here discussing the future of our child with these three people, while Adam, the father of said child, still knows nothing of his or her existence.

I'm upset at Adam for making plans for his—for our?—future without discussing them with me. Yet isn't that what I'm doing at this very moment?

Ranae

"BUT THE DILEMMA REMAINS," I say around the angry tightness in my throat. "It takes two to fight for a marriage, Hugo. Or any semblance of a relationship." I shoot him a pointed look. "And that's not happening here. Adam has never wanted children; he's made that abundantly clear." I avoid Dani's eyes, not because what I'm saying isn't true, but because it sounds harsh when spoken so plainly. I want so badly to protect her, but I'm afraid I might just be adding to her pain. And yet, I feel compelled to say what no one else seems willing to. "I think you're right, Dani. He's going to believe the worst about all of this, and he'll accuse you of getting pregnant on purpose."

"So?" Gran says, tough love oozing out of every pore. When her values are challenged, it can be like arguing with a rock. "It doesn't change the fact that she is, indeed, pregnant, and that he is, indeed, the father, and that he, too, should have the opportunity to choose his child's wellbeing over his own."

"But that's it, Gran. He won't. He won't even choose his wife's wellbeing over his own, the woman he vowed to love and cherish above all others. And by 'all others' that includes himself." I scrub my hand through my hair, frustrated at how ridiculous this all feels. How sanctimonious. I gesture at my friend. "Dani would lay down her life for him, but while she's busting her butt bringing other people's babies into the world instead of her own, he's out there buying new cars and a bachelor pad." I make air quotes and speak the words with as much derision as I can muster.

"How do you know he won't?" Gran persists. "How can you be so certain he doesn't want to be the man he once was, the husband he once was? What if this is the wake-up call he needs, Ranae?"

I push back from the table in frustration. I have seen the changes in my friend since she married Adam, and they haven't been good in a very long time. "The kind of husband he once was? He's never been any better of a man than he is right now, Gran. Never. Dani deserves better." I turn to my friend and grab her arm, my throat tight. "You deserve better. You and this baby."

"Ranae Niemeyer, enough." Gran's voice is firm, and I stiffen in my seat, pulled up short by her reprimand. I cross my arms tightly, press my lips together, and clamp my jaws shut.

I want to scream. I want to throw something.

I want to hit the backspace button because I know she's right. I've gone too far. I can see it in Dani's shuttered expression.

I know what's stirring up in me, and it's not just over Dani.

I know what it feels like to be set aside. I know how soul-crushing it is to believe in happily ever after, to be promised forever, only to have forever ripped out from underneath me. And I hate that Dani is going to have to walk that road, too.

I want to hurt Adam. For both Dani's sake and my own. For her baby's sake... and for my baby's sake.

"I'm not even sure he's going to be home tonight." Dani's voice is small, and something shifts inside of me. I need to focus on her right now, not on my own past hurts and disillusionments.

"I'll go with you," I tell her.

"I don't think that's a good idea," Gran interjects. "Not in the state you're in."

"Not to talk to him," I clarify. "And I'm not in a state, Gran." My denial rings false, even to my own ears. I take a quick, sharp breath and say, "I'll drive with her to make sure he's home. If he's not there, Dani, you're coming back with me."

"You don't have to do that," she begins, but Hugo is nodding, and my grandmother halts her protest to look at him.

"I'll follow you," he says. "You two take Dani's car so she doesn't have to drive alone. If Adam is there and wants to talk, you can ride back with me, Ranae." He eyes us both, but to Dani, he says, "You're not going home alone, and it probably wouldn't hurt for Adam to see us drop you off, either." He doesn't say it, but the unspoken words are there just the same. *In case Adam is in a less than amicable mood.*

Gran is frowning, but she doesn't argue, and neither does Dani.

Fifteen minutes later, while Dani is upstairs saying goodbye to Ruby and Millie, Hugo and I head out to the driveway. He's brought his truck tonight, which is how he got back here so quickly after dropping us off in the cart. It's a sturdy old Ranger, and although it gets better gas mileage than most full-size trucks, he usually rides his bike the few miles in good weather or walks the trail he and Chloe forged through the woods from their place on the backside of Fair Havens property.

"Is Adam dangerous?" he asks when we're out of earshot of the house. We stop between his and Dani's vehicles and turn toward each other. Muted sounds of Gran's television show drift out through the screen door.

"Not that I'm aware of," I tell him. "I honestly think it would require too much effort, too much of an investment, for him to be dangerous." I know I sound contemptuous, but that's the best I can do right now. I feel a lot more than contempt for the man. "Which is why, I'm sure, he's just making plans to cut and run. He's not even going to attempt to fix things because that would take too much effort, too. Cut and run. Pretend nothing ever happened." I grimace, the night before Dani's birthday party sharp and toxic in my memory. "That's Adam's modus operandi."

"So you're saying you really like the man," Hugo says.

"He's my all-time favorite," I quip back at him, a half-grin tugging at my lips without my permission. I absolutely love Hugo's dry sense of humor.

He brings a hand up between us like he's going to touch my arm, or even my face, but he falters, then reaches around to rub the back of his neck. He glances past me at Dani's Forester. "You okay to drive? You were pretty upset in there."

I shake my head, a little embarrassed now. "No, no. I'm fine. She's my best friend, you know. And he's hurting her. So yeah, I was pretty upset. I *am* pretty upset. But that's nothing new." I cross my arms and lift my shoulders to my ears. "I've been pretty upset at Adam for quite a while now."

Hugo nods, as though he understands perfectly. "If he's there, don't engage with him, okay? Just get out of her car and get into my truck. It's going to be difficult enough without our interference."

"I'm not going to interfere." I tighten my clasped arms. He lifts one eyebrow, doubt written all over his beautiful, scarred features. "I won't engage," I assure him again. "I promise I'll behave."

He does touch me then, a quick squeeze of my shoulder. It's more than I usually get from him, and I want to reach up and cup my own hand over the place his palm rested momentarily, a silly attempt to hang onto the sensation.

"You're right, you know. He doesn't deserve her," he continues, unaware of my desperate emotions. "But then, none of us deserves the unconditional love of another person, do we? That's what makes it unconditional."

I make a half-hearted attempt at a teasing glare. Anything to ease the tension. "Are you always this sensible? This reasonable?"

It seems to work. He grins down at me, a good six inches taller than I am.

I shake my finger at him, then quickly pull it back when he makes to grab it. With a snort, I say, "You must drive everyone around you crazy." I'm unable to say Chloe's name.

Dani hurries down the porch steps, looking long and willowy in the fading twilight. She's brushed her hair, and I recognize the look on her face for what it is. Impenetrable. She asks me to drive. "I need to call the Thornburghs before I get home," she explains.

She spends a good portion of the drive on the phone, but when she finally ends the call, she turns to me and says, "Thank you."

I know what she means without needing clarification; I'm grateful for her in my life, too. "I love you," I say. "Bon Jovi or Def Leppard?" Without waiting for her answer—she won't care which one we listen to—I select the Def Leppard playlist on my music app. It's been cued up since I got behind the wheel and plugged my phone in. Her sound system is amazing, and I have to play my arena rock every time we ride together in her car. It's tradition.

I pull Dani's Forester into the garage, and Hugo pulls into the driveway behind us, leaving his truck idling. Adam's Escape is parked in his spot in the garage, and I resist the juvenile impulse to run my keys down the length of it. Instead, I hug my friend tightly, and ask her one more time if she's sure about this.

Hugo revs his rumbling truck engine a few times. I roll my eyes at Dani; talk about juvenile. Then it occurs to me that he's making his presence known, not to us girls, but to Adam.

"You two are the best," Dani murmurs before she pushes open the door that leads from the garage into her kitchen.

I take a cue from Hugo and make my presence known, too. "Call me later, girlie," I call loudly as I duck out of the garage. "Cool your jets, Hugo!" I'm shouting now, partly to be heard above the roar of Hugo's engine, but also to make sure Adam knows exactly who is dropping his wife off. "I'm coming!"

Ever the gentleman, Hugo is out of the truck and holding open my door by the time I reach the passenger side. He offers me a hand up, and I take it. My attention is focused on the house, but my palm tingles in his solid grip.

We sit there, idling for several moments, as though waiting for some kind of a cue that it's okay to leave. Dani's dining room window blinds are open, and we watch her move to stand against the counter that divides the kitchen from the dining room. She appears to be talking to someone, but Adam remains out of our line of sight. She turns and gestures with a broad wave in our direction, then she moves quickly, hurrying around the counter, her hands up as if trying to stop something from happening.

Hugo is already stepping down from the truck again when Adam marches out onto the porch and strides down the walkway toward us. Hugo stands just inside the open truck door, feet braced apart, but loose and casual, like he's greeting an old friend.

He doesn't fool me. I can practically feel the pulsing air emanating off him. The man is ready for anything. I'm primed and poised, too, my hand on the door handle, but I can hear Hugo's voice in my head, telling me not to interfere. Not to engage.

Followed by my promise to behave.

I just watch; Hugo can handle Adam just fine without my help.

"Is there something I can do for you?" Adam asks, his tone curt. He's not even pretending to be polite.

"Adam." Hugo offers his hand, but it's ignored. I wonder if Adam notices the fist that Hugo makes as he lowers his hand back to his side. "We just dropped your wife off."

Adam turns and looks pointedly at the Forester inside the open garage. "Doesn't look like she needed anyone to drop her off. Her car seems to be running just fine."

"She wasn't feeling well," Hugo states matter-of-factly. "We wanted to make sure she made it safely home."

"Why didn't she call me?" Adam asks, glaring past him at me now. Dani steps out onto the stoop and calls his name. He ignores her. "Was she with you?" he asks me through the open door.

"She was with us." Hugo answers for me, his calm demeanor belying his forceful presence. "Out at the farmhouse." He steps to the left to block me from Adam's line of sight.

Adam stands silently for several moments, but Hugo doesn't say a word, either. Finally, unable to hold out any longer, Adam points at Dani who is still waiting just outside the front door, and says, "Well, she's home, safe and sound, as you can see, so you can both get off my property now."

For just a few tense moments, I think Hugo may be the one who interferes. His fingers curl into a fist again, and in the glow of the cab light, I can see the ripple of flexing muscles in his shoulders. But then he nods at Dani, gives Adam one last lingering look, and climbs back in behind the wheel. He pulls his door closed and backs out of the driveway without another glance at the angry man still standing at the edge of the lawn.

"I don't like this," he mutters, running a hand through his hair as we make our way to the end of the street. "I hope we did right by leaving her there with him."

"He's too much of a chicken to hurt her, Hugo," I assure him, and I'm certain it's true. Adam is a blusterer. His words are lethal weapons, indeed, but he's all bark and no bite. He may raise his voice, but he can't be bothered to raise his fists.

"You seem awfully calm now," Hugo says, angling a look at me.

"She's going to call me in one hour. Or text me if she can't call." That should be plenty of time for her to tell Adam about the baby, and for him to react however he's going to. "If I don't hear from her in an hour..." I let the words hang in the air between us. "Regardless, I'm planning on coming back to get her at that point. I have a gut feeling that Adam will take off again," I confess.

Hugo makes a low sound of disapproval at the back of his throat, then asks, "How is Millie getting home tonight?" The question comes out of nowhere, and for a moment, I can't recall who Millie is.

"Oh. Right. Um, Millie." She's only been my daughter's best friend for the last decade. "Her mom is picking her up at nine. School night." I reposition myself so I'm turned toward him. How nice it is to be able to watch him unabashedly. If he looks over and sees me staring, well, I'm just being attentive, is all.

"Would you like me to wait for her with you?"

I'm confused again. "Um, you don't need to do that."

"I'd feel better about it, though. We can go grab coffee and maybe a slice of pie—" He breaks off and grimaces. "We just had coffee and pie. Never mind. But maybe we can find some place to wait in town rather than driving all the way back to the farmhouse, I mean," he finishes lamely.

"Oh!" It finally occurs to me that he's not talking about waiting with me for Millie's mom. He means waiting with me until I hear from Dani. "You don't have to do that, Hugo. It may be fifteen minutes or three hours, for all I know. I was just going to head home and keep myself busy until she calls."

"I don't have anywhere else to be," Hugo tells me. "Might as well be with you."

If I hadn't been looking right at him, I might have been offended. But even in the low glow of the dash lights, I can see his self-recriminating expression. He obviously didn't think about how it would sound until after it was out there. I make light of it, trying to put him at ease. "Now there's an offer a girl can't refuse." I flick him playfully in the bicep.

"I'm sorry." He grips the steering wheel with both hands. "That was badly done. Let me try again."

I laugh softly and tuck one foot up underneath me. "Go ahead. I'm all ears." I like the way his cab smells. Upholstery, engine oil, a hint of cedar aftershave. A little good, clean dirt, even if it's likely graveyard dirt.

He smiles at my teasing, but his tone quickly grows serious. "I don't feel good about you going back to Dani's house alone, Ranae. I'd like to wait with you until she calls, and then drive you over there myself. Would that be all right with you?"

I blush at his sincerity and will myself to not read anything into his concern for me. "That would be fine," I tell him, hoping I don't sound as breathless as I feel. "Are you sure you don't need to be back?" I have to at least ask.

"I'm sure." Then he turns and grins over at me. "What about you? Are you allowed to be out late on a school night?"

From my passenger seat, I can't see his scars, and I can almost believe they're not there. But the thought of him without them somehow feels disrespectful, and I focus on the way his hair falls forward over his brow, the sharp angle of his nose, and the crinkles at the corners of his eyes.

He turns on his blinker and heads toward town. "Where would you like to go?"

"Go? Um...." My mind is suddenly blank. I have no clue where the two of us should spend the next hour or more together. It feels completely different than the hours upon hours we spend alone together at Fair Havens. "Why don't you choose," I tell him, suddenly not quite sure what this is. Is it just two friends killing time while waiting for a call? Or is it an excuse to spend a little time together, just the two of us, outside of work?

He nods and a semi-comfortable silence settles around us, giving me the opportunity to relish in the moment. Who needs a magic carriage when a girl can ride in a truck that smells like her man? Not that Hugo's mine, of course. It's a hypothetical question. But I try not to be too obvious as I sniff the air, filing away the scent in my mental Hugo file.

When we pull into a parking lot in front of a coffee place, I grimace. "Um, I don't think I should have any more coffee tonight."

"Nor I," Hugo says. The cab goes quiet when he pulls the keys from the ignition.

"Nor I?" I tease, filling the silence with my voice. "You and Gran sound like you're right out of the Renaissance Period. Blackguards and nor I's."

He shrugs and turns his beautiful smile on me, apparently in no hurry to get out of the truck. "I'm old-fashioned, remember?" Then he does something that isn't old-fashioned at all. He reaches across the console between us, hooks a finger under my chin, and rubs the pad of his thumb along the curve of my bottom lip.

I'm pretty sure my heart stops. Or maybe my lungs collapse. Or maybe I've died and gone to heaven, and it just hasn't sunk in yet.

A moment later, his hand is gone, and I quietly suck in some oxygen. My heart is suddenly pounding so loud I can't hear my own thoughts, and I think my eyes are too wide when I look at him.

"You had blackberry sauce," he said, holding up his thumb to show me. "Right there." He touches the corner of his own mouth, and my eyes follow the movement like a tractor beam.

"Oh," I manage to squeak out before forcing my gaze away to glance out the window. Next to the coffee shop is a charming little bookstore. I've been in the place before, but it's been years, and from what I can tell through the large front window, it's been spruced up a bit since I last visited.

"You like books." It isn't question. He knows that Ruby and I are avid readers.

I don't turn to look at him, afraid of what he'll see on my face. "I do," I concur, then I have to squelch the thoughts of white lace gowns, flower girls, and unity candles that those two words conjure. "Love books, I mean. This looks perfect."

And it is perfect. We somehow manage to commandeer a little sofa tucked into one of the many little reading nooks throughout the shop. The armrests are frayed at the seams, and the seat back cushions could probably do with a good re-stuffing, but it's comfortable and homey feeling, and when the two of us sit together on the little sofa, I find the way I'm most comfortable is turned sideways with my back to the armrest, my legs crossed under me, facing Hugo. If I hold my book or magazine just so, I can steal glances at him without him noticing.

Except that he always seems to notice. I can tell he knows I'm looking at him because he's smiling almost every time I do. It's not his mouth that gives him away—I'm on his left now, and the scars that cover this side of his face tug the corner of his lips down. No, it's the crinkles at the corners of his eyes that give him away.

We end up splitting a coffee from the cafe next door after all, along with a piece of pumpkin spice cake, and while we're talking about the small pile of books we also purchased, my phone rings. It's been an hour and fourteen minutes since we left Dani's place.

"I won't need to be picked up, after all," she says. I want to put her on speakerphone so Hugo can hear what she has to say, too, but it's too loud in the coffee shop. I send him an apologetic look across the little table we share.

"He has surprised me, I have to admit," Dani says, sounding calm, if a little sad. "Adam isn't terribly upset about the news. He's not exactly thrilled, either, but we've had a good talk already, and now he's in the shower. He's not going anywhere tonight, at least."

I press my phone closer and plug my other ear so as not to miss anything she says. I have no clue what to make of what she's telling me, but Adam's uncharacteristic behavior leaves me feeling unsettled. Should I let things be for the night? Or should I pay attention to the red warning lights flashing in my mind?

Hugo holds up his keys and gestures toward the parking lot.

"Hold on, okay?" I ask her as I gather up my books and nod at Hugo. In less than thirty seconds, he's helping me into the truck. "Sorry," I tell Dani. "We're at a coffee shop, and it's too loud to hear well inside. I'm putting you on speaker, okay?" I tap the speaker icon just as Hugo climbs in on the driver's side.

"We?" Dani asks, her voice suddenly dripping with honey. Apparently, she didn't catch the part about putting her on speaker. "As in you and Hugo Heartthrob?"

Mortified, I frantically fumble for the mute button too late.

"Hello, Dani," Hugo says, leaning toward me over the console so my phone will pick him up better. A gentle wave of his man-smell envelops me, and I close my eyes briefly. "Hugo Heartthrob here."

"Oh." Her voice is small on the other end of the line, and all I want to do is cry. "Well, there you are, indeed. Hello, Hugo."

"That's Mister Heartthrob to you," he teases her, then nudges my shoulder with the back of his hand. "Hey," he whispers.

"Sorry," I whisper back, covering the mouthpiece of the phone with my thumb. I barely manage to meet his gaze before closing my eyes in disgrace again.

Hugo starts the truck, the rumble of the engine not terribly loud inside the cab, especially after the cheerful bustling noise of the cafe. "Are you cold?" he asks, then turns the heat on when I nod.

"What are you two whispering about?" Dani asks.

"Nothing," I tell her, then change the subject back to her. "So, can you repeat what you just said to me? About Adam and your plans for tonight? I want Hugo to hear it, too."

As she tells us once more about Adam's tepid reaction, it's all I can do not to demand she pack a suitcase and wait for us out on the front lawn. But Dani seems willing to accept the way things are for the moment, and Hugo, although he remains silent throughout most of the conversation, shakes his head at me when I start to suggest she let us come pick her up, anyway. Don't interfere. Right.

"Fine, we won't come kidnap you tonight," I finally promise her. "But you need to call me first thing in the morning, you hear? Or any time throughout the night if anything changes," I add. Knowing Dani, if Adam left in the middle of the night, she still wouldn't call me until morning.

"I will, I promise. By eight. I know you have that funeral." She sounds exhausted, almost resigned, which really bothers me. I'm reluctant to end the conversation. "I'd better go," she says. "I still have charting to do before bed. It's been a long day, and I need a good night of sleep."

"Dani?" I wait for her response.

"Yes?"

"I love you."

"I love you, too."

"And I love that baby already."

"That baby loves you already, too." She doesn't choke up when she says it, but I do.

"Call me," I reiterate.

"I'll call. I promise." Then she's gone.

We sit in silence for several moments, and I let loose the growl of impotent frustration and worry that's been building in me all night. It's only Hugo, and he's seen me vent a few million times over the years since we've known each other. I ache for my friend; this should be the happiest night of her life, discovering she's pregnant with their first baby.

I'm still holding the phone out between us, my elbow resting on the console, but Hugo takes it from me and sets it into one of the cup holders. Then he curls his large, calloused hand around mine and holds it gently the whole drive home.

Dani

IT'S BEEN MORE THAN a week since I told Adam about our baby, and although we're spending most evenings at home together, we're both tiptoeing around each other and all the things we haven't said.

It's not as though we haven't had the opportunity to talk. I've cooked several of his favorite dinners, hoping to inspire important conversation. He politely acknowledges my efforts and helps with cleanup after every meal, yet somehow, we still manage to avoid the topics we should be discussing.

Perhaps it's just me tiptoeing. I feel like I'm waiting for him to respond, react, *do* something. Anything. I could just come right out and ask him if he plans to stay or go, but for some reason, I can't bring myself to do so. I suppose I'm afraid of what his answer will be, especially if I put him on the spot.

My positive pregnancy test seems to have triggered a hormone release, and every day this week, I've been battling morning sickness. Except that it's all day, not just mornings, and it seems to catch me off guard every time. I've taken to carrying around a plastic bin everywhere I go, just in case, even though I've only actually vomited once since that first day at Ranae's. Fortunately, although I have several prenatal appointments with clients, I have no babies actually due over the next month, and I'm grateful. Maybe by then, I'll have figured out what triggers the nausea and will have some ideas on what I can do to manage it. My goodness, but do I have a renewed empathy for mothers who have suffered with this.

Gail sets me up for my first prenatal appointment with Tracy Rogan, one of the midwives I work with at the birthing center. I don't even suggest to Adam the possibility of us having our baby at home. He may be open to the idea if he decides to stay, but again, since I'm not sure what his plans are, I feel more comfortable preparing for a birth at Breathe. It's a thought I don't allow myself to dwell on for too long; it makes me sad to think of delivering anywhere but in the comfort of my own personal space. Our birthing center is wonderful, and we've made it as home-like as possible while still having all the basic accouterments of a hospital available to us, and for many of our families, knowing the hospital is less than two blocks away is a huge comfort. But it's still not home. Not *my* home.

I have Ranae and Ruby and their adorable midwife Rose Bergmann—who took me under her wings and taught me far more than I learned in school—to thank for my choice of vocation. It was my experience as Ranae's home birth partner that not only convinced me to pursue midwifery, but also planted in my heart the desire to have my own home births.

Either one of my parents would be thrilled to be my obstetrician, of course, but we've had this conversation several times over the years, and they understand my birth plan wishes. They'll both want to be at the birthing center when I deliver, I'm certain, but as participants, not providers. They insist they'd rather be grandparents first, doctors second, to any child of mine, which eases my mind.

I pull up outside the perfectly manicured home my parents have lived in since moving back here more than twenty-five years ago. It suits them to a tee; the house is painted in neutral earth tones with a few splashes of color on doors and window trims. The lush lawn is bordered by a low limestone retaining wall since their property sits a little higher than the home next door. There is a large pagoda dogwood tree in the front yard, a flowerbed under the front bay window where a few hydrangea bushes hide a spigot and hose reel, and their white mailbox with its bright red flag looks like it's been freshly painted.

No one would guess at the fierce, bold spirits who dwell inside, people willing to go to remote and dangerous ends of the earth to provide medical care to those far less fortunate than themselves.

I've come to tell my parents about my pregnancy. It wasn't meant to be only me, but late this afternoon, Adam called with the news that he had an emergency parent/teacher meeting this evening, and suggested I go ahead without him. He came home for a quick dinner, showered and shaved, and then headed back to work. Right before he left, he pulled me close and kissed me in a way that made my heart race, and for a few brief moments, I wanted to believe that he really did have a school meeting to attend and would rather stay with me than go. That spark of hope only lasted as long as it took his car to leave our driveway.

So I'm here now, platter of homemade brownies in hand, wondering how my parents will react to our news in Adam's absence. Wondering if they'll believe me when I tell them how happy we are about this surprise pregnancy, this baby.

This baby. I still catch myself stumbling under the weight of those words. My father opens the door before I can ring the bell. His left eyetooth on top is slightly crooked, and when he smiles, it rests jauntily on his lower lip. I used to wish for a crooked tooth of my own, and he'd tease me about getting his straightened to look like mine. He never has, thank heavens, and I suddenly wonder what kind of teeth this baby will have. I smile at the thought of a snaggle-toothed infant, a bubble of protective mummy love swelling inside my chest.

"Hello, Danielle," he says. I lean forward, the plate of brownies between us, and kiss Dad on the cheek while he pats my back affectionately. "I see you brought your old dad his favorite dessert. I've got ice cream, of course."

"Of course." Brownies and ice cream. More American than apple pie, he insists. He takes the plate into the living room while I head for the kitchen where I know I'll find my mother.

Mum greets me with a quick hug. "Hello, Danielle," she says, sounding just like Dad. She studies my face for a moment before I look away, but I don't miss the flicker of concern in her eyes. "Adam's not coming?"

I shake my head. "He had an emergency parent/teacher meeting and the teacher requested he be there." I don't make a practice of lying to my parents, so I repeat exactly what Adam has told me. They'll figure out the truth of the matter soon enough; we all will.

"Tea is ready," she says, not missing a beat. She moves her pretty teapot to a large tray that already holds three tea settings, along with a few ramekins of condiments. Has Adam's absence become so predictable? "Did I hear you brought brownies? Would you like to dish us up some ice cream?"

"Of course." I make quick work of filling three bowls with some gourmet Vanilla Bean ice cream they keep stocked year-round. Mum maneuvers the unwieldy heavy tea tray out to the living room with the grace that comes with years of practice.

"Michael, are you already eating a brownie?" I hear her ask my father. "Put that down and pour for us, won't you?"

Her accent, like mine, has become less pronounced over the years she's spent in America, but she has not given up her favorite PG Tips black tea, and still prefers it loose leaf, even though the pyramid bags will do in a pinch.

Ten minutes later, we're settled comfortably in front of the gas log fireplace. I pass on the ice cream but add a spoonful of honey and my mother's homemade clotted cream to my tea, turning it into an indulgent treat all on its own.

Suddenly, my father asks, "Where is Adam? I thought he was coming with you this evening."

It's not strange that it's taken him this long to notice my husband's absence. Adam often finds excuses for not joining me at my parents' home. Tonight, I'm calling it what it is. Excuses. Legitimate or not, he has always seemed to have a ready supply of good—and not so good—reasons to send me without him. I know he feels like he has nothing in common with my Mum and Dad, yet they've never treated him with anything but kindness and affection.

Maybe he and his black heart can't handle all the goodness in this house. The toxic words drift through my consciousness like a bad smell, and I actually wave them away with my hand. I won't let myself assume the worst. Not yet. I repeat Adam's excuses to my father, and when he frowns, I pray he doesn't ask me to expound. But Mum doesn't let us linger on the topic of Adam.

"I'm pleased you're visiting tonight, Danielle," she states. "We just so happen to have some exciting news to share with you. We were going to ask you two over for dinner this weekend anyway, but this works out just as well."

I wonder dryly if their news is as exciting as my own. "I can't wait to hear it."

Dad sits forward, setting his empty dessert dish on the coffee table in front of him, and resting his hands on his knees. My parents are usually rather reserved about most things, but his eyes are lit up with excitement, and I can't help but smile. "We've been asked to head up a Doctors Without Borders team in Beira next summer. After all this time; can you imagine?"

"It's been more than thirty-five years since we've been back there," my mother adds. "So we're quite giddy about the prospect."

"That's wonderful!" I exclaim, getting to my feet to hug each of them in turn. The exchanges are both a little stilted and awkward, especially with my father who can't decide whether to accept my embrace sitting or standing, so we end up looking like two rugby players in a huddle, bending at the waist, arms around each other's shoulders. But we are all sincere in our affections, nonetheless.

When I return to my seat, they tell me how the trip came about, that a mutual colleague commandeered a specialized team of obstetricians and gynecologists to open a new women's clinic in Beira. When he said he could think of no two people he'd trust more to oversee the launching of the clinic, my parents jumped at the chance to return to their old stomping grounds.

Seeing the anticipation and excitement on their faces now, I ask why they've not gone back before this. I've heard the stories of their missions to Beira all my life. In fact, I've always assumed they'd go back at some point, so the only element of surprise in it for me is why it hasn't happened sooner.

"Well, we've considered it over the years, darling," Mum says, smiling at the question. "But there has always been one reason or another for us not to. The timing is simply right this go around."

I drop my gaze to the cup in my hand. Next summer. My baby is due early next summer. I wonder if they'll still consider the timing right when I tell them my news, and as seems to have become a habit of mine, I start to question whether or not I should tell them at all.

"When do you leave?" I ask, not looking up. From the corner of my eye, I see my mother stiffen ever so slightly. Can she really sense something, or am I just being paranoid?

"The end of May," my father says, leaning back against the cushions behind him, relaxed again now that he's divulged his exciting news. "The clinic is scheduled to open June first, so our group needs to be there about a week before to make sure everything is ready, then we'll stay for the first month to see that the operation runs smoothly."

I still don't lift my gaze, not wanting them to see my distress, but my mother rises and comes to sit beside me on the sofa. "Danielle?" She doesn't touch me, but she's close enough that I can smell her Light Blue perfume. "Is it Adam?"

I start to shake my head, then stop. Of course, it's Adam. It's Adam and this baby and my parents' trip and some stupid bachelor pad and a Mrs. Granger who isn't me.

"I'm pregnant," I blurt out, and before either of them has time to react, I add, "And I'm due around the 15th of May."

"Then we won't go, of course." my mother says, without a moment's hesitation. She lays a hand on my back and leans forward to try to catch my eye. "This is wonderful news, Danielle." It's a statement, but I hear her questions in every word.

"No, of course we won't," my father confirms. He's sitting forward on the edge of his chair again, his eyes lit with a completely different emotion. "Pregnant? Are you sure? A baby?"

"Of course I'm sure, Daddy. A baby, yes. And of course you *will* go," I declare, ignoring his suspiciously bright eyes. "I am not going to be the reason you two pass on such a fantastic opportunity." I am adamant, a little angry that they'd even consider sacrificing this once-in-a-lifetime trip because of me.

Are you willing to sacrifice your own happiness, your own wellbeing, for your child's?

Suddenly Gran's words echo in my mind, and it's as if a thousand-watt bulb has just blinked on over my head. I turn to stare at my mother, my eyes wide. "Am I the reason you've never gone back to Beira before now?" The question tumbles out sounding a little like an accusation.

Its only for a moment, but she does hesitate only briefly before rushing in with a quick denial. "Oh, darling. Of course not," she insists, shaking her head, and I almost believe her. But then she darts a look at my father, and when I see his deer-in-the-headlights expression, I know I'm right.

"It *is* because of me, isn't it?" I ask again. "I don't understand. Was I so helpless as a child?" I always thought I was frightfully independent. I don't ever remember even being afraid of the dark.

My father finally speaks, but his voice is a little strained, like he's trying to sort through his words to find the right ones to give me. "Well, I suppose you're right to a certain extent. We have, of course, had several chances to go back over the years, but as your mother said, until now, it simply hasn't worked out. When you were younger, you were, indeed, one of our primary reasons for not going, but extenuating circumstances always played a large role, too. When we lived in London where you might have stayed with your Aunt Adele it simply wasn't possible because of your mother's position at Queen Charlotte's; her contract wouldn't allow her to take that kind of leave. Then once we moved back here, we didn't have family close by for you to stay with, and we didn't feel compelled to have only one of us go without the other." He clears his throat. "That, my dear, had nothing to do with you. Call us selfish and sentimental, but we wanted to return together as a team, or not at all."

"You have never been helpless," my mother says, her fingers fluttering over my shoulder and down my arm before she returns her hand to her lap. I am unsettled by her furrowed brow, and I lean back a little to look at her more closely.

"But..." I prompt, growing more agitated by the second. What is going on?

Mum sighs softly and lifts her hand as if to touch me again, but instead, she plucks at a non-existent crumb on the knee of her pale blue trousers. "But for a long time, you stopped being... fearless."

The word swirls out of her mouth like a smoke ring, drifting down over my head and shoulders until its wispy tendrils tighten around my chest. It's a sensation my mind remembers—a sense of overwhelming dread—but I can't recall what caused it. I subconsciously bring a hand to my abdomen, an innate desire to protect my baby from the truth of it. "What happened to me?" I ask, certain there must have been some terrible tragedy or an act of treachery against me. "Did something—someone—?" I can't put the question fully into words.

"No, no, darling." My mother reaches for my hand and clasps it tightly. "No," she insists again. "You were just a very brave girl who started to believe that the world wasn't kind to brave girls, that's all. You went from being outspoken and inquisitive to analytical and, well, perhaps a little lost. We worried for you, and we simply felt it best that we put off gallivanting around the world until...." She stops and shrugs one slender shoulder in a gesture I've never seen her do before. Mum is not a shrugger.

"Until you found your place again, honey," Dad finishes for her, the warmth in his smile not quite reaching his eyes.

I feel like I'm missing something. "It makes sense to me why you wouldn't go when I was a child. Fine. But I'm thirty-four years old. You might have gone at any time over the last twenty years. Even in high school, I could have stayed with Ranae's family. Did you not trust them or something? Was it the boys?" I could understand why they might be concerned about Ranae's handsome older brothers. I'd had a mad crush on Nolan for many years before I met Adam.

"That's not it at all, Danielle. The Niemeyers are wonderful people, and those boys have always behaved above reproach," my mother declares, almost sounding offended by the question. "Carl and Noralee have been your alternate emergency contacts from the time you were sixteen years old."

"Then I don't get it. What are you not telling me?" I lurch to my feet and stand near the fireplace, putting distance between us. Another exchanged look confirms my suspicions that there's more.

My father straightens his shoulders, and a furrow forms above his eyebrows. "There is nothing to get, Danielle. More often than not, as you will soon discover, and as I'm sure you've seen with Ranae and Ruby, parents make difficult decisions based on what they believe is best for their children. Your mother and I have made many hard choices over the years that we have not told you about, primarily because they weren't your burden to bear."

"So the answer is yes, then. I am the reason you haven't returned to Beira until now. Why? Was there something wrong with me?" I know I sound belligerent, and I want to suck the words back in. I'm usually far better behaved, especially with my parents, but I can't fight the feeling that the lovely tapestry of my life is quickly unraveling around me.

Then again, I don't know if I can handle this tonight. I'm rather sick of secrets, and I'm not so sure I want to uncover any more this week. Or maybe for the rest of my life. "Never mind," I say in a clipped tone. "Keep your secrets. I don't want them." I cross my arms and take a deep breath in through my nose, then pant a little as a wave of nausea sweeps over me. I wonder if I'll have to make a mad dash to the bathroom, but I manage to ride it out by standing perfectly still and taking short shallow breaths until it passes.

"Danielle, please." My mother remains seated, but her posture is stiff, tension practically radiating off of her. "Come sit down. You look quite pale."

I hold up both hands. "I'm fine. I've had terrible morning sickness all week."

"Who is your doctor?" my father asks. "Or your midwife? Are you going with one of your partners at Breathe?"

I tell them about my first visit with Tracy next month. "If my calculations are right, I'll be around ten weeks along, so we'll do an ultrasound then, too."

My mother asks the question I haven't had the courage to voice. "Is Adam going with you?"

I sigh and cross my arms again. "I don't know. He said he'll try to get off work, but he might not be able to." Which is ridiculous. Unless he's lying about other things, he hasn't used any of his sick days in more than a year.

My father surges to his feet, startling both Mum and me. "Just a minute. Let me get something straight. Adam was supposed to be here tonight, with you, to tell us about your pregnancy, but he called off because he had to work, correct?"

I grimace slightly and nod, already knowing where he's going with this. I resist the urge to defend my husband. I've been doing far too much of that over the years, I think.

"Now he's not going to your first prenatal appointment because he has to work."

"He said he'll try." I sigh, long and loud, the omnipresent exhaustion of early pregnancy getting to me. I just want to go home and crawl into bed. I want to close my eyes and let sleep carry me away from this—this chaos that my life seems to have become.

"And last month, he couldn't make it to Breathe's annual open house because he had to work."

"Correct."

"Michael," my mother says, but it's only a half-hearted attempt to stop him. I can see her mentally checking off the same list, too.

"No, no. I want to get this right." My father is now pacing back and forth in slow steps between his chair and the bookshelf behind it. "July 4th with the Niemeyers, Adam had a conference to attend in Las Vegas." He holds up a hand and starts ticking things off on his fingers. "He didn't come to Ruby's seventeenth birthday in June because he had another conference up north. Indianapolis, I believe? A one-day event, right?"

The expression on my mother's face upsets my stomach almost as much as the morning sickness, and I make my way back to the sofa to sit beside her. I offer her my hand, and she takes it between both of hers. I can feel a slight tremble in her fingertips, and I find myself wanting to comfort her, even though I'm the one who should be falling apart. But I've got a significant head start on my parents; I've had far more time to process all of this, and none of what my father is saying is revelatory news to me.

"Your anniversary." He stops pacing and returns to his seat, folding his hands together in a white-knuckled grip. "You had to cancel your anniversary trip because he had to work."

"No, no." I lift my free hand, holding up a finger to stop him. "We had to cancel because he got too sick to travel. The plan was that we were going to tack on a few days to the end of a weekend conference he wanted to attend on the west coast, remember? Then he got sick the day before we were supposed to leave."

When Adam told me about wanting to attend the conference in California, I'd presented him with the idea of me going with him, and of taking a few extra days and making it a short vacation to celebrate our eighth anniversary. I'd never been to that side of the United States, I had an uncharacteristically small patient load at the time, and since he was going to go anyway, why not tag along with him? He'd been reluctant, telling me he didn't think he could take extra time away from work. So as a surprise, I put in the request for vacation time for him and it was approved without a hiccup. Imagine my own surprise when he arrived home that evening, red-faced and fuming, and practically threw the vacation time approval form at me, telling me I had no right to go behind his back like that. We made up before the trip, but when he got sick right before leaving, and then went back to work instead of taking those vacation days with me, I couldn't help wondering if it was all a big farce, if he was in some awful way, punishing me for taking matters into my own hands.

"But he's promised me that we're still going to take that trip," I chirp, my voice drenched in false cheer. "Any day now."

"So he worked instead of taking you away for your anniversary," my mother concludes solemnly.

"Exactly. He had to work," Dad persists, using his fingers to make air quotes around his words. His face is flushed, and not from the heat of the fireplace. He clears his throat and narrows his eyes at me, his expression fierce, reminding me of the way Hugo looked at me at Gran's table the other night. "Listen to me, Danielle. If you need to come home, come home."

I feel my mother flinch beside me, but I'm fairly certain it isn't because she doesn't support my father's offer. I think it's because he has said exactly what she wants him to say. "It's okay, Dad. Thank you, but Adam and I have some things we need to work out before either of us makes any kind of a move." I almost laugh at my own words. I wonder if Adam got that memo.

"I'd like to go with you to your appointment if Adam won't be there," my mother says. "Unless, of course, you have someone else you'd like to take. Maybe Ranae is planning to go with you?"

"Mum." I squeeze her hand to stop her. "I'd love to have you there. And Ranae, too. You know how it is at the birthing center. The more, the merrier." I turn to my father. "You're welcome, too, Dad. Whether Adam shows or not."

"I almost hope he *does* have to work," my father mutters.

"Michael."

"I'm with you, Dad," I say, smiling sadly at him. "I don't really want anyone there who doesn't want to be there, you know?"

"I want to be there," Mum reiterates.

"So do I," Dad insists, rather angrily.

I want to do a little insisting of my own, particularly about my parents' trip with Doctors Without Borders, but I keep my thoughts to myself for the moment. We will have many more opportunities to talk about the women's clinic in Beira, I'll see to it, but at the moment, I'm afraid I might fall asleep on my parents' couch if I stay much longer.

It isn't until I'm pulling into my garage that I remember the other part of our conversation. The part with the exchanged looks and evasive responses. The part that feels like old secrets and unanswered questions.

Adam's parking spot is empty; apparently, his emergency parent/teacher meeting has lingered well into its third hour.

Ranae

IT'S BEEN A FEW weeks since we found out we're having another baby in the family—Dani's going to be a mama!—and joy bubbles up in me every time I think of holding a tiny infant in my arms again. I refuse to let Adam's behavior taint this happy news, even though he hovers over all of this like a gray cloud.

Dani is suffering terribly from morning sickness, but Gran has concocted an herbal tea blend that actually seems to help a little. She also whips up large batches of homemade ginger snaps for Dani to nibble on. "These will do you far better than any cardboard biscuits in a box from the grocery store," she insists. Although I don't remember my own morning sickness being anything like my friend's is now, Gran's ginger cookies were a staple during my Ruby's gestation.

Memories of my pregnancy have been washing over me, and I catch myself falling through time and reliving every precious moment I can conjure up.

Solomon McCray. The first time I laid eyes on him was a Sunday morning in mid-August, right before classes started at USI. I was running late to church as usual, and my parents had gotten fed up with waiting and left without me, but not before my father let me know there'd be hell to pay if I didn't show up in time for the sermon.

I thought the threat rather ironic.

Then my car wouldn't start—in my haste to get in under the wire of my Saturday night curfew, I'd left the door ajar, and the overhead light had stayed on until the battery ran out of juice. I knew my father, though; he wouldn't cut me any slack for the car. So I called Dani and begged her to come pick me up. "You don't have to go to church with me," I assured her. "I just need to get there. I'm already busted for being late, but if I ditch altogether, it'll be really bad." I'd woken her up much earlier than she'd planned; but then, I'd also kept her out much later than she'd planned the night before, so she had every right to be disgruntled with me. "Please, please, please, please, please," I chanted into the phone. "I'll make it up to you, I promise. I'll trick Nolan into taking you out."

"Oh, great. That's exactly how I want to win him over. By trickery."

But good friend that she was, she crawled out of bed, threw on a hooded sweatshirt, and was at my door in less than ten minutes. It might have had more to do with my promise that if she picked me up, she could come to Sunday dinner at our house. She loved the big spread we had, and the hodgepodge of people who sat around our table—there were always random guests to feed at Sunday dinner. And besides, Dani could sit across the table from Nolan and stare longingly at him the whole meal.

I made it to the church service right before the pastor started his message, slipped past my stone-faced father, got a good-for-you wink from my gorgeous mother, and settled into the empty seat she'd saved for me. Jordan no longer attended church with us; he was a young associate pastor at the church where he'd met his wife, Shelly, but Nolan, at USI at the time, sat with several of his University pals in the row in front of us. Most of the guys I recognized, but two of them had that just-off-the-bus look that shouted, "Hey, I'm a freshman!" There was never any shortage of college students at our church; Evansville was home to two Universities, a college, and several tech schools, and students often migrated toward our local churches for a semblance of family and home.

Nolan, jerkface that he was, reached over the back of his seat to thump me on the knee. "About time," he mouthed over his shoulder.

"Hey!" I whispered harshly, grabbing his wrist and refusing to let go. The commotion ended abruptly when my mother flicked Nolan in the side of the head, her long, lacquered nail making an audible thwack against his skull. I had to release him so I could cover my mouth to stifle my laugh, not just at the injured look on his face, but also at how all five of his buddies turned his way at the sound of his hollow noggin. The shoulders of one of the freshmen started to shake, then he dropped his head forward, and for the next ten minutes, I knew he, too, was fighting an uncontrollable fit of laughter. Throughout the rest of the service, it must have crept up on him at least half a dozen times, sending me into sympathetic paroxysms of my own.

I didn't even have to see his face to know I just might be done for.

But then I did see his face, and I was, indeed, absolutely done for.

At one point, he turned and murmured something to the guy beside him, then glanced past him over his shoulder at me. Our eyes locked for one of those out-of-body time warp moments, and I couldn't look away. My face heated, my pulse did this odd little polka clog dance, and to my utter mortification, I actually shivered. A full-on tremor. It was like I'd touched a live wire.

Then he smiled. I'm pretty sure my body forgot that oxygen was necessary for survival, because for what seemed like an eternity, it would only allow me to take short, shallow breaths that made me go a little lightheaded. Thank goodness he returned his gaze to the pastor, freeing me from the spell he'd put me under. I sagged against the back of my seat, fanning myself with my mother's church bulletin, and prayed that the makeup I had on didn't make me look too trashy. I really wanted that church boy to like me.

Apparently, he did. At least three more glorious times, he found a reason to turn in his seat enough so he could glance down the way at me. And every single time, I was certain my heart would clog dance right out of my chest and crash into the back of his head.

At the end of the sermon, we all stood to sing one last song, and the row of guys in front of us formed a wall of broad shoulders and blue jeans. "Oh my," my mother murmured beside me. Appalled, I glanced over at her, half expecting her to be appreciating the very male lineup the same way I was. "I can't see a thing, can you?" she asked, leaning toward me.

Oh, yeah, I could see just fine, thank you very much.

As soon as the pastor dismissed us, Nolan turned around and stuck out his lip like a pouting toddler. "Ow, Ma. That really hurt," he said, rubbing his temple with the heel of his palm. "Child abuse, and in church, no less."

"Be nice to your sister, and I won't have to do it again," she told him, flashing him her big warm smile and patting his cheek. "Hi boys," she said to Nolan's friends who were lingering nearby. "You all have a place to go for Sunday dinner?"

That was my mom, always looking out for someone in need of a home, a meal, a hug, even a thwack on the side of the head.

Nolan ended up bringing three USI schoolmates home with him that day. One I already knew, Shane Dunes, and then there were the two freshmen, Toby Heppenstall and Solomon McCray.

It was Solomon McCray who kept busting up over my mother's assault on my brother's hollow head.

It was Solomon McCray who kept glancing my way throughout the church service I'd almost missed.

And it was Solomon McCray who kept finding reasons to engage me in conversation throughout the afternoon, even after a well-rested and fresh-faced Dani arrived, and I was no longer the odd man—or woman—out.

At the dinner table, it was Solomon McCray who claimed the empty seat next to me, Nolan on my other side. Dani sat across from us—across from Nolan—just as I'd promised, and the whole meal long, we sent each other silent messages with foot nudges and facial expressions. We weren't as subtle as we thought, though. At one point, Nolan even asked a mortified Dani if she had something in her eye.

Having Solomon sitting so close was something akin to torture. The subtle smell his spicy cologne made me a little lightheaded, and his elbow nudged mine far more often than seemed necessary, sending waves of gooey warmth spreading over me. When he talked, his deep voice vibrated through me, making me want to shut my eyes and simply *feel*.

He told us about his past: his home, his family, about the long line of Scottish McCray immigrants that had made something of themselves in America. He took great pride in his roots, fully accepting the mantle of being the only son of an only son. "I'm actually the fifth generation Solomon Louis McCray here in the U.S.," he told us, without vanity, but with heartfelt family pride. "The fourth to go to college, and the third to go to the University of Southern Indiana."

He talked about his future, how excited he was to make a difference in the world. "I may be just a farm boy in the end," he said with a cheeky smile. "But I'm designing a whole line of specialized equipment for organic farming." He explained he wanted to create tools and implements that would work just as effectively as fuel-powered machines, but that would also be affordable for the new generation of small farmers and ranchers who were making great strides in bringing land use back to its roots. "It's a whole new world out there, and we're all seriously looking back to the old ways of doing things," he exclaimed, his passion for the subject making him easy to listen to. "I aim to make Solomon McCray Farming Equipment a household name on every farm and ranch across America. And beyond," he added with a little flourish, his cheeks flushed with his fervor.

Then there was his laugh. Lord, his laugh. You knew it was coming by the shaking of his shoulders first, the clenching of his jaw, like he was trying to keep it trapped inside. But soon enough, it rolled out of him, a battering ram of a laugh, relentless and full-bodied, until tears formed at the corners of his eyes, and he had to stand up to catch his breath. The whole group of us, including Jordan and Shelly who'd also joined us for dinner, sat around the cleared table playing Fictionary, a game—when played with the right people—that could send everyone into gales of laughter, but witnessing Solomon let loose was a borderline religious experience for me.

He was just so... so *much,* and I wanted to sit there and take him in. He fascinated me, the way he gave himself over to the things he was passionate about. Solomon was charismatic and genuine at the same time, magnetic, yet transparent about why he thought and felt the way he did.

At the end of the afternoon, it was Solomon McCray who found an excuse to get my phone number. "I have to buy my sister a birthday gift this week," he said quietly as we sat around recovering from the game with a second round of cobbler. "I figure you probably know this town a little better than I do. Can I bribe you with a cup of coffee in exchange for helping me find her something?"

"Ahem," Nolan cleared his throat before I could completely comprehend the invitation. "Dude. Did you just ask my little sister out? Right in front of her two big brothers?" My parents had made their excuses before the last few rounds of Fictionary. They'd left to take their regular Sunday afternoon drive out to see my mom's mom who lived in a skilled nursing facility on the east side of town. Dementia had stolen her memories, and Grandma no longer recognized us kids. Sometimes the confusion of seeing strange faces in her room sent her into an uncontrollable tantrum that often ended in the administration of sedatives for her own safety. After an especially awful episode over the holidays the year before, Mom tearfully asked us kids to stop visiting altogether.

I threw a spoon at my brother's head, but Nolan just batted it away, not taking his eyes off Solomon.

"Do you think I'm an idiot, man?" Solomon asked, shaking his head in denial. His words cut through me, but under the table, his foot nudged mine, and my protest stuck in my throat.

"Actually, I do," Nolan shot back, his narrowed gaze darting back and forth between us. "Jordan?" he prodded. "Any thoughts?"

Jordan toyed with his water glass. "Sure. I have one in particular. My sister is seventeen. Seventeen, Solomon Louis McCray of the Clan McCray. Got it?"

Solomon sobered, but didn't cave. "Got it. It's coffee and birthday gift shopping." He dipped his head in my direction, his confident grin never faltering. "Your sister reminds me of my sister. The way she dresses, her jewelry." Then he turned to look at me. "You could help me pick out something she'd like." Once again, his foot bumped mine, then lingered there, the toe of his sneaker against the back of my heel. The... caress? Was that what it was? It felt like one. The caress took the sting out of his glib remark.

"She reminds you of your sister?" Shane asked, a dubious smirk on his face. "Really, Sol?"

"Yes, really?" Dani asked, one eyebrow up. If my legs had been a little longer, I'd have kicked her under the table.

"Her style, yes." Solomon opened his mouth to say something else, but Nolan cut him off.

"Actually," my brother said. "I think it's good that she reminds you of your sister. Let's keep it that way, okay?"

"Excuse me," I interjected, waving both hands in the air. "I'm right here!"

"We see you, Pippy," Nolan said, reaching over and ruffling the top of my head. Pippy, not for Longstockings, but for Pipsqueak. I didn't usually mind the nickname, but today, I wasn't so sure about the motives behind it, at least not in this instance. I felt like he was reminding me that I was still just a child.

I snatched up a pen and one of the scraps of paper we'd been using for the game and scribbled my number on it. "Here." I held it out to Solomon. Our eyes locked, and I lifted my chin a little higher.

Without hesitating, without shifting his gaze from mine, he took it from me, folded it in half, and slid it into his shirt front pocket.

"Call me," I said, then pushed up from the table and excused myself. But not before intentionally elbowing Nolan in the back of the head as I turned to leave. "Oops," I said as sweetly as I could muster. "Sorry about that, big brother." I dodged out of the way before he could grab me.

Dani, my best friend in the whole wide world, was already on her feet and making her way around the table to join me.

We were tentative with each other at first, Solomon and I; like my brother had so glibly pointed out, I was still only seventeen. Solomon, on the other hand, was almost twenty. He was my brother's peer, and I was Nolan's kid sister. He was in university; I was in high school. Solomon hailed from Kentucky across the Ohio River, with roots in Owensboro as deep as mine were in Evansville.

By the beginning of October, we were sleeping together, Solomon as passionate about his love for me as he was about everything else. But honestly, he stirred that same passion up in me, too, unlike anything I'd ever experienced before. There was never even a question in my mind that I would tell him no, and he never made me regret it.

Except that I was still only seventeen. A minor. And he wasn't.

So we kept our clandestine affair a secret from everyone—except Dani, of course—both of us desperate for the day, the hour, the moment I turned eighteen so that we could proclaim our love to the world. We were already planning our future together: where we would live, what we would name our children, what kind of pets we'd have. What was six months in the grand scheme of things?

"I'll die if I can't have you now," he must have murmured against my skin a thousand times.

On December 7th, I discovered that despite our diligent use of condoms, I was pregnant. On December 10th, per my request, Solomon met me under our favorite tree on campus. We were stealing every moment we could find to spend together, knowing we'd be apart for almost three weeks over the upcoming holidays. Greeting me with a bear hug and exuberant kisses, he was nearly impossible to resist, but I finally broke away and stepped back, breathing hard from a combination of passion and panic. Not sure my shaky legs would support me, I leaned against the trunk of the tree, then I unceremoniously blurted out that I was pregnant.

If there was any hesitation on Solomon's part, it was only the time it took to register what I'd said. I saw nothing but delight and joy—no fear, no anger, not even a hint of doubt—in the expression that spread across his features.

He grabbed me up against him again, his big arms wrapping tightly around me, and kissed me like I'd just made him the happiest man in the world. Then he set me back on my feet, backed me up against the tree and pressed his forehead to mine. "Well, I guess there's no reason to keep this thing between us a secret anymore." He kissed me slowly, gently, then he chuckled against my lips before pulling back so he could see my face. "Think your parents will give us their blessing to get married? Or will they just have me arrested? Or shot at sunrise?"

I jerked back, banging my head against the rough bark behind me, and gawked up at him while rubbing the tender spot. "Ma—married?"

Without further ado, Solomon dropped to one knee in front of me, lifted the back of my hand to his lips, then said, "Ranae Aileen Niemeyer, will you do me the honor of becoming my wife?"

I stared at him, wide-eyed and open-mouthed, my heart screaming at me to throw myself into his arms and tell him yes, a thousand times, yes. But my mouth seemed to have a mind of it's own. "You're crazy. Get married? Now? How are we going to live?"

Solomon let loose one of his rumbling laughs and said, "Laws, Ranae. How are we going to live if we're not together? Haven't I told you a million times that I'll die if I can't have you? " He pulled me down so I was kneeling in front of him. He cupped my face in his big hands and made me look into his eyes. "Everything will be all right, as long as we're together. You'll see. We'll figure it out." He shrugged one shoulder good naturedly. "Sure, it may get harder before it gets easier, but as long as we have each other, we won't have to face any of it, the good or the bad, alone. Please say you'll marry me. I'll talk to my parents as soon as I get home next week. I want to do it in person; they deserve that much. But I also want to ask my dad for my grandmother's ring. I want you to wear it, Ranae. Then after I tell them, I'll drive up here and we can talk to your family together, okay?"

"Aren't you even a little afraid?" I asked him, an electric pulse pinging just below the surface of my skin. "A baby, Solomon. We're not just talking marriage. We're talking about a baby, too."

He kissed my forehead between my eyebrows. "Not as long as she frowns just like you with your furrowed brow." He kissed my cheeks. "Not as long as she blushes the color of sun-kissed Georgia peaches." He kissed the tip of my nose. "Not as long as she flares her nostrils when she laughs."

My nostrils flared as I laughed, helpless to resist his charm.

He kissed my lips. "As long as she is yours and mine, I am not afraid."

His tender words made my emotions well. "What if she's a he?" I murmured, letting him brush away the tears that wet my face.

He kissed me again, then stood and pulled me up with him. He leaned back a little and struck a pose, chin in the air, chest puffed out. "Well, let's hope he looks like me, then."

"Let's hope he's as wonderful as you are," I whispered.

"Well?" he prodded, pressing his forehead to mine again. "Don't leave me hanging. Is it a yes?"

With a shy smile, I said, "Yes, Solomon Louis McCray, I will do you the honor of becoming your wife."

But Solomon didn't come back to Evansville after he left school on December 16th. Nor did he return any of my calls. He didn't come back to USI after the holiday break, either.

The day after school started, I learned from an uncharacteristically somber Nolan that Solomon had been in a car accident while taking his mother and sister Christmas shopping. The women walked away with a fractured wrist and a couple bruised ribs between them. Solomon had died on impact.

I wandered around in a fog, somehow able to continue breathing and sleeping and eating. It was only because of Dani and her constant companionship that I was able to endure getting up each day and going to school, but it was all a blur, a farce. The real me curled into a tiny, misshapen lump behind my ribcage, unable to accept a future without Solomon, unwilling to live without him.

And yet, somehow, I did. We did; me and the baby growing inside me.

The second week in January, a letter came in the mail requesting a meeting between the McCray's attorney and me. Because I was still a minor, I had to bring a legal adult with me, so I first went to Gran and told her the whole sordid story. She didn't let me off the hook, though, but sat beside me while I repeated everything to my shell-shocked parents, who were far more gracious toward me than I'd anticipated. They were, in fact, relieved to finally have some insight into why I'd been so distraught over the past several weeks, especially at Christmas, even though I'd done my best to pretend I was as excited as always for my favorite holiday of the year. Oh, they'd asked, of course, but I'd told them I was fine. I'd thought they believed me.

My father and I met with Mr. Arthur Vancour at the Law Offices of Frederick and Vancour in Owensboro, Kentucky, on a bitterly cold, blustery day the end of January. He handed us a folder and gave us as much time as we needed to read over the documents inside, then went over everything with us. In what sounded like carefully rehearsed lines, the lawyer informed us that Solomon had, indeed, told his parents about us and our baby, that he had asked for his grandmother's ring and had been refused, so he'd gone shopping with his mother and sister to buy me one of my own. According to his mother's report, Solomon had practically flaunted his purchase in her face, "...behaving in a manner completely out of character for him." In the heat of the moment, Solomon ran a red light, swerved sharply to avoid cross traffic, and plowed into a utility pole.

When all was said and done, his family blamed me for his death.

"Due to the brevity and nature of the relationship between you and Mr. McCray, my clients are questioning its validity." The note of kindness in Mr. Vancour's voice belied the cruelty of his words.

"Excuse me," my father cut in, a hand raised to stop the man. "What exactly does that mean? My daughter is pregnant with that young man's child. I'm not sure how much more valid a relationship can be."

Mr. Vancour nodded patiently. "They are not questioning the validity of the pregnancy, Mr. Niemeyer. Solomon assured them the child was his, and they have chosen to believe him without requiring proof."

"Proof! Proof?" Aghast, my father stood, bracing his hands on the edge of the man's enormous mahogany desk. "What *are* they questioning, then?"

"Please sit down, sir," the lawyer said, not even flinching in his seat, although his hand slid under his desk where I thought there might be a gun. Didn't every good ol' Midwestern boy have a gun close at hand at all times? Or maybe just a panic button; I'd seen the brawny security guard posted just inside the door of the large building that housed a myriad of businesses like Fredericks and Vancour. "I understand this is a very difficult time for all parties involved. It is my primary goal to equip you with the information you need to make the decisions being presented to you today."

The room fell silent while he waited for my father to take his seat again. Anxious for a distraction, I let my gaze wander over the surface of the attorney's desk. There was surprisingly little on it. A black leather Day Planner, a phone, a framed photo facing him, presumably of his family, and a wire mesh tray with a neat stack of manila folders in it like the one I held in my hands. Directly in front of him was another folder with McCray/Niemeyer written in block letters on the tab and laying perfectly lined up beside the folder was a black lacquered Cross Townsend pen exactly like the one Dad used at his desk at Niemeyer Mortuary when signing documents with his own clients. Behind the man was a large window that looked out over a nearly empty street. The window was flanked on either side by built-in bookshelves, but no matter how long I stared at the book spines, I couldn't make out the titles. I saw and recognized individual letters, but my mind seemed to have lost the ability to put them together into words.

My father finally settled, and Mr. Vancour continued. "To be succinct, they are not convinced that a marriage between their son and you, Ms. Niemeyer, would have come about were it not for this pregnancy. Last month, Mr. McCray told his parents that the two of you had been dating for not quite five months, and that at that time, you were already three months pregnant. Is that correct?"

Stated so starkly, we sounded like stupid children. I supposed in the eyes of his parents, we were just that. "That's correct, yes," I said, with as much courage as I could muster. I did not try to defend my love for Solomon to this man.

"It is the short duration of time you and Mr. McCray had together that concerns my clients. In light of how quickly things progressed, they believe there is some question as to your motivation for pursuing their son."

"Their son pursued me, too," I interjected, my bravado withering under the cloud of shame being cast over me. "I didn't seduce him for his money, if that's what they're suggesting."

The attorney didn't deny or confirm my allegations. "Their primary concern now is that they be allowed to grieve their loss without interference from you."

"Interference?" The word came out a harsh whisper, and I glanced over at my father as if needing him to clarify for me. He was no help, red-faced and wide-eyed, his mouth opening and closing in mute offense. I touched his arm briefly, silently begging him to maintain his cool so we could get through this nightmare as quickly as possible. "How do they presume that I'll interfere?" I finally managed to ask, wounded sarcasm coloring my words. "Throw myself on the coffin or tear my mourning clothes open to show my pregnant belly?"

"No, no," Mr. Vancour said, shaking his head slowly. He cleared his throat quietly, then continued. "Let me try to make this succinct. They do not feel that they are in a position to accept you into the family at this time."

My father made a strangled sound beside me.

"That is definitely succinct, Mr. Vancour," I said, clinging to the remnants of my dignity. "Honestly, I don't think I *want* to be accepted into their family," I continued. "I have a family of my own already, thank you very much." I took my father's clenched hand and held on tightly. He still hadn't uttered a word, but I could feel him vibrating next to me. "However, this is their only son's child, Mr. Vancour." My voice cracked over the words, but I managed to go on. "I can understand why they're not thrilled about me being in their lives, but surely they don't consider their grandchild to be an in—interfer—" I couldn't finish.

Once again, the attorney circumvented a direct response to me. "My clients are, indeed, aware that your baby is their son's only child. They have asked me to offer you a compromise."

"A compromise?" I asked, baffled by the new direction. "A compromise about what? If they don't want us in their lives, that's fine by me."

"A choice," he said. He seemed a little unsettled by what he was about to say, and I narrowed my eyes at him. He slid two envelopes toward us, both embossed with the Frederick and Vancour logo, and took a deep breath. Tapping the envelope under his right hand, he said, "My clients understand that you are a minor and are still in high school. They know that having a baby at this time in your life can present some nearly insurmountable difficulties. They'd like you to consider allowing them to adopt the baby as their—"

"I'm not giving them our baby." I gasped, the words coming out tight and high-pitched. "Do you think I want this child being raised by people like them?"

He tapped the envelope again and kept talking. "The check in this envelope will more than cover your maternity and delivery costs, and will still leave you with plenty of money for a college education, plus enough to live on for many years to come, if you manage it well."

"No. I don't want their dirty money."

"We don't need their money," my father said at almost the exact time.

"They can provide your child with everything he or she can possibly need or want—"

"Except for a mother and a set of grandparents who will pour love into that child's life." The words burst out of Dad like fists; I couldn't remember the last time I'd seen him this affronted and angry.

"They are committed to raising this child as their own," Mr. Vancour said in response. "They have—"

"Stop. No," I interrupted. "She—or he—isn't theirs. That isn't an option I'm willing to consider, not even for a moment," I said with finality, shoving the envelope away. I turned to my father. "Daddy, get me out of here."

"Please hear me out, Ms. Niemeyer. There is a lot at stake here, and the McCrays want to do this the right—and legal—way."

I stared at him, aghast at how glib his words were. "They are offering to purchase our child, Mr. Vancour. How right and legal is that?"

"They are offering to provide for you *and* for your child, Ms. Niemeyer," he corrected. With another soft throat-clearing, he added, "And they are prepared to file for full custody if you do not give him or her up willingly."

I gaped at him. "Excuse me?" His words had my heart pounding like a kettle drum. "They don't even know me!" I croaked out. "On what basis are they going to try to take this child from me?"

"This is ludicrous!" My father's voice shook. "There is no way in hell they can win a custody battle against us," he ground out, pointing a trembling finger at the lawyer. "And you know it."

"Maybe not," Mr. Vancour said, rubbing his temple briefly, obviously ill at ease with this whole situation. "But they can make it very costly for you to defend your rights to keep the child." He held up both hands before either one of us could respond. "Please hear me out. There is another offer."

"Oh, I can't wait to hear this," my father scoffed.

Mr. Vancour tapped the other envelope. "This envelope contains a check for one hundred thousand dollars, a one-time payment in lieu of any and all financial support that you might expect from the McCray family. If you cash this, you are agreeing to release the McCrays from any further financial obligation to you or the child." He was relentless in carrying out his part in the obscene performance.

My father started to rise, but I squeezed his hand to stop him, and he paused, waiting for me to respond. In the back of my mind, I wondered what this whole encounter was doing to him. My poor father.

"What part of 'We don't want their money' do you not understand?" I asked, my tone weary in spite of my angry words. I clenched my hands over the folder in my lap and ignored the envelope, staring straight into Mr. Vancour's eyes instead. I was shocked beyond measure by the callousness of the people who had raised someone as beautiful as Solomon. "I am not interested in accepting any form of payoff from those awful people. I want nothing—*nothing*—to do with them, not me or my baby." It was the first time I intentionally referred to the baby as mine, not ours. With Solomon gone, she or he belonged to no one but me.

The attorney nodded, but left the envelope on the desk between us. "If you are not willing to allow them to adopt the child—"

"I'm not," I snapped. "Let me make this perfectly clear. They cannot have our baby. I don't care how much money they squeeze out of me; I will not simply hand over our—*my*—baby to them."

"I understand, Ms. Niemeyer. Please hear me out," Mr. Vancour repeated. "Perhaps the rest of this second offer will suit you better."

"I seriously doubt they could offer me anything that would suit me in any way."

He ignored my scathing remark. "If you agree to permanently relinquish any and all rights to Solomon McCray's name, then my clients will agree to permanently relinquish any and all rights to the child. That means no birth certificate or any other legal paperwork with his name on it, nothing that would tie his name to you or your child in a court of law."

"Wa—wait," I stammered, unable to fully grasp what he was saying. "So now they *don't* want this baby? I thought they were going to fight for custody?"

"This is the only way they will agree *not* to fight for custody," he started to explain. "If you agree to not make any claim to their son's—."

"So, that's the real truth of it," I interjected rudely. "They want nothing to do with us. Me or this baby. No ties, whatsoever. All or nothing, is that it?"

After a moment's hesitation, Mr. Vancour nodded. "That about sums it up, yes. But it must be done legally. In a legal and binding contract."

And I thought I'd seen the worst of them. Mr. and Mrs. McCray's son was dead. *Dead.* And they were more than willing to give up all rights to his only child, their only grandchild by their only son. I couldn't fathom it. What kind of people wouldn't ache for any trace of evidence of their son's existence in the features of his own child?

"Which also means you and your family must agree not to press any form of criminal charges against their son."

Ah. There it was. They knew I had them and their high and mighty reputation in the palm of hand.

"Criminal charges?" My father's voice sounded hollow, echoing with the pain I felt over this whole situation. "Why on earth would we press charges against their son? He's the only one in that family who isn't turning his back on Ranae and their baby. And he's dead, for the love of all that is holy! What kind of people do they think we are? What kind of monsters are they?" He put his arm around me and pulled me close. "My daughter loved that boy and he loved her; you remind them of that, Mr. Vancour. They want to be left alone in their grief?" he scoffed, the words sounding like tumbling gravel. "Alone in their greed, is more like it. Those crazy people don't even know what grief is, they're so wrapped up in their greed and self-preservation, even in the face of such a great and tragic loss. No sir. We can *not* be bought. We don't want their money and we're not signing anything." He turned to me and started to rise again. "Come on, sweetheart. I will hire an attorney of our own to go over all of this with us. As soon as we leave this nest of vipers and get back home."

There was that cleared throat again. "You should know, sir, that if you opt not to sign either of these options today, they will begin the process of filing for custody of this child. They have bottomless resources, Mr. Niemeyer, and although they may not be able to win custody in the end, as you have conjectured, they can certainly cost you everything you have to defend your right to keep the child." Mr. Vancour sounded terribly sad, as though his words weighed heavily on his spirit.

As well they should. But I refused to feel sorry for him. I straightened in my seat and put out a hand toward my father. "Wait, Daddy." For the first time since sitting down across from Mr. Vancour, I had discovered a glimmer of hope in his words. "They are agreeing to relinquish any and all claims to my child? Permanently?"

"Permanently."

"What if one of them needs a kidney one day? Or a blood transfusion?" It was a far-fetched possibility, but I needed clarification.

"If you agree to release them for any and all responsibility for this child, then they agree to relinquish any and all of their rights," the lawyer repeated.

It still blew my mind, the thought that they would just write off their grandchild, but I no longer cared what kind of people they were. If I understood this man right, I would never, ever have to worry about what kind of people they were, and neither would my child.

"Forever? Even after my baby is old and dead? What about his or her children? Grandchildren? Will they have any claim or any reason to connect with them after this paper is signed?"

"We should see an attorney, Ranae," my father said, his voice low, tight.

"Forever," Mr. Vancour confirmed. He didn't exactly ignore my father, but he directed his responses to me. As he'd done with the check, he slid the expensive pen toward me. "If you sign the documents relinquishing any familial claims on

Solomon McCray, then they, in turn, will relinquish any and all familial claims on your child."

"We will be dead to them?" I prompted, wanting to be a hundred percent certain of what he was telling us.

Mr. Vancour closed his eyes briefly, but then met my gaze and nodded.

I waited, not looking away.

As if he could read my mind, he grimaced, then said, "In so many words, yes. You will be dead to them."

"Good." I narrowed my eyes at him and asked the question that scared me the most. "Am I allowed to tell my child about Solomon?"

Mr. Vancour sat forward and rested his forearms on his desk. His face drooped a little, making him look weary, even sad. My heart remained hardened toward him. "No one can stop you from telling your child about Solomon McCray. But these documents are my clients' guarantee that you and your child will not claim any legal right to him, his family, and his name. In light of that, I would advise you to consider carefully what you say, how you say it, and to whom you say it."

Relief washed through me, because there was no way on earth that I wouldn't tell our child all about her amazing father. I smiled—actually smiled!—at Mr. Vancour. "It seems I can be bought after all." I picked up the pen and signed the earmarked pages before handing everything to my father to do the same.

"You're sure," Dad murmured, his eyes holding mine. It wasn't really a question, though.

I nodded and turned back to the lawyer. "The McCrays are dead to me now, Mr. Vancour." My voice came out steady and sure for the first time since stepping into that office. "That is my purchase price. Their death for my child." I silently begged my father not to argue.

My father sat with his pen poised over the first signature line. "Signing this means we are finished here, right?" he asked the attorney, in need of his own assurance. "There will be no recourse on either side?"

"It ends today with your signatures." Mr. Vancour confirmed.

My father signed the documents and slid the folder back across the desk to Mr. Vancour, who scanned the pages to make sure he had all the signatures he needed. "I'll have certified copies of these documents delivered to your address."

I wanted to ask him how it was possible to have both Niemeyer and McCray names on this legal document since the contract stated we were not allowed to be linked in any way, but I bit back the belligerent words. The whole situation was ludicrous, as Dad had said.

I had just agreed for my baby to be disowned by half of his or her family.

We started to rise, but the attorney held up a hand to stop us. "There is one more thing, Ms. Niemeyer." He pulled a small velvet box out of the top drawer of his desk. "Solomon's sister, Sarah McCray, informed me—she insisted—that this is yours. She said to tell you that Solomon couldn't wait to give it to you." He held it out to me, and in a gentle voice, said, "Ms. Niemeyer, please know that I am deeply sorry for your loss."

With trembling hands, I took the box from him and held it to my heart. I would not open it in front of him. I would not give him the privilege of witnessing my reaction when I did—that moment belonged only to Solomon. But I thanked him with a broken voice, told him I was sure his job must be one of the most difficult in all the world, then I slipped my hand into the crook of my father's arm and let him lead me from the room.

The whole drive home, I wept silently in the passenger seat, my hand resting protectively over my abdomen where a new life, already marked by the cruelty of this world, grew inside of me. Dad gripped my other hand, his big fingers wrapped around mine, and the one time I glanced over at him, there were tears on his cheeks, too. We were two tragic peas in a pod, my father and me, hearts breaking over the wrongs done against our children, against us, and doing the best we could to forge on anyway.

That evening, I lay in the guest bed at my grandparents' house with my knees drawn up, my body curled around my baby, Solomon's solitaire diamond on my finger. Dani, quiet and solemn, lay on her side facing me, holding my left hand in hers, toying with the beautiful ring.

She'd come to the farmhouse immediately after school let out and sat on the porch swing in the cold watching for us, while Mom waited inside with Gran and Opa. She'd hurried down the steps the moment we pulled into the driveway and had hugged me silently after I'd staggered out of the car. She, of all people, knew there was nothing anyone could say. No words would bring back Solomon, no platitudes and condolences could set things right ever again. She'd simply stayed close, ready with anything I might need. A glass of water, a box of tissue, a cold washcloth, she had them at the ready before I even had to ask.

The next night, after my father had gone to bed, my mother tiptoed into my room and handed me a soft, leather-bound journal. "I know you're not supposed to claim Solomon publicly or legally—and I will curse the McCray family until my dying breath," she interjected with impotent rage. She tapped the cover of the journal. "But your heart doesn't know that, my sweet girl. This is so you can claim him privately. Write down everything you know about him, everything you love about him, everything you dreamed of with him. That way, when you're ready to tell your child about him, you'll have everything locked away in here." She smiled sadly. "It might be hard at first, but the words will come, I promise." I knew journaling had helped her through her miscarriages before they adopted me. On my sixteenth birthday, she'd gifted me with the flowery notebook that she'd kept over the first three years of my life as she got to know the person I was.

I returned home the next day, and with her parents' blessing, Dani sacrificed her perfect attendance record to stay home from school with me for the rest of the week.

During that time, our moms took an afternoon off work to put together an enormous gift basket for me. It was loaded with everything from prenatal vitamins and body butters to help fight stretch marks, to the softest nightgown in the world, and a matching bathrobe and slippers. Amid the foot soak salts and herbal teas were gift certificates for maternity clothes at a few local boutiques, and an amazing telescoping back scratcher I probably used more than anything else in the basket. Not counting the enormous U-shaped pregnancy sleep pillow; but that wasn't actually *in* the basket.

Francis handed me a small stack of pamphlets and books to read as I was able, then she went over everything I could expect to happen to my body over the next several months. She explained to me how important it was for my baby that I not only take care of my changing body, but also my mind and heart. Perhaps it was her gentleness and kindness, even while speaking so plainly, but for the first time since losing Solomon, I felt like I had something to hold onto, a line in the sand, a place to start, and I loved Dani's mom more in that moment than I ever thought possible.

It wasn't Dr. Francis Nelson I went to for my prenatal care. Everything about this pregnancy felt cocooned in a blanket of intimacy, perhaps because of how rooted it was in my unrelenting grief, or maybe because of the sordid secrecy surrounding it, created by my deal with the McCrays. I simply couldn't bring myself to go sit in a waiting room with other pregnant women where I'd have to dodge questions and birthing war stories. I felt raw and vulnerable all the time, like the top layer of my skin had been peeled off. The idea of climbing up onto an exam table and propping my feet into stirrups made me want to vomit, and for the first time in my life, I was suddenly, inexplicably terrified of going to a hospital. The sterility and routine of it all was at such odds with the exposed nerve endings of my circumstances, and at one point, I told my mother that I wanted to have my baby in my own room in my own bed with only people I knew and loved around me.

It was she who suggested I talk to Dani's mom about using the services of a midwife. Francis gave me the names of three midwives she knew and respected. One of them happened to be Gran's good friend, Rose Bergmann, and when I asked Gran what she thought of me having Rose as my midwife, she insisted I go with no one else. We met at the farmhouse over herbal tea and Irish scones—different from English scones, according to Gran, but I had no clue why—and I fell in love with the stout German woman who cupped my face in her large, rough hands, and prayed a blessing of peace and comfort over me. Before she knew about Solomon, she recognized the condition of my heart, and I felt safe in her hands.

By the middle of March, I was no longer able to easily hide the fact that I was pregnant. I wasn't ashamed of my pregnancy, but not being able to talk about the circumstances surrounding it made facing my classmates extremely difficult. So I opted to finish my senior year of high school at home on an independent study track. When Gran and Opa invited me to live with them, it seemed like the perfect solution, and before the end of the month, I had moved into the lovely upstairs bedroom that overlooked Gran's garden and the woods beyond the expansive back yard.

The farmhouse has been home to Ruby and me ever since.

I still have Solomon's ring and the black velvet box it came in. I keep it, along with a few pictures I have of the two of us, our faces radiating our shared happiness, and the journal my mom gave me. I filled the notebook from cover to cover over the duration of my pregnancy and well into the second year of Ruby's life. Everything is tucked away in a wooden box—one of those fancy fruit or wine gift boxes with a slide-out lid—under my bed, along with a few other treasures I kept from that same time period. There's an ugly, jagged stone inside a Band-Aid box. One day while we walked in the park, Solomon had kicked the rock absentmindedly, and it ricocheted off a tree and hit the back of my hand, drawing blood. We'd both laughed so hard at the improbability of it all, that my pain was all but forgotten. By me, anyway. He made up for it the next time I saw him with the large Band-Aid box filled with chunks of my favorite chocolate-covered honeycomb candy. There's a heart-shaped leaf he gave me in lieu of a ring on the day he asked me to marry him. An empty glass bottle of Mountain Dew with a rolled up love letter inside. It's the only thing I have with his writing on it, and I cherish it.

At first, I kept my copy of the papers from Frederick and Vancours in the wooden box, too, but after realizing the sight of that pale linen envelope with the attorney's logo in the corner made my hands shake and my bile rise, I handed them over to my father. They are now in our family's safe deposit box in an expandable folder marked Ruby Noralee Niemeyer. In that folder is also the account information and the quarterly statements from a CD my dad set up for Ruby using the cashier's check Mr. Vancour sent along with the legal documents.

"For her college education," Dad had insisted when I told him I didn't want it. "It's what Solomon would have provided for her had he been able to." How could I argue with that?

Ruby and I periodically take out the box and pour over the contents. Over the years, I have told her everything I can possibly remember about Solomon, but I have kept my part of the bargain with the McCrays, and I have not divulged his family's name to her. Because of the mature nature of some of the things I wrote in the journal, I waited until her last birthday, when she turned seventeen, to share it with her.

She was so hungry for it by then, she has read it cover to cover multiple times in the six months it's been available to her.

Sometimes it seems that she looks the most like him after she's been reading from those pages.

Ruby has asked about her father's family, but I tell her I have no information about them that I can give her.

I have never once doubted my decision to sign those documents.

Dani

"Dani?"

"Yes, Adam." Who else did he think might answer my phone at eleven o'clock at night?

"I'm staying at the lake house tonight. Paul, Cherona, and I headed over to Mancini's after our meeting, and I had a few drinks. I'm going to play it safe and not try to drive home. I just wanted to let you know where I am."

I am at a complete loss as to how to respond. It's as if now that I know about his apartment, he has no qualms about telling me he's using it. And yet, if he has been drinking, he's doing the right thing by not driving the thirty-plus miles home from Mancini's. To boot, this is the first time in months that he's bothered to explain his reasons for staying away. His call sounds almost solicitous, as though he actually wants to set my mind at ease.

"Where is your place?" I ask. I'm not sure that I want to know, but in my weariness, my filters are down and it's the first question that comes to mind. How far did he drive inebriated?

After only a breath of a hesitation, he says, "It's only a few minutes from the school. I made it here safely, don't worry, but I'm not comfortable getting on the expressway. I'm not drunk, I assure you, but that meeting this evening took it out of us, and I just want to put my head down and go to sleep."

He does sound tired, and against my better judgment, my heart begins to soften toward him. When I go through a difficult birth, I don't want to talk about it, I don't want to dwell on it, I just want to burrow under my covers in our darkened bedroom and let the rainy day noise machine lull me into mindless oblivion. I don't even mind Adam slipping into bed behind me and pulling me up against his hungry body, as long as he doesn't ask me any questions.

"I'm sorry," I say now, still trying to put things into perspective. It feels a little twisted, but I'm not sure why. I'm not exactly sure what I'm sorry for, either. The rough meeting? The fact that he's not coming home? That he's had too much to drink? Or that he has somewhere else he calls 'my place' when talking to his wife?

Don't forget that he wasn't by my side to tell my parents about our baby, the little voice in my head reminds me. I lean my head against the back of the sofa and take a deep breath to quell the quick surge of resentment in my belly. I should wrap this up and go to bed.

"I'm sorry, too," he says, his voice softening in a way that causes a tiny flutter of desire—or is it despair?—somewhere behind my heart. I press the heel of my hand over my sternum, willing whatever it is to be still. He doesn't expound, and I can hear his own questions filling the silence between us.

I want him to ask how things went with my Mum and Dad, then it dawns on me that he might be waiting for me to ask him how things went at the meeting. Unlike me, Adam does like to rehash his tougher cases, even though it goes against his "Don't bring work home" rule. I don't mind it. By nature, I'm a good listener, and I know it helps him process. "Do you want to talk about it?"

He speaks at the exact same time. "I spoke to your folks this evening."

"You—you did?" This is news to me. I left their place shortly after eight, so it's certainly not out of the realm of possibility. But if Adam called my parents, it might be the first time since he asked for my hand in marriage more than six years ago. "Why? I mean, what did you say?"

He chuckles, the low rumble making that little fluttery thing in my chest lift its head. "I apologized for not being there with you and congratulated them on becoming grandparents."

"Oh. Wow. Thank you." This conversation keeps getting stranger. Everything about it feels so out of character for the Adam I've been living with lately.

"They seemed pleased with the news," he adds, ending on a note that makes his statement sound unfinished, like he wants to say more. But he falls silent.

"Yes, I believe they are," I finally agree, wondering how we got here, this place where we're so stilted and ill at ease with each other. I draw my knees up close to my chest and tug my soft jersey nightgown down over my folded legs. I know it looks ridiculous, all 5 feet 9 inches of me accordioned inside my shift this way, but I've done it since I was a little girl, and for some reason, it comforts me. I used to tuck my head inside my neckline and tell my parents I was a doodlebug—or a roly-poly, as Ranae calls them—but now that I'm an adult, I draw the line there.

I want to ask Adam if he's pleased with the news, too, but instead, I thank him again for calling them.

"Don't act so surprised, Dani. It was the least I could do after bailing on you."

"I'm not surprised," I declare, then frown at how easily the lie slips out. "I just appreciate you taking the time to do so in the middle of what you had going on this evening, that's all."

"I told you I'd make it up to you."

He had? I don't remember any such promise. "I know." Another lie. "I just didn't expect it to be tonight, that's all."

Over the phone, it sounds like Adam's moving around, probably getting undressed. I hear the telltale clink of his belt buckle, the swish of fabric against fabric. My mind conjures up a visual of my husband as he unbuttons his pale blue Oxford and pulls the undershirt free from the waistline of his trousers that settle low on his hips, his belt already discarded. Long and lean, his stomach is flat and taut, the narrow line of dark hair dividing his torso symmetrically and disappearing beneath the band of his boxers. I swallow hard.

Pregnancy hormones, that little voice tells me, and if it had eyes, I'm sure they'd be rolling.

When he still doesn't speak, I fill the void, desperate to get control of my thoughts.

"I—" My voice cracks, and I swallow again. "I'm sure it means a lot to them that you called, Adam."

For a moment, I wonder if he's put down the phone, but then he says, "Does it mean a lot to you?"

"Of course," I assure him quickly. "You know it does."

"Are you in bed?"

The sudden change of subject catches me by surprise, and I answer truthfully. "Um, no." I straighten, sliding my legs out of my nightgown and lowering my feet to the floor. "I was reading. In the living room. But I was just getting ready to call it a night when you telephoned." I can't decide whether I want him to think I was waiting up for him or not.

"What are you wearing?" His voice has turned molten, and my cheeks grow hot. "Under your pajamas, I mean."

"Adam," I murmur, trying to keep the censure from my tone.

"Well, exactly how much does my phone call to your folks mean to you, sweet Dani?" His tone is heavy with suggestion, and I can practically see his left eyebrow arch in request. "Come on, baby. I miss you."

"Really?" I ask, then pull the phone from my ear and stare at the screen for a moment, my brow furrowed. I have no objection to a little conjugal creativity with my husband when the real deal isn't an option, but the man is half an hour from home. "Do you want me to come and get you, Adam? I don't have anything scheduled first thing in the morning. I can take you to work in the morning, or to pick up your car."

He is silent on the other end of the line for so long, that I wonder if he's ended the call. "Adam? Are you there?"

"Nah. Never mind," he finally says, and I can hear a thin ribbon of steel in his words. "I'm tired, so I'm going to bed now. I'll see you tomorrow after work."

"Adam," I cajole. "Don't do this."

"Don't do what?"

"I'm sorry, okay? I just thought the real thing might be better."

"And I thought you appreciated what I did for you tonight."

His words are like a bucket of ice water upended over my head. "For me? For us, you mean, right? This is our baby, not just mine."

"It's *your* parents," he shoots back, as if that explains anything.

I press the heel of my palm to my chest again, a dull ache now settling in where that fluttery thing has turned to ash. I can't believe I'm having this conversation. I can't believe Adam wants me to repay his act of husbandly chivalry with drunken phone sex. I can't believe what started out as an unexpectedly nice call has turned so sordid and sour.

And yet, I can believe it. All of it.

"Good night, Adam," I say, then hang up.

Not for the first time, I'm grateful for the overwhelming fatigue brought on by this pregnancy. In spite of my churning stomach and aching heart, I'm asleep within minutes of my head hitting my pillow.

Six hours later, I'm awakened by the sound of Adam's ring tone on my phone, a Taylor Swift song from our dating days. I open one eye just long enough to accept the call. "Hello?" My voice is husky with sleep, and I'm struggling to free my mind from the murky waters of the dream I was having.

"Dani. It's me."

"Adam?" I crack an eye open again and pull my phone away to check the time. Just after 5 AM. "What's wrong?" He sounds terrible, and I'm almost afraid to hear his answer.

"Baby, I feel rotten about last night. I've been lying here awake for an hour, waiting to call you. I hate that I was that kind of guy on the phone to you."

I roll to my side and reach for the pillow from Adam's side of the bed, then tuck it under my head. The scent of his aftershave stirs my senses, and I turn my face into it and breath him in. "It's okay," I murmur, more out of habit than because it is. It's not okay, actually, but I'm not clearheaded enough to have this discussion right now.

"I should have come home—" he begins.

"You'd been drinking," I tell him, cutting him off. "You made the right choice not to drive." Why am I letting him off the hook? I can only imagine what Ranae would say if she could hear me now.

"But that whole phone call, Dani."

"It's all right. It's fine."

He's quiet on the other end of the line and I can feel my muscles twitching as my body attempts to settle back into sleep.

"Sorry if I woke you," he finally murmurs. "I just couldn't wait another minute to tell you what an ass I am."

I chuckle sleepily. "You didn't need to wake me up to tell me that."

"Yeah, I know." He sighs loudly, and I roll onto my back, my eyes still closed. It's comforting talking to him here in the dark, even if he isn't in bed beside me. "But I wanted you to know that I know it, too."

"Well, thank you for that."

"You're welcome."

I know I should still be upset, but I'm not. Either I'm too tired to be, or this situation simply isn't important enough to me. Right now, I'm not sure which, but I'm going to put off mulling over it until after I get more sleep. "I'll see you tonight at dinner, okay? I'm drifting off; forgive me."

"Of course. Go back to bed. I shouldn't have called so early."

"It's okay," I reassure him again, then release the jaw-cracking yawn I've been holding back. I almost tell him that I appreciate him making the gesture, but I realize how formal that sounds. Instead, I say, "I miss you."

For a moment, he doesn't respond, but finally, his voice catches around his words as he says, "I miss you, too, love."

I don't bother checking to see if he's still on the line. I shove the phone under my pillow and slip back into the blissful nothingness of sleep.

Ranae

"DANI, THIS IS CAROLINE. Caroline, Dani," I say, gesturing between Dani and the woman whose makeup I'm doing. Dani lifts a hand in solemn greeting and moves to perch on a stool nearby, scrutinizing the array of cosmetics on the counter in front of her.

"Can you hand me that big powder brush? The pink-handled one." I hold out my gloved hand toward my friend.

Dani plucks it from my collection of makeup brushes and hands it to me. "She looks nice," she says, acknowledging my efforts. I'm not the artist my mother is, but I've been trained well by her, and I know how to put a little color back into a corpse's face without making her—or him—look like a stage actor. "I like the way you fixed her hair. Looks just like the picture."

I have a photograph of Caroline pulled up on my desktop monitor, a recent one, thank goodness. One of my pet peeves is when I'm given outdated pictures and I'm expected to make a loved one's face look twenty years younger than he or she actually is. It's already a bit of a stretch to make them look their age, depending on the circumstances of their death, but I always do my best to accommodate. I'm proud to say there have only been two times when my efforts did not meet expectations, and only one of them was my fault.

Two years ago, I picked up a young man's body from a hospital where he'd spent the last few weeks of his life with a brain tumor. His parents brought me a photo of him that was obviously several years old; when I picked him up, Jamison sported a full black beard and long hair, while the picture showed him with short, tousled hair and a clean-shaven face. They didn't feel comfortable tending to his body themselves, so with their written requests on file, I agreed to shave their son's face and cut and style his hair to resemble his picture as close as possible. Jamison's shave and a haircut turned out really nice, in fact, and his parents were thrilled; he was quite a handsome young man under all that hair. His mother wouldn't stop gushing over how wonderful he looked.

Then his girlfriend of almost five years showed up.

Alice wore a colorful maxi dress, no bra or shoes, and there were beads and silver trinkets woven into her waist-length dreadlocks. When she saw what I'd done to her beloved partner, she broke down and wept into her henna-tattooed hands, mourning the loss of Jamison's hair as if he'd been Samson, and the haircut, not the brain tumor, had been his demise.

The other incident occurred much earlier in my career when I was still learning the finesse of 'less is more'. The body I was working on had taken on a rusty yellow-orange hue, and instead of toning down the color with a contrasting concealer first, I went straight to my stock of theatrical creme and cake makeup. By the time I was finished, the poor man looked like he'd had been made up by an over-exuberant little girl who'd gotten hold of her mother's makeup, and I'd been in tears. That was before the man's wife and children came by with his clothes. His twenty-something-year-old son started laughing when he saw his father, and no matter how hard he tried, he couldn't stop, and tears streamed from his eyes. His daughter and wife cried, too, but without the cackling, and I couldn't stop apologizing between my own sniffles. Fortunately, this was back before I had my own studio at Fair Havens, and my parents swept in and rescued us all. The man ended up looking just like his photo, and the tears shed at his funeral were due to grief over his loss, instead of dismay over his appearance.

I've already bathed Caroline's body in one of my signature herbal body washes; this one is a base of witch hazel and distilled water infused with lavender, rosemary, lemon, and tea tree oils. I like it because it's crisp and clean smelling, but I have several options, knowing some people have strong fragrance preferences. It seems people either love or hate the smell of lavender, so I use it sparingly. One of my other favorites is infused with cedar and marjoram. I use it on most of my male subjects.

Caroline is wearing a beautiful cotton dress that looks like it came right out of a 1950's Good Housekeeping magazine. It's a lime-green gingham with a full skirt and a Peter Pan collar trimmed in a red satin ribbon, and on her feet are the cutest little red kitten heels. I've arranged her bleached-blonde hair into a French twist that covers the worst of the structural damage at the back of her head, and I curled her bangs over her bruised forehead to give her a Betty Paige vibe. Her husband, Troy, is a vintage car mechanic, a gentle giant of a man who rolls his t-shirt sleeves up and sports several Sailor Jerry tattoos, and he's bringing their two young daughters and their large extended family by this afternoon for a private viewing before the funeral tomorrow. Troy built a gorgeous cherry wood casket for her, and he wants to lay her in it himself. Caroline, ironically and oh-so-tragically, was killed in a car accident.

I'm already a mess just thinking about the couple. I can't help it—I automatically cry whenever men cry, and I have yet to meet with Troy when he hasn't had tears streaming from his eyes.

I also can't help comparing Troy to Adam, not with Dani sitting across the room from me. In short order, I'm telling Dani about how wonderful Caroline's husband is with his girls, how obvious it is that he loves them and cherishes them with every breath he has left in him, even more now that he's lost their mother. It's not fair, and I know it, but I wish Dani would take her blinders off and see Adam for what he is—a selfish man-child who wants the privileges of being married without having to act like a married man.

"You know," Dani says slowly, and I can hear the warning edge in her voice. Sheesh, but that girl sees right through me. "I've been thinking about what I'm going to do. My appointment with Tracy is tomorrow—you're coming, aren't you?"

I nod. "Of course."

"Good. Because Adam isn't going to be there."

"Why not? What does he have that's so—"

"Please don't," she says, holding up a hand to stop my questions. "He's just not, and that's all there is to it. My parents are coming, but I really want you there, too."

She pauses for several moments, but I can tell she has more to say, so I just nod again and busy myself with digging through the makeup bag Caroline's husband brought in.

Sure enough, Dani continues. I don't look at her lest she hesitate again or chicken out altogether. "I'd like to ask you to be my official birth partner," she says, her voice quiet, but firm. "Right now, Adam is being pretty great, all things considered, but I simply can't be certain he's going to stick around for the long haul, so I've decided to make plans without him. Just in case."

I straighten on my stool, a lip brush coated in cherry red lipstick in one hand, and I meet her eyes. "You don't even have to ask, Dani. You were there for Ruby and me. I'll be there for you and your—"

She holds up her hand again, and I frown. I don't like being hushed, not by anyone, even Dani. "Before you agree, let me lay a few things out on the table first. One, I love Adam."

My eyebrows twitch and I turn back to Caroline, not wanting Dani to see the sneer that's trying to take over my features. I know she loves him. Any fool can see that. It's *why* she loves him that has me so baffled.

"I can hear you," she says.

"I didn't say anything," I shoot back at her, keeping my eyes averted.

"I can hear you anyway, loud and clear." She sighs loudly and takes a long sip from her water bottle. "I still love my husband, Ranae, and I've decided that I'm not ready to be the one who leaves. I readily admit that I don't like how things are right now, how he's acting. I certainly don't like the idea of him setting up an alternate life, or whatever it is he's doing, but I'm not ready to give up on the one we still share."

"Okay," I say with a slow nod. My best friend is nothing, if not loyal. "What does that have to do with me being your birth partner?"

"Well," she says, absentmindedly straightening a row of foundation bottles in my enormous makeup kit so that all the labels are facing the same direction. "If at any time, Adam decides he wants to start participating, I want him to be included, and I don't want him to feel like he's a third wheel."

I frown as I focus on applying an even coat of color to Caroline's blind-stitched lips. I'm ecstatic at the thought of being there to share the joy of birth with Dani, but I selfishly don't want to share that experience with Adam. What if he makes *me* feel like a third wheel? He's very good at that.

"What do you think?" she asks when I don't respond right away. "Am I asking too much of you?"

I shake my head, still not trusting my voice, but not willing to bow out, either.

"It is, I know it is," Dani says with an unhappy sigh. "Would you rather I ask my mother? Or Gail? I'll be delivering at Breathe anyway—"

"Stop, please," I finally say, tossing the lip brush onto the counter near me and swiveling on my stool to face her. "Dani, I want to be there, okay? This is about you and what you want, not me. I have figured out how to share you with Adam all these years already, haven't I? Trust me to be ready and willing, albeit maybe a bit grudgingly, to share you with him for the birth, too." I shoot her an ironic expression. "This is his child, after all."

She studies me, her expression both sad and relieved, and I'm reminded of how she looked at me the morning after her surprise birthday party. My friend is counting on me to be strong with her. Not for her, not instead of her, but *with* her. I can do that.

Things seem to be at a standstill with her and Adam. She says he's not upset about the pregnancy, but he certainly doesn't act very thrilled about it, either. He still insists she knew he was going to buy the car last spring, and she has stopped insisting she didn't. He also says she's making too big of a deal about his lake house bachelor pad, the one he refers to as their investment property, but he won't take her to see it because he wants it completely ready before he shows it to her. "It was supposed to be a surprise," she explained to me without any detectable sarcasm. "I think he's kind of proud of what he's accomplished on his own. Like he's proving something to himself, maybe even to me."

Whatever it is that Adam is trying to prove is beyond me, and Dani won't call his mother to confirm if she is, indeed, the Mrs. Granger who is helping him pick out French Country window treatments. That might be all the "proof" she needs, and it's what I would have done first thing.

Dani has acknowledged that she's having a hard time believing anything he tells her, but it's obvious she's still hoping to find a way to the other side of this season with her marriage intact. "I'm honestly just too tired right now to fight," she tells me with a wry smile. "All I want to do is sleep and barf and eat stuff with ginger in it. Or drink stuff." She lifts her water bottle in a salute and sighs. I'm pretty sure there are chunks of fresh ginger floating in the bottom of the stainless-steel canister. "My poor patients. Half the time they're giving me advice on how to get through this. I'm sure I instill a lot of confidence in them."

I want her to kick Adam out. I want her to at least give him an ultimatum. That man cave or bachelor pad or lake house or whatever the heck it is needs to go—now—or he does. But she has made it clear to me that although she understands my concern, she is handling things the best way she sees fit for now.

I take a deep breath and turn back to Caroline. The woman is only two years older than we are, far too young to be laid out on my gurney, and I can feel the burn of tears at the back of my throat again. Preparing a body for his or her last momentous occasion in the land of the living is an aspect of this job that I have grown to cherish, but it's also the most difficult emotionally. Every single body that ends up in here has a story, and while some are truly lovely and garner deep respect and appreciation from me—those who come to me after a long life well-lived, surrounded by a circle of friends and family—there are also the Carolines and Jamisons, or the children and infants I must nestle into a favorite blanket in one of the woven willow or bamboo caskets who break my heart.

When I worked for my father and Opa at Niemeyers Mortuary, I seemed better equipped to distance myself from the personal lives of my clients. Maybe it was because there were always other people around while I worked—one of the secretaries, Dad, Mom, my grandfather. My brothers were often in and out of the place, Jordan in the capacity of a young pastor, Nolan sniffing around for free food or a pretty young mourner to comfort. Or a sister to tease. Nolan and I have what has always been something of a love-hate relationship. He loves to tease me, I hate to laugh when he does. But somehow, he can always get a smile out of me, no matter how dark my mood.

On the surface, Nolan is the quintessential bachelor. He's devilishly good-looking, he has a sharp sense of humor and a ready laugh, and more friends than any person has the right to. He's the kind of guy who dates women just long enough to give them hope, then moves on right before that moment when heartache becomes heartbreak, somehow managing to stay friends with almost all of them. But underneath his easygoing, middle child manner, Nolan is a solid sort. There is a reason that he has so many people in his life, and it's not just because he's a lot of fun to be around. Nolan can be counted on. Maybe because he's content with who he is, and that makes others feel safe with him.

Right after Solomon died, I know he felt some burden of responsibility for me, and then Ruby, too. With my parents' support, I had made the decision to tell my brothers about our relationship, regardless of the contract Dad and I had signed. He once came upon me standing at the window in our dark living room late one night, my hands cupped over the small, tight bulge starting to form at my abdomen. I'd just felt Ruby move and I was crying, imagining Solomon behind me, his own hands covering mine, his warm breath against my neck as he whispered how much he loved us both. Nolan came to stand beside me, and for several moments, he, too, just stared out the window into the moonlit yard. Finally, he turned toward me, his chin dipped contritely, his own eyes glistening suspiciously, and apologized for ever introducing Solomon to me. In a fit of rage and despair, I hauled off and slapped him with all the emotions a disowned grieving pregnant teenager could muster. I would never be sorry for having known Solomon, for the precious, blissful eternity we shared in those few short months we had together, for loving him with every fiber of my seventeen-year-old being. A stunned Nolan lunged at me, not to tackle me as I half-expected, but to wrap his arms around me and crush me up against him. I came undone there in my big brother's tight embrace, my body shaking and juddering against him, and he just held me as I soaked the front of his t-shirt with my misery. He only complained once, and rather vehemently, I might add, when I used the sleeve of his shirt to blow my nose.

Now, here in my own small schoolhouse basement preparation room, I often work alone, spending long contemplative hours over the body of someone leaving behind friends and family who will mourn them. And it's here in this quiet sanctuary that I find myself thinking of Solomon as I share in the grief of those who have lost someone they love. I wonder who cared for his body, who put him back together after the accident. I know he was laid to rest in the McCray family cemetery on their own land. I've seen a picture of his tombstone on his sister's Facebook. *Beloved Son, Brother, and World Changer.* They'd left off *Father* and *Fiancé*, but then again, to those who buried him, Ruby and I don't exist.

World Changer, indeed. Solomon certainly changed my world, and he left me with far more of him than they'll ever have.

True to my promise, I've never reached out to any members of his family. But Sarah McCray's profile is public, and every once in a while, when the dull ache of Solomon's absence in my life grows a spur, I open an incognito browser and do some clandestine lurking. I see Solomon in her face, in her smile, in the way her eyes turn down when she laughs.

I see Ruby in her, too. The full, bow-shaped lips and ready smile, her narrow, straight nose that doesn't sport a ski-jump tip like mine. All three of them—Solomon, Sarah, and Ruby—have eyes the color of sweet tea when the late afternoon summer sun shines through it. Those eyes are Ruby's claim to Solomon's name, no matter what any court of law says.

And no matter what happens between Dani and Adam, her baby will have a claim to Adam's name, too, I remind myself firmly.

Because of her severe morning sickness, Dani is spending only a few hours a week on site at Breathe. She's put a hold on taking any new patients, especially those with delivery dates close to her own, and other than a birth at the center earlier this week, she's only had a few home prenatal visits to go to. It's obvious she doesn't want to be alone, and we're always happy to have her loitering about the place, even in her somber mood.

We are all on high alert: Gran, Hugo, and me. Quiet and watchful, we are taking our cues from her. On the rare occasion she wants to talk about Adam, we let her talk about Adam. If she doesn't, we don't bring him up. She's spending most of her down time out here with us at the farmhouse, cooking or gardening with Gran, helping Ruby with her homework, or just napping wherever she falls asleep. Sometimes, like today, she comes over to the cemetery and keeps me company down here in my workspace or walking the woods with me while I make my rounds. If Hugo is around when she shows up, he puts her to work with a pair of gardening gloves and tools, busying her with mundane tasks so she doesn't go crazy with her runaway thoughts.

She's getting that sad, broken-winged bird look again, and I wave an eyebrow pencil at the computer. She needs a distraction. We both need a distraction. "Have you seen the comments on our Facebook page today?"

"Not yet," she says, leaning one elbow on the counter near the computer keyboard. "I haven't been online much lately."

"I'm pretty much done here, and I have the small version of Caroline's picture on my phone, so I can refer to that if I need to. Pull up our Facebook page and check it out." We just shared on our podcast last week that she's pregnant, and congratulations and advice have been pouring in. There have been some less than appealing comments, but it's impossible to have a platform on any social media forum without gaining a few trolls, no matter how harmless our content.

"Be wary of GottaPanda4U," I warn her.

"Why?" Dani asks, straightening a little and scooting closer to the keyboard. She turns the monitor toward her.

"Harmless enough," I assure her. "Just kinda gross and creepy. He—or she—wants to know if you're going to post Kardashian pics of your pregnancy."

She makes a dry heave gagging sound and I'm not sure if it's authentic or not. "Of course. Anything for our fans," she mutters, rolling her eyes.

"Well, I'm glad we don't have any scary stalkers or major weirdos. That we know of, anyway. It kind of surprises me we don't, what with the rising numbers of death enthusiast communities out there."

"Nah," Dani says. "I think you make it pretty clear you're not all into that Dark Lord and heebie-jeebies stuff."

"Dark Lord and heebie-jeebies stuff?" I ask with a giggle.

"You know what I mean, woman." She throws a makeup sponge at me, but I duck out of the way with ease. I did grow up with two older brothers.

With her long fingers flying over the keyboard, Dani pulls up our Life and Death email account. "Goodness," she whispers. "Look at all these messages. There are so many."

The atmosphere lightens as she starts scrolling. At least two-thirds of them are for Dani, and as she skims through the kind and encouraging words, her eyes glisten brightly. She's been so much more emotional than usual, and although she knows it's her wacky hormones, she hates not being able to keep them in check. But it's just the two of us right now, and I know better than to even acknowledge her tears, which in turn, gives her the freedom to let them fall.

I put the last finishing touches on Caroline's lovely face and gently tug the protective drape from where I tucked it in around her collar. Then I straighten her dress one last time and whisper a prayer of gratitude for the honor it is to do my job as I cover her with a lightweight linen sheet. With quick, practiced moves, I unlock the wheels of the gurney and roll it over to the refrigeration unit across the room. I bought the cooler from my father when he upgraded to a larger unit at the mortuary. It works great for my needs, thanks in part to Hugo, who keeps it in tip-top shape, and it's a simple task for me to single-handedly transfer Caroline on her body board into the cooler. I close the heavy door, double check the latch, then with a quick glance over my shoulder to make sure Dani is all right, I head to the bathroom to wash up.

"I'm going to put on some coffee upstairs," I tell her when I duck back into the room, rubbing a homemade medicated balm into my working-girl hands. "Would you like something? More water?" I'm lazy about using gloves out in the woods, and my hands tend to get a little rough and ragged doing the heavy-duty groundskeeping tasks, but I'm fastidious about wearing my sterile gloves while working with cadavers here in my workspace. It's more for the sake of my clients than my own, though. Touching a dead body with bare hands is rarely cause for alarm, and indeed, I encourage family members to do so, especially if they're preparing their loved one at home. But the gloves mark me as a professional, the way a lab coat does a medical practitioner, which is something people like to see when they first come to what seems like a rather rustic setting. I keep my basement spotless and smelling of herbs and a hint of bleach, a combination of aromas that subconsciously denotes a sterile environment. But the tradeoff is that my hands can get pretty irritated if I wear the sterile gloves too long, and the balm I use is good for both protection and relief.

"I'm good," Dani tells me, clearly distracted by the comments she's reading. I'm glad to see the gentle smile on her face as she waves me off.

I'm heading back down the basement stairs a few minutes later, my steaming coffee cup in hand, when I hear her call my name. "Ranae?" Her voice warbles, and I hurry to see what's wrong.

She's sitting bolt upright, staring at the monitor, her face pale. When she turns to me, her eyes are wide. She holds out a hand toward me, beckoning me forward, and her expression, although obviously shocked, is one of uncertainty and concern.

For me.

"What's up?" I ask, trying to tamp down the fear spiking through me. I take her hand in mine and her fingers are trembling slightly. "Good grief, Dani. What is it?"

She says nothing; just flaps her other hand at the screen. Dani is still perusing our Matters of Life and Death email inbox, and at the top of the list of emails is one from someone named Sarah McCray Crawley. Part of the first line of the message body shows next to her name. *This message is for Ranae Niemeyer. I don't know if you remember me, but my name is...*

"What on earth?" I ask as I set my coffee cup down on the counter, the contents sloshing over the top and searing the skin on the back of my hand. I barely feel the burn as I drag my rolling stool over next to Dani. She's still holding my other hand, squeezing it hard.

"Do you want me to open it?" she asks, her voice just above a whisper.

I can only nod.

I don't know if you remember me, but my name is Sarah Crawley. My maiden name is McCray and I am Solomon McCray's sister. If you're still reading this, I promise to keep it short, as I'm sure I'm one of the last people in the world you'd want to hear from. I know what that awful contract says, but I don't care. I'm hoping you'll give me chance to do what I can to set things right. My mother has recently passed away, and my father is aware that I am writing to you. Ranae, I'd like to meet the woman my brother loved so intensely, and I'd like to meet your child one day. My brother's child. And although I have no legal right to claim her, my niece. It is with great hope that I send this, Sarah.

She included her mailing address, her phone number, and a few of her social media links, along with a postscript: *You can find out more about me online if you'd rather start there.*

"No," I say, pushing to my feet, my stool skittering away from me. My voice sounds rough and hard, as unforgiving as my spirit is. "No. She does not get to drop in out of the clear blue sky and insist I let her into our world."

"What about Ruby?" Dani asks quietly, almost hesitatingly. "What do you think she'd want?"

I know what my daughter would want. She'd jump at the chance to meet someone from Solomon's family. Not because they're so wonderful, but because she has no idea how terrible they are. I shake my head, locking eyes with Dani. "It doesn't matter what she'd want because she'll never be given the option. Never." I reach across her for the mouse, but Dani moves it just out of my reach.

"Please think on the situation before you do anything rash," she says quietly, her British accent and her formal phrasing irritating me for no apparent reason.

"There's nothing to think about and the only rash thing I'm considering doing is filing a cease-and-desist claim with Frederick and Vancours." I lean forward again and hold out my hand for the mouse Dani is still clutching. "Give it to me."

"What are you going to do?"

"Junk it. Mark it as Spam. Delete it permanently. I don't want to see any trace of it in our inbox." I step back and cross my arms, glaring back and forth between the monitor and the ominous email and my friend who isn't being such a great friend right now. "You know I can erase it at any time, right?"

"Come now, Ranae. Why don't you sleep on it, all right? Give it until tomorrow morning before you decide what to do with this email."

But I'm having none of it. I spin on my heel, grab my phone off the other end of the counter where it still shows Caroline's smiling face on the screen, and pull up our email account. In two swipes, I've not only trashed the note, but I've deleted it from existence. At least on this end.

Dani

I insist on picking Ranae up for my appointment today. She was so upset after receiving that message from Sarah McCray, and I'm worried about how she's doing. I want to catch her alone before getting to Breathe where she'll have to play the role of excited best friend in front of everyone. I still don't know if Adam is going to make it or not—I didn't bother reminding him this morning. The date is clearly marked on the calendar hanging beside the refrigerator. But my parents, and Gail and Tracy, they all know Ranae well enough to be able to tell if something is wrong, especially if she's bursting at the seams with suppressed emotions. I'm certain she had to keep things bottled up last night, although perhaps she shared with Gran. We can talk in the car on the way, get it out of her system so that she can concentrate on being excited for me. Then maybe we can do lunch together after. We can't make it a late lunch; I have an afternoon appointment with a patient who is ready to give birth any day now, and Ranae needs to get back to Fair Havens to help Hugo start prepping the two buildings at the cemetery for fresh coats of paint. A week from Friday is this month's Live and Let Die Bonfire Night, and the two of them will spend the next several days going over the place with a fine-toothed comb in preparation for visitors.

I almost laugh when I pull into the driveway at the old farmhouse, but I restrain myself. Ranae is pacing back and forth on the faded lawn in front of the porch, an almost visible cloud of agitation trying to keep up with her. Her faithful Blimey is sprawled like an enormous heap of gray fur on the top step, and he lifts his head just enough to twitch his ears and narrow his eyes in my direction, then flops back down again. I roll my window down, not bothering to get out. Ranae is already stomping toward me. "Hey there," I call out as she rounds the hood of my Forester and yanks open the passenger door.

"Hey," she murmurs, then lays her head against the back of the seat and lets out a restrained growl.

"Buckle up," I tell her, knowing she'll spill when she's ready. I'm not even out of the driveway when she starts.

"How could she? Doesn't she realize how selfish her request is?" Ranae twists in her seat so she can look more directly at me. "Why now? Why not wait until Ruby is eighteen? She couldn't give us one more year?"

I'm glad to hear that Ranae has been thinking about Sarah's motivations. Perhaps if she can sort through this from that perspective, she may be more open to the idea. I, too, have thought about the situation, relieved to have something other than my own issues with Adam to mull over, even though I feel a little guilty that it's at my friend's expense. But the more I consider things, the more I believe that Ruby has the right to be included in this decision. I'm just not certain how to express that opinion to my raging friend right now.

"Maybe it's because her mother has died," I suggest. "Perhaps she feels that her daughterly obligations have been met now that her mum is out of the picture, and she is free to look for what she perceives is her lost family." I glance over at Ranae and grimace. Her expression tells me she doesn't really want to be reasoned with at the moment. I continue anyway. "She did say she's doing this with her father's blessing. With Solomon's father's blessing."

"I know who he is, Dani. He's the same man who signed a legal document that stated he had no familial obligation to us. By his own choice, he is nothing to me, and by his own choice, he's nothing to Ruby, either. Which means, by association, Sarah McCray is nothing to us, either. We are under no obligation to even respond to her, no less to meet her demands."

"She didn't sound like she was demanding anything, Nae."

"Whose side are you on anyway?" Ranae shoots back, narrowing her eyes at me. I can practically feel the heat of her glare against my cheek.

"Yours. And Ruby's." I know she's not angry at me. I don't really believe she's angry at Sarah, either. I believe she's afraid of what might happen if she opens this Pandora's box. She's afraid of getting hurt by Solomon's family again. Even worse, she's afraid of Ruby being hurt by them. Afraid of trusting them with her daughter's heart the way she once trusted them with her own.

But I have faith in both of them, in my friend and her precocious, effervescent daughter.

"Well, it doesn't matter what that woman wants of us, or whether she's demanding it or not. She's not getting it." She crosses her arms and stares out her passenger side window, and I have to press my lips together to keep from smiling. She looks so much like a sullen teenager—like our own sweet-and-sour Ruby—and I am momentarily swept back in time to the silly arguments we used to have back in high school. We never could stay angry at each other for more than half a second, and although this isn't really a silly argument—reconnecting with Solomon's family is about as serious as things can get in the grand scheme of things—I'm not worried about the two of us sorting this out. She's talking to me about this because she trusts me, and even though she may not like my opinion, I truly believe she wants it, nonetheless.

I hesitate, but only for a moment before forging on. "I am thinking of Ruby in this, Ranae. She's asked you about Solomon's family before, so you know she wants to know. It isn't just information about the man who was her father. It's part of who she is, too."

"Come on, Dani. You and I both know that our identities are not determined by our bloodlines. Sure, our chemical and metabolic makeup is, maybe even our sense of style since clearly, you didn't get yours from your parents." She makes a quick full body sweep hand gesture at me and lifts an eyebrow. I'm wearing a soft patchwork skirt that's so long it almost drags on the ground behind me, and a bright pink lace tank top under a sheer butterfly-sleeve blouse. It's an outfit my mother—and certainly not my father—would never be caught dead in.

I know what Ranae is saying. Over the course of our friendship, we've spent hours and hours discussing the pros and cons of being adopted. We've heard the horror stories, the glorious reunion tales, and have been regaled by the terrifying and pitiful and tragic and triumphant from our social media fans and followers, and we both soundly agree that we are among the fortunate ones. We two were given the best that adoption has to offer, and the freedom to be the best that we can be because of it. Ranae and I were not handed our identities. We got to discover them for ourselves, and for that gift, we are both grateful.

And yet, I can't help but wonder why I've spent so much of my life feeling a bit untethered, or *lost*, as my parents described it the night that I told them about my pregnancy. They spoke of it as though it was a thing of the past, like I've regained my fearlessness, but the more I think about it, the more I'm not so sure they're correct. I still feel rather lost and scared most of the time. I'm really only brave when I'm not alone.

"I don't know, Nae. I believe that if I were given the opportunity, I would want to know more. I'm not about to pursue it for myself. I don't need it," I say, my mouth pulling wide as I emphasize the word *need*. "But if someone told me they held my back story in their hands and asked me if I wanted to read it? Well, I'd say yes. I might want to think about it first, talk to my parents, of course, and certainly discuss it with you, but in the end, my answer would be yes."

"No one has asked Ruby, and that's the way it's going to stay."

I glance over at her and frown. "And doesn't that tell you something about Sarah? The fact that she came to you first, that she's asking your permission, Ranae? That shows respect and wisdom. She could have waited until Ruby was eighteen and gone straight to her."

Ranae shook her head vehemently. "No. The contract wouldn't—"

"Did she sign it?" I ask, cutting her off. "Did Ruby?"

Ranae doesn't respond, but I see the uncertainty and perhaps a little fear in my friend's expression, and I know my point has been made.

"What are you afraid of?" I ask, although I already know the answer. I push her anyway. I want her to speak the words, to nullify them by putting them out there. "Ruby is not going to switch loyalties. You know that, right? Nor is she going to look for something that's been missing from her life. You've already given her father to her in that journal you kept. The rest of them—these other McCrays that this Sarah woman is part of—they are the peripherals. The extras."

"Hold up," Ranae says, lifting a hand between us to stop me. "You don't seem to understand, Dani. I've given Ruby *my* half of Solomon. And it's not even half. My five months of Solomon. The five months of him that were mine. They have the other nineteen-plus years of Solomon to give her. Don't tell me she's not going to be chomping at the bit for them to fill up a bottomless well of emptiness in her. A well my tiny part of Solomon can't even begin to fill." Her voice catches, and I realize there's even more going on than I'd thought.

I'm nearing the birthing center, but we are a good fifteen minutes early, so I pull into an empty parking lot half a block away. I turn off my ignition and shift in my seat so I can see her face. "What about you?" I ask. "Don't you want to know about the other part of Solomon McCray? Don't you want to know what—or who—made him into the man he was when you met him?"

"He was hardly a man," she scoffs, roughly swiping her fingers under her eyes.

"He was man enough," I shoot back, refusing to let her dodge this bullet. "Man enough to love you. Man enough to impregnate you. Man enough to choose to marry you."

"I get it," she mutters.

"Well, what if Sarah can give you the big picture of who he is? Or his father?"

"And what if the picture they give me isn't the Solomon I loved? What if Sarah paints him as someone else altogether? I couldn't bear that, Dani. I couldn't. His memory is sacred in my heart, as well as in Ruby's, and I want to keep it that way. I won't let his family taint my memories of him. Of us."

"But..." I begin, then hesitate, wondering if I should let things rest for a bit.

"But what?" Ranae isn't going to let me hold back, even though I know she won't like what I'm going to say.

I soldier on. "But what if your version of Solomon is the tainted one?"

Ranae narrows her eyes at me and shakes her head, a quick, decisive back and forth motion. "Nope. Not possible. He was as transparent and genuine as they get. I knew him, Dani, because he knew himself. He lived out loud, transparent and real."

"Then what are you afraid of?" I repeat, reaching over to take her hand. "These people are an extension of Solomon. They're not going to taint or change him to you. But they can give you more of him."

"Stop, Dani." She jerks her hand from mine and starts scrambling for the door handle like she's going to get out of the car. "I can't do this. I can't. Not now." She glances out the window, and I see her shoulders twitch in sudden awareness. She's been so preoccupied with her inner turmoil that she's just realized we're not in the parking lot at Breathe. "We'd better get to the center before you're late for your appointment."

I take a deep breath and start the car up again, but before I pull out onto the street, I try one last time. "Will you do something for me? Because I love you and I really do want only good for you and Ruby?"

She crosses her arms and studies me, her expression hard. It hurts my heart to look at her. "I'm not going to make any promises."

"Will you think about it a little longer? Will you consider talking to Ruby about this and finding out what her thoughts are? At least let her know that the option is there for her when she turns eighteen?"

Ranae rolls her eyes at me. "Really? And how well do you think that's going to go over? Here you go, daughter of mine. A big, fat, juicy carrot, one you've always wanted." She lifts a hand, her finger and thumb pressed together like she's dangling something between us. "But you can't touch it, taste it, or even think about it for another year." Her voice is drenched with sugary sarcasm.

I nod, agreeing that the scene she's painting is ugly. But that's not what I'm suggesting, and she knows it.

"And why on earth is that a favor for you?" she asks before I can expound, her brows furrowed angrily. "This doesn't have anything to do with you."

Her words are like a slap, and I actually flinch. I don't look at her, though. I have a feeling she's already feeling remorse and wishing she could suck them back in. I put the car in drive and pull out onto the quiet street.

"You and Ruby are mine, Ranae," I say, my voice steadier than I expect. "It's a favor to me because your happiness and well-being mean everything to me. And it's a favor to me because if I were offered the chance to know more about where I came from, and why I'm so different from the people who love me and raised me—parents who I'm eternally grateful for, to be certain—I'd grab it with both hands. It wouldn't change who I am, but it might help me *understand* who I am a little better."

We are silent the short distance to the birthing center, but when I go to open my door, Ranae puts a hand on my arm to stop me. "I'm sorry for being a jerk. I understand what you're saying, Dani. I really do." Her features are soft, pleading for me to hear her heart. Her voice. "I just don't know if I'm brave enough to accept the risks that come with letting them back in."

"You're not alone in this, Ranae," I tell her, still hurt, but forgiving her anyway. "You have Ruby, you have me, and Gran, and your amazing family. Even Hugo. He's got that lovely set of shoulders to unload on," I tease. "You wouldn't be accepting any of the risks on your own. We'd all stand by you."

But she's shaking her head before I'm finished. "I just can't," she murmurs. "I can't."

I cover her hand where it rests on my forearm, and we sit in silence for a few painful moments.

She takes a deep breath and blows it out hard, then pastes on a wide, grim smile. "Shall we go inside? See what kind of creature Adam has implanted in your womb?"

I gather myself and give her a shaky grin back. I've got a secret of my own that I've been holding in, and for a moment, I almost tell her what I have been hearing on my home Doppler all week. Not one, but two heartbeats. I'm not absolutely certain, but I've listened to a lot of heartbeats in my career, and I'm half-afraid, half-giddy over the possibility—no, the probability—of there being two tiny babies growing inside of me. *You'll never be alone again.* I have whispered those words in my heart again and again. I clamp my lips together, though, and hold the secret in my heart for just a little longer.

My mum and dad both get to their feet when we walk through the door. Mum texted me a few minutes ago to let me know they were already there, but there is no sign of Adam and no message from him about whether he's coming. I filled out all my paperwork before my appointment, and after a quick urine test, we decide to start with the ultrasound. It's what we're all here for, really. The rest of my visit with Tracy will consist of blood work and vital checks and letting her know my birth plan preferences. All things I can do with Tracy on my own, freeing my parents up to get back to work right away.

Tracy is all smiles as she leads us back to the ultrasound room. Along with the exam table, the ultrasound machine, and the large desktop monitor on the ultrasound cart, there is also a grouping of chairs for loved ones, and a second huge monitor mounted on the wall where everyone can view the images projected there. Typically, the midwife or technician performing the scan will view things first, then once the important images are captured, it's projected onto the large screen for everyone else to view. But I've already let Tracy know that I'd like to be included in every step of the process.

So while Ranae and Gail help me up onto the exam table, Tracy is making sure the wall monitor is live. I lie back on the paper-covered mattress, feeling a bit awkward viewing things from this position, but after I tug the waist of my skirt down and bunch my top up just below my bra, I look up at all the beaming faces who have gathered around me. These are the people I love so much. I truly am grateful.

I have a small hole in my heart over Adam's absence, however, and it seems like I'm losing blood from it in tiny, immeasurable drops. I know that eventually, all those tiny, immeasurable drops will add up to a puddle deep enough to drown in if I don't figure out how to plug that hole soon.

"Look at you," Tracy says as she slathers my abdomen with warmed gel. "You already have a little baby bump, girl. How far along did you say you were?"

"It's because she's so thin," Ranae interjects. "That baby has nowhere to hide."

There are a few titters around the room, but I glance over at my parents to catch them exchanging wide-eyed looks. They must be thinking the same thing I am, that the fact I'm already starting to show is a good indication there might be more than one baby in there. "I'm about ten weeks, I think. Maybe eleven?" My nausea seems to be waning in ferocity a little, or maybe I'm just getting accustomed to always feeling a bit seasick. The worst of it is in the hours after I first get up, and then again at the end of the day, or when I go too long without eating. But I'm able to get through my days now without too many dashes to the loo. I'm struggling with headaches from the surge of hormones and increased blood volume coursing through my system, but they're tolerable if I drink enough water and eat plenty of fresh fruit. I haven't gained any weight since I discovered I was pregnant almost a month ago, but now that I'm not trying to heave up everything that goes down, I'm expecting that to change.

Tracy starts moving the wand, and then I hear my mother gasp softly.

"Um, Dani?" My midwife holds the wand in place and turns her monitor so I can see it better. But I've already seen the images on the large screen on the wall, just like everyone else.

I look up at Tracy and nod, unable to hide my delight. We are looking at an image of not one, but two little heads bumping gently against each other. They're in separate amniotic sacs, but from what I can see, they share the same placenta. Which, combined with my advanced age of thirty-four, makes this officially a high-risk pregnancy. When multiples share a placenta, they share the same food source, and there is the potential for one baby to absorb more nutrients, causing a failure to thrive in the second baby. It's providential that I've decided to give birth at the birthing center after all—we are well-equipped at Breathe for high risk pregnancies, and in case of an emergency, we are only a block away from the hospital where my parents work.

Tracy moves the wand again. There's one tiny spine, then another, a thigh bone, two, then the other baby's legs. One heart beating, then the other. The swishing rhythms flow from the speakers and I believe it's the sweetest sound I've ever heard.

"Twins?" Ranae has her hands pressed to her cheeks, and tears are gathering in her eyes. "Twins? Dani, you're having twins? Oh my gosh, did you know?" She's full-on crying now, but laughing at the same time, and she starts bouncing up and down on her feet as she stares at the monitor, too. "Oh, look at them. They're so cute already. I think they have my nose."

I laugh at the absurdity of her statement, but part of me wouldn't be surprised if some bits and pieces of Ranae show up in my offspring. She has been closer than a sister to me for almost two decades, and if osmosis actually worked that way, these babies would be hers, too.

I look back at my mother to find tears trickling from her eyes as well, my father's arm around her. He leans forward and rests his smooth hand on my shoulder, beaming at me.

"You're also not ten weeks along, my dear," Tracy says, eyeing me with a curious expression. I look over at the monitor and frown. "See here?" she says, moving the wand to get a better angle on one of the babies. "Look at the hands, fingers, feet, and joints. Clearly defined internal organs, veins, and distinct facial features. I'm going to do measurements, but I'm thinking you're already at least twelve, maybe thirteen weeks."

"What? No, I can't be." I frown, studying the monitor more closely. But Tracy is right. The babies are measuring about the size of large plums, not strawberries, and the development of each one is well past the ten-week stage.

"We might be a little limited on the screening tests we can give you if you are, indeed, past thirteen weeks," Tracy begins, but I wave her concerns away. I only want tests that are absolutely necessary, and although I'm not going to say so in front of my parents, that will include a full sexually transmitted disease panel, just in case Adam has done more about creating a separate life for himself than just buying a car and a bachelor flat. The thought momentarily dampens my spirits, but I force myself to focus on the joy of the moment. When one of the babies moves a hand like he or she is waving, I lift my own and wave back. *You will never be alone again.*

When the new due date is determined to be April 24th instead of May 15th, I turn to my parents. "There you go, you two. It's all working out beautifully. Now you'll be free to go to Beira. By then, we'll all be old hats at this." I wave at my stomach and smile bravely. I can't help wondering if my *we* will include Adam or not. Mum and Dad share another one of their silent communication looks, and I frown. "What is it? Did you already tell your colleague you're not going?"

"No, no," Dad assures me, but he doesn't expound.

Mum finally adds, "We haven't given him a yes or a no yet. We have until the end of this month to decide."

"Then call him and tell him yes," I demand. "You're going, you hear?"

Gail steps in and wipes my stomach clean before helping me sit up. I sway a bit and don't immediately let go of her hand. "Lightheaded?" she asks.

I am, but it passes quickly, leaving behind an uncomfortable wave of nausea. It's not a very threatening one, though, and other than the dull headache I can't seem to shake, I'm doing all right.

Not quite an hour later, Ranae and I are heading back out to my car to go get something to eat. My headache has gotten worse, and after the adrenaline rush of this morning, I'm suddenly ravenous. "I'm craving Mexican food, something with a little kick," I tell her.

"How about El Gato Goro?" My friend knows me so well.

"They have the best green salsa," I say with a nod, linking my arm in hers as we cross the parking lot.

"I'm sorry Adam didn't make it," Ranae says once we're buckled into my car. Her tone is kind, and I know she means it. "He really missed out."

I nod, but say nothing. I'm angry that he has been a no-show today, but I suppose I'm hesitant to give my friend any more ammunition to use against him than she already has, mainly because if she's right about him, then what kind of a fool does that make me?

"Do you need to call him? Or are you going to wait to talk to him when he gets home from work?" She pulls out her phone and glances at the time. "Maybe you can catch him on his lunch break." Her tone is careful, but I can all but hear the things she isn't saying.

"I'm going to wait to talk to him." I'm not going to tell him we're having twins over the phone, but that's not really why I don't want to call him. I don't want to give him any information at any time if he doesn't want it, and his absence today is a good clue as to how he's feeling about things. "He's got a crazy load at work today." The words come out like a bad habit. Why am I defending him?

"Why are you making excuses for him?" Ranae asks, echoing my thoughts. It makes me a bit angry that she is so quick to assume that's what I'm doing, even if she is right. "What on earth is so important about his job that he can't take an hour away from work to come see his babies' first ultrasound with you?" She doesn't raise her voice, but her ire rolls off her in waves.

She's right to be upset for me—I'm upset for me, too—but because I can't answer her question, I feel backed into a corner. "Do you know what he does for a living?" I ask, my voice a little sharper than I intend.

"Why, yes," she shoots back. "Yes, I do." But she doesn't say more.

"A lot of people depend on him at his school, Ranae." I try to soften my tone, but I want to bite my tongue. I sound like one of those stereotype abuse victims. Adam doesn't abuse me, but I still feel this irresistible urge to defend his bad behavior, especially to my friend.

"And you depend on him here at home, Dani." She's still speaking quietly, but I don't miss the hard edge in her voice. "He should have been here today."

I have no rebuttal. She's right. He should have been here. I feel the prickle of tears, but I don't want to cry. I want to celebrate. I want to revel in the knowledge that I'm having twins, and that from what we can tell, they're both healthy. *I'm* healthy. I want to focus all my attention on those little ones bopping around in my uterus right now, and I certainly don't want to argue with Ranae anymore today.

She sighs, sensing my turmoil. She knows me so well. "Let's not talk about Adam, okay?" she says, reaching over to lay a hand on my shoulder. "Or the evil McCrays."

"Agreed." I shoot her a quick smile.

The tension between us lingers, shadow-like, but by the time our food arrives, we are laughing over a story Gran told Ranae about going bra shopping with two of her elderly church friends. Half an hour later, Ranae receives a call from someone wanting a tour of Fair Havens, so when we finish lunch, I drop her back off at the farmhouse, then head home to take a nap. The nausea may have abated a little, but I feel like I could sleep twenty out of the twenty-four hours in any given day. I'm exhausted all the time.

I wake to the sound of Adam calling my name. "Dani? You here?"

I know I've been asleep quite some time already, and that I really should get up and start thinking about dinner. I push up to the side of the bed and wait there while my head clears and my stomach stops flip-flopping. "I'm here," I call back, my voice husky from sleep. I feel lethargic, like I've been drugged, and my mouth is terribly dry. I reach for my glass of water on my bedside table, but it's empty.

"Hey," Adam says, appearing in the bedroom doorway. "Were you sleeping? It's almost five o'clock."

I lift my head to look at him blearily, not bothering to answer. It's fairly obvious, isn't it?

"What's for dinner?" he asks, then frowns and shakes his head. "I'm sorry. That made me sound like a jerk. Let me rephrase that. Would you like me to go pick something up for dinner?"

I dart him a forgiving half-smile and hold out my glass to him. "Would you be willing to get me some water first?"

He's back in a few minutes with a clean glass. There are even a few ice cubes in it. "Here you go," he says, crouching down in front of me with it. "How are you feeling? Busy day at Breathe today?"

I stare at him for a few moments, trying to figure out what game he's playing. I take the glass and mutter, "Thank you," then sip slowly at the chilled liquid, closing my eyes in pleasure. Finally, I simply say, "Yeah, I've had a pretty eventful day."

"Me, too." He moves to sit on the bed beside me and drapes an arm around me, pulling me gently against his side. "A nap, hm? I'm glad at least one of us got to put our feet up for a little while today."

I want to pull away from him, to stare at him like he's gone round the bend. I open my mouth to respond, but snap it shut again when I realize I'm at a complete loss for words.

Apparently, he doesn't need any response from me. "Are you hungry? I'll go call in a pizza, okay? Do you want Papa John's or Luigi Romero?" He slips out of his sports coat and hangs it in the closet. "Sausage okay?"

"Get whatever you want," I tell him, a little bowled over by his fervor. "I'm not sure I can handle pizza, though. I had Mexican food at lunch today and had heartburn all afternoon." I press a hand to my chest. "I might need to stick with something a little blander tonight."

"You went out to eat for lunch?" he asks, his tone a little too casual. "With your girls from work?" He leans out of the walk-in closet to look around the open door at me.

Why is he playing dumb like this? I don't try to hide my consternation. "No, Adam. With Ranae. We went out to get a bite to eat together after my ultrasound appointment at Breathe this morning."

I actually see the jolt of understanding hit him. "Your—your ultrasound was today?" he asks, frowning darkly at me. "And why was Ranae there?"

Is he serious? "Why weren't you there?" I ask, instead of answering his stupid question. "Even my parents showed up."

"Well, you didn't invite me," he says, stating the words slowly. He emerges from the closet and closes the door behind him, then leans his back against it. His expression has gone carefully blank, but his eyes are blazing.

"Invite you, Adam? To *our* ultrasound? You didn't come today because I didn't extend you a personal invitation?" I am flabbergasted by his response.

"Exactly," he shoots back. "I would have been there if you'd asked me. I didn't know I was allowed to go."

"You're kidding, right?" I gawk at him.

"No, I'm not kidding," he exclaims loudly. "If I had known I was supposed to be there, I would have been there."

I shake my head in disbelief. "I told you about this ultrasound appointment, Adam. Three weeks ago. I wrote it on the calendar. I even brought it up at dinner last night."

He nods. "Yeah, so? Putting something on the calendar is not the same as asking if I want to be there, is it?" He crosses his arms and glares at me. "I put stuff on the calendar all the time, but if it's something I want you there for, I tell you. I ask you to come with me. I make sure you know that you're invited."

"But Adam, these are—this is your baby, too." Right now is not the time to tell him about the twins. "Today was our first time seeing the baby, hearing the heartbeat. Why on earth would you think you shouldn't be there?"

"Oh, no, no, no." He shakes his head vehemently. "Don't you put this on me. Why on earth *would* I?" he retorts. "I've never done this whole pregnancy thing before. I've never really even thought about it. You know this is all new territory for me. How am I supposed to know what I am and am not allowed to do? For all I knew, this was one of those invasive female exam things that are just between you and your doctor." He lurches forward a step, then stops with his arms out, his hands lifted at his sides. "Your dad was there, too? Your *dad*?" He suddenly looks like he might cry. "He must think so highly of me right about now."

I stare at my husband, forcing myself to step back from the situation, and to try to see things from his perspective. Is it possible he really has so limited an understanding of modern-day birth culture? Have I, a midwife who is all about naturalizing the birth experience for the whole family, been so remiss? A wave of sympathy surges through me.

"Oh, Adam," I say with a sigh, my shoulders sagging. "I'm sorry. I just assumed—well, I assumed you'd at least know that this pregnancy is as much yours as it is mine, and that you are not just invited to participate in everything as much as you possibly can, but that I expect you to." I wrap my arms around myself and add, "I was so hurt that you weren't there today. I thought you'd forgotten. Or that it wasn't important enough to you to be there."

For a moment, his expression softens, and I find myself hoping for a truce, at least. Then he shakes his head again, this time in disgust. "You know, sometimes I feel like you want to assume the worst about me," he says.

I frown up at him. "That's not true," I insist. "In fact, it's just the opposite. I'm always ready to give you the benefit of the doubt. Always."

"Oh yeah? Then why the ongoing questions about the lake house? Why do you keep bugging me about the new car? I can see what's going on in your head. You think I'm cheating on you, don't you?"

"What?" I ask, shocked to hear him speak the words out loud. The very words that I have, indeed been thinking to myself.

"I know you, Dani. I know how you operate. You're building your case in your head about me, compiling a whole Plan B that doesn't include me. You won't come right out and ask me if your assumptions are right or wrong. Oh, no. You're just going to believe and prepare for the worst."

"Stop it, Adam. That's not true." But in essence, it was the exact truth. Just yesterday, I'd asked Ranae to be my backup plan. Even before my high-risk status had me opting for the birthing center for my labor and delivery, I'd had Breathe as my back up plan because I didn't know if I could count on Adam to want to do it at home. I never even bothered asking him about any of it before I was already setting up my contingencies.

"It's not?" he retorts, his head cocked angrily to one side, his chin jutting forward at me. "Are you sure?"

"Try to see things from my perspective, Adam. Think about how it looks to me. I feel like lately I can't count on you for anything. You have bowed out of so many things lately, and often at the last minute. Like the other night when we were supposed to tell my parents about the baby. Or our anniversary trip that we had to miss—"

"I got sick!" he interrupts, gesticulating wildly with both hands. "You're going to tell me you can't count on me because I got sick?"

"No, of course not." I grimace at his raised voice, but I try to explain anyway. "But you did say we would do something else for our anniversary, didn't you? That was months ago, and we still haven't celebrated. Other things, too. Family things. Birthday parties. The Fourth of July."

"You miss stuff, too, you know," he spouts back. "You've bailed on doing stuff with me. Date nights. Work parties. Whenever one of your patients calls, you just drop everything and go."

I stare at him, dumbfounded. "That's the nature of my business, Adam. I can't exactly tell a mother to hold off on her labor pains while I finish my date night."

"And I can't just leave some poor kid and his parents hanging so that I can attend some teenager girl's birthday party, can I?"

"You weren't working that day," I challenge back. "You simply didn't want to go. And Ruby is not just some random teenage girl."

"Do you know why I bought that car?" Adam asks, changing the subject so abruptly, my head spins.

"No," I finally say, morbidly curious about this new direction he's taking our conversation. Do I want to hear his reasons? "I suppose I thought—"

"Exactly," he cuts me off. "You assumed. Well, let me tell you why, even though you haven't bothered to come right out and ask me. I bought it because my old one only had two doors. Why? Because I knew you wanted to have children one day, that's why. I figured if I got a car that was more family-oriented, you'd see proof that I wasn't completely averse to the idea of having a family. I didn't buy a sports car; I bought a compact SUV. A family car, Dani. Did you ever consider that?"

"No," I murmur, a bubble of shame welling up inside me.

Except that I had, indeed asked him why on earth he'd bought that car. And he'd said nothing about the Escape being a family car back in March.

"I—I thought—" I stammer, and try again. "Why didn't you tell me all this before you bought it?" I ask, befuddled by his explanation. It seems so out of character for him. But then, if he's right and I do assume first and ask later, if at all, then maybe I don't really know him like I think I do.

"And the lake house? You want to know the truth about that?"

I just nod. I try to ignore the little voice whispering that whatever he has to say about it probably isn't the truth.

He clears his throat, then in a choked voice says, "You act like you're getting ready to leave me, Dani. You're distant and closed off. You don't include me in your life, and I'm not talking about the events you go to without me. I'm talking about your heart." He thumps his chest. "Our conversation at dinner is about everything, but us. We used to laugh together over meals, cook together, dance in the kitchen, have wild, monkey sex several times a week."

"Wild monkey—? Really, Adam?" Joking about our sex life—he *is* joking, isn't he?—doesn't seem very appropriate at the moment, and referring to it in such crass terms does not endear him to me. Is that really what he thinks of our lovemaking?

He continues without acknowledging my interruption. "Lately, you tell me you're too tired to do anything more adventurous than missionary style, and even that doesn't happen very often. You close your eyes when we're together, and I have no clue if you're with me or—or someone else."

"Adam," I murmur, appalled at what he's suggesting. "There is no one else. And I'm tired because I'm three months pregnant. I'm tired because this is my busy season and it's been a hot summer. I would love to cook and dance with you, but we're rarely home at the same time to do those things anymore."

"Exactly. It's felt like this marriage hasn't been a priority to you in a long time, Dani. You say you can't count on me?" He crosses his arms and widens his stance like he's digging in for the duration. "Well, maybe it's your own fault. Maybe I'm doing a little of my own preparing for the worst. You push me away, you don't include me, you neglect to tell me the important things, and then you wonder why I'm not participating in us." He lifts one hand to wave a finger back and forth between us.

I should stand, get on his level, but I'm not sure my legs will hold me. I lift my chin a little higher and hold his gaze, silently imploring him to believe me. "You are always my top priority, Adam. You and this marriage. I make every effort to be here for you and with you whenever I can. I try to cook food I know you love, I do my best to please you in bed, even when I'm so tired I can barely keep my eyes open, and I don't bug you about doing anything you don't want to do." I want to defend myself, but even more than that, I want to keep my marriage intact.

"But you assume I don't want to do anything. Like today's ultrasound. When I wasn't there, you just assumed I didn't want to be there, didn't you?" He grabs his phone from his back pocket and holds it out to me. "You didn't call me and ask me where I was. You didn't text me to remind me about it. You didn't even mention it this morning when we ate breakfast together. It feels like you just set me up to look bad, Dani. To all *your* people," he adds, emphasizing the possessive pronoun.

"That is not the way it happened," I say, pushing to my feet now. I hate sitting while he's standing during an argument. It makes me feel subversive and inferior, and shaky legs or not, I must get up. "I always feel like my requests are a nuisance to you. I know you didn't want this pregnancy, and I don't want you to feel obligated to do anything you don't want to do. I certainly don't want to guilt you into doing stuff."

"Too late for that," Adam snaps. "You made me feel three inches tall over that car, and I felt so terrible for disappointing you, that I bought the lake house from George with the sole intent of getting that money back as quickly as possible. Real estate is always a good investment, Dani."

I nod slowly, although that line sounds rehearsed to my ears. "That's exactly what Ranae said when I told her about it."

"Ranae," he scoffs, practically spitting her name out of his mouth. "The rock in the shoe of this marriage. I've never measured up to her, have I? She's poisoned you against me from the very beginning. I don't know why you didn't just marry her. You'd be much happier together than we are, that's for sure."

My bladder feels like it's about to explode, and I want to be finished with this conversation. We're not resolving anything at this point. "I'm sorry," I finally say. "This all feels like a huge misunderstanding. I'm not leaving, Adam. There is no one else. Please believe me."

For a few moments, I think he is going to argue some more, but he finally turns away and starts toward the bedroom door. He pauses to glare at me over his shoulder. "So now that everyone else has seen our baby, when do I get to?"

This is something I can do for him. "I'll call Gail first thing in the morning and set something up. I'll need her help to do the ultrasound. Can you get off work a little early tomorrow or Friday? Plan on at least a half an hour. I'll have her reserve whichever time works best for you."

He considers my words for a few moments, his eyes narrowed. "I can't this week, but what about next Friday?" he finally says. "I can meet you at Breathe at 4:30 next Friday. Then we'll go out for dinner afterward."

For someone so put out about not being included in today's appointment, he's in no hurry to get in for another ultrasound. The extra time will give us both a chance to calm down, though, and allow me time to figure out how to give him the news that there are twins before the appointment. I assure him that next Friday will work fine, all the while wondering why he looks so pleased with himself.

It isn't until he's gone to pick up his pizza that I figure it out. Next Friday is Ranae's Live and Let Die Bonfire night, and I have never missed a single one. Until now.

Ranae

"I HAVEN'T SEEN HER since her ultrasound," I tell Gran when she asks about Dani as I'm slipping into my corduroy jacket. I have a fleece pullover in my office in the schoolhouse just in case I need an extra layer later tonight. It's nice out right now, but I know that once the sun goes down, the temperature will drop dramatically.

October is my favorite month for a bonfire, barring inclement weather, of course. We typically have lots of dead wood to clear from the trails and around the buildings and parking lot, and the nights are cool enough that people tend to gather in close, making it a cozy event. During the summer, it's harder to keep folks from wandering off into the woods, and I'm always grateful for Hugo's watchful eye. It's rare that he doesn't have to round up at least one or two curious sightseers who circumvent the ropes across the trail heads. A few years ago, we finally put in solar lights along the first fifty feet of the Wild Rose Trail and opened up that section so that folks could at least take a look at a few of our grave sites, but it's never quite enough to satisfy everyone. Someone always has to be corralled back from beyond the barriers. However, it happens less often as the nights get colder and darker.

"She wasn't here for your radio thingy last Saturday, either," Gran says, dipping a finger into a mixing bowl of chocolate batter to test it. She's making the last of another enormous batch of brownies to put out for visitors at Fair Havens. She took over providing the goodies after the first bonfire night nearly three years ago when I laid out trays of store-bought cookies and candy. I let her without a word of resistance. There are some things I'm good at, and some things I'm not. I'm pretty good with anything on the grill, and I can whip up a mean pot of spaghetti, but things that require finesse in the kitchen? Not so much.

Although I'm exceptionally skilled at eating them.

Gran will head over a little later with this last batch of goodies, bringing Blimey with her, too, but I'm meeting Hugo in ten minutes, and I don't want to be late.

"Fortunately, we do have a few back up podcasts we've got pre-recorded for times like this, so I had something to post today." I tell Gran. She couldn't make it earlier this week on Monday when we had our regular recording session scheduled, but her excuse felt contrived to me. Dani had texted to let me know she had a busy work schedule that was keeping her way too busy and exhausted.

I'll be there for the next session, I promise, she assured me. When I texted back asking her if she wanted me to bring her lunch later in the week, she said that might be nice, but that she would call me to let me know what day worked best for her.

When she hadn't called by Wednesday, I phoned her. Then I called her again on Thursday. Both times, she had what seemed to be valid reasons for not being available.

"Well, if it doesn't happen before," I told her Thursday evening, "then I'll just see you at Bonfire Night." I was excited for her to see how pretty the chapel and schoolhouse looked all freshly white-washed for the coming winter.

She hesitated, then said quietly, "I won't be there, Ranae. I'm sorry. I'm doing another ultrasound at Breathe with Adam, then we're going out for dinner after."

I'd been left at a complete loss for words. I'd even forgotten to ask how Adam had handled hearing about the twins—I assume she's told him already and isn't waiting until he sees the ultrasound for him to find out.

"It'll be nice to see her tonight. I'm worried about our girl," Gran says.

"She won't be here," I tell her as nonchalantly as I can manage, then hurry on before Gran can voice the questions in her eyes. "She and Adam have plans."

"Ah. Well, that's commendable, don't you think, honey?" Gran's voice is gentle, but direct. "Spending time with her husband?"

When she says it like that, I have to tether my rebellious tongue to the back of my throat. I want to snark that there's no such thing as commendable when it comes to Adam. Instead, I say, "That's why I'm not angry at her for not being here. But I am worried about her, too, Gran." I'm unsettled by her withdrawal from me, especially when I know things have been so rocky in her home. Is this Adam's doing? Is he giving her some kind of ultimatum? I can imagine him offering her some absurd deal, like, 'If I'm going to accept this pregnancy and stick around, then you can sacrifice, too, and be home more often.' And Dani, not one to rock the proverbial boat, might just agree to such a rotten bargain.

It's been almost a whole week since I've laid eyes on my friend. I don't remember the last time we've gone this long without seeing each other. Maybe not since Dani's honeymoon. On top of that, I've been a bit of an emotional wreck myself this week. I haven't told anyone else about Sarah McCray's email, and even now, the thought of it makes my skin go hot and prickly, and not in a good way. It's not anger exactly—at least, not anymore. It's more like an allergic reaction. I am desperate to talk to Dani about it, to use her as a sounding board, but since she's been out of reach, I've had to keep it all bottled up inside of me.

Ruby appears at the top of the stairs, and I turn to gaze up at her. "You look nice," I tell her, lifting a curious brow. She loves the bonfire nights across the creek, but she's usually pretty casual about her appearance. Today, however, she's wearing a pair of form-fitting black jeans, a sheer scarlet off-the-shoulder peasant blouse over a black tank top, and the patent leather turquoise Doc Martens she got for her birthday back in June. Her hair is now tipped in shades of aquatic greens and blues, and her wide, full lips are painted the same shade as her blouse. She looks stunning... and it's a bit overkill for Bonfire Night. "Got a hot date?" I tease her.

She lifts her chin as she comes down the stairs, like she's going to deny it, but I don't look away. I have a feeling I'm not far off, and when I cock my head quizzically, she cracks. A slow smile pulls at the corners of her cherry red lips, and she ducks her head, like she's suddenly shy.

"Hot date! Hot date!" Gran chants gleefully from the kitchen. "Who's the lucky guy, girlie?"

"Geez, Gran," Ruby says, rolling her eyes. But she's still smiling, and now her cheeks have turned a color only a few shades lighter than her bright red shirt.

I link my arm with her and kiss the side of her head. "You'll introduce me, right?"

"Of course."

"Should I tell Hugo to bring his gun?" Gran asks over her shoulder. She's spreading batter into a large, shallow sheet pan.

"Gran!" Ruby squawks.

"Just for show, sweets. Just for show. Since Opa isn't here to do it."

"He's not a hot date, okay?" Ruby says, tugging nervously on the bell sleeve of her top. "He's just a guy from school. He's new this year. Me and Millie and a couple of the others were talking about Bonfire Night today, and he overheard us. His locker is near mine." She shrugs prettily, and I want to tell her she'll be cold with her shoulders uncovered, but I leash the helicopter mom rearing her irritating head inside of me. Ruby is old enough to know how to dress in all kinds of weather, and it's not like she can't dash back to the farmhouse if she needs to add another layer. "He asked about it, so I invited him."

"But is Just-A-Guy-From-School hot?" Gran persists, sliding the huge sheet pan into the oven, then circling the end of the counter to come stand in front of us. She licks her finger and holds it up in front of her, making a hissing steam noise.

"Oh, my gosh, Gran. Please, please, please don't ever do that again." Ruby pulls away from me to hug her great grandmother tightly. "Yes, he's super hot, and I think I really like him, but if you lick your finger and touch him, he won't sizzle. He'll run screaming."

"Got it." Gran pats Ruby on the cheek. "No licking your boyfriends."

"He's not my boyfriend!" Ruby declares.

"No licking your future boyfriends, then."

"Gran!"

I'm laughing at their antics as I turn to head out. This guy must be something special for Ruby to be ready so early. "Is Millie coming?" I ask before pulling open the back door. The house is warm and cozy, already hunkering down for the coming winter, and I don't want to let the heat out, or the Autumn chill in.

"She should be here any minute now," Ruby confirms. "And Will is coming, too. Is that okay?" Will is Millie's on-again-off-again boyfriend, and although Ruby doesn't care much for the guy, she tolerates him whenever he's on again. For Millie's sake.

I get it. I feel the same way about Adam. I tolerate him for Dani's sake.

But the fact that Will is coming means there's potential for the foursome to become two couples. "Of course," I tell her. "Just remember what the night is about, okay?"

"People will be grieving," Gran says, and for a brief moment, I think she might actually be serious. "So if you want to make out, you'll need to go behind the schoolhouse or out into the woods where no one will see you."

"Gran!" Ruby and I both screech in unison, almost drowning out the old woman's chortle.

To my surprise, I am back at Fair Havens before Hugo, but I'm not too worried. He's put in long hours this week, getting the place looking it's best, and I take a moment to relish in the beauty around me.

There's about an hour of daylight left, and this time of the year, between sunset and full dark, we get an extra hour-plus of twilight. The woods seem to glow with an inner fire as the sun, low on the horizon, shoots golden beams through the red and amber treetops. The early fall breeze sets everything in motion, and I lift my nose to breathe in the earthy smell of leaf mold, resin, and the hint of woodsmoke that permeates the air. This place, this haven, is fair indeed, and in moments like this, I am overwhelmed with gratitude for all with which I have been entrusted. Not just this land and those laid to rest in it, but also for Gran and Opa and the farmhouse where I have never known anything but love, my beautiful, beautiful daughter, my parents who chose me to be theirs, and my brothers, of course, although I'd never tell them that.

The people who will gather around our bonfire tonight, certainly. Family and friends, both old and new.

In spite of whatever the disquiet is that seems to be lingering between us, or maybe because of it, I'm especially grateful for Dani. I already miss her presence, and the event hasn't even started.

And where would I be, where would Fair Havens be, without Hugo and Chloe Beckenbauer? Their fingerprints can be found all over this sanctuary.

I lower myself to one of the stone benches at the back of the outdoor chapel and close my eyes, listening to the wind whisper secrets to the trees. I feel the bite in the air now that I'm sitting still, and I shiver and wrap my arms around myself.

"Here."

My eyes snap open in surprise, and I let loose a little "Eep!" Hugo has approached from behind me, shucking out of his canvas barn coat, and before I can berate him for sneaking up on me, he settles the garment over my shoulders. I close my eyes briefly again, relishing life the warmth of the flannel and fleece lining, and I breathe in the scent that is Hugo. Woodsmoke—was it his fireplace I smelled a moment ago?—cedar, and something green. Moss, maybe? It's all just so *Hugo;* I think I would recognize him blindfolded by his smell alone.

"Thank you," I murmur, then look over at him as he sits beside me. "The place looks great, doesn't it? We did good this week. You did good."

He just smiles and bumps his shoulder against mine. He's wearing a dark blue thermal under a worn flannel shirt, and he doesn't seem to mind the cold at all. I can practically feel the warmth radiating off of his body, and I want to press closer to him.

I wonder if there's a way to stop time so that I can sit here beside him in this sacred place forever. But I suppose I'd get hungry at some point. And I'd need a bathroom, too. "Never mind," I mutter under my breath.

"Hm?"

Oops. Said that out loud. "Nothing. Sorry. I was commenting on my own thoughts." *Brilliant, Ranae.*

"Yes," he says.

"Yes... what?" I ask, feeling awkward and a little lost.

He chuckles and nudges my shoulder again. "Yes, it does look great, and yes, we did good."

"Oh." I'm such a dork.

After another moment, he asks, "Dani be here soon?"

Sometimes I catch him looking at my friend and wonder what he sees there. She's so beautiful, all long and lean earth mama with her peaches and cream coloring and wide blue eyes. And there's that accent, too. What guy wouldn't be just a little in love with the whole Dani package?

I ignore the ridiculous pinprick of jealousy at the thought. I hate that I feel so possessive of someone who doesn't belong to me. "She's not coming tonight." I straighten my shoulders and lift my chin, still trying to resolve my feelings about Dani's absence. "She's spending the evening with Adam."

After a long pause, Hugo echoes Gran's sentiment. "Good for her. I applaud."

"I don't," I readily admit. This is Hugo I'm talking to, after all.

He laughs quietly. "Really? I'd never guess."

"Seriously," I shoot back. "Do you know what they're doing tonight?"

"No, and it's not really my business."

"I don't care. I'm telling you anyway." I push to my feet and pull the lapels of Hugo's jacket around me, no longer chilled, but not ready to relinquish it. "She's going to give him a special screening of their ultrasound since he didn't bother to show up for the first one over a week ago."

"Sounds nice. A private showing between a mom, a dad, and the babies they made together."

"Oh, stop being so reasonable. No," I insist, my shoulders hunching up toward my ears in frustration. "It doesn't sound nice at all. He bailed last week, Hugo, remember? A no-show. Didn't even bother calling to tell her he wasn't going to make it. Just didn't show up. Then he demands a replay? At *his* convenience?" I can feel myself getting wound up, and I know I should cool my jets, but again, this is Hugo. He can handle my rants.

He says nothing; he just watches me as I begin to pace.

"And I know he planned it for tonight on purpose," I continue. "She hasn't missed a single Live and Let Die since its conception. Not one." I hold up one finger and jab at the sky. "I mean, they could come over here after the ultrasound, right? But no, they're going out to dinner. They're not coming here. He's purposely keeping her away from me."

Hugo stands, and I instinctively take a step back, not because I'm afraid of him, but because I'm afraid of being so close to him. I'm already unnerved when I'm around him these days, and sometimes I feel like I can't breathe right when he's too close.

"Hey now. Do you really believe that?" He shoves his hands in his front pockets and cocks his head to look at me. I stop pacing and stand with my back to the woods. The burnt orange sunlight filtering through the trees behind me makes patterns dart and dance across his face. It's hypnotic to watch, and for a moment, I forget what he's asking.

"Actually, yes," I tell him, blinking hard. "I have no doubt in my mind that Adam knew exactly what tonight was, and that he chose it, not because it was convenient for him, but because it would prevent her from being here tonight. No doubt whatsoever," I reiterate.

Hugo frowns, studying my face in a way that makes me terribly uncomfortable, and at the same time, feels way too intimate right now. Like he's trying to read my innermost thoughts. "Is there something else going on with you, Ranae? You've been..." He pauses and shrugs. "I don't know. On edge, I guess? A little more manic than usual?" He's smiling now, teasing me, but I know his question is serious.

"I'm fine," I say quickly. "It's been a strange couple of weeks, that's all, and Dani not being here makes things feel weirder. I don't know why, either. She usually just comes and hangs out. But I count on her for moral support, you know?"

Hugo dips his head so he can look me in the eye.

"What?" I ask when he doesn't say anything.

"I'll be your moral support for tonight, if that's what you need."

Flustered, I tug his jacket off my shoulders. "It's not really the moral support I'm missing, Hugo. It's Dani. I know it sounds selfish, but I think she should be here for me. She's always here. I count on her." I hold his jacket out to him. "Here. Thank you. I'm good now."

He doesn't take it right away; he just continues to study me. "May I ask you something? Without you snapping at me?"

"I'm not snapping at you," I snap, then roll my eyes at my contradictory behavior and shake the jacket between us. "Here," I say again. My frustration has heated my blood considerably, and I'm definitely not cold anymore. I do, however, feel a little unraveled, kind of wispy around the edges.

He grins and nods like he doesn't believe me, takes his coat from me, and drapes it over his arm. "Okay." He pauses a fraction of a second, then in a careful tone, says, "Do you want Dani's marriage to succeed?"

I'm surprisingly ready with an answer for that question. No thinking required on my end. "Not the marriage she has."

"So you want her marriage to fail?"

"No." I shoot him a hard look. "I don't want anything in her life to be a failure. I want her happy, and I'm convinced that Adam doesn't make her happy."

"You're sure about that?"

"Of course, I'm sure. That's what being convinced of something means," I snap again. I want to suck the words back in. Instead, I continue with my little tirade. "I've known her for almost twenty years, right? I think I know my best friend by now."

"Better than her husband?" He's like a dog with a bone.

"Absolutely. Yes, yes, and again, yes." I can't stay still a moment longer and start shifting from foot to foot in my agitation. "If you want to continue this conversation, we'll have to do it inside. I need to make sure the refreshments are set up."

I turn toward the schoolhouse where I've cleared the front part of the room and set up long serving tables. A myriad of finger foods are already laid out on serving platters and covered with old-fashioned flour sack towels. We aim for a minimal waste venue, so there's no tin foil, no plastic wrap, and we only provide paper plates and napkins that can be tossed into the bonfire after use. No plastic utensils, hence, the finger foods. We have trashcans set up for folks who bring stuff with them, and although they're usually full by the end of the event, we're always pleased by how little trash we generate with so many people in attendance.

Hugo steps around me as we approach the schoolhouse and reaches for the door to hold it open for me.

"Thank you," I mutter, not feeling very convivial toward him at the moment. I don't like his line of questioning, and I was kind of hoping he'd find an excuse to stay outside.

"My pleasure." His rumbled response as I pass by so close to him makes my skin vibrate.

Once I'm inside, he follows right behind, and hangs his coat on one of the pegs running the length of the back wall. He circles around to the other side of the table where I'm standing so we're facing each other again. Apparently, he isn't finished. "Wasn't she happy with him at some point?"

I frown at him, straightening trays and peeking under towels just to give my hands something to do. "I honestly don't know. I suppose at the beginning, she was. At least, she seemed to be. And I was happy for her, too, you know?" I frown and shake my head, reminding myself of all my misgivings about Adam. "But I don't know how real that was. I mean, she loved him—she says she still does—but that doesn't automatically translate to being happy, does it?" I step back and scan the room for anything left that needs doing before folks start showing up. "She's loyal, Hugo. Once she's decided to love someone, she'll love them forever, whether they deserve her or not."

"And you don't think he deserves her."

"Nope." My reply is immediate and without reservation. I have my back to Hugo as I move across the room to one of the windows, but I'm sure he can see the stiffness in my posture. I glance over my shoulder at him and shake my head. "I *know* he doesn't deserve her," I insist.

The room falls silent, and I have a sudden impulse to make as much noise as I possibly can. Yell, stomp my feet, clap my hands. Anything to break up this rising tension in me. I finally turn for the door; I need to take one last look at the chapel, too.

His voice, low and gentle, stops me. "Are you jealous, Ranae?"

"What?" The word comes out sharp and spiked with offense. "Jealous of her? And Adam? No. Absolutely not. I wouldn't want a marriage like that for anything."

"That's not what I mean."

I pause at the door and turn around to glare at him. "Then what, exactly, do you mean?"

He is blushing. *What on earth?* His scars stand out almost silver against his ruddy cheeks.

"I see your face when she's around, Ranae. Your eyes light up. You two share wordless conversations when you look at each other." His words sound a little like they're tumbling out of his mouth, and I find myself scrambling to keep up with the direction he's going in. "Are—are you in love with her? Did Adam take your place in her life?"

I stare at him aghast, my mouth opening and closing impotently, but I can't seem to come up with any response. Does he actually believe what he's asking? That I'm in love with my best friend? I mean, I know it happens, but seriously? Does he not know us both—know *me*—better than that? Has he not seen the way I look at *him*? "No," I finally manage to get out, but it's little more than a harsh whisper. I try again, but my throat is still too tight. "No."

I don't care if he heard me or not. I turn on my heel and push outside, pulling the door closed firmly behind me in what I hope is an obvious cue for him not to follow me. I pause on the stoop and take in several deep breaths to settle the demented butterflies in my stomach, then make my way on shaky legs to the chapel. Once inside, I lock the double doors behind me. I need a few minutes alone, and if I know Hugo, he'll want to clear the air before people start showing up. But I can't talk to him right now. I can't face him. Not now, not knowing that he's been thinking my heart belongs to Dani—to *Dani!*—all this time.

I'm such an idiot. Such a fool. I thought I was more transparent than that. I mean, that's what everyone always says. But apparently not, at least not where my feelings for Hugo are concerned.

I stay cloistered inside the chapel as long as I can, finding things to keep me busy while I work to get my emotions under control. Of course, I'm crying. Stupid tears. I feel misunderstood and abandoned by both Dani and Hugo, and because I do, I also feel childish and immature. "Get it together, Niemeyer," I order myself out loud, knowing I have to meet and greet visitors who will be arriving any minute now, many of them with far better reasons to cry than I have. I straighten the unbleached linen shroud laid out in the model woven bamboo casket on the oak table at the front of the room. I shift the floral arrangement from one side of the small dais to the other. I run a finger along the keys of the electric piano, checking to make sure it's off and the electrical cord put away out of sight. Children can't keep their hands off it, but when they realize it won't make any noise, no matter how many buttons and keys they push, they soon lose interest. I turn the sound system on and select the Live and Let Die playlist that Ruby updates periodically for me. So far, she's only made me cringe a few times, but not badly enough to warrant taking on the tedious task myself.

Most of the wooden benches are lined up against the walls to keep the room clear, but I've left two in place at the front. I sit down on one of them as the soulful notes of Adele singing low and sweet break my heart like they do every time. I bow my head and close my eyes, and sternly remind myself why I'm here.

Fifteen minutes ago, I was sitting on a stone bench in the outdoor chapel, overwhelmed by beauty, love, and gratitude, and I want that back. I take a deep breath and blow it out slowly, then another, forcing my body to relax and my mind to stop clamoring for answers I don't have.

I push open the chapel doors and step outside. The sun is dipping low—it'll be gone in less than fifteen minutes—and it's time to welcome my guests. While I've been locked away, Hugo has started the bonfire, and a cheerful blaze leaps and cavorts in reckless jubilation, sparks drifting skyward like shooting stars.

Hugo stands close to the fire ring, his eyes on the flames, conversing with a young man I recognize from a funeral we held back in May. Joel, if I recall correctly. His father passed away, and his mother, Jenny, chose Fair Havens as her husband's last resting place. I remember Joel being quite impressed with our cemetery, and I wonder why he's here tonight. I glance around in search of Jenny, hoping to see her pleasant face; it's not uncommon for spouses to follow each other in death after decades of life spent together. But she's here, I'm relieved to discover, making her way out of the schoolroom with a small plate of treats and a cup of coffee. I wave and start toward her, but not before I glance back to find Hugo's eyes trained on me. His expression is unreadable, and I turn away.

Over the next hour, the usually quiet clearing comes to life. There are tears, group hugs, laughter, and sloppy singing along with whatever songs are being piped through the sound system speakers mounted under the eaves on either side of the chapel doors. Someone brought a huge basket of marshmallows, chocolate bars, and graham crackers to share, and I keep refilling the treat platters inside until there are no more reserves left. Dani usually helps me with drinks, and I feel her absence acutely, but I don't let it bring me down. I just hope she's having a nice time with Adam tonight.

It's the truth, I realize. I pause in my activities as the thought occurs to me; I genuinely do hope their evening is going well.

Ruby introduces me to Gideon, a tall, slim young man with James Dean hair and a deep-set, confident gaze that's more often than not, fixed on my daughter. I greet Millie with a hug, offer William a more reserved greeting with a pat on his shoulder, and tell the four of them to enjoy themselves.

I manage to avoid Hugo all night. Almost.

Around 8:30, the McCartneys' "Live and Let Die" bursts through the speakers like a call to arms, and as usual, almost everyone surges toward the bonfire to join in singing along with the survivors' lament, as we call it. It breaks me every time, and even though I'm singing at the top of my lungs with everyone else, laughing with and hugging on the wonderful folks around me, I always cry with the best of them, too. I stopped wearing mascara on my bottom lashes years ago, which has made my ugly cry not quite so scary. A tip from my beauty queen mother, of course.

Besides, I kind of like how a little extra compensatory makeup on my top lid gives me a vintage, plump, Hollywood starlet look.

By nine o'clock, most of our visitors have taken their leave, including Gran and Blimey, who headed back over the footbridge to the farmhouse right after "Live and Let Die." They were escorted by one of the gentlemen from her church, Abe Bruckner. He comes to these events to see Gran, not Fair Havens, but I don't mind. She says they're just friends, but Abe is markedly attentive to her, and he's single, to boot. He and Opa were great friends and fishing buddies, and I don't think my grandfather would mind if Abe were to make his move. On the other hand, maybe Abe and Gran are fine with the way things are, content in the knowledge that they have someone out there who cares what happens to them.

Must be nice.

Enough with the maudlin thoughts, Niemeyer.

I scan the remaining stragglers for Ruby and her gang. I saw them loitering around the private church graveyard right after Gran left, but they're nowhere to be seen now. Maybe they went back to the house, too. I'm not worried, but I could use their help taking all the platters and trays across the way. I head inside the schoolhouse and text Ruby to come back over, then start packing up the remaining goodies and the empty dishes into boxes. If the kids prefer, they can load everything onto the golf cart and do most of it all in one trip.

Ruby doesn't respond to the text, though, and when she doesn't pick up my phone call, either, I dial Gran.

"The kids aren't here, honey," she says, her voice tired. It occurs to me that she's probably already in bed. She dismisses my apology and insists I call her back when I've found them so that she won't worry, then I hang up and head back outside.

I don't see them among the group still mingling around the campfire, the fenced graveyard is empty, and they're not in the chapel, either. I check the parking lot around the side of the buildings, but it's empty except for two compact cars, Hugo's truck, and our Fair Havens van. I make my way around to the back of the schoolhouse where we park the golf cart, but there's no sign of them there, either. Standing under a lamppost, I call my daughter's name loudly a few times; maybe her phone is dead. Still no response.

For some reason, my Spidey senses—my Mom version—are on high alert, and I don't like the way my scalp is tingling. I turn in a slow circle, my eyes peeled for anything that feels amiss. My gaze lands on the wide, white cellar doors butted up against the back of the schoolhouse that once led to the cellar stairs. They now open to reveal a hydraulic stretcher lift I installed for getting bodies in and out of my workroom in the basement. I move closer, checking the locks, but nothing looks disturbed. Ruby knows where the keys are, of course, but I don't want to believe that she'd outright disobey me just to impress a guy. She's forbidden to take anyone downstairs without me there, no exceptions, but I have to check.

Ruby and her friends aren't in the basement, either, and although I'm relieved, I'm really beginning to worry. She's a big girl, and it's not even ten o'clock on a Friday night, but it's not like her to take off without letting me know what her plans are. Dismissing my earlier reticence, I approach Hugo, who is making quick work of spreading out what's left of the wood still smoldering in the stone circle of the fire pit. He's conversing with a young couple about what kind of trees to plant for shade in the back yard of the new house they've just bought.

"Excuse me," I say when there's a brief lull in the discussion. "Hugo, have you seen Ruby?"

It's the first time I've spoken directly to him all evening, and his gaze on me is guarded and maybe a little wounded. So he knows I've been avoiding him. *Suck it up, big guy,* I want to tell him. *You gutted me tonight, too.*

It's not a fair response, though, and I know it. Dani and I do spend an excessive amount of time together—at least we have up until recently—and it's true that I do love her more than most human beings. But that gooey, drooling expression he sees on my face? That's because of him, not her. I guess I just hide it better when he and I are alone, and I don't have Dani there as my buffer. So, yes, I can see why he might think I have a thing for her. But then, I can't imagine how he's missed the fact that the thing I have is actually for him. Everyone else in the whole world seems to have noticed. Even Ruby teases me about him on occasion. She's joking, of course. She'd be appalled if she knew there was nothing funny about it. She's too committed to Chloe to ever let me usurp the woman in Hugo's life.

"Not for a while now," he says, his eyes not leaving my face. "They were hanging around by the chapel last time I saw them. At least half an hour ago?"

The couple he was talking trees with cuts in to thank us for the evening—Hugo, especially, for his tree suggestions—then they make their farewells and head out. There is one other forty-something couple and their teenage daughter still lingering in their camping chairs on the other side of the fire pit speaking to Tom Sedgewick, a semi-retired Farmers Insurance salesman who lost his partner a little over a year ago. Tom is at a lot of our bonfires—he and Jasper used to come together back when Jasper found out he was sick, and Tom has continued the ritual almost every month since. I've never heard a hint of an insurance sales pitch come out of his mouth, but he seems to make connections with people every time he's here, and I'm sure some of those connections have turned into clients. I can speak from personal experience; Tom is my insurance man, too. Tonight is no different. The woman he's conversing with now is tucked against her husband's side, dabbing at her eyes with a crumpled napkin, and their pretty daughter is sitting on the ground in front of her parents, resting her head on her mother's lap as she watches Hugo with something akin to adoration.

I feel you, girlie.

"Ruby isn't answering her phone." I hold mine up to him like I'm offering proof and add, "She hasn't read her texts, either."

Hugo's eyes dart across the way to the Wild Rose Trail, and I follow his gaze. The solar lights casting a glow along the first several yards of the well-marked path have started to lose their luster, and from here, I can no longer make out the sawhorses we use to block off the rest of the trail that meanders deeper into the woods, or the sign hanging from them that clearly says, 'No Entry Beyond This Point.'

"She's not back at the house?" he asks calmly, but I don't miss the note of concern there, too.

"No. And I've looked pretty much everywhere else." I start toward the path, my emotions in a turmoil. If Ruby has taken her friends past the barricade, she's going to have some 'splainin' to do. She knows it's off limits during the bonfire nights, and she also knows there are no exceptions to this rule.

"I'll go," Hugo says, stopping me with a hand on my shoulder. I flinch and step back, and he drops his hand. He frowns slightly, but doesn't acknowledge my reaction to his touch in any other way. "You stay with your guests. That way you'll be here if they show up."

"No. She's my kid. You stay. Please," I add, realizing I'm ordering him around. I start toward the trail again, and this time, he lets me go. I can't decide if I'm relieved or disappointed. I'm upset at him, but it's because I'm hurt, not angry. I want him to *see* me, to know me, maybe even one day to love me. But now I feel a chasmic disconnect with him, like he doesn't get me at all.

I grab one of the rechargeable LED lanterns we put out in a basket near the trail head. They're an extra precaution for guests to use on especially dark nights, and I make a quick count. There aren't any missing. Maybe the kids haven't gone into the woods after all. Of course, they all have cell phone flashlights, so it's probably wishful thinking on my part.

I hear quiet footsteps behind me and dart a glance over my shoulder. I'm not surprised to see Hugo.

"Tom is going to watch the fire for us," he tells me. He's got an industrial-sized Maglite with him, and he turns it on, shining the high-powered beam among the trees. We get to the blockade at the end of the open section of trail and pause there to call for Ruby. I'm not panicking yet, and I don't want to embarrass her by shouting hysterically, so I try to keep my tone casual. There is no response, though, so Hugo moves aside one of the sawhorses, and into the woods we go.

Ten minutes later, his flashlight beam lands on William, who is ducking clumsily behind a tree. When he realizes he's been spotted, he lifts one hand up to shield his eyes. "What's up?" He looks guilty. But then, I think all teenage boys look guilty. Probably because I have a teenage daughter.

"Where are the others?" Hugo asks before I can speak.

"Up the trail a way." William gestures with one hand, the other tucked behind him like he's hiding something.

"Is Millie with you?" I ask, hoping she's not. But why would the others leave him behind alone?

"Nah." The way he says it makes my skin crawl. "I started back without them. Gotta get home."

"Not fishy at all," I mutter under my breath, and beside me, Hugo grunts softly.

"What do you have there, brother?" Hugo asks, waving his flashlight beam at the arm still held behind William's back.

"Nothing." The kid now looks like he's trying to shove something in his pocket. He's so obvious, it seems almost cruel to call his bluff.

"Let's see," Hugo says, stepping off the trail toward him.

William lifts both hands like he's being held up. "I'm serious, man. I got nothing."

We can all smell it though, the sweet, grassy smoke of cannabis. Hugo shines his light on the ground at William's feet. He doesn't spot anything, but in a deceptively casual tone, he says, "You'd better be sure there isn't any trace of that stuff left behind, *man*." The words are heavy as they fall from his mouth. "You don't want to start a fire in my woods. I really, really don't like fire." Then Hugo tips his head to the side and flashes the light over the scars marbling up his neck and jaw from under the collar of his shirt. I feel my eyes go wide at this rather aggressive scare tactic. I've never seen Hugo intentionally direct anyone's attention to his marred flesh before.

I don't correct him about the ownership of the woods issue, either. William says nothing, but I can see his jaw clench tightly in frustration, and if he's smart, a healthy dose of fear.

"Let's go." Hugo stands aside and waits for William to move ahead of him back onto the trail. "How about you stay close to us until we find the others." Hugo says in that terrifyingly casual voice. It's not a suggestion.

"But I gotta go," William grumbles, sounding much younger than his seventeen years.

"But you gotta stay," Hugo corrects him, then shines the flashlight on the trail in front of us. "How about you lead the way." It's not a suggestion, either.

I keep my mouth closed and let Hugo take care of this since he's doing a much better job than I would. I'm glad he didn't let me wander in here alone. I'm seething inside, angry at Millie for taking William back, especially if she knows about his clandestine recreational habits, and I'm absolutely furious at Ruby for bringing them out here.

William mutters something foul as he shuffles past us, brushing against me a little too roughly, forcing me to sidestep into Hugo. The man moves so quickly, I stumble in surprise. Before I realize what's happening, Hugo is gripping one of William's wrists behind his back, and Hugo's other forearm is wedged against the kid's neck, the heavy-duty flashlight resting parallel to his smooth young jaw. William yelps, more in surprise than in pain, as the two march up the trail a bit, putting a few feet between us. I am certain Hugo has no intention of hurting the kid, but when he speaks quietly into his ear, William is nodding agreeably even before Hugo finishes talking.

Then he releases William with a gentle shove forward. The boy starts to turn around toward me—is he hoping I'll rescue him from this mad woodsman?—but Hugo shines the flashlight directly in his eyes. "Don't even look at her."

We meet Millie, Ruby, and Gideon quite a bit further up the trail, just as William said. They are making their way back toward the main clearing. Ruby, who is now wearing Gideon's denim jacket around her previously exposed shoulders, and Gideon are walking on either side of Millie, using their phone flashlights to light the way. One look at Millie's smeared makeup and puffy eyes confirms that things have not gone well between her and William this evening.

I am hit with simultaneous waves of relief and anger when I see they're safe, and for a moment, I can't decide if I'm going to hug my child or yell at her. I do neither. She's got her phone, and the flashlight is on, which means the battery is working just fine. She has chosen to ignore me for the last half an hour.

"You're grounded," I say flatly. "Effective immediately."

"Mom!" I can't tell if she's arguing or just embarrassed. She's a smart kid; she knows this lark won't go unpunished. I turn to Millie.

"Did that boy drive you here tonight?" I flap my hand in William's direction, but I keep my eyes fixed on Ruby's best friend.

"No," she whimpers. "My mom dropped me off. And I'm sorry, Ranae. I really am."

"I'm glad to hear it. On both counts. Did he hurt you?"

"No," Millie insists. "I'm okay. Really."

"You sure?" I ask again, not willing to let my frustration over their disregard for the rules take precedence over the possibility of something worse.

Millie nods affirmatively, her eyes locked with mine, despite her obvious contrition. I think I believe her, but I'll know better when we get out of the dark woods.

"Mom," Ruby snaps. "Do we really have to do this out here?" She glances sideways at Gideon.

So she's embarrassed. Poor, poor baby. "Right here. Right now," I say, then turn to Gideon. "And you. How did you get here tonight?"

"I drove," he responds. "My car is parked back at your house." I hear no trace of disrespect in his quiet words, and I'm listening for it with my whole body.

"Did you smoke any of Will—"

"No, ma'am," he interrupts. *Careful, son.* I do not like being interrupted. "I did not. None of us did." He indicates the three of them and doesn't spare William a glance.

"So which of you is responsible for coming into the woods?" I ask, narrowing my eyes at my daughter. If she doesn't raise both hands high into the air and take full responsibility, she's going to be in a lot deeper than she already is.

All three of them start talking at once, each ready to throw themselves into the gauntlet for the others. As upset as I am, I recognize in that moment that my daughter has good friends. With the exception of William, of course.

"Stop, you guys," Ruby says, stepping forward, lifting both arms at her sides like she's holding back the tide. "I am, Mom. It doesn't matter whose idea it was, I'm the one who let it happen." She grabs my hand and squeezes it. I don't squeeze back, but I don't pull away, either. "Please, can we get out of here first? Please?" she whispers, her eyes darting toward William and then back to me again. "Away from him?" she adds so quietly I almost miss it. And then I see the tears in her eyes, too.

I pull her against me and hug her—hard—then let her go just as quickly. "Back to camp, then. Time for a Live and Let Die meeting at the bonfire." Thinking I'm pretty clever, I add, "We'll decide who lives and who dies."

"Mom," Ruby growls under her breath. I would laugh if I weren't so angry.

"Ranae, I'm going to get this guy home," Hugo says, resting a hand on the back of William's neck. There's nothing casual about it. "Think you can make it back to the clearing in one piece without me?"

"Yes," I tell him, and I see the three teenagers beside me nod in unison. "Thank you, Hugo." I honestly don't care what he does with William at this point, as long as the kid is off my property. In fact, I wouldn't mind if he got the police involved. "I'll have these three help me finish with cleanup so you don't have to come back." I know he will anyway.

"But my truck," William argues. "I'm not leaving it here."

"You won't be needing it tonight," Hugo states. To me, he says, "I'll be back." Then off they march again, several paces in front of the rest of us this time, the Maglite beam bouncing along the trail ahead of them.

Silence settles around us, and I know I should say something... well, *parental*. But now that I know everyone is safe and accounted for, I'm not quite sure where to begin. I lift my lantern high and wave the three of them ahead of me. "Let's go."

Dani

I LOST MY COURAGE and wound up not telling Adam about the twins over the weekend as I'd planned. I kept waiting for him to ask about the ultrasound results, but he never did. I suppose I can understand his reticence. He probably wants to wait to see the thing for himself, especially if he truly has no clue what an ultrasound is. Of course, he could always Google one and educate himself, but I'm not going to be the one to suggest it. Adam doesn't like to look stupid, even in front of me. Maybe especially in front of me.

In fact, I have the sneaking suspicion that he is playing me for the fool that I am. That this whole ignorance angle he's taking is actually his way of setting me up to take the blame for his bad behavior.

My head spins when I try to read between the lines that Adam is feeding me. I'm pretty sure that's what they are—lines—but he seems so sincere, so genuine, and I find myself waffling, even against my better judgement. I *want* to believe him.

He's my husband, the man I promised to forsake above all others, and I want to believe him, and to trust that he is choosing to stay true to his promises, too.

So in spite of us spending most of last weekend together, we hardly talked about important matters at all. Oh, we chit-chatted, of course. I told him about my parents' plans with Doctors Without Borders, and we discussed putting in different landscaping along the side of the house where everything gets far too little sun. Adam told me about a new Indian curry place he wants to try, and I suggested we go see a movie Sunday afternoon. We found one we both agreed on, which then gave us enough conversation fodder to get us through the evening meal. Sunday night, we sat on the couch and watched a few episodes of the Netflix series we're currently hooked on. I started drifting off before the end of the second episode, and to my surprise, Adam agreed to call it a night early with me.

I finally tell him about the twins on Tuesday night over one of his favorite meals, Chicken Marsala. I don't know why I waited, why I thought putting it off would make it easier.

He is livid when he realizes that I've known for several days and haven't bothered filling him in. "Does Ranae already know?" he demands, her name spilling out of his mouth like it's toxic. I want to remind him that he would already know, too, if he'd bothered to show up last Friday, but I bite my tongue and just nod.

Adam takes off for a few hours, but when he comes back to the house just as I'm going to bed, he apologizes and tells me that his exclusion, intentional or not, leaves him feeling unmanned.

The thing is, I kind of believe him when he says he didn't show up because he wasn't invited. He's always expected special treatment—from his parents, from his peers, and of course, from me. I knew that when I fell in love with him. I, too, was an only child, and understood that unique need for validation that seems to be the bane of only children. Knowing Adam, he probably was, indeed, waiting for me to specifically invite him.

I do, however, struggle to fully accept his insistence that he knows nothing of the process of pregnancy and birth. He continues to play that card, making me feel like I have somehow been holding out on him, denying him information about it all.

I am a midwife and the daughter of two OB-Gyn practitioners, for goodness' sake. My husband, of all people, should be thoroughly educated on all things labor and delivery.

Except that his ignorance, for lack of a better word, is self-imposed.

Adam has made it no secret that his interest in children at work is just that: work. He doesn't want children of his own right now, so why would he care to educate himself—or let me educate him—on anything to do with pregnancy, labor and delivery, and infants, for that matter? None of his students are younger than five years old.

Knowing Adam's ability to compartmentalize his life, it's not too big a stretch to believe that he really could be unaware of how monumental that first ultrasound can be.

On the other hand, all he had to do was ask about it, and we wouldn't be in this predicament. I don't like that it seems he set me up to be the bad guy, but that's exactly how I feel.

And once again, I find myself bending over backwards to convince him that not only am I the good guy, but so is he.

Maybe if we spend more time together like we have in the last few days, we'll rediscover our sweet spot and start believing in each other again. I love my husband, even though there are a lot of reasons not to like him very much right now. I'm more than willing to see this thing through, if not for my sake, then for that of our babies.

I've spent most of the week at Breathe trying to sort out my schedule for the months ahead. Because this is considered a high-risk pregnancy, I will be getting ultrasounds every two or three weeks to monitor the babies for growth and development. It also means I need to be prepared for anything, including reduced activity or complete bed rest at any point during this pregnancy, or even an early C-section, worst case scenario. So I'm organizing my patient visits to correspond with the schedules of the other midwives in our group, just in case I end up needing one of them to cover for me. I'm also handing off a few of my brand new clients to the others in the group since I have a feeling things could get pretty unprofessional with me trying to bend over a home water birth to catch a baby when I'm more than seven or eight months along.

Then there is the amount of time I'll need to recover and get accustomed to caring for twins. The earlier due date means that Adam will still have about two months of work before the school year gets out. I really need a straight answer about his plans for us and our future, but regardless, I'm probably going to need a lot of help from someone other than my husband after I deliver.

I know I can count on Ranae and Gran, but unfortunately, my best friend has become a raging sore spot for Adam lately, and I'm not about to bring up her name any more than necessary right now. They've never gotten on very well, Ranae and Adam, but some of the things he has said about her lately have been so awful. He isn't cutting her down, exactly, but every time her name comes up, he accuses me of measuring him against her, and that he inevitably falls far short in my eyes. I insist I do no such thing, but he still insinuates that maybe she has too big of a role in our marriage.

So I'm lying low for now, keeping close to home, especially when he's around. And I'm giving him lots of details of how I'm spending my time when he's not with me, not because he's asked me for them, but because I want to reassure him that he and our marriage are my number one priority. I want Adam to believe me when I say I want him to stay. Ranae will always be my best friend, and I know that she, of all people, understands Adam's weaknesses, so I hope she can also understand why I'm keeping my distance right now.

I suppose Ranae would say that Adam is my weakness.

It's now a little after eight on a Friday night and I am struggling to keep my eyes open and my focus on the conversation we're having. Adam and I sitting across from each other in a booth at Flask and Flounder, Adam's favorite seafood restaurant. The smells in this place are overwhelming, but I've been able to keep the nausea at bay by sipping on my ginger-infused water and nibbling on the basket of fancy oyster crackers on our table.

I order halibut in a lemon butter sauce, and the first several bites go down fine. But then a waiter walks by with an enormous tray of dishes for a group at a nearby table, and the combination of those smells sends me bolting for the bathroom. Adam is frowning when I return, but he asks if I'm okay. I assure him I am, but I don't bother trying to get more fish down. "I'm just going to stick with the crackers."

He's not pleased about it, I can tell. I think he's purposely taking his time eating his salmon just to punish me for... well, for any number of things. He's one of those people who pays for the experience at restaurants, not just the food, and tonight, he seems determined to get every single penny's worth at my expense.

I watch him carefully separate the last of his salmon steak into several bite-sized pieces on his plate. He swirls a chunk of the pale pink meat in creamy dill sauce, and I'm suddenly reminded of a wound management class I took years ago. In particular, the PowerPoint presentation of the different stages of bed sores. I close my eyes, but the images flash even clearer behind my dark eyelids, so I quickly open them and peer around the room, desperate for a distraction. I'm clutching my napkin to my mouth when I spot a little girl a few booths away, leaning against her daddy's shoulder, and watching me with a sweet smile. I lift the napkin a little higher to cover my eyes, then lower it quickly and mouth, "Boo!" at her. She giggles and her father glances over at me, too.

"What are you doing?" Adam asks, looking around to see who I'm interacting with. Of course, it's at the exact same moment the girl's dad acknowledges me, and my husband turns back to me with narrowed eyes. He doesn't say anything, but his expression tells me he believes he just caught me flirting.

In that moment, I am overwhelmed by both physical and mental weariness. I just want to go home and slip into my soft pajamas. I want to crawl in bed next to my husband and have him wrap his arms around me and tell me that he loves me. I want to press my belly against his back and have him marvel along with me at the miracle of our babies growing and developing and thriving inside me. I want to close my eyes and not have to wonder for one more minute whether Adam is going to misread, misjudge, or misinterpret my actions. Or worse, leave me guessing altogether.

Earlier at Breathe, while Gail operated the ultrasound machine, I talked Adam through what we were seeing on the monitor. The twins performed beautifully for him, kicking and waving, and at one point, they looked like they were trying to high-five each other. But Adam seemed completely unimpressed by it all, asking questions like, "Why are their heads so big?" and "What is that?" while pointing at one of the baby's beating hearts. He really couldn't tell from the rhythmic pumping and its position in the fetus? I saw the bemused concern in Gail's eyes, and when she caught me looking at her, she gave me an encouraging smile.

Adam wanted to know their genders, but with them moving around so much, it was hard to hold a position long enough to get a clear shot. Thirteen weeks is a little early to be a hundred percent accurate, anyway, at least in my experience. If it had been Tracy, with her radiology background, or Wendy, our part-time ultrasound tech, one of them might have been able to work the machine a little better. But with me flat on my back, and Gail following my instructions the best she could, the only thing I could tell him was that I didn't think I saw any boy parts.

That seemed to be Adam's cue to lose interest, so we wrapped things up after only twenty minutes. I thanked Gail as we headed out past her desk, accepted the tissue she tucked into my hand, and dabbed at my eyes quickly after Adam closed my passenger side door for me and hurried around to his side of the car. By the time he was settled in behind the wheel, I was smiling bravely again.

"Do you have any questions about all of that?" I asked, wondering if he'd felt awkward in front of Gail, and if perhaps that had been the reason for his glaring lack of excitement over what he'd just witnessed and his insensitive questions during the scan that even now, made me uneasy.

"I don't think so," he said with a quick shake of his head. "I mean, I had a hard time seeing most of what you ladies were talking about. The heads, the spines, the hands and feet, they all look like they're supposed to, right?"

I nodded. "Yes, and all the internal organs, too."

"Like I said, you know better than I do." He reached over and patted my thigh. "You hungry? We're pretty early for our reservations. Do you want to go get a drink first? I know you can't drink, but I wouldn't mind a little pick me up. We can get you a Shirley Temple," he said with a condescending wink.

It's been two hours since we left the birthing center, and we haven't discussed the ultrasound, my pregnancy, the babies, or our future. And if I have to endure another minute in this loud, odiferous environment, I'm going to lose my mind. Or the contents, what little there is left, of my stomach. "I'm not feeling very well, Adam. I think I need to step outside and get some fresh air. Is it okay if I wait for you in the car?"

"Absolutely not." He glances around at the other patrons, then leans forward and says in a lower voice, "Everyone will think you walked out on me."

"But—but I'm not walking out on you," I say, surprised at his vehemence. "I'm pregnant, Adam, and I'm having a real struggle with nausea. We've been here a long time, and the noise and smells in here are all pretty overwhelming."

"But no one here knows you're pregnant," he argues. "They'll just see you get up and leave."

I sit back against the seat cushion and study him. Will he make a scene if I just get up and go? I suppose if I do that, then I actually am walking out on him.

Fortunately at that moment, our waiter, Patrick, approaches and asks if we are enjoying our food. I assure him everything was delicious, not bothering to explain my barely touched meal, and then I look pointedly at Adam.

"What?" he asks impatiently, taking another slow bite of fish.

"May we have our bill, please?" I ask the waiter, embarrassed for all of us.

Patrick digs through his black ticket folders and sets ours at the edge of the table between us. "Are you sure I can't tempt you with any dessert?"

For a moment, I'm certain Adam is going to ask him to see the menu, so I jump in. "No, no. Thank you, though. We need to be somewhere."

Adam's eyebrows rise in feigned surprise, and I half-expect him to contradict me, but thank goodness he's too busy chewing and can't swallow fast enough to do so.

"I'm going to the bathroom," I say when Patrick moves away. "Can you please try to finish your meal while I'm gone so that we can go straight out to the car?" I no longer care if I upset him. I just want to get out of here.

Adam makes a sound that might be agreement, but I don't wait for clarification. When I emerge from the back hall several minutes later, my husband is gone, and our table is cleared. "I should have gone to the bonfire tonight," I mutter under my breath as I head toward the front door of the restaurant.

Adam is outside pacing lazily back and forth on the sidewalk while talking on his phone. I watch him for a few moments. He's smiling, an expression I've hardly seen all evening, and talking animatedly to whoever is on the other end of the line. When he sees me pushing through the glass door, he quickly wraps up his conversation and shoves his phone into his back pocket. "What took you so long?" he asks as we start across the parking lot to his car.

He stays one step ahead of me as we walk, and it suddenly occurs to me that this has become our new normal. When did it happen? And was Adam the one who stepped out in front? Or was I the one who fell behind?

I don't bother responding to his question, and he doesn't seem to notice. I glance at my watch. Who was on the phone with my husband at this time of the night? It's not terribly late, but it's Friday, and we're on a date. If I'd been the one to receive a phone call, he would have thrown a tantrum. I want to ask him about the call, but I already know it won't matter what he says. I won't believe him anyway.

I hope Ranae's evening is going better than mine, I think to myself as I settle into the front seat of Adam's Escape. It's actually quite comfortable, and the synthetic new car smell does wonders for my over-stimulated olfactory system. I breathe in deeply and close my eyes, letting the vibration of the engine lull me into a sleepy haze. I somehow manage to stay awake until we get home, though; I've never liked the disorienting sensation of falling asleep in the car at one location and waking up in another.

"I think I'll head over to the farmhouse in the morning after I get up," I say sleepily, as I move past Adam who is holding open the door for me from the garage into the house. I drop my purse on the kitchen counter before filling a glass with cold water from the dispenser on the fridge. "Find out how things went tonight. Do you have plans for tomorrow?"

"Actually, yes I do. I was planning to spend the day with you," he says, as though I should already know that.

"Oh. All day?" I glance over my shoulder at him. It's rare that we spend Saturdays together, so I'm not prepared for his response. He likes to get up early and go to the gym or watch sports, things that he enjoys doing alone. If I'm not out on a call, I often head over to Ranae's, even if she's got a funeral going on. I like the serenity of the services and enjoy the time spent outdoors in the beautiful Fair Havens preserve. I haven't seen her in over a week, and I miss her.

"If you'd rather spend time with Ranae, be my guest," Adam says glibly. "I'm sure I can find something to do on my own."

"Wow, Adam." I try not to scoff, but this poor little lonely boy act doesn't sit well with me. He's never vied for my time like this before, not so vehemently against my friend in particular. "Seriously?"

"Wow, Dani." He mimics both my tone and my accent. "Yes, seriously. You're always asking me to spend more time with you on my weekends off, and now that I'm finally able to do so, you go off gallivanting with your gal pal." The way he says *gal pal* is full of accusation and derision.

"Adam." I send him a look of censure. "Why must you be so ugly about Ranae?"

"I want to spend time with you, but you want to spend time with her." He loosens his tie and lifts a challenging brow at me. "Up to you, babe."

I shake my head in frustration. Didn't I just choose time with him over Bonfire Night and Ranae? I turn and head down the hall. "I'm going to bed," I call over my shoulder. "Goodnight, Adam." I should thank him for the evening, I suppose, but stubbornly, I keep my mouth clamped shut. The last several hours have been all about him; he's seen to that. He should be the one thanking me.

"Are you going to spend the day with me or Ranae tomorrow?" he asks, his voice raised to be heard above the sound of the television he's just turned on.

"I'm spending the day with my husband, of course," I tell him, then make a beeline for our bathroom. Fifteen minutes later, I crawl between the cool linens on our bed. The television is still playing loudly in the front room, but my hormone-induced weariness all but blocks it out. By the time my head hits the pillow, I'm halfway to Dreamland already.

Ranae

I shoo the girls and Gideon ahead of me on the path, and when we arrive back at the main clearing, Tom is alone at the bonfire ring, waiting for us. As soon as he sees us, he gets to his feet. "If you don't need me," he says. "I'm off. Thanks for yet another incredible evening, Ranae." Clearly, Hugo has told him we have things to sort out here.

I give him a quick hug and send him on his way while the kids settle onto a few of the split log benches Hugo built from a black cherry tree felled by a tornado years ago. When I turn back to face them, it's Gideon who speaks first.

"Ms. Niemeyer," he begins, but I hold up my hand to stop him.

"Hold on." I say, then move around to crouch in front of Millie. I put my hands on her knees and wait until she meets my eyes. "Honey, I just want to ask one more time. Did William hurt you in any way?"

"No," she insists. "He's just a jerk. So I guess he hurt my feelings, but that's all." I glance over at Ruby for confirmation.

"He's just a jerk, Mom," she echoes. "That's why we weren't with him."

"I'm really sorry, Ranae," Millie says again. "This whole thing is my fault."

"No, it's not," Gideon cuts in. "I'm the one responsible, Ranae—"

"That's Ms. Niemeyer to you." I have drilled into Millie's head that she should call me Ranae, but that doesn't automatically mean it's a free-for-all.

"Mom." Ruby covers her face with her hands.

Gideon clears his throat. "Sorry, Ms. Niemeyer. But I saw the sign posted, and I went in anyway," Gideon continues, undeterred.

"We all went in," Ruby interjects, lowering her hands to her lap where she toys with the hem of her top.

"Yeah, but only because we were trying to stop William, you guys." Millie straightens her shoulders and wipes her eyes. "He wouldn't listen to us, and I didn't want him to do anything stupid out there," she says. She, too, is twisting her hands together in agitation. "I mean, he's such an idiot. I was sure he was going to get lost or fall in a creek or something."

"Did you know he had weed with him?" I ask, sitting on another bench nearby.

"No, Mom," Ruby insists, scowling at me like she's offended I'd even ask. "Not until we caught up to him."

"And you didn't think that was a good time to haul your backsides out of there? Let Hugo know? He could have taken care of William right then, and we could have avoided all of this." I made a circular gesture in the air.

"We didn't want to disrupt the party," Gideon said. "And that's my fault. I thought I could handle him. I know his type. He talks a big game, but when push comes to shove, he's full of crap."

"Not tonight, he wasn't," Ruby mutters.

"What does that mean?" I ask, narrowing my eyes at her, remembering how William had shoved by me earlier.

"When we tried to get him to see reason," Ruby begins, but Millie cuts in.

"I tried to take his stupid pipe away," she says, her voice stronger now. "We kinda wrestled a little, and I fell." She must see the flare of anger on my face, even in the dimming glow of the dying embers of the bonfire and the solar lights around us, because she quickly adds, "But he didn't hurt me, I promise. I was just shocked. And—and embarrassed. My skirt kinda, you know." She makes a flipping motion with her hands. "He got a big kick out of that."

It's all I can do to keep my composure. I want to punch someone in the throat right about now, and his name starts with William. "Do you want to press charges?" I ask. "You have witnesses."

"No," she insists. "It's not like he pushed me. I should have let go of the stupid thing, but I didn't, so when he jerked it away from me, I went backwards." She reaches over and grabs for one of Ruby's hands. "Rubes told me to leave him be, but I didn't listen. She wanted to get Hugo; I promise. I was too embarrassed about the whole thing and wouldn't let her, and then I was crying and didn't want to go back right away where everyone would see us."

"And once again, I didn't insist," Gideon says. "My fault."

I eye the three of them for several moments before I finally say, "Are you guys for real?"

"What does that mean?" Ruby asks, her expression letting me know that she's not any happier with me now than she was ten minutes ago.

"You sound like good kids who made a couple of stupid mistakes." I can see it playing out exactly as they claim it did. William taunting and a little too rough, soft-spoken Millie trying to convince him to be good and come back to the bonfire. Ruby insisting they get the adults involved, and this new kid, Gideon Moore, playing superhero, trying to save the day. And their dignity.

"That's because we are," Ruby shoots back. "William is an idiot, Mom. We only went further up the trail to get away from him. But you saw us. We were on our way back when you found us. Wasn't it obvious?" She's no longer embarrassed. She's angry.

"Watch yourself, Ruby," I tell her. I hate it when she uses that tone with me, like I'm a clueless mom. I'm not. I know very well what being seventeen feels like. Sometimes I think part of me has been trapped there my whole adult life.

She doesn't apologize, but that's okay. I also understand her frustration. I'm glad she made Millie's emotional condition priority, and I commend them for walking away from a potentially volatile situation. But that doesn't change the fact that they went past the barricade in the first place.

"Am I still grounded?" she asks, her voice tight and small.

"You are. You went into the woods." I don't have to reiterate to her all the reasons it's off limits after dark.

Ruby crosses her arms and turns away from me.

"I'm sorry, Ranae," Millie says again.

"I am, too, Ms. Niemeyer," Gideon echoes.

I pause, hoping my daughter will offer her own apology, but it doesn't come. With a sigh, I stand and gesture at them to follow me. "Help me pack up the refreshment stuff. As soon as Hugo gets back, I'll take you home, Millie."

"Do you want me to stay or go?" Gideon asks, and once again I'm impressed by his composure.

I point to a shovel and the wheelbarrow of dirt nearby. "Do you know how to put out a fire with dirt?"

"I do. I can take care of this." He grabs the shovel and spreads the few pieces of still-glowing wood around in the fire pit just like Hugo was doing earlier, chopping at them to break up the larger chunks. When he starts scooping the dirt over the top, I turn to follow the girls to the schoolhouse. Ruby and Millie are already several paces ahead of me.

"Ruby, can you bring the golf cart around?" I call out. "We'll load it up, and you can drive the stuff over to the house in one or two trips."

"Ms. Niemeyer?" Gideon's voice stops me.

I turn back to face him. He's leaning on the shovel handle, his eyes following Ruby and Millie. "Yes?"

He blinks rapidly, tellingly, then shifts his focus to me. "I'm really glad Ruby invited me here tonight. This place is pretty amazing; everything about it. And I am sorry about what happened. I hope—well, I like your daughter," he says, his voice dropping so the girls can't hear him. "I hope you'll let me come back again and see all of this in the daylight."

I eye him warily. "How old are you, Gideon?"

He straightens and says, "I just turned nineteen a few weeks ago. I'm a little older than most of the other seniors, I know. I had a football injury back in tenth grade and got held back a year," he explains casually, but I wonder if perhaps his age is a sore spot for him, and that's why he's so quick to explain.

But it's his age that explains his surprising maturity, I think. He reminds me a little too much of Solomon, but in the best of ways. His coloring is completely different—Gideon has that rough and tumble, boy-next-door appeal to him with his dirty blond hair and slightly crooked front teeth. But his smile is ready and genuine, he looks me in the eye when he's talking to me, and he's quick to take responsibility when it's his to take.

Even when it isn't.

I nod slowly. "You're okay in my book, Gideon." I leave it at that. A lot will depend on how Ruby handles things over the next few days. She, too, needs to take responsibility when it's hers to take, and no matter what the motives for doing so, the rules of the night were broken on her watch.

When we're all back at the farmhouse, I release Gideon from dish duty. He looks noticeably relieved, and I have to smile. He did a good job with the fire, and he remained polite and attentive throughout what must have been a very awkward cleanup session. He says a quiet goodbye to Ruby at the front door and leaves in his truck. Millie stays to help wash dishes with Ruby, then Ruby and I drive her home, too. I promise I'll let her tell her mother about William, but only after making her agree that she needed to do so.

Ruby says a perfunctory goodnight to me from the top of the stairs, then closes herself up in her room. When I knock on her door fifteen minutes later to say goodnight, there is no response.

I open her bedroom door and approach the bed. "I love you, Ruby," I murmur softly, touching the silky hair at her temple. "I'm glad you and your friends are all right."

Her breathing is steady and even, her eyes are closed, but I know she's awake. "Sleep well, sweet baby of mine."

By the time Hugo returns, there is nothing left for him to do over at Fair Havens, and he finds me sitting on the porch swing at the farmhouse. I knew he wouldn't head home without one last check on the bonfire, but I'm out here on the porch because I also knew he'd come looking for me to set things right between us. I'm not sure I'm ready to talk to him, but I owe him my thanks for all he did tonight, not just for the Live and Let Die Bonfire event, but for me and my kid and her friends, too.

"How are you?" he asks as he mounts the front steps, pausing on the top one as if unsure how I'll respond if he comes any closer. I'm going to assume he's asking about the kids now and not referring to our earlier conversation, because I'm not going there, I've decided. Not tonight, anyway.

"I'm all right, although Ruby isn't ready to forgive me for embarrassing her yet." I push the toe of my shoe against the wood plank flooring, setting my swing in motion. "Millie is all right. Her tears were more out of embarrassment and shame than anything else. I think she's finally taken off her rose-colored glasses where William is concerned."

"And the new kid?" he prompts when I pause. "Gideon?" Of course Hugo knows his name.

I don't answer right away. Not because I don't want to tell Hugo, but because I'm battling some of my own demons where Gideon Moore is concerned. I finally say, "He's a nice guy. Polite. Respectful. Seems like a good kid." Keep it safe. Simple.

"Right. I got that vibe, too," Hugo says, nodding sagely. He props his backside against the porch railing and crosses his ankles out in front of him. He braces his hands on either side of him, making his shoulders, outlined in the moonlight, look broader than they already are. It's a very masculine pose, and I have to lower my gaze to Blimey who is resting on his pillow nearby so that I don't stare. Or drool. "Which makes him a bit of a threat. At least to me," he adds.

I frown up at him. "What do you mean? To you?"

Hugo chuckles softly and holds my gaze. "He's the kind of kid who might just have what it takes to steal Ruby's heart away from us."

I nod slowly, unnerved at how he's put words to my own fears so succinctly, as well as by the collective 'us.' We sit in silence a few minutes longer, then he pushes away from the rail and crosses over to sit beside me, stilling the motion of the swing. He leans forward, rests his elbows on his knees, and gazes out toward the driveway where the golf cart is still parked. I'll take it back in the morning.

Finally, he speaks. "I'm sorry for what I said earlier, Ranae. I didn't mean to offend you. I only wanted to be sensitive to what might be a sensitive issue."

"There's no issue," I insist, my tone a little harder than I'd like, but I don't want to talk about this right now. "I'm not in love with Dani, okay? I really mean it."

"And I'm really glad." He sounds like he means it, too. I'm not sure what to make of him right now. I want to be upset still, to hold on to my wounded pride, but it's clear he wants to make amends before we end the night.

And also, he smells ridiculously yummy.

I need to change the subject. "Did you see Abe hitting on Gran again tonight?"

He chuckles softly, straightens to sit back against the seat cushion, and starts the swing moving again. His legs are much longer than mine, and I let him take over. "That old boy must have a steel rod for a spine. Or steel plates in his head. It takes nothing short of a man's man to have the courage to pursue Gran."

"Do you think he's really pursuing her? Or is it just comfortable companionship? Gran insists they're just friends."

Hugo props his elbow on the swing back and nudges my shoulder with the back of his hand.

I turn to look at him. "What?"

"Have you seen the way he looks at her?"

I scoff playfully at him. "Yeah, and remember what happened the last time you made an assumption about the way people look at each other?" I point two fingers at my eyes, then shake my head. "Stop playing Cupid, Hugo Beckenbauer. You stink at it."

He laughs out loud and it's such a lovely sound. I've heard it a lot more lately, and I'm glad. Hugo's physical scars healed a long time ago, but the wounds of the heart can take forever to mend. I should know.

"Touché" he says, then sobers quickly. "Are we all right?" he asks, touching my shoulder again, more gently this time. "You and me?" I can feel him studying me, but I can't bring myself to meet his eyes.

"We're all right," I tell him, relieved that he seems as anxious to put the misunderstanding behind us as I am. "I'm still worried about Dani, though, and I'm sad about the way things went down with the kids—oh!" I snap around to look at him. "What happened with William?"

He hesitates just long enough to make me worry, but then he says, "I hired him to do a job for me."

"You what?" I narrow my eyes at him. "A job here? At Fair Havens?"

"No, no," Hugo is quick to assure me. "I have some work to do on my place, and he needs a productive way to spend his time. I made him an offer. He could come over every day for a few hours after school for the next several weeks and help me get it done, or I could hand-deliver him to the police station where I'd press charges for disorderly conduct, attempted arson, and physical assault. He opted to come work for me."

"Smart boy," I murmur. "But I'm not so sure I can say the same thing about you. Why would you want to have him hanging around your place? He's trouble."

Hugo reaches up to rub the back of his neck, almost like he's thinking about the vice grip he had on William earlier. "He's not such a bad kid, Ranae. Just a little lost right now. His home life isn't anything like Ruby's or Millie's."

"Right. I seem to recall as much."

I met William's mother at the Fall Festival downtown last year. William had come upon the three of us—Millie and Ruby were hanging with me as we wandered the booths one night, gorging ourselves on deep fried foods and processed carbs... although, I'm pretty sure they opted to stay close because I had money and they didn't—and then suddenly, his mother was there. Megan or Maggie, I can't remember now. She was mad as a wet hen because she couldn't find her husband, and she let everyone know about it. I saw the mortification on William's face as he tried to calm her down. She'd wanted none of it. "Who are you?" she'd asked me in a sharp, unfriendly manner. Her eyes ran up and down my body in a way that made me glad I wore my thick, shapeless poncho. I quickly learned she had nothing against me, as long as I didn't know her husband, and William assured her I didn't.

"Everyone needs someone who still believes in them when he or she gets lost." It's a statement that brooks no argument, and I wonder if Hugo isn't referring to himself as much as to William.

I nod slowly. "Well, good for you." Maybe it will be good for both the guys to put a little sweat equity into making something like new again. I still have my reservations about William being so close by, though. "But you need to know he's not allowed on this property until further notice."

Hugo nods solemnly. "I told him the same thing. If I catch him even lurking at the edge of the woods, our deal is off." He asks me if it's all right to leave William's truck parked in our driveway overnight. "I'll ride my bike over in the morning and pick it up first thing."

I nod again, knowing I can trust this man to look after our best interests here at the farmhouse.

Hugo keeps the swing moving gently back and forth. The night is cold and clear, the stars twinkling brightly in the dark sky. The moon is a crescent tonight, but it still takes center stage over our heads. The song of the night creatures rises and falls in rhythmic pulses beyond the circle of light from the lamppost in the yard, the melody accompanied by the rustle of the wind in the trees. Blimey snuffles in his sleep like the old man he is, making me smile.

"He was impressed by my scars," Hugo says without preamble. He shoots me a cheeky grin and runs his fingers along the puckered skin under his jaw.

I roll my eyes at him. "Yeah, I saw your little scare tactic back there. Like the poor guy didn't think you were scary enough already?"

"You mean scar tactic?"

"Oh, no." I shake my head. "No, no, you didn't." I laugh at his horrible joke anyway, then push to my feet and release a contented sigh. Life is hard sometimes, but people like the man sharing this peaceful moment with me make the hard times manageable. "It's been a long night for you, Hugo. I'm sorry we've kept you out so late, but I hope you know how much I appreciate you."

"It was a good night, in spite of the way things ended with the kids. And that will all work itself out in the end, Ranae, you'll see." He sits forward again, bracing his hands firmly on his knees, and looks up at me with a warm smile that makes my pulse lurch. I cross my arms in self-defense; I ache for him in every cell of my body.

Yes, for him. I don't just want my own Hugo Beckenbauer. I want *the* Hugo Beckenbauer. This Hugo Beckenbauer who sits on my swing gazing up at me in the moonlight.

"Go home," I murmur softly, hoping he doesn't hear the longing in my voice. "Get some well-deserved sleep."

Hugo gets to his feet and pulls me into a quick, unexpected hug. But before I can uncross my arms to wrap them around him in return, he releases me and steps back. "And I appreciate you, Ranae." He juts his chin toward the front door and adds. "Ruby and Gran, too, of course."

"Oh. Right. Of—of course," I stammer, glad for the dim light so he can't see the blush warming my cheeks. "Thanks for being our friend." I take a step backward and trip clumsily over the corner of Blimey's dog pillow, but Hugo reaches out and grabs my hand before I land on my backside.

"You okay?" he asks, and I can tell he's doing his best not to let his smile turn into a full on laugh.

"Aren't I always?" Not even embarrassed, I step around the dog who has gotten to his feet to follow me inside. I'm a klutz, and this man already knows it. "Goodnight, Hugo. Thanks for making another Bonfire Night amazing."

"My pleasure. See you around."

Upstairs in my room, I want to text Dani. I want to tell her all about tonight, the highs and lows, the tears and the laughter, and about how Hugo swept in and saved the day with the kids. I even want to tell her about him thinking I was pining for her, because maybe with Dani, I can laugh about it.

But my gut tells me that a text—no less, a phone call—might not be a great idea. There's a reason Dani hasn't been around much, a reason why she missed tonight's event, and that reason is probably laying in bed next to her. Besides, Dani is probably sound asleep.

I call her at nine on Saturday morning, around the time we usually connect, but she doesn't answer, and I don't leave a message. Maybe she's sleeping. I know this pregnancy is really doing a number on her. I wait until ten before I text her, but when I don't get a response, I try calling again. Still nothing.

Great. My daughter won't speak to me. My best friend is ignoring me. Her husband hates me, and Hugo thinks I like women. I can't help feeling rejected by everyone I love.

I finally hear back from Dani just before noon. She won't be coming out to the farmhouse this weekend, but we agree to get together early next week.

Ruby stays in her room most of the day, and even though she has her phone in there and is probably texting with her friends about what a monster her mother is, I give her the space she needs. She's not really a kid anymore and the grounding is less about punishing and more about reminding her that there are consequences to her actions and choices. Like I said, she's smart. She knows this is the way things work around here. We've had many a spat between us, but we always find our way back to each other.

Besides, she'll have to talk to me at some point if she wants to know how long she's grounded for. I'm not going to offer the information to her unsolicited.

Gran left first thing in the morning with some ladies from her church to attend a two-day craft fair and auction over in Amish country this weekend. She's not super crafty herself, but she loves spending time with her friends. It's something they go to together every year, usually spending the night in a bed and breakfast nearby. Without Dani or Ruby keeping me occupied, and no funeral services scheduled for the weekend, things are uncharacteristically quiet around here. I finally decide to head over to Fair Havens to make sure there isn't more cleanup to do after last night. I'll take Blimey with me. Give the old boy a little exercise.

I remember the golf cart in the driveway, but when I step out onto the porch, it's gone. There's a folded note under a piece of fieldstone on the top step where I can't miss it.

Ranae - I was here early to pick up William's truck. Went ahead and took the cart back over to Fair Havens, too. Didn't want you to think it had been stolen. Have a great day. H.

I press the note to my chest and sigh dramatically. "I love you, Hugo," I murmur under my breath, then fold it into a small square and tuck it into my bra. Over my heart. Only because I don't have pockets in my leggings or in the sweatshirt I'm wearing, of course.

"Come on, Blimers," I call to my dog, urging him to follow me down the driveway to Kirchwood Lane. "We'll walk this way today."

Dani

Ranae has called twice this morning, and both times, I let her go to voicemail. I'm sitting on the sofa watching a sports network show with my husband, and I have no clue what or who they're talking about. But Adam seems to have strong opinions about everything the newscasters are saying, and his passionate rants are far more entertaining than the show itself. Even so, I know answering the phone now would only cause a row.

A few minutes later, I get up to use the bathroom, and while I'm there, I check my texts. Three from Ranae, two of them inviting me over, the third asking if she should be worried about me not responding.

I quickly key in that I'm fine, that I'm just spending the day with Adam, and she returns the text with a thumbs up sign. I know my friend well. The fact she only texted a sticker tells me she's got a mouthful to say and is biting her tongue to hold it in. She uses emojis all the time, but usually just to break up long, wordy texts.

Maybe we can do lunch next week, I key in.

Monday? Her short answer is not very encouraging.

Maybe. I have to check my schedule at Breathe.

She texts right back. *Check it now and let me know.*

But I don't have it with me, at least not the altered version. I usually keep everything updated on my phone, but I haven't had time to confirm all my schedule adjustments with the other midwives yet, so I haven't made anything official. I text back, *I'll check first thing Monday morning and call you.*

Another thumbs up sticker. Oh dear.

I return to find Adam sprawled lengthwise on the sofa, his feet up on one armrest, his head on the other. He doesn't seem to notice when I enter the room. I wonder if he noticed when I left.

"Do you need anything?" I ask, picking up my water bottle and heading for the kitchen to refill it.

"Sorry, babe," he calls after me, sitting up quickly. "Habit. I'm not used to having you watch this stuff with me. Come sit. I'll get that for you."

"I've got it," I tell him, disarmed by his warm smile. Sometimes I think I might be losing my mind. One minute Adam treats me like I'm nothing but a great big disappointment to him, then the next minute, he does everything right, bending over backwards to make me feel like the love of his life. Last night, I was convinced I disgusted him, that my pregnancy and all the wonderful and awful things that come with it—like this insane nausea I can't seem to conquer—revile him. I kept waiting for him to tell me that he was leaving, that becoming parents now wasn't part of our plan, or at the very least, to ask if I did this on purpose, getting pregnant behind his back. Then this morning, he woke me up with a cup of hot ginger tea and a plate of soda crackers. I didn't know he was even aware of my before-I-even-get-out-of-bed routine to quell the dry heaves. When I came out of the bathroom, he was waiting for me in bed wearing nothing but a smoldering smile. A tender, lazy bout of lovemaking followed, after which we migrated to the sofa where we've been for the last two hours.

One minute I fear he loathes me, the next, I'm clinging to the belief that he still loves me.

Ranae would tell me it's a game he's playing, a means to manipulate me, to keep me grasping at hope. Part of me knows she's right, at least on some level, but a much more adamant part of me insists that if hope does indeed exist, then it's worth hanging on to.

I fill my water bottle and return to the sofa, curling up on one end with my toes tucked under Adam's thigh. I've just started a delightful new book about an exotic pet sitter written by one of my favorite cozy mystery authors, and I open to my bookmark. I try to pick up where I left off, but although I'm enchanted by the sassy young protagonist, it's hard for me to fully immerse myself into the story with the television up so loud.

"I think I'm going to go sit outside on the porch with my book," I finally say.

"Do you want me to come out with you?" He points the remote at the television and mutes his show.

"No, no. I'm fine. I just need some fresh air." I pat my stomach. "Morning sickness."

"It's almost noon," he responds with a frown.

"I know. I get it off and on all day. A lot of women do, especially with multiples. Twice the hormones and all that." I try my hardest to keep the irritation out of my voice. This isn't the first time I've explained this to him.

He nods, getting momentarily distracted by a commercial with a big truck driven by a long-haired woman in tight jeans and a dirty white cowboy hat. It doesn't bother me, the way Adam's eyes wander, not really. Not anymore. It probably should, I suppose, but half the time, I don't think he even realizes he does it.

I push to my feet, pausing to let my roiling stomach catch up, then scoop up my book and water bottle and start for the back door.

"You should call Ranae back," he says, his tone deceptively casual.

I pause at the door and smile sweetly back at him. "I told her we'd catch up next week sometime." Then I push open the slider and make a deliberate show of setting my phone face down on the patio table where he can see it. I don't care who calls or texts me today. I'm not answering it unless it's an emergency delivery. In fact, that goes for the whole weekend. I will not give Adam any reason to question my desire to be right here with him.

I hear the television come back to life as I settle into a lounge chair and open my book. I can practically feel his eyes on me, but I don't turn to look at him. I can't help but wonder if my nausea is a result of an increase in hormones or stress.

Adam and I haven't always been like this. When we first met, I wasn't immediately attracted to him. He was lovely to look at, indeed, but what drew me to him was his ability to make me feel comfortable in a setting that would otherwise have me feeling overwhelmed. We met at a Christmas party for the hospital staff where our parents are colleagues, and while I thrive in more intimate, one-on-one situations—it's one of the reasons I love being a midwife—social events like large parties leave me feeling overstimulated and drained. Adam's company that evening turned something I'd been dreading into a thoroughly enjoyable affair for me. Over the course of the meal, we found we had a lot more in common than just our parents. He, too, was an only child, we were both finishing up doctorate degrees in our respective fields, and both heading into careers involving children. We ribbed each other over the psychology behind our mutual fascination with family units, and in particular, siblings, and the fact that both of us always wished we'd had brothers and sisters.

The best part about it was that not once throughout the evening did Adam make any kind of romantic or suggestive pass at me. At that time, I was far too focused on completing my education and launching our birthing center business to have time for a dalliance of any kind. By the end of the party, I felt like we were fast friends. I left the event with his name and number in my phone and his promise to call the next time he was down from Indianapolis to visit his folks.

He did exactly that. Two weeks later on a Friday morning, he texted to let me know he was coming down for the weekend. We met for coffee at Smolder and Brewed, a combo coffee and craft whiskey bar, where we enjoyed our visit so much that we decided to make it a tradition. We met there once or twice a month for over a year before Adam even hinted at wanting to take things to the next level.

At first, I played ignorant. Our Sunday afternoons were such a respite from the insane amount of pressure on me, admittedly mostly self-inflicted, and I was hesitant to let things change. I didn't want anything to go wrong, to sour what had become an easy friendship between us.

Then one evening when the days had grown short again and the nights had turned cold, when once again, we'd lingered over our coffee longer than usual, Adam had walked me to my car the way he always did.

He did not unlock my door and open it for me as usual. Instead, he took a single step closer to me and dropped my keys into his coat pocket. When I laughed at his game and held out my hand for them, he caught mine in his own and planted a warm, soft kiss on the inside of my wrist. Then he pulled me, ever so slowly, toward him before cupping my face in his and leaning forward to kiss my mouth.

All my thoughts of resistance fled at that moment, and even now, my stomach still tightens at the thrill of it. He'd swept me off my feet without me even realizing it was happening.

These days I'm swept off my feet by Adam all the time, but not for the same reason. My imbalance has more to do with him repeatedly ripping the rug out from under me.

I want to give him a reason to leave the rug put. To come stand beside me again, not behind me, analyzing my every move, and not out in front so I feel like I'm being dragged around on a leash. Beside me, together, equally yoked. A team. I do believe we can find those people we once were. Underneath the mess of what we are today, I am holding out hope for the Adam and Dani who fell in love once upon a time. Surely, they've just gotten lost along the way somewhere.

If spending more time with him when he's available will help us find our way back to each other, then that's what I'm going to do. Ranae and my parents will understand. And even if they don't, they'll support my decision to do so.

Sweet birdsong accompanied by the whisper of drying leaves dancing in the autumn breeze soothes my spirit—and my stomach—and it's not long before a tentative sense of well-being settles over me. I open my book and lose myself in the story of a young woman who discovers the new man in her life isn't exactly who he says he is.

Ranae

By the end of the weekend, Ruby and I have reached something of an impasse. I finally bribed her out of her room with lemon bars and a romantic comedy on Sunday afternoon, then while she showered and picked out her outfit for school the next morning, I made a huge pot of spaghetti and pulled up *The Walking Dead*. We've been binge-watching it whenever we can over the last few months, hoping to get through all the seasons by Halloween, and it's tradition—we always indulge in some kind of noodles and red sauce while watching zombie shows. We critique, brutally and loudly, the death and gore special effects. If anyone knows what death and gore looks like, it's a mortician and her teenage daughter.

Granted, I don't see a lot of badly damaged corpses these days, mainly because I'm not equipped to do any major reconstruction at Fair Havens. It's an adrenaline rush I don't miss.

In spite of the movies and zombies and yummy food, however, Ruby still isn't ready to be my buddy again. In the car on the way to school on Monday morning, I remind her that she needs to come home directly after school. "I'll be waiting for you. Don't dawdle."

"You don't have to remind me," she says, barely sparing me a glance from the passenger seat. "So how long am I grounded for?"

I force myself not to smile. I knew she couldn't hold out much longer. "Through Wednesday. I want you to come help me at the cemetery after school for three days, then you're off the hook." I reach over to take her hand, but she pulls it out of my reach. "I'm proud of you for looking after Millie," I tell her, ignoring the sharp pang her rejection causes. I was going to tell her about Hugo and William just in case she runs into him at school, but I'll wait until she's home this afternoon. I hope he avoids her today—she might be even more angry at me if she finds out from him and not from me. "I like Gideon, by the way," I add. "I'm looking forward to getting to know him."

She arches a brow and in a dry tone says, "Who says you're going to get to know him? Do you really think he'll want to come hang out with me ever again? After how you embarrassed him Friday night?"

I know it's Ruby who's embarrassed, and I know she's dreading seeing him again. I'd like nothing more than to put her mind at ease by telling her what Gideon said to me. But first things first. "You can't talk to me this way, Ruby. It's not right, and you know it."

"Well, I don't think the way you talked to us on Friday was right, either, but no one made you stop. Accusing us of getting high and all."

"I didn't accuse you of getting high. I simply asked if you'd smoked with William. I think that's a pretty reasonable thing for any parent to do, don't you?"

"How about trust, though?" she asks, her voice rising in pitch the way it always does when she's frustrated with the world. "I mean, was there any reason for you to assume the worst of us the way you did?"

We're getting close to her school, and we need to wrap this up before she starts crying. No high school girl wants to show up on a Monday morning in tears. "Ruby, yes. There were several reasons for me to question what was going on. *Not* to assume the worst, which I didn't. Reason number one, the one that tossed the whole notion of trusting you out the window, mind you: you and your friends broke the rule about going out into the woods. Second, we stumbled across William, who was hiding in the trees with his head in a cloud of cannabis smoke. Third, you and Millie and Gideon were even further down the trail, having left William to get high out there on his own. What if he had started a fire? Or gotten lost? Our woods aren't huge by any means, but spending the night lost and alone out there, especially with the colder nights now, would not be fun for anyone." I force myself to loosen my grip on the steering wheel. I'm not telling her anything she doesn't already know, and it irks me that she can goad me so easily. "And last, but not least, you didn't answer any of my calls or texts."

"That's because reception stinks in the woods," she cuts in. "I didn't get any notifications until we got back to the bonfire."

"One more reason for you not to have been out there," I shoot back as calmly as I can. "It's not like you didn't know about the poor reception before Friday. You're lucky I haven't taken your phone away, Ruby. Think about it."

She folds her arms tightly around the messenger bag in her lap and says nothing until her school comes into view.

"I did trust you, Rubes," I try again. "I do trust you. That's why I *asked* you if you'd been smoking, too. I trusted you to give me a truthful answer, and I trusted you when you said you hadn't."

She still says nothing, but now she's biting on her lip, and I can see her throat muscles working hard to swallow back her emotions.

"Should I drive around the block again?" I ask when she doesn't respond. "I'm not going to leave it like this and just drop you off."

She releases a dramatic huff of breath. "I'm sorry, okay? I'm just so ticked off at William for being such a stinking pile of poop, and I'm mad at Millie for taking the loser back and bringing him to Bonfire Night so he could ruin it for everyone. And I'm mad at myself for not being able to keep everything from getting out of hand—because I did try my best to do the right thing, you know." Her tone is still cutting, but I can tell she's letting off steam now.

"I know." I want to reach out to her, but I don't. I know she's fragile right now.

"And I'm especially mad that you came out there and dragged us back in like naughty little kids." She kicks the underside of the dash. Not hard, but it makes a satisfying thunk. "I'm not a little kid, and you made me feel like one. I'm as old as you were when you got pregnant with me, when you thought you were old enough to marry my dad. I'm practically an adult, you know?"

I want to tell her that things are different, that times have changed, that I was much more mature than she is now, but of course, none of that is true. She's right on one count; she is practically an adult. And even adults make dumb mistakes. It's how we figure out the whole adulting thing. "I didn't mean to make you feel like a child, Ruby. I was just worried and scared and upset."

"Well, you did, Mom," she huffs. "And in front of Gideon, too. He's important to me, and you made me look like a stupid little kid in front of him."

I don't remind her—again—that had she not been out there in the woods in the first place... It won't help matters. She knows what she did, and she knows why I'm doing what I'm doing. But she's afraid she might have messed things up beyond repair with this guy she really likes, and she's pointing fingers at me because she wants it to be anyone else's fault but her own. I get it. And I can take it. "I'm sorry, Ruby. I could have handled things differently."

She says nothing, so I continue.

"I want to tell you something," I say, lowering my voice like I'm imparting some big secret. "But you didn't hear this from me."

She turns away from me to look out her window, but I don't miss the way her hands still. I can almost see her ears twitching in anticipation.

"At the fire pit Friday night, Gideon apologized again for what happened and said he hoped I'd let him spend more time with you in the future."

Instead of letting her off in the long line of cars near the front entrance, I pull into a parking spot and let the car idle while we finish our conversation. It'll take me longer to get out of the parking lot now that I've lost my place in line, but I don't mind.

"Did he really say that?" she asks, still keeping her gaze averted. But there's a hesitant note of hope in her voice now. "And what did you tell him?"

"Yes, he did. And I told him he was all right in my book." I smile over at her, hoping she sees it from the corner of her eye. "Those were my exact words."

She reaches for the pearl charm hanging from the necklace she's wearing. She slides the bauble back and forth on the delicate gold chain, something she does when she's nervous or deep in thought. Or both. Finally, she turns narrowed eyes on me. "Why didn't you tell me this earlier? Why wait until now?"

"You were hardly speaking to me all weekend, Ruby. I mean, you said more words to Rick and the zombies than you did to me. Besides," I add, although I'm aware my next words might not sit well with her. "I didn't feel like you were remorseful about breaking the rules, and I wasn't going to reward you for your bad behavior."

"Who says I'm remorseful now?"

I want to roll my eyes, but I restrain myself. "No one did. However, the fact that you're talking to me now tells me that you want to work this out. That's the first step. And if you weren't at least a little remorseful about things, none of this would bother you so much. I'm counting on you and all that's good in you to get to the right place in your heart and mind. It may not be today, or even tomorrow, but I'm expecting to have another version of this conversation by Wednesday, at the latest." I pause, then add, "Unless, of course, you want to extend your grounding for another few days."

Ruby doesn't contradict or challenge me, but just sits solemnly with her book bag on her lap and stares out the window.

Please don't cry, I bolster her in my head. *Keep it together until you get home. For your own sake.*

Her eyes glisten suspiciously, but she manages to keep the tears at bay.

"I love you, Rubes. You'd better go, or you'll be late." I stroke her arm with the back of my knuckles and this time, she doesn't pull away.

"Yeah," she mutters, opening her door and sliding out. Right before she closes it behind her, I hear her say, "Bye."

It's a far shot from 'I love you, too,' but I'll take it.

I don't feel like going straight back to the farmhouse, even though I typically take Mondays off from work. It's my personal catchup time—catch up on laundry, paying bills, meal planning and grocery shopping, and whatever else needs my attention to kick off the week right. But Gran was still in bed when Ruby and I left the house, and I don't want to wake her busying around the house before she's ready to get up. She loves her weekend trips with her friends, but it often takes her a day or two to recover from them.

It's also a little too early to have heard from Dani yet. That said, if I don't hear from her in the next hour, I'm going to start calling her.

I'm not really dressed for work in my leggings and sweatshirt, my unruly hair held back with the wide headband I use when I'm doing my makeup or washing my face, but I head for the cemetery, hoping I won't run into Hugo. He officially has the day off, too, as Fair Havens isn't open to the public on Mondays, but the man can't seem to stay away from the place any more than I can.

I am both relieved and disappointed when he's nowhere on the premises after all. "Even Hugo doesn't want to spend any time with me," I mutter, sticking my bottom lip out since no one is around to see me. I thumb a quick text to him. *Happy Monday. You by any chance at FH this afternoon? Ruby needs to fill three hours every afternoon for the next few days. Got any suggestions?*

Hugo isn't big on texting, so I don't wait with bated breath for a response. Sure enough, about ten minutes later, he calls my cell. "Hugo here," he says in that gravelly voice when I answer my phone. Like I don't know it's him. "I'll be there when you get back with Ruby. Had some things to do here to prepare for William coming."

"Hm." It's the best response I can make when it comes to wee wicked Willie right now. I change the subject before I say something I shouldn't. "Right. So Ruby. I can put her to work mopping, dusting, and polishing in the church and schoolhouse, but if there's stuff she can do outdoors, I'm sure she'd prefer it."

"Well, Rusty Jacobson called this morning." Hugo's tone is thick with tenderness. It's one of the things I love about him. He's so stoic and reserved on the outside, yet there always seems to be this wealth of emotion rippling just beneath the surface. I wonder if he ever lets his guard down, if it ever gets to be too much to contain. I think I want to be there when he finally cracks open. I think I want to stand in the path of whatever it is that pours out of him when he finally lets go. "Echo is home on hospice, and Rusty says it's going to be quick."

"Oh no," I murmur, pressing a fist to my chest. Echo and her son, Rusty, came to Fair Havens a few months ago and selected her burial plot, so the news isn't a surprise, but it still hurts my heart anyway.

"Maybe Ruby can help me prep the site so that it'll be ready when it's time. It's pretty overgrown along that section of the trail, so there's a good amount of cleanup and clearing out to do."

"Of course. That will be good for her," I agree. "Prepping a grave is always a little sobering. Might help her put things in perspective."

There's a smile in his words as he says, "I'll be sure and remind her how good she's got it being on the handle end of the shovel."

He will, too. He talks more with Ruby than he does with most people, but his real magic is in the way he can get her to talk to him. Whatever conversations they'll have at Echo's grave will be meaningful. Of that I'm certain.

"Thank you." I hesitate, then say what's niggling at the back of my mind. "Question. If William is working for you after school, does that mean you won't be around in the afternoons for a while? I hadn't thought to ask you how that was going to work with your schedule."

"I'll be around."

"Do you think it's wise to leave William alone at your place?" I am more than skeptical about how that's going to turn out.

"I'm hiring him, Ranae. Not babysitting him."

"Right. Sorry."

"And I'm not leaving him alone at my place, either. He'll be working with me for a couple hours in the evenings three or four times a week."

"Sorry," I repeat, ashamed at my presumptions. I turn toward the woods and gaze in the general direction of the Beckenbauer property. In the dead of winter, when the trees are bare and the sky is clear, I'm certain I can see the glisten of lights coming from their home. It's not quite three miles by road, but less than a mile through the trees as the crow flies, and it's a comfort to know who resides on the backside of our woods. "You're a better man than I am, Hugo."

He soft chuckle thrums through me even over the phone. "I believe that's a good thing, Ms. Niemeyer. You're a better woman than I'll ever be."

"You know what I mean," I shoot back, but I'm grinning as we say our goodbyes, my spirit lifted considerably.

I pull up Echo's file to see if there is anything I need to do to help facilitate my part in the woman's last days. Rusty has asked me to help them prepare her body after she's passed, but I don't need to be there before then. She will have a host of loved ones gathered around her when her time comes, and they are as prepared as they can be to say goodbye to their matriarch. When she visited Fair Havens, Echo did more than just choose her burial plot; she also purchased a beautiful willow casket, brought in a handwoven wool blanket with which to line the casket, and she gave me a letter she'd like me to read to her friends and family during her service. With her blessing, I've already read it myself so I know what to expect, but it won't matter. I'll cry over the woman's wise and tender final words, anyway. Echo made her living as a weaver, but she is an artist in every fiber of her being, and her words are just as beautiful as her Navajo rug designs.

There is a reason the threads of our lives are woven together, and the tighter we cling to each other, the more beautiful the design of our tapestry. We must make the most of each time we cross paths with another soul. Never let misunderstandings turn into misgivings, because they'll inevitably become missed opportunities to love and be loved.

Oh, Dani. I miss my best friend too fiercely to let whatever misunderstanding or misgiving there seems to be between us turn into a missed opportunity. I pick up my phone and shoot off a quick text to her. *Happy Monday! Want some donuts?* Anything can be patched up with donuts.

I let fifteen minutes pass by before I call her. I only get her answering machine. Surprise, surprise.

Perched on the edge of my desk, I stare out the schoolhouse window toward the little family graveyard, until it occurs to me that I am simply waiting for people to make time in their lives for me. "Or waiting for people to make time in their deaths for me," I mutter wryly to myself. I don't mind spending time alone, but I need people in my life. Even more, I need to be needed. And right now, no one seems to need me. No one even wants to be around me.

What is wrong with me?

It's that old wound from all those years ago when Solomon's family turned their backs on me, on *us*, I know. When they wrote us out of their lives without even bothering to meet us. Dismissed, rejected, unloved, unwanted. Ugly words that can still pierce my heart even now. Sarah's untimely email has stirred things up in me that I thought were long dead.

With an ugly grunt, I lurch to my feet. I'm not getting anything done here, sitting around waiting like this. I head back to the house, determined to be as quiet as I can so Gran can sleep in longer.

But when I push open the front door, I find her in the kitchen making a fresh pot of coffee. Granted, she's got some remarkable bedhead, and she's wearing mismatched socks and Opa's navy blue bathrobe, which tells me she probably stumbled out of bed only minutes ago. But she smiles warmly at me, even though she doesn't speak. Like all the Niemeyer women, conversation doesn't come easy until we've downed at least a few sips of the magic brew.

For the next hour, I putter around the house aimlessly, until Gran grabs my chin and tips her head back to look through her reading glasses at me. "Child, you're acting like a caged chicken. I'd offer you a cup of coffee, but I'm not sure that would be such a good idea, not with you being so agitated already. What's gotten into you?"

I hesitate just long enough for her to give me a gimlet eye, then I drop into a chair and tell her what happened with Ruby and her friends.

"And Dani missed her first Bonfire Night, too," Gran says with gentle sympathy. She's joined me at the table and is toying with the edge of the woven place mats that are always laid out at each place on the table.

"And Dani missed her first Bonfire Night," I echo. "Ever. On top of that, she won't answer my phone calls, and even her text replies are vague and noncommittal. I don't know if she's mad at me—if that's all it is, then we can fix that—or if Adam is keeping her from me. Maybe from everyone." My tone is scathing, and I sigh. "I know you think it's a good thing, but—"

Gran holds up a hand to stop me. "Now wait a minute, Nae-nae. I said it was commendable for her to be spending time with her husband. I did not say it was a good thing for him to be keeping her isolated." There's that gimlet eye again.

I shrug. "Well, I don't know which it is, but it's not like her to ignore my calls. It was bad enough she ditched Friday night; if that's all it had been, though, especially because of the ultrasound, I would have forced myself to be okay with it. But this is more than that. There's something going on, and I don't believe her when she says she's busy and tired. That's just excuses." I'm not ready to tell Gran about Sarah McCray's email, but I seriously doubt our little tiff over my refusal to respond to it is the root of this disconnect between us.

"Have you considered just driving over to her home and asking her directly? Instead of second-guessing what's wrong?" Gran's hands are shaking just the tiniest bit as she laces her fingers together on the table in front of her. She really is tired, and I should let her rest.

I nod. "Yes. In fact, she was supposed to call me today after she got into Breathe, but so far, I've heard nothing from her." I reach across the table and rest my fingers on Gran's arm. "I think I'll head over there now, though. Pick up some super fattening negotiation treats on the way. You should get some more rest while the house is quiet, Gran."

"You know, I think that sounds like a great plan." She doesn't even argue about the resting part, and that worries me a little.

"I mean it, Gran. Go back to bed. I'll be back in time to warm up spaghetti for lunch. I made a really good batch last night with lots of leftovers."

I stop at The Bean Machine for a strong cup of coffee for me, a foo-foo herbal tea for Dani, and a box of pastries—a fancy word for donuts. I order a dozen, not just for the two of us, of course, but enough to share with whoever else happens to be at the center this morning.

I don't see Dani's car in the parking lot, but I'm not deterred. With my pastry box in one hand and a drink holder in the other, I use my shoulders to push through the front entrance. From inside, I hear Gail's voice telling me she's coming to help, and a moment later, she pulls the door open for me.

"Um, hi," she says, her voice stilted and anxious.

"Hey, girl." I greet her with a warm smile and hold up the box. "Rough Monday already? I brought the cure."

"Um," she says again, this time a little more drawn out. "A really strange Monday." She tips her head toward the small waiting room just out of sight of the foyer where we're standing. She takes the box I hand her and leans forward to whisper, "I'm freaking out a little. Go see for yourself."

"What on earth?" I have never seen Gail so out of sorts.

She opens her mouth to speak, but no words come out. She just shakes her head and then starts back to her desk, leaving me to trail behind her with my treats.

Breathe's waiting room is set up to look like a homey living room. A chunky couch and complementary love seat with colorful throw cushions, a padded rocking chair with a matching foot stool, and a low teakwood coffee table compile most of the furniture. Built-in shelves on one wall are filled with books, magazines, puzzles and games, along with baskets of toys on the bottom shelves where kids can get to them. Three primary-hued beanbag chairs are grouped together on the black and white checkerboard area rug in front of the shelves.

I step into the main office and glance over at the only other person in the room, a woman sitting on the couch. "Oh! Hey, Dani. You waiting for these?" I tease, holding up the pastry box. No wonder Gail is flustered. Why on earth would Dani be lounging in her own waiting room?

But the woman who looks up at me isn't Dani.

She dresses like Dani in a flowing colorful skirt and a white crocheted top. Her long blonde hair is swept away from her face like Dani wears hers, pulled into a loose messy bun at the back of her head, and she's wearing gladiator sandals on her feet—I'm pretty sure Dani owns a pair just like them—even though it's late October, and it's definitely fall weather outside. Her eyes, that strange blend of green and blue that I've only ever seen in one other person, study me studying her. Then she smiles, and I think my heart is going to stop.

"Hi," she says in Dani's voice, but without the British accent. "Sorry. Not Dani. Jolene." She waves politely; even her hands look like Dani's.

"Hi," I somehow manage to squeeze out. "Right. Sorry. My mistake."

Gail is at my side again. "Here. Let me take those for you." She acts like she's grabbing the sweets box, but she wraps her fingers around my wrist and leads me away. "We can put all of this in the kitchen."

I follow her without resistance, taking another quick glance over my shoulder at the woman on the couch. She's engrossed in the magazine she's holding again, and I have to tear my gaze from her lest I run into a wall or knock something over. "Who—what is going on?" I whisper. I'm not sure I've spoken loud enough for Gail to hear, but she already knows what I'm thinking.

"She's a new patient," Gail tells me, and her voice is almost as shaky as mine. "She's here to see Tracy, thank goodness. Can you imagine what would happen if she somehow ended up with Dani? But Dani should be here any minute now." Gail covers her mouth when a hysterical little giggle slips out. "Oh my gosh,

Ranae. What should we do? How is this possible?" She's rambling, her words spilling out at a fast, nervous clip.

"But who—who is she?" I stammer, setting my box on the kitchen counter. "What's her name?"

"Jolene something. Sanderson, I think, but don't quote me on that. I'm just a little freaked out right now." Her eyes are wide, and I can see her pulse fluttering in the hollow at the base of her neck.

"Um, Dani's supposed to be here, you said? We need to catch her in the parking lot or something," I say. "Prepare her, at least. I mean, I'm pretty freaked out, too, and that's not even my doppelgänger out there." I grab Gail's hands and give her a little shake. "Gail, that woman is Dani's clone."

"I know!" she says in a hushed, but emphatic voice. "And I have to tell you, Ranae, I'm already a little worried about Dani's state of mind, as it is. You should have seen how Adam was acting during the ultrasound on Friday night. It was so strange and awkward, and she looked like she was on the verge of bursting into tears the whole time. This might just be more than she can handle today."

"Okay." I straighten my shoulders and take a deep breath. "Okay," I say again, taking the drink carrier that Gail is still clutching. "I'm going to go sit outside with these and run interference. I have no clue what I'm going to tell her, but I'll think of something. She just can't walk in here without any warning."

But I'm too late. Just as I round the corner from the back hallway, the front door opens and in sweeps Dani. She, too, is dressed in a long, flowing skirt and a pale, ivory sweater. Her hair is held in place at the back of her head with a spider clip, loose tendrils softening the angular features of her face. I panic and jerk to a stop, my eyes darting back and forth between her and Jolene.

Distract her, Niemeyer! My brain is screaming at me to move, take action. *Save Dani!* But I just stand there like a deer in the headlights.

I have a clear view of Dani's face from this angle, and I watch the color leach from it as she stares, wide-eyed at the woman on the sofa who's wearing the exact same expression on her face as she stares back at Dani. Jolene slowly stands, the forgotten magazine sliding to the floor at her feet.

It's like I'm watching one of those mirror pantomimes. Dani reaches up to cover her mouth at the same time Jolene does. Dani's hand slides down the front of her neck to press against her heart, and Jolene's hand follows the same motion, coming to rest over her own heart.

Then my friend's eyes flutter in a strange way, and I finally, *finally* charge across the room toward her. I catch her just as her knees start to give out, and although she weighs far less than I do, there's no way I can support her now that she's gone completely limp. Gail is at my side in an instant and helps me lower Dani to the ground, and then Jolene is there, too, sliding a cushion under her head.

"I—I didn't—" Jolene stutters and stalls, then whispers, "I'm sorry."

"Maybe you'd better sit down." Gail puts a hand on her arm and gestures back toward the sofa.

"No, no." The woman shakes her head. "I'm fine. Really. Should I call 911?"

I shake my head. "Not yet. I think she's okay." Dani's already starting to come around, and I'm ninety-nine percent sure she's not hurt. "Maybe step back a little, though. Give her some space?"

"Sure, of course." Jolene and Gail move toward the seating area a few feet away. Gail's hand still hovers near the other woman's elbow, just in case.

"Hey, Dani." I bend low over my friend and smooth a few strands of hair from her face. "It's Ranae. Can you hear me?"

Her eyes pop open, and she immediately tries pull herself up to sit.

"Whoa!" I twist my arm free of her grip and take her shoulders, gently pressing her back down. "Lie still a minute. Get your bearings. You fainted, Dani. Let's make sure you're okay before you get up."

"I fainted?" I can tell she's still trying to put all the pieces together, and when she turns her head to look toward Gail and Jolene waiting nearby, it all clicks. "What—what is going on?"

"My goodness," Jolene gasps, her hands on her cheeks. "You even sound exactly like me, but... but with an accent?" It comes out more of a question, and I want to set her straight. She's the one with the wrong accent.

"Who are you?" Dani asks, turning onto her side and leaning into her elbow so she can sit up slowly. She's still a little pasty, and I keep a firm grip on her shoulder, just in case. She doesn't take her eyes off Jolene.

"She's here to see Tracy," Gail offers, far too brightly. "A new patient."

"I'm Jolene. Jolene Sanderson. Um, Jolene Winston Sanderson?" Her full name comes out as a question, and she adds an emphasis on *Winston,* as if there might be an explanation for everything in the name. "My friend, Wendy Bubeck, recommended this place to us. She worked with Tracy a few years ago and couldn't stop talking about how wonderful her experience was." Jolene's hands move to curve around the small baby bump under her skirt. "She told me there was a midwife here who looked a whole lot like me, and wow. She wasn't kidding, was she? I mean, I saw your pictures on the website, and it was a little surreal, but also pretty cool, right? I thought it would be fun to meet someone who looked so much like me. Compare stories, and all that." Nervous energy is pouring out of her with every word she babbles.

I watch Dani's face as she maneuvers into a sitting position. She seems to be okay, as far as I can tell; she's not flinching or wincing in pain.

Dani's twin waves a hand back and forth in a frantic flutter. "In real life, though? I mean, this—this—well, it's uncanny, isn't it?"

Dani's twin. *Dani's twin.* The words explode into my consciousness like a Fourth of July firework show. Dani's twin.

This woman is either a freak of nature lookalike—they say everyone has at least one unrelated doppelgänger out there—or she is, indeed, my *adopted* friend's biological, if not identical, twin.

Dani's identical *pregnant* twin.

Suddenly I'm a little lightheaded, too. This is all too bizarre.

"I think—I think I'm going to be sick." Dani turns to me, her eyes glazed with shock. "Trash can," she whispers urgently.

I lurch to my feet, but Gail is quicker; she probably deals with this stuff on a regular basis. A few minutes later, she and I help Dani down the hall to the staff bathroom, leaving Jolene alone in the waiting room.

She assured us she would be fine, although her hands were trembling as she waved us off. "My husband should be here any minute now. He was finishing up a phone call in the car."

It isn't until I'm sitting across from Dani in her office, with her still looking pale and perplexed, that she finally says anything about the woman sitting in the waiting room.

"Jolene Winston," she murmurs contemplatively. "I know that name."

Dani

"Wait. You know her?" If Ranae's eyes get any wider, they might just pop out of her head and roll across the desk. My stomach lurches at the lurid thought.

I take a few long, slow breaths to settle my stomach and calm my nerves. "I don't know her." I flap a hand toward my closed office door. "I've never met that woman in my life. It's her name. I feel like I know it."

"Her name? Who cares what her name is. Dani, you two are like carbon copies of each other. Right down to your toenail polish. Is she—are you twins?"

"Please!" The word comes out sharper than I intend, but I need her to stop talking so I can think. "That name rings a bell. That's all. I feel like I should know it, but I just don't remember from where." I don't acknowledge the part about us being carbon copies. It really was like looking in a mirror out there. I search my memory. A letter, maybe? A legal document? No, that doesn't sound right. Jolene Winston. Jolene Winston. Winston. Where have I seen that name before?

The look on my friend's face reflects my own confounded thoughts.

Muffled voices drift from the front reception, and I eye the door. Ranae, seeing the direction of my gaze, reaches over and cracks it open just a hair so we can hear more of the conversation. I'm not usually one for eavesdropping. I've learned with Adam that sometimes it's best *not* to listen in when I haven't been asked to participate; one might hear something better left unheard. But Ranae has always bolstered the diminutive rebel spirit in me, and besides, she's the one who opened the door. I'm just an innocent bystander, right?

"I feel terrible about all of this. Is she going to be okay?"

I'm listening to *me*, even though that version of me is talking like a Midwesterner. I wait for Gail's response, but she speaks so softly, I don't understand more than a few words.

"... morning sickness... busy... fine."

There's a man out there, too, presumably Jolene's husband. In a pleasant enough voice, he asks, "Is it possible for us to speak with her?"

"I'm not sure. I'd have to check; make sure she's up to it right now." This time, I can hear Gail clearly, and I get the feeling she's speaking louder to give me fair warning.

"I know. And I totally understand if she's not," Jolene responds quickly. "This is all such a shock. And again, I'm so sorry. But... but could you at least ask if she'll see us? Or just me, if she'd rather? Is that okay, babe?"

"Of course, Jo. Of course." The man's deference to his wife—and to me and my preferences—is obvious even from several rooms away. I don't want to think what Adam's response would have been had it been the two of us out there. I'm certain he would have taken it as a public dismissal.

A lump of shame wedges itself against my heart over my disloyal thoughts. We weren't always like this, I remind myself, my husband and I.

After a brief pause, Gail tells them that on second thought, maybe now is not a good time. "It might be best if I give her your contact information. Then she can reach out to you when it's a better time for her."

"Oh, no, Gail," I moan, dropping my head into my hands. "Don't put this on me."

Ranae is poised like an attentive statue in her chair, her head cocked to better listen to the conversation out at the front desk, too. Her silence, however, does nothing to mask her thoughts. *This already is on you, Dani. You're the one hiding in the back office.*

"I really don't want to see that woman again," I say in response to her unspoken challenge. "There isn't going to be a better time. Not today, or next week, or—or maybe not ever."

She finally moves, shifting in her seat so she can lean forward and brace her forearms on my desk. "You don't have to make any decision today, Dani. You get to call the shots. Gail is buying you some time so you can process."

"I don't need to process anything. Even if that woman—" I can't stop calling her that. "Even if she is somehow related to me, I'm not interested in any more upheaval in my life right now. My plate is full to overflowing."

"I know, Dani. Really, I understand how crazy this all is. And the timing, too." Her voice gets softer as mine rises, and I recognize what she is doing. It's one of her Ruby tactics; when her daughter gets riled up, the worst thing Ranae can do is yell back. Instead, she snuffs out the fuse with quiet, gentle words, giving Ruby space to pull herself together without feeling backed into a corner. I wonder if this is something all mothers learn instinctively. I've seen Noralee do the same with Ranae, and my own mum with me over the years, and I can't help wondering if I'll pick up on that same kind of intuitive mothering.

An image of an angry Adam flashes across my mind, and I realize with a touch of disquiet that I already employ the same diffusion tactics with my husband. I can't remember the last time I raised my voice in response to his tirades.

"Maybe..." Ranae begins, sliding a hand across my desk toward me. I don't return the gesture. I already know I don't want to hear what she has to say. "Maybe you should talk to your parents. I mean, you guys have to be twins, Dani. Sisters, at the very least. It's crazy obvious. Talk to them. Ask them what—*if*—they know about her."

"My parents? They were there, Ranae, remember? If I have a twin, they'd know. And therefore, I'd know."

Ranae presses her lips together as if contemplating whether or not she should say what's on her mind. Then in stops and starts, every sentence ending with a question mark, she continues. "But maybe, well, maybe they haven't told you? Everything, I mean? Your birth mom did want things closed after the adoption was final, right?" Her voice trails off.

I cross my arms and sit stiffly in my chair. I don't like what she's suggesting, that my parents have kept a secret of this enormity from me. My stomach isn't roiling anymore, but I feel flushed and prickly, the adrenaline still coursing through my system. I'm desperately curious about that woman out there. Who is she? Why does she look like me? *Exactly* like me. How is it possible that we're not twins? Because we can't be... can we? And if she is, if we are, then how do I not know about her?

The questions fly round and round in my head like a swarm of angry bees, and try as I might, I can't seem to pull one out of the air to put into words. I shake my head slowly. "No. They wouldn't keep something like that from me," I finally manage to get out. "No."

Ranae sighs softly, her eyes never leaving my face. "Even so, you can't just ignore her and hope she'll go away. You've seen her with your own eyes. You have a sister. A *twin* sister, by the looks of it. This should be good news, Dani. Great news.

And... well, you can't just pretend she doesn't exist," she repeats. "Because she does."

And those are the words I need to find my backbone. "I don't have to pretend she doesn't exist," I tell her, lifting my chin a little higher. "She can exist all she wants. Just not in my life."

"Oh, Dani." There is a boat load of censure in those two short words.

"Don't you dare judge me right now." I uncross one arm to shake my finger at her, my jaw muscles tight as I speak. "I am—" I pause, searching for the right word, but the only one that comes to me seems pithy and impotent. I use it anyway. "I am overwhelmed by all that has been heaped on my plate over the last several months." I lower my hand to my belly, and without consciously doing so, I cover my heart with my other one. "I don't have it in me to face any more surprises right now. Good, bad, or otherwise."

Ranae nods slowly, but I can tell she still wants to argue. "I agree. I really do. You have a lot going on. But I also know you, Dani. This is going to eat you up until you face it. Face her."

I narrow my eyes at her. "Wait a minute. Wait just a wee minute, deary. Aren't you the pot calling the kettle black here? What about you and your Sarah McCray? It's okay for you to ignore her, to pretend she doesn't exist, but it's not okay for me to put off that woman out there?"

"That's not the same thing, Dani. And we're not talking about me. We're talking about you," she says in that calm, maternal tone that suddenly sounds like metal on metal to me. "I just think you should talk to your parents before you make any decisions about Jolene."

"Don't talk down to me, Ranae Niemeyer. I am not your daughter." I can hear my voice getting louder; I feel like the seams of my self-control are coming apart, and all my innards are threatening to spill out of me. "You don't get to sit there all sanctimonious and tell me what I can and can't do. Not while you're wallowing in the same mud pit."

Ranae holds up both hands in surrender. "Okay. Message received." She's still speaking low and soft, but her wide eyes tell me she's as surprised as I am by my outburst.

I can't seem to rein in the volcano of emotions roiling inside me, and even though I can see she wants to end this volatile conversation, there are more words spilling out of my mouth before I can catch them. "You know, all you ever do is tell me what I should and shouldn't do." I sound like a raving lunatic, and now I'm waving my hands around in the air so that I look like one, too. "You should do this. You shouldn't do that. You should. You shouldn't!" I smack a hand flat down on the surface of my desk. "Who died and made you Queen of Everything?"

Her eyebrows have disappeared up under her fringe as she stares at me aghast, and then I see the telltale wobble of her chin.

"No, no, no. You don't get to cry right now," I tell her, standing up and shoving my chair back too hard. It crashes against the bookshelves behind me and bounces back, hitting me behind my knees, and it's all I can do to keep from collapsing back into it. My head spins a little, and I pray I'm not going to topple again. "This is not about you. This is about me. That woman, that *stranger* out there—"

Ranae cuts in, her voice like razor wire. "Her name is Jolene, and she is obviously not a stranger, no matter how loudly you proclaim it. She's your mirror image." Her shock and hurt over my attack have turned to anger and wounded pride, and she stands, too.

I lean forward, my palms slick where they're pressed against the smooth glass top of my desk. "That woman," I say again, enunciating each syllable, "does not get to just show up here and throw a hand grenade into the middle of my life. And you." I jab a finger at her, almost poking her in the forehead. "You don't have the right to tell me what I should or shouldn't do. About her, about my babies, or about my husband."

"You're wrong, Dani," Ranae somehow remains calm, even while I'm screeching like a banshee. "In all of this. I love you and so I do have the right to speak when I am worried about you. I may not always choose the right words, but you know me. You *know* me." She thumps her chest with her closed fist. "You know I only want the best for you. I hate seeing you like this."

"Like what? You hate seeing me stand up for myself? Or you hate seeing me tell you you're wrong about something?"

Ranae picks up her coffee cup and her purse and starts toward the door.

"And now you're going to walk out in the middle of this argument. Can't handle a little conflict?" Lord, I sound like Adam. Spiteful. Hateful, Baiting, goading.

"This isn't an argument, Dani. This is an attack." Her next words echo my own thoughts so exactly that my knees go weak. "You sound just like your husband."

She closes the door softly behind her, and suddenly, I'm shaking like a leaf. I reach behind me for the arm of my chair, pulling it close so I don't end up on the floor if my legs give out.

I want to run after Ranae, to stop her, but I can't. It would mean coming face to face with that—with Jolene Winston Sanderson, and there's no way I can do that right now. I shudder violently, then sink into my seat, my face in my hands. What have I done? What do I do now?

There's a hesitant knock on my door, but I ignore it. If it was Ranae, she wouldn't be knocking. Which means it's Gail or maybe one of the other midwives, and I'm in no condition to speak to any of them. Especially if it's Gail asking if I'll meet with the Sandersons.

I don't respond, hoping whoever it is will just go away. Perhaps I'll hide in my office all day. I have several water bottles stashed under my desk, the hot tea Ranae just brought, and if I'm not mistaken, a box of pastries, too. "A loo," I mutter in disgust. "I can't go all day without a bathroom." Who am I kidding? I can't go more than an hour without one.

"What am I going to do?" I moan, flopping back in my chair and closing my eyes against the recessed lighting overhead.

"Dani?" The door starts to open, and I quickly straighten and set my features into what I hope is a neutral, if not exactly pleasant, expression. Gail doesn't come in, but peers around the door at me. "Three things," she says, lifting three fingers next to her head. "One, Ranae told Jolene and her husband that you were not available to meet with them. Two, Tracy just got here, and they're in with her now, so if you want to duck out, now is your chance. And three, I want to make sure you're okay. Ranae didn't look so good."

Gail doesn't pull any punches. It's something I usually appreciate about her. But right now, her words rankle me. Even after me telling her to stop trying to orchestrate my life, Ranae is still acting on my behalf. And Gail, *my* assistant, not Ranae's, allowed her to do so.

"And here are my three things. One," I hold up my index finger, and before I give myself a moment to consider the consequences of my words, I say, "It's not Ranae's place to tell them anything. That's your job. It's what I pay you for. This is my territory. They're the ones who don't belong here, and I'm not ducking out like I've got something to hide." I hold up another finger. "Two, Tracy should refuse to see them. It's a conflict of interest, as far as I'm concerned, so you can be sure I'll be speaking with her as soon as they're gone." I force myself not to cringe at the toxic vitriol pouring out of me.

Gail's eyebrows shoot up. I've gone way too far. Once again, I sound like I'm channeling Adam. Is this how he feels all the time? Out of control and angry, defensive about everything anyone says? At least I have the excuse, weak as it is in light of the havoc my emotional vomit is wreaking, of my hormones being all out of whack. What's his excuse?

And now I'm angry at Adam, too.

"And three," I plow forward like an out-of-control Omnibus, taking out everything in its path in wide, sweeping arcs. "I'm fine. Couldn't be better."

"Hmm." Gail steps into my office, pulling the door nearly closed behind her. She eyes me with the same steady expression she wears when one of my laboring mothers insists that she can no longer do the whole birthing thing. "You know, I think you might want to reconsider sticking around, boss." Her words, although casual in content, are decidedly serious, and her use of my title is clearly not meant as a form of respect. "You don't have any visits scheduled here today."

I glare at her, but Gail just cocks her head and smiles back at me. She is one tough lassie, Ranae's Gran would say of her.

I feel like an angry child, and I know I'm behaving terribly. There's something in me that feels like it's waking up, stretching against its confines, pushing me from the inside out, and I can't bring myself to relinquish my self-righteous indignation. "Fine." I stand too quickly, but cling to the edge of my desk until the darkness at the edge of my vision fades, and the room stops its seasick wobble. Then I begin to gather my things. As I circle the desk, I snatch up the box of pastries. "I'm taking these with me.

Gail opens my door for me and holds it wide. She is still smiling. "I'm sure that's what Ranae would want."

I narrow my eyes at her. Is that sarcasm? Or is she pulling some kind of reverse psychology tactic on me? "Oh, really?" I feel like I'm watching myself as I turn and drop the box and my full cup of hot, delicious herbal tea—and I so wanted that tea!—into the trash bin beside my desk, before I stalk out into the hall and head for the front door.

Outside on the sidewalk, I glance over to where I'd seen Ranae's car parked earlier. Of course she's already gone, but the empty spot makes me a little queasy. I've made a right mess of everything and it's not even noon. My Forester, parked at the back of the lot with the other employee cars, seems miles away, and I hesitate before stepping off the curb, wondering if my shaky legs will carry me that far. I move a few feet away from the front door so Gail can't see me, and lean a shoulder against the solid brick wall for support.

I pull my phone from my purse and stare at the screen. I feel like I need to call someone, to tell someone what's just happened. But who? Ranae? Ha! She may never speak to me again.

Adam? I release a harsh scoffing sound. I'm having a hard enough time trying to handle my own reaction to all of this. There's absolutely no way I can handle his, too.

Mum and Dad.

Of course! What am I thinking? My mother and father. They'll know what to do.

They'll know...

My mother and father. Who were there when I was born.

If that woman sitting in Tracy's office is my twin... then... they were there when she was born.

The world as I know it begins to tremble beneath me.

Lies. Secrets and lies. My parents have been lying to me my whole life.

The blackness at the edges of my vision is there again. "You will not pass out," I grind out between clenched teeth. There's a city bench under the shade of a tree in the parkway just down the sidewalk, and I manage to make it there, thankful beyond measure for whatever person had the foresight to have it installed outside our birthing center. Leaning forward with my head down—there's no way I'm going to put it between my knees lest I topple over out here all alone—and take several slow, controlled breaths until I feel steadier.

A few minutes later, I manage to stumble to my car and climb in, pulling the door closed behind me. I lean my head back and close my eyes, relishing the cocoon-like stillness around me. Finally, I pick up my phone and start to dial my mother's number, but it occurs to me that I won't be able to speak if she answers. I can hardly breathe, let alone get out a coherent accusation or two.

I thumb in a text instead. *Do you by any chance know someone by the name of Jolene Winston Sanderson?*

No, that's too nice. I delete everything, then tap out a different question. *Do I have a twin sister?*

I send it before I can chicken out, then I sit there in the stillness of my car and stare at my screen, willing it to light up with an answer.

There is none, but then, she's probably with a patient. About ten minutes later, unable to stand waiting another second, I pull up Dad's number and type in the same question. But before I can send it, Mum responds.

Where are you, Danielle?

I stare at her non-answer, desperate for the letters to rearrange themselves into different words.

Betrayal. Rage like I've never felt before. Grief. Oh, my Lord, the grief that wells up inside me is an eruption I am not equipped to handle. A cry that I almost don't recognize as my own pours out of me, rising higher and louder as years and *years* of pent-up longing consume me. That hollow place in my heart, that inexplicable need to share myself with someone who knows me as well as I know myself. The countless nights I've dreamed of reaching out toward someone who is reaching back to me... only to awaken alone in my bed, or worse, with my husband's rigid back to me.

I don't know how long I sit, wailing into the suffocating bubble of my car. When my voice finally becomes raspy and weak, I find that I am spent, but not satiated. I feel faded and somehow diminished, as though the tears have washed out all the color in my life. I know I need to speak to my parents, to get the real story they've kept from me all these years. But I also know there is a distinct possibility that when I stand before them and open my mouth, my words will once more meld together into that terrible, keening cry of despair.

Having ignored the multiple texts and calls from both Mum and Dad, I shove my phone into the inner pocket of my purse, then root around in the console compartment for my travel pack of tissue. I blow my nose, wipe away the worst of my makeup smears, and start my car. I have nowhere to go but home. Home to my empty house, alone.

A sharp jab pushes up against my rib cage, and I grunt softly, pressing against the spot with the flat of my hand. I am amazed at how much movement I feel from these babies inside me, now that I'm into the beginning of my second trimester. I know it's because there are two of them bopping around in there, taking up more of the limited space than one baby would, and the secret words of my heart come to me again. *You don't ever have to be alone again.*

I am not alone, either. Not while I have these two precious gifts whom I have been entrusted with.

"Did I scare you, wee ones?" I smooth my fingers over the curve of my belly, marveling anew at how it seems to grow measurably every single day. "I'm sorry I'm such a mess. I'm so sorry," I murmur softly. "I love you both already. So much."

I sigh loud and long, expelling my breath in a woeful gush of self-pity. If I sit here much longer, I may end up seeing Jolene and her husband after all. First visits are unpredictable. If a pregnant mama has educated herself in what to expect from her midwife and doula, and if she is comfortable with her body and what is going on in her pregnancy, then those first meetings between us and our patients can be relatively short. I secretly hope Jolene knows nothing, not just because her ignorance will give me more time to get out of the parking lot, but because it would set us apart from each other in some way. *See? We're not exactly the same after all,* I could say. It's a childish thought, I know, but it's there, nonetheless.

When I pull into our driveway, I'm glad to see Adam's space in the garage is empty. He's not supposed to be home today, but lately things have been so unpredictable with him that it would be par for the course, especially with the way this day has gone so far. I stumble inside and drop my purse and keys on the kitchen counter, but I leave my work satchel out in the car. I already know I won't be getting anything done this morning. I need to calm down; in spite of the cortisol and prolactin the body releases with emotional tears, my heart rate is still racing, and I'm sure my blood pressure has spiked, at least temporarily. My untempered reaction can't have been good for me or my babies, and although I know my weeping and wailing hasn't caused my dehydration, the fact that I am dreadfully parched tells me I am not taking good care of my body. "You have one job to do right now, Dani," I tell myself sternly. "And that's to keep this incubator in top working order."

My thoughts keep spinning relentlessly so that I am unable to focus on any one thing for very long. I don't want to think about how I unleashed my fury on Renae, nor do I want to dredge up the image of her face as she sat there, speechless, under my assault. Her every thought is written clearly in her expressive features, her wide, ocean-deep eyes, and if I think about the way she looked at me, I will come apart again.

I don't want to think about how rude I was to Gail, my tried-and-true sidekick. She won't quit on me, of that I'm certain, but I don't deserve her. How on earth can I make this day up to her?

And I certainly don't want to contemplate what Jolene and her husband might be saying to Tracy at this moment. Are they asking about me? Telling my business partner about how unhinged I am? I force myself to stop circling that Pandora's Box for now.

Nor can I let myself dwell on the knowledge of what my parents have done, because surely, they have, indeed, lied to me all these years. Either they were there, they delivered both of us baby girls into this world, then participated in separating us from each other, and then went on to lie about Jolene's existence, even if only by omission... or they weren't there, and they made up all those precious stories of my beginning.

I can't bear for either option to be true, and yet I know it's one or the other.

Adam. My husband. What should I tell him about all of this? He'll use this against my parents somehow; I know he will.

Why do you have to tell him anything? The voice is quiet, almost a whisper, but I recognize it as my own. *Can you even trust him enough to tell him?*

Before I make the conscious decision to do so, I am already planning my strategy for pretending there's nothing wrong when he gets home. I will cook something that requires my attention up until the very last moment, perhaps stir-fry and beef sate, a meal that is best eaten hot, and one that he loves. Then I can truthfully claim fatigue and head for an early bedtime. It's something that has come in handy lately, this unending craving for sleep.

If I weren't still in the first half of a high-risk pregnancy, I'd go for a short run. It's not something I do regularly, but sometimes the rhythmic movement and the tap-tap of soft rubber soles eating up the asphalt is as calming as a hypnotist's pendulum. But I have been warned off any kind of high impact exercise for now, so I pull out my yoga mat instead. I know it will take me much longer to quiet my spirit than a two-mile jog, but it's not like I have anywhere else I need to be right now.

I also know I will not be able to settle down if I'm allowed to sit inside my head immersed in own tumultuous life story, so I pull up my library app and search for a Kristan Higgin's audiobook to listen to. Her writing makes me happy, and she always has the best narrators.

An hour later, I step out of the shower and pull on a pair of high-waisted leggings and a cropped charcoal cashmere jumper, one I absolutely adore. It has a deep turtleneck that cups my jaw and keeps my long neck warm, and the pattern down the front is classic Irish cable knit. There's a lovely autumn nip in the air, which means I get to wear bulky, soft clothes that smooth out my hard lines and sharp angles. The sweater will soon be too short to cover my baby bump, so I'm glad I can still wear it a few more times before I have to put it away until next year. I slip on a pair of fluffy socks and pad into the kitchen to make a pot of chai tea, heavy on the ginger, then I'm going to crawl into bed and fall asleep listening to my audiobook. It's a story I already know will have a happy ending, and I could use a happy ending right about now. I am exhausted from the morning's roller coaster ride of emotions, and even though I'm feeling much calmer than I was when I first got home, I'm not yet ready to think about what I'm going to do next.

"Hide, that's what I'm going to do right now. Maybe I'll stay in bed all day, and when Adam gets home, I can just pretend I'm still asleep—"

My phone rings, startling me so that I almost drop the teakettle. I haven't checked the thing for calls since I barreled inside. The clock on the microwave tells me it's not quite noon. I'm sure it's my mother still trying to reach me. A flush of emotion makes my cheeks warm; she must be frantic with worry. Do I want to speak with her right now? Before I can talk myself out of it, I root around in my purse for my phone and answer it.

"Hey, baby."

For a moment, the unexpected male voice confuses me, and I don't immediately respond.

"Dani? It's me. Adam."

"Oh," I say, still feeling flustered. "Adam. Right. Hi."

He chuckles, but it's not a very nice sound. "Were you expecting some other man?"

"No, no. Of course not. I—I thought you were my mum," I say in all honesty.

"Your mum?" he mimics, and I cringe. When he pokes fun at my accent, it always sounds more like he's mocking me. "What is she calling for?" He suddenly sounds quite serious. "Is everything okay with you? The babies?"

"Yes, yes, the babies are fine." I quickly reassure him, softening at his concern. "And I'm all right, too. Just tired after the eventful last few days. It was a nice weekend, though, wasn't it?" I ask it without really thinking, but the moment the words are out of my mouth, I know I'll regret them.

"It sure was," Adam responds, his voice slowing to a raspy hum. "Do I know how to show my lady a good time, or what?"

I want to say, "Or what," but I press my lips together so that the words don't escape. The thing is, Adam does know my body well, and with the increased hormones coursing through my system, my appetite in bed is noticeably increased, and my husband is rather appreciative. We did, indeed, have a nice weekend compared to most other weekends, but I still spent much of the last three days walking around on pins and needles, always on high alert to what Adam would or wouldn't do or say.

In saying anything in the first place, I only meant to take the edge off me telling him I'm tired. I seem to claim fatigue all the time these days, and Adam has taken to rolling his eyes whenever I do. So I only say, "Yes," and leave it at that. It's not a lie. He does know how. He just doesn't actually put that knowledge into practice much these days.

"So what's wrong with you, then?" he asks after a moment's hesitation. "Why are you calling your mom?"

I scramble for a vague answer, but all I manage to get out is, "We are trying to find a time to get together. You know, for coffee, or lunch or something."

"What about tonight?"

"Tonight?" For a moment, I think he's suggesting we invite my parents over for dinner. I pull open the refrigerator door to see if I have the veg that I need to make enough stir-fry for four instead of two before I realize what I'm doing and stop myself. They are not coming over here this evening. Not to have the talk we need to have, anyway. "I don't think I have enough chicken," I quickly tell him.

"I meant why don't you go over there?" he says. "Offer to grab takeout on the way. My treat."

Ah. I get it now. "You're not coming home for dinner?" I ask, my voice going flat.

There's that slight hesitation again, and I want to throw my phone across the room. Right at my favorite framed picture of Adam on the mantle. These violent urges are so foreign to me, yet I want to give in to them more than anything in the world right now.

"I need to stay for a meeting, Dani. I won't be late, I promise. I can probably make it home by eight. I mean, I'll really try. Why don't you go do something with your mom?" When he says mom instead of mum in his fake accent, I know he's working some kind of angle. And then I know what it is. He's suggesting my mother because he doesn't want me spending the evening at Ranae's.

"I don't know," I say, keeping my voice as nonchalant as possible. "I was thinking about going out for a cup of tea with Ranae. I told her we'd catch up this week, remember?" I am baiting him, full stop. I have no intention of spending a moment with Ranae, not until I get a few things sorted on my own first. I know I was wrong in the way I treated her today, lashing out at her the way I did. But I was right about the fact that she is always, *always* telling me what I should or shouldn't do, and honestly, as awful as I feel about hurting her, it also felt kind of liberating to put it out there. I need to clear my head a little, sort through these conflicting emotions so that I'm in the right frame of mind when we talk.

I'll even apologize first. I always do.

"Ranae?" Sure enough, his tone tightens noticeably. "Do you have to see her tonight? That means you won't be home when I get there, right?" He's whining. Like a little boy.

"No, Adam, I don't have to see her tonight," I say, stressing the words *have to* the way he does. "But it sounds like it will work out perfectly since you won't be around anyway."

"But I was going to cut things short so I could be home with you," he tells me. "I said I'd be home by eight."

"I can be home by eight, too," I say, almost flippantly. I'm not going anywhere tonight, but he doesn't need to know that.

"What about your mom, though?" he tries again. "Don't you need to get together with her anyway?"

"Actually, I do, but I'm waiting to hear back from her because we're trying to get together this afternoon for tea, and I need to know whether I should go to the hospital or their house," I explain, realizing as I say so that it's exactly what I want to do. "In fact, I need to get off the phone so I can get ready, Adam." There is a tense silence on the other end of the line, and I can't seem to help but poke at it with a proverbial stick. "Is that why you were calling me? To tell me you aren't going to be here for dinner again?"

"Yes," he grumbles. "But honestly, I don't know why I bothered. You clearly already had plans for the evening. Without me." He makes a sharp scoffing sound into the phone, and I hold the speaker away from my ear. "Glad I could be so accommodating," he adds.

"Well, I appreciate the phone call, anyway." I'm not going to rise to the bait and argue with him. "I'd better get going."

"Okay then," he says, and now he's sounding flippant. "I'll see you sometime tonight."

"At eight, right?" I ask, casual as can be. "We'll both be back by eight?"

"I don't know." I can practically see him shrug noncommittally. "I suppose there's no reason for me to rush back, now."

"So," I prod, knowing I shouldn't. "Does that mean there's no reason for me to rush back, either?"

Why does this feel so exhilarating right now? I'm playing Adam's game, and it feels like I'm besting him at it.

"Of course not. I mean, of course there is." He huffs loudly. "You know what I mean."

I know exactly what he means. I've gotten rather skilled at reading between his lines. He's definitely not going to be home by eight, and I've just given him the out he was hoping for, but at a price he's not so thrilled about paying. "Look, Adam. Why don't you *not* cut things short tonight? We spent all weekend together. You shouldn't feel guilty for wanting to spend some time hanging out with your buddies." And with those words, I've just backed him into a corner, and I am practically buzzing with glee. If he turns down my offer, then he hands me the right to be upset when he doesn't make it home by eight—and I already know that won't happen, regardless. If he accepts my offer to let him off the hook, then he has no reasonable excuse to insist that I don't spend the evening with a buddy of my own.

And the best part of it all? I get the house to myself for the next—I glance at the clock again—eight or more hours.

"Maybe I'll do that," he mutters, and I don't ask him to clarify which of the "thats" he'll do.

"Sounds good. We'll see you whenever you get home, Adam," I say inclusively, patting my little baby bump. My voice is full of cheer, but I don't care if Adam can tell it's false or not. "Have a nice evening with your friends. And drive safely."

The other end of the line is quiet for so long, I think he might have hung up. Then he says, "Okay. Love ya. See you later."

It's not until I've hung up that it occurs to me that he didn't say he loved our babies. It's petty, I know, but I have the oddest notion that he forgot they existed after that initial moment of concern at the beginning of our conversation.

And "Love ya?" When did he start tossing that one out? Not "I love you," or even "Love *you*." It was little more than a sign-off.

The bigger question that bears asking is why am I not more bothered by the whole conversation we just had? I'm not falling apart over what ordinarily might feel like his desertion or rejection. In fact, I'm a bit giddy over his pending absence, already planning what I'm going to make for dinner—and dessert—and what shows I'm going to watch since I'll have control of the TV remote.

There are three texts from my mother, a missed call from my father, and a text from Gail. Nothing from Ranae, although I'm not exactly surprised. I wouldn't have texted me, either, if I were her. I tap on Gail's message. I'm pretty sure I already know what it will say, but just in case it's about a patient, I start with hers.

Just checking in, making sure you're okay. You're a good boss who's having a bad day. I love you, Dani. Let me know how I can help.

Even Gail says "I love you" properly.

I key back that I'm fine and offer her a sincere apology for being so rude. *Did you rescue Ranae's pastries from my waste bin?*

You know it, girlie! And they were bomb delicious. Tracy and I ate them while we gossiped about you. She most likely isn't kidding.

I'm glad. They smelled amazing, I'm not too proud to admit.

Come in tomorrow and we'll talk. I have a patient on hold right now. Gotta go.

I promise her I will, then listen to Dad's brief worried message. "Danielle, please answer your mother's texts or calls. We're very concerned and we want to speak with you as soon as possible. I love you, sweetheart. If you know nothing else, know that."

I refuse to cry at the rawness of his tone. I squeeze the bridge of my nose with the thumb and finger of my free hand. Mum's texts say little more, just that she's worried about me, wants to know where I am, would I meet them for lunch somewhere, and then finally, asking me to meet them whenever and wherever I want. *We must talk,* she adds at the end of her last text. I take a deep breath, blow it out through pursed lips, then key in my response.

I'll be at your house in one hour.

That will give me enough time to figure out what I'm going to say to them, and them enough time to get out of any obligations they might have. I don't allow myself to feel guilty about disrupting their workdays. I selfishly cling to the claim that my workday disruption far outweighs theirs, and they can just deal with it.

I head to my room to change, then decide that my sweater is just fine. I trade my thin leggings out for black stretch jeans that used to be big on me and now are so snug, I'll not be able to wear them much longer, either. Then I tug on a pair of lace-up ankle boots over my thick socks, and I slick my hair back into a severe knot at the back of my neck. I am determined to be taken seriously today; none of my flamboyant colors or jingly-jangly jewelry. I apply only a quick swipe of mascara and tuck a tube of clear lip gloss in my back pocket. I'll apply it after I figure out something to eat that won't make my stomach even more upset than it already is. Toast and chicken noodle soup sounds like a winning combination at the moment.

They are already there when I arrive at my parents' home. Dad greets me at the door and for the first time, I see him as something other than steadfast, dependable, and unwavering in his sense of purpose. He's no longer the biggest and strongest man in the world; isn't a girl's father supposed to be just that? Now he seems fallible, ashamed, and somehow shrunken by remorse.

"Hello, Danielle," he says, patting my shoulder when I pull away from the side hug he offers. "Come in, please." He sounds so tragic, and when I finally meet his gaze, I am moved against my will by the misery I see there. I shuffle past him quickly, lest I give in to the weak part of me that wants to assure him everything is going to be okay. Because I'm not so sure it is.

The heady, sun-sweet floral aroma of jade Oolong tea fills my nostrils; Mum is brewing the good stuff. I stop short at the sight of her when I come around the corner into the kitchen. When did she grow old? Her shoulders are curved forward, more bony than slender, the ridges of her scapulas distinct under the thin blouse and cardigan set she's wearing. I wonder if she's lost weight recently. Her eyes, like my father's, are also dark pools of suffering, and when she comes forward to greet me, I am shocked by how pale she is. Her skin is almost transparent today, and although her eyes are dry at the moment, they're swollen and red. She's been crying, and not just a few quick tears. I cannot pretend that my stoic mother and father aren't nearly as distraught as I am.

Have my parents both changed so much since the last time I saw them? I was just here in this kitchen a week ago as we talked about the surprise of discovering twins during my ultrasound, and I didn't notice anything remiss then. The memory of that conversation now turns my stomach.

Lies. Secrets. So many secrets for so many years. I lift my chin and square my shoulders, sucking in a quick rush of air through my nose. It ends here. I am so tired of secrets.

We settle warily around my parents' small dining table, the teapot, a corpulent referee squatting on a trivet in the middle of the smooth surface, each of us with our cups clasped like shields—or weapons—in front of us.

"I'm tired of secrets," I say, not waiting for them to begin first. I rally my anger and allow a chill to seep into my next words. "Especially the secrets that are really just lies."

"Oh, Danielle," my mother murmurs, her voice breaking in a way that pierces my heart.

"I want answers," I say, soldiering on. "And I want the truth. All of it."

She nods quickly. "Of course you do. We owe you nothing less." She turns a pleading look toward my father.

He clears his throat and begins, Mum filling in details she feels are important.

Yes, there were twin girls born that day to a young woman named Jennilyn Winston. No wonder that name seems so familiar to me. I *have* seen it before. Not Jolene Winston, but Jennilyn Winston. There have been a few letters to my parents from her over the years, explained away as correspondence from an old friend from before I was born.

"We had every intention to adopt both of you girls, our babies, our daughters. It had been our plan all along. We'd never considered any other option. But Jennilyn had a change of heart just days before she went into labor." My father's voice is steady in the telling, but he is bouncing his right heel up and down rapidly, the way he does sometimes when sorting out a dilemma, and I can feel the table jiggling rhythmically. "She'd thought things through thoroughly, had even spoken to an attorney of her own, and when the time came, she told us we could be there for the birth of the first baby only—" He makes a sound a bit like a wounded animal, but straightens his shoulders and opens his mouth to continue.

"Me," I interject, the single word coming out like a fresh wound.

"Yes, sweetheart," Dad says, nodding solemnly. "We were there to welcome you into the world. Into our world. But then we were ushered out of the room and—" His voice breaks, and he clears his throat abruptly, making my mother flinch. "We never got to meet her. We didn't get to say goodbye, either." There are tears shimmering in his eyes, and I want to reach across the table to him, but I can't seem to break free of the need to rage at someone, anyone, and it just so happens that my parents are the ones in front of me.

My mother must sense what is going on inside of me. "There was nothing we could do, darling. Believe me, we tried, but the law was on her side. She wasn't a bad person, just a young woman, all alone in the world with no one to help her, who wasn't ready to be a single mum of twins. She had the right to keep you both, and we were so afraid she would take you from us, as well," she says, every word trembling precariously.

"Even though she requested we cut off all contact, through our attorney, we were able to help set Jennilyn and your sister up in an apartment of their own. We paid her rent for a whole year so she could get her feet under her."

"We wanted to pay for a nanny, too," Mum adds. "But Jennilyn turned us down. She believed we meant to plant a spy, someone who would feed us information about her mothering skills, or lack thereof. She was certain we would do anything to take the baby from her."

"And we would have," Dad declares harshly. "Had we found or heard anything even remotely questionable, we would have taken her to court and fought tooth and nail to get your sister back."

Mum places her hand on his arm. The table stills for a few moments, and I watch Dad pull himself together as my mother picks up the tale. "When we were certain that we'd done everything we could for them, we tried to accept the tragedy and move forward, but not more than two months later, we received the first letter from Jennilyn telling us that she'd made a mistake, that she wanted to talk to us. We thought she meant she was ready to let us adopt your sister. Elated, we had our attorney reach out to her, only to find out that she wanted you, too."

"Or so that's what she said at first," Dad interjects. "It soon became evident that what she really wanted was more money from us."

"It broke our hearts all over again." Mum's voice is little more than a whisper. "Our attorney recommended we cut off all communication with her, and it was at that time that I received the job offer for the position at Queen Charlotte's and

Chelsea in London. It seemed providential in every way. Moving took us out of the dreadful mess we'd become entangled in with Jennilyn, and London gave us a place to begin again. Nothing would ever be the same, of course."

Once again, my father picks up the story. It's like listening to a string duet, the instruments taking it in turns to carry the melody, weaving in and out of each other's way, yet never cutting each other off. "We couldn't stay here, knowing our baby girl was so close, and yet completely beyond our reach. Knowing Jennilyn would try again and again to make us pay for what we could not have."

"Our grief over the loss of your sister was nearly unbearable, darling," my mother says. "We saw it in you, too. You'd reach an arm out in your sleep, your tiny hand opening and closing like you were grasping for something—or someone—that wasn't there. As soon as you learned to speak, you carried on incessantly, whether there was anyone to talk to or not."

One side of my father's mouth curves up in a sad smile. "We soon realized that as far as you were concerned, there was always someone to talk to. You even named her, do you remember?"

"Elle," I say, my pulse racing. "I was Dani, she was Elle, and together, we were Danielle. Two parts of a whole."

"It's why we've always called you Danielle," my mother says. "You have always been whole to us."

I shake my head slowly. "Saying so doesn't make it so, Mum. I've never been whole, not truly, have I? You both knew it and never told me. I have lived all these years knowing—" I thump my chest with a closed fist. "Knowing in here that something was missing. I thought…" I hesitate and chew on my bottom lip, dredging up all my old feelings that now make sense. "I just wanted a sibling. I thought that if there was another child, a sister or a brother, that would be enough. I would have been content with that, I think."

"We tried," my mother begins, and my father covers her hand with his.

"I know," I say, shaking my head again. "You didn't choose to not have another child. But you did choose to not tell me about the other child you already had."

After a stream of sentences practically falling over each other, almost like they've been begging to be let out for decades, the room is suddenly, almost abruptly, silent.

I am surprised at how simple their explanation is. Shocked at how few words are needed to give me the truth I have demanded from them. In less than ten minutes, the story of my life as I know it has irrevocably changed. In the amount of time it takes to steep a pot of tea, my world has been turned upside down, shaken hard, until all the details of who I thought I was have spilled out in one big mess.

I wonder who is going to be responsible for cleaning it up.

My mother looks like she's caving in on herself across from me in her straight-backed chair. My father's expression is bereft, one hand laid on the table near Mum, not touching her, but there in case she needs something to cling to. He sees me looking at it and leans forward, reaching toward me with his other hand.

I cross my arms and press my stiff spine against the back of my own chair. This man whom I thought could fix anything, no longer has the power to do so. It seems that I, and I alone, am going to be in charge of putting my life back together.

"We thought—we thought it was best," my mother whispers. It's a statement, but I see the doubt in her eyes, even though she's looking at my father, not at me. I see it in his, too, the uncertainty, even though he nods in agreement.

"It was such a terrible situation, sweetheart," Dad says, nodding at me, like he's hoping I'll agree with him. "We were heartbroken, and in our grief, we made what we felt was the best decision for everyone involved."

"Except for me," I counter. "And my twin." That woman—Jolene—and I are suddenly on the same team.

No, we've always been on the same team. Except my twin and I have been playing this game in the dark, not knowing we were never as alone as we thought we were. "No one has ever asked either of us if the decisions you all made were the best for us. Maybe, just maybe, what you did was understandable when we were infants, but you should have set the record straight as soon as I was old enough to understand. Maybe even as soon as I started talking to Elle." I swallow hard to hold back the sob that is climbing up the back of my throat. "I gave her the other half of my name," I rasp. "Couldn't you see how lonely I was? How... how *disconnected* I always felt? I thought there was something wrong with me. I thought there was no one else in the world who would ever understand me."

"We hoped... kept hoping that we would be enough for you," Mum murmurs, her voice trailing off as though she just now realizes how futile that hope has proved to be. "And then there was Ranae."

"Don't put her in the middle of this. Not anymore. Ranae might have saved my life in many ways, but it was you who jeopardized it in the first place." I square my shoulders and take a deep sobering breath. I eye my father, then my mother, and in a surprisingly calm voice that belies my tumultuous emotions, I say, "You were wrong not to tell me about her. About my other half, my twin. My *twin*!" I practically shout it out, and both of them flinch as if the word is a slap. "Maybe not when I was too young to understand, but later, when I was so lonely, so out of place everywhere I went. Couldn't you see how miserable I was? Why didn't you tell me then? When we came back here to the United States? Jennilyn found out we were back, didn't she? I know she wrote to you when I was in high school. I remember letters from her. Her name." I tap the side of my head. "What did you tell her to get her to leave us alone?"

My father shakes his head. "Nothing, Danielle. We never wrote back. She simply stopped writing. That's all."

"That's all? That's *all*? Didn't I have the right to know about her? About Jolene?" There's nothing they can tell me now that will make this better. "Were you ever going to show me Jennilyn's letters?"

"Our hands were tied," Dad begins, but I shake my head so hard my vision blurs.

"But they weren't." I plow forward, momentum an angry bull pushing relentlessly against my flagging self-control. "No one tied your hands or stitched your lips closed. No one made you sign any kind of agreement or contract." I can't help but think of Ranae, and my chest aches for her and Ruby, for the young Solomon, and yes, even for Sarah McCray. "You didn't tell me because of your own fear."

Dad opens his mouth to speak, but nothing comes out, and he drops his chin to his chest, his eyes closing in misery.

"You're right, darling," Mum finally speaks up, resting her long trembling fingers on Dad's forearm before he can defend himself again. "We were afraid. We made the choices we did because we were afraid. Afraid of losing you. Afraid of what might become of you if—if she tried to find you. We were even afraid of how much we loved you and of the power of the grief that consumed us. Yes, we were afraid." She swallows hard and meets my gaze. "We—we couldn't bear any more than what had already been forced upon us."

The momentum of my anger pushes me forward, even as I ache for them both. "So you are forcing me to bear it, instead."

My parents sit across from me, overwhelmed by a new kind of grief. I can see that they believe they've lost me after all, in spite of their best, if misguided, efforts.

Out of nowhere, an intense weariness washes over me like an endless wave, dousing the intensity of my rage. It's all I can do not to put my head down on the table and close my eyes. "I need to go," I finally say, sliding my chair back and pushing slowly to my feet. My limbs feel leaden, and I wonder if I'll make it home without passing out behind the wheel. "I need to process all of this." Without another word, I head down the hall to use the bathroom and wash my face, hoping to wake myself up a little before getting into my car.

When I return for my purse, my parents are standing side by side, both of them looking terribly frail to me.

"Are you all right to drive?" Mum asks me, her physician's eyes studying me carefully in spite of her heartache. "You can stay here if you need to rest. Your room is always ready for you."

"I'm fine," I assure them. "I'm going to go sleep in my own bed. Adam isn't coming home until late," I add, not caring what they think of him at the moment. They have no right to point fingers at anyone. I start for the front door, but my father's voice stops me when I reach the small foyer.

"She's beautiful, Danielle. Just like you are." His voice has gone tender. "Your sister."

I slowly turn to face him. "How do you know?"

"We spoke to Ranae," my mother jumps in quickly, as if that tidbit will make everything okay. "When you didn't respond to any of our texts or calls, I phoned her, hoping you were with her."

"You asked Ranae about Jolene? Before you talked to me?" They have no idea how things are between us, but that does nothing to dull the sharp stab of betrayal at Mum's words. How much more can I endure?

"Oh, no, darling," she counters, holding her hands in front of her like she wants to reach for me but knows better than to try. "It wasn't like that. We just asked if you were okay. After your text, we were so worried, and then you wouldn't respond back to either of us. She filled us in on what little she could." She is watching me with a wary tilt of her head. She clearly senses that something about what she's saying isn't sitting well with me, but never in a million years would she think my best friend and I are on the outs. "She sent us a picture of Jolene," she adds. "From Facebook, I believe."

Which means Ranae has connected with Jolene Winston Sanderson on social media. How could she? The stab of betrayal now feels like an evisceration. It's too much.

I narrow my eyes at my mother. There is a hint of something in her tear-bright gaze, something that makes my stomach knot. Longing? Hope? Anticipation?

"Oh, no," I declare, softly at first, then a little louder, firmer. "Oh, no. Don't even think about it. You have no say whatsoever in what happens between me and Jolene anymore. If—and it's a very big if—I decide to connect with her, it will be for me, and me alone. You don't get to be a part of any of it—that's what you wanted, remember?"

"It was never what we wanted," my father counters firmly. He stands taller at my accusation, meeting my angry gaze with a surprisingly steady one of his own. He reaches for my mother's hand and laces his fingers with hers, clearly speaking for both of them. "We are deeply sorry for withholding the truth from you, and we can see that we chose wrong. We hope you can forgive us, that you will believe us when we say we have always only wanted what was best for you. For Jolene, and even for Jennilyn, too. And yes, for us." He pulls my mother a little closer to his side. She is nodding in agreement to everything he says. "For all of us. We trust that you will do what you feel is best, too."

"I need some time," I finally say. "I need—I'll call you when—*if* I'm..." I leave the rest of the disjointed sentence unfinished. "Please don't call Ranae about me or my sister. She clearly doesn't know when to keep her mouth shut. I'll let you know what's going on when I'm ready to tell you."

Tears slide in thin rivulets from the corners of Mum's eyes, but she nods slowly. Dad says nothing, but his brown gaze speaks volumes. I can feel their love for me radiating off of them, and I have to steel myself against its magnetic pull.

I start forward and then pause one more time, my back to them. I close my eyes and count to five. Then ten. I want them to stop me, I suppose, to beg me to stay. To tell me that everything will be all right. We've always faced things together, the three of us, and the frightened little girl in me who still shows up now and then is worried that if I step foot outside their front door, I will truly be on my own.

Alone.

But neither of them speaks. I know they're still behind me. Waiting, hoping, themselves. Allowing me to go my own way if I so choose.

I grimace in frustration. I can't leave like this, no matter how much I want to. With my hand still on the doorknob, I rotate on my heel just enough to face them.

Yes.

Hope.

It's written all over their faces. Hope, and the deep, abiding love of a parent for a child. I recognize it for what it is, and my hand goes instinctively to my abdomen.

I take another deep breath, and the words come out easier than I expect them to. "I love you, Mum and Dad, but I feel a lot of terrible things toward you right now." I swallow hard, but I don't look away from them. "I know you love me, too, and that's what makes this deception and betrayal so much harder to bear."

"Oh, darling," my mother begins, then she covers her mouth with her hand. My father wraps his arm around her and pulls her against his side.

I am gutted to realize that he is protecting her from me.

Traitorous tears well as I watch them practically meld into one before my eyes. My voice trembles as I say, "I couldn't wait for my childhood to be over. Do you know why? As far back as I can remember, I knew I wanted what you two had. I wanted to grow up fast so I could be like you. You have always been each other's other halves." I have to swallow hard before I can keep going. "And then there was weird, ugly duckling me." I press my palm to my sternum. "All I ever wanted was to be someone's other half."

It seems I've run out of breath. When my gulping inhalation turns into a shredded sob, my father lurches forward. Before I can stop him, he wraps his arms around me and pulls me tight against him, one hand on the back of my head, pressing my face into the crook of his neck. I am surprised at how solid he feels, at the sudden sense of certainty I have that I can, indeed, lean on him, and he will not stumble or give way under the burdens I foist on him. He holds me, rocks me, nothing awkward or stilted in his embrace now.

"Oh, my sweet girl," he murmurs against my temple. "Forgive us. We love you so much." Then he releases me slowly, gently, and steps back to stand beside Mum, once again wrapping his supporting arm around her waist. It's her turn to lean into him, to draw on his solidness. It's easy to see that she knows she can count on him to hold her steady, too.

My father, it seems, may not be the biggest man in the world, but he might possibly be the strongest man I know, after all.

Ranae

I HAVE JUST RETURNED from picking Ruby up from school, and after the fifteen-minute ride with my still sullen teenager, I dropped her off at the farmhouse with explicit instructions to put her things away, get a snack, and head over to Fair Havens. I then drove over myself, rather than walking, with the intention of grabbing a few extra minutes to rally my patience. She and I are going to be spending the afternoon working together, and I'm not looking forward to three hours of scathing glances and rolling eyes. After our conversation this morning in the car about her disrespect toward me, she probably won't try either one to my face, but a mother knows what goes on behind her back.

A quiet rap on my driver's side window startles me. I let out a little shriek and drop my phone, and it slips between my knees to the floorboard under my feet.

I turn to find Hugo standing there, his right hand now braced against the top of my car, his other one shoved in his coat pocket. He doesn't have to hide it from me, but it's a habit of his, keeping his scars out of sight. He often wears fingerless gloves when others are around—he dons them on most Bonfire Nights—and Ruby tells him it makes him look like a woodsman biker, which always makes him laugh.

He's grinning in at me now, the twinkle in his eyes letting me know he saw me jump like a scared rabbit. And heard my chicken squawk, too.

I roll down my window and shade my eyes as I look up at him. "Hey." Using my foot, I nudge my phone toward the center console so I can reach down around the steering wheel to pick it up.

"Didn't mean to startle you," he says. He waits for me to contort myself into a pretzel to retrieve my phone, then adds, "Didn't mean to interrupt, either."

"No, no." I shake my head quickly, trying to play off what I know is probably a sheepish expression. "You didn't interrupt anything." I shove my phone into my coat pocket and attempt a casual smile. "I mean, not really."

I was, in fact, perusing Jolene Sanderson's Facebook profile for the zillionth time, still a little freaked out by the uncanny—Jolene called it right on that count—resemblance she shares with my best friend. I found a picture of Jolene's mother, Jennilyn Winston, who apparently passed away a few years ago. The woman in the picture looked like she'd lived a hard life, and I had a hard time finding any resemblance between her and Jolene.

But if Jolene is not adopted—if Jennilyn Winston is Jolene's birth mother—then Jennilyn Winston is also Dani's birth mother.

Yikes. That's a subject I'm not quite ready to sink my teeth into.

But there is no denying that Jolene and Dani are twins, no matter how much Dani wants to deny it. Not a fluke of nature doppelgänger, but a real live twin. It wasn't a fluke that they were dressed alike and wore their hair in the same messy up-do. Albums of photos dating back at least ten years depicts a woman who mirrors Dani in almost every way. The colors in their wardrobes. The styles of shoes in summer, boots in winter. The sharp elbows and long, elegant feet and hands. The narrow, straight noses and enormous blue eyes, and those matching wide, toothy smiles… although Jolene's seems to flash more readily than Dani's. Jolene even has a hunter green car the same color as Dani's, but hers is a RAV4, not a Forester.

It's Jolene's husband, Pete Sanderson, however, who has me seriously rattled.

Pete and Adam could be brothers, or at least cousins. They're not, of course, but the similarity in their appearances is quite unsettling. Both are male-model-handsome with slashing eyebrows over deep set eyes, strong jaws, and broad shoulders.

There is one huge difference, though. In every picture of Jolene and Pete, the man is smiling or laughing, or looking adoringly at his beautiful wife. Who looks exactly—and I mean, *exactly,* freakishly so—like Dani.

I accepted Jolene's friend request on Facebook a few hours after I left Breathe. She wasn't in the waiting room when I headed out, but even though we weren't officially introduced, it wouldn't take a genius to figure out who I was. Not only do we have the popular podcast, Matters of Life and Death, but all Jolene would have had to do was search Dani's name online to discover our intertwined social media channels.

In hindsight, I probably shouldn't have clicked that 'accept' button. I admit that in spite of my best intentions, I am exactly what Dani says I am. I'm a fixer, a nurturer. I'm a pseudo-mom to anyone who needs one. It's my nature to love readily and single-mindedly, yes, maybe even to hover, to protect and defend, especially those who can't, or won't protect or defend themselves. But I consider those qualities to make up my good side.

Every coin has two sides, though, I know. The flip side of who I am, the side I war with on a daily basis, is a meddler, a backseat driver. Actually, I simply take the wheel when I think Jesus is too busy.

You should. You shouldn't.

Those words will be engraved on my tombstone, I'm certain.

Jolene sent me a private message within minutes after I accepted her friend request, apologizing again for the way things played out this morning, and asking me if there was anything she could do to make amends. *I so desperately want to know Dani, Ranae. Although I only learned about her today, I realize I have missed her my whole life.*

I wanted to tell her that Dani has missed Jolene her whole life, too, but I didn't respond, hoping she'd feed me a little more info about herself without me having to ask for it.

Did she really not know about Dani? Was choosing to go to Breathe for her birth plan truly just a coincidence? She'd admitted to seeing photos of Dani on the birthing center's website before coming in. Was it possible, in this day and age, with search engines databases at our fingertips, that she hadn't Googled Dani before today?

I jumped the gun today, begging to see her even after the way she reacted to me. My husband warned me not to push, told me to reach out carefully, maybe by email or letter first, but I'm so afraid she'll block me, or simply refuse to communicate with me.

There was a pause, then a new message popped up. *That said, Ranae, if she really doesn't want to meet me, even now after knowing I exist, then I will back off.*

How was I supposed to respond to that? Jolene's husband is right; this is treacherous ground they are treading, and it might very well be slow-going for a while. Dani clearly isn't ready to face the situation, not right now. But hopefully one day, maybe soon, she'll have a change of heart. I am not about to make a call like that for Dani, though.

Again, I left the message unanswered.

Finally, almost half an hour later, Jolene gave it one last, and rather sad, effort. *You're her best friend, right? You know her. Is there hope?*

What is it with us humans? We are so quick, so willing to circumvent the direct course of action when we don't get the answers we want, too impatient to wait for the ripples to cease after we drop our stones into the water.

Taking pity on her, I finally texted back. *There is always hope.*

Even those few words reeked of betrayal.

I know I am already on shaky ground with Dani, and I do not want to be the reason things go from bad to worse between her and Jolene. I don't want to give false hope where there is none, but I also can't get Dani's words out of my head, the ones she said to me just a few weeks ago while trying to convince me to respond to Solomon's sister. "If someone told me they held my back story in their hands and asked me if I wanted to read it, I'd say yes. I might want to think about it first, but in the end, my answer would be yes."

I am dying of curiosity about Jolene's side of the story, but I have no doubt that if I ask the woman even a single question, things between my best friend and me will likely go from bad to irreconcilable.

Give her some time, Jolene, I finally added, then closed the app so I wouldn't show up as being available to chat.

When Francis called me looking for her daughter shortly after my exchange with Jolene, and she told me about Dani's cryptic text to her, I gave her an abbreviated version of what had happened at Breathe. After listening quietly, Francis simply asked if I believed Jolene was who she said she was.

"No two women could look more alike," I told her plainly, then offered to send her a photo. Although she quickly agreed that she'd like that very much, I'm fairly certain Dani's mother was crying by the time we said goodbye, which meant, of course, that I was crying, too.

Everything has gotten so messy so quickly. I sigh and squint up at Hugo standing at my window, a quizzical look on his face. He has on a knit cap with a rolled rim, and the afternoon sun highlights the bronze undertones in the curls sticking out beneath it.

"You alright?" he asks, his expression growing serious.

"I'm fine. I was just wasting time online," I assure him, patting my coat pocket where I tucked the phone. "Sitting here thawing out from the icy blast of my daughter's cold shoulder," I add with a grim smile. "She's going to meet me at the schoolhouse in about fifteen minutes to put in her child labor hours." I explain, my fingers making air quotes around *child labor*.

When he says, "I see," I can't help wondering what he sees. Hugo, like Dani, like Gran, like—well, like everyone who knows me even marginally—can practically read my mind. But still. A woman needs to believe she has at least some air of mystery about her, doesn't she? With my people, however, I am no enigma, and sometimes that bugs me to no end.

He cocks his head. "Haven't seen much of Dani around here lately."

And there you have it. Mind read.

However, our last conversation about Dani pops unbidden to my mind. I still can't believe he thought I had a thing for her. Apparently, he can't read my mind so well after all.

I want to wave off his concern, but when I open my mouth, the only thing that comes out is a long, drawn out, "Uhhhh."

He nods slowly, his brows furrowing in concern. "Anything I can do?"

I scrunch my nose and shoot him a side-eyed squint. "Do you have a magic wand? Maybe one that specializes in cleaning up my messes?" I seem to be leaving a trail of wounded in my wake these days, good intentions or not.

"You? Make messes?" he teases, but his smile is kind. "My magic wand is in the shop right now, but I have at least one good ear." He taps his unmarred right earlobe. He glances around, taking in the beautiful fall day festooned in its gemstone colors. "Want to go sit out in the chapel?"

"Sure." I might as well bend his ear until Ruby gets here. Maybe he can give me some insight into what role I should play with Dani and Jolene, and I want to ask him what's happening with William, too. I climb out of my car and am reaching back inside for my purse and water bottle, when Dani's car pulls into the driveway, her tires crunching on the gravel as she comes to a stop behind me. By the time I close my door and straighten beside Hugo, she is out of her Forester and striding toward us.

It doesn't take a mind reader to see that she is not happy, and I feel every muscle in my body tense.

"How could you? Was this all your idea? Did you and Jolene cook up today's little meet cute? Is that why you were there at Breathe with your tea and pastries?" She shoots off her questions in rapid fire progression, and I feel the impact of each one. "And sending pictures to my parents? I thought you were my friend.

I thought—" Her voice breaks in spite of her anger, and her face crumples momentarily before she squares her shoulders and lifts her chin. "I thought I could trust you."

Hugo says nothing, but I feel the light pressure of his hand at my low back, a silent show of support. I dart a quick glance up at him to find his brow furrowed, expression concerned. Poor guy has no clue what's going on, but it's pretty obvious things aren't okay between Dani and me.

Dani halts in front of me, one hand on her stomach, the other on her hip. She's changed her outfit since this morning; she's wearing black skinny jeans, black biker boots, and a charcoal gray turtleneck sweater with not an ounce of color anywhere. Her hair is slicked back into a severe bun, not even a single loose tendril wisping around her face. She's rather intimidating, truth be told, a description I don't think I've ever applied to her before now.

"Dani," I finally say, my voice sounding a little strangled. "I had nothing to do with Jolene's appearance today. I didn't even know she existed until maybe five minutes before you did, and that's only because I walked into Breathe five minutes before you did."

"You really expect me to believe you? Seeing as how you're all chummy-chummy with her on Facebook? Why does everyone keep secrets from me? Am I really so fragile? My parents, Adam, and now—now you." She lifts a finger to point at me, practically spitting her next words. "I hate secrets!"

Hugo takes a step forward, his hand still on my back, but when he opens his mouth to speak, Dani turns her narrowed eyes on him, then her pointy finger, too. I don't think I have ever seen her this livid, so I know he hasn't either.

"Don't even think about stepping in, Hugo Beckenbauer." I love Hugo's last name; it always makes me happy to say it. But when it leaves Dani's mouth, it's like gunshots. She waves that same aggressive finger back and forth between us. "This is between Ranae and me."

Hugo, brave, brave man, doesn't back down. "Clearly, there's a misunderstanding. This isn't like you two."

"A misunderstanding? Is that what we call lying and keeping secrets these days?" Dani is so worked up, I'm actually beginning to worry about things like blood pressure, hyperventilation, and other potentially unhealthy side effects that might endanger her health or that of her babies.

Or mine, for that matter, if I'm being honest.

Hugo's too, if he's not careful.

What can I say to make her calm down so we can talk about this rationally? Surely, she can't believe that I would, or even could, keep something this monumental a secret from her. "I assure you, Dani," I try again. "I had nothing to do with her showing up like that today. You have to believe me. I'm telling you the truth."

"Oh, but you were in an awful hurry to get all cozy with her on social media, weren't you? I saw the picture you sent Mum, Ranae. Straight off Facebook." Her eyes are glistening with unshed tears, but she's so hot under the collar that they're probably evaporating too quickly to fall. "I know for a fact that her account is private, so the only way you could have gotten a hold of it is by befriending her."

Hugo turns to look at me, his eyes now more concerned than confused. I'm sure he's wondering if that's what I was doing when he startled me in my car a few minutes ago. Guilty as charged. He doesn't even know who Jolene is, but it's not hard to guess that she has somehow come between Dani and me. This all feels a little high school to me, except that Dani and I never had any altercations like this in high school, either.

"You're right," I admit, more indignant than remorseful. "I did accept her friend request online, and yes, *she* messaged *me* immediately," I say, making it clear which of us reached out first. "But I did not get all cozy with her, as you put it. In fact, I told her to give you some time."

"Oh great. So the two of you had a little chat session about me, did you?" Her hands are both on her hips now, her shoulders back in a stance that thrusts her little baby bump forward. If she wasn't so angry with me—if I wasn't starting to get angry back at her—I'd reach out and rub it. "You want me to just step aside and let the two of you sort out my life for me? Oh, and I'm certain my parents would love to be in on that, too. You'll have to set them up with a Facebook account, but hey, you don't seem to mind butting in where you're not wanted, so that shouldn't be a problem for you." She's practically snarling at me. Where on earth is all this rage coming from? And why is it directed at *me*?

"You know what? I don't need this," I snap. "You, of all people, should trust me a little more than this. You should know that as your *best friend*, I only want what's best for you. Excuse me for going about it in what you apparently think was a heavy-handed manner, but my intentions are good, and I'm standing by them."

"Heavy-handed is right," she bites back, then raises her own hands in the air like she's giving up on me. Or maybe singing in some gospel choir. I've never seen her so emotionally demonstrative. "I don't know why I'm surprised, truly. I mean, this is your usual modus operandi, isn't it? You and your god complex. You decide what's best for everyone, whether they agree or not."

"What do you mean by that?" I ask, feeling more attacked and offended with every word she spews. "You, Dani, you said yourself that you would jump at the opportunity to meet your birth family if it arose. Well, Jolene isn't just some random member of your birth family. She's your twin. Your identical twin!" I hear Hugo's surprised grunt beside me, then I raise my voice to make another point. "And you blew her off like she was some creepy stalker stranger."

"She *is* a stranger, Ranae. I don't know her from Adam." She stiffens at the euphemism she's just let slip out, and I want to throw a fist in the air in cruel delight over the irony. I can't help thinking that perhaps Adam is partly—or wholly—to blame for Dani's irrational anger toward me right now. She's the only one who can't seem to see his true colors. Or maybe she does see them, but simply refuses to admit it.

Just like she's doing now with Jolene.

"And for all we know, she *is* a creepy stalker!" Dani continues, practically shouting, pointing her long finger down the driveway as if Jolene is even now sneaking through the bushes to spy on us. "You expect me to believe that she just shows up at Breathe by chance? Out of all the midwives in the Midwest, she just happens to choose our group?" she rants. "Practically wearing the same outfit as one I have on in a picture on our website? Like that's not more than a little creepy?"

In any other circumstance, the scenario might ring false, but I'm not going to give Dani an inch at this point. "She's not a creepy stalker, Dani, and you know it. You were wearing an outfit very similar to any one of the outfits Jolene is wearing in every single picture of her online. Sorry, but I don't think that's creepy at all. I call it cool. It's cool, okay? Freaky, maybe, but also cool that you two have never met, and yet you're so much alike. And not just in the way you dress. Your features, your postures, your style, the tone of your voices is identical. Why are you denying all of this so adamantly?" Now I'm pointing at her, and she narrows her eyes at me. I get the feeling she'd like to snap my finger right off. *Feeling's mutual, baby.* "And why, in the name of all that is good and holy, are you angry at me? I don't keep secrets. And I certainly am not responsible for you and Jolene not knowing about each other."

"Wow. Just... wow." Dani throws her hands up again, but before she can continue, I cut her off.

"You know, all I did today was try to keep the peace. You practically kicked me out of your office—"

"You stormed out," she interjects.

"No, I walked out after you started doing what you're doing now. Attacking me."

"Oh, please," she says, rolling her eyes with as much drama as Ruby does. "I wasn't attacking you; I was standing up for myself, which is actually what I'm doing now."

"Seriously?" I ask, and now I sound like a teenager, too. I flap a hand at her. "You charge onto my property all riled up and start hurling accusations at me. What happened to talking about things? Friendly communication? Asking me for my side of the story?" I can't decide whether I should be more angry or hurt right now, and the tremble in my voice makes it obvious to anyone who might be listening that I'm on the brink of breaking. "What is wrong with you?"

Dani spreads her arms wide in a grandiose gesture and guffaws sarcastically. "What is wrong with me? What is wrong with *me*?"

We're both shouting now, and I can feel tension radiating off Hugo beside me. He clears his throat, but if he thinks he's going to get a word in edgewise, he's going to have to be a little quicker on the draw.

"I'll tell you what's wrong with me, wee little Ms. Niemeyer." She starts ticking things off on her long fingers. At least they're not pointed at me anymore. "I'm married to a man who can't remember where home is. I'm pregnant with not one, but two of his children whom he can't decide if he wants or not." She takes a quick, harsh breath. "My mother and father have lied to me about my identity all my life, and now you, my supposed best friend, betray me by befriending some woman who shows up on my doorstep claiming to be my long-lost twin. How's that for starters? Or do you want more?" She is visibly trembling, her emotions in so much turmoil.

"Okay, ladies," Hugo says, stepping forward and slightly between us. "There has to be a better way to handle this."

Dani and I simultaneously shoot daggers at him; on this, we're united. He should probably butt out, if he knows what's good for him.

She speaks first. "Actually, Hugo, darling, that's the problem, isn't it? Ranae shouldn't be *handling* any of this. It's my problem to handle. My parents, my husband, my sis—my situation," she amends. "Not hers. But oh, no, no, no. She knows what's best for everyone, right?" She points past Hugo at me. "You're just like my parents with all your selfish and self-protecting secrets."

"I don't keep secrets," I repeat stubbornly. I am fighting back tears with every ounce of will power, but I know I can't hold out much longer.

Dani glares, one eyebrow arched coldly. "Not keeping any secrets, are you? Have you told your daughter about Sarah McCray yet? Have you mentioned that her daddy's family wants to meet her? Or are you going to wait until she's thirty-five, and some hungry-eyed woman walks up to her and introduces herself as her long-lost aunt?"

"What?" The half-screech bursts out from behind the schoolhouse a nanosecond before Ruby does. My daughter's eyes are wide with shock, and red-rimmed like she's been crying, and my heart lurches at the sight of her. Who knows how long she's been back there listening? I'm sure her tears are a result of hearing Dani and me go at each other the way we are, but the look of stunned despair is due to something else altogether. I start across the gravel toward her, but she takes a step back, her hands out in front of her to stop me from coming any closer. "What is she saying, Mom?" Her voice is shrill and as sharp as broken glass. "Is it true? Is what she's saying true?"

"Oh, baby," I begin.

"Don't 'oh, baby' me!" she shouts back, crossing her arms tightly around her body, as if she's holding herself together. "I'm not a baby. I'm almost eighteen, remember? The exact same age you were when you decided you were old enough to screw around and get knocked up, and oh! Then get married, too. Remember?"

I actually flinch as her anger hits me like a bowling ball to the chest. I am being hit on all sides right now, and I don't know if I can bear it. I stiffen my spine and face my daughter. "Ruby, you've got to listen to me. I didn't think—"

"No, you listen to me for once," Ruby interrupts. "I have asked and asked about Daddy's family, and you have told me over and over that you know nothing about them. But that's not true, is it? You know a whole lot more than what you've told me, don't you?" She's so hot under the collar, I'm pretty sure I see sparks shooting off the tips of her curls.

But I am sick unto death of being yelled at, and I spin on my heel and point my own finger at Dani. Mine isn't nearly so long and elegant as hers, and my chipped cobalt blue nail polish only adds to the overwhelming feeling of inadequacy and failure washing over me. The tears that have been held at bay, purely by the force of my indignation, suddenly fill my eyes and spill over. "How could you?" I rasp out in a strangled voice.

Dani has her hand over her mouth, her eyes as large as Ruby's. And Hugo? The man is just standing there, his fingers laced together at the back of his neck, his head bowed. I can't tell if his eyes are closed or not.

"Is it true?" Ruby shouts again, her breath hitching between every word. "Sarah McCray? Is that her name? My—my aunt?"

"Oh, Ranae," Dani murmurs, her blue eyes glistening, pleading with me. Her voice is no longer toxic with fury, and I know she must be reeling over what she's done, over what is unfolding before her. I turn my back on her to face my daughter. I won't give Dani the chance to show me her remorse. Right now, I don't care what she's feeling. I don't care if she walks off Fair Havens' property and never sets foot here again.

All I care about is my daughter and the look of utter betrayal on her face. A look directed at me. I take another step toward her.

"Don't come any closer to me," Ruby says between clenched teeth. "I want the truth, and that's pretty much all I want from you right now."

"Ruby-girl, come on." Hugo starts to move toward her.

She scuttles backward a few paces and thrusts her chin in the air. "Don't Ruby-girl me, Hugo. You are a backstabbing pushover, too. You—you hired that loser jerk, William, to work practically next door to me, but I have to hear it from him?" She phrases it as a question, but she doesn't wait for an answer. "Thanks a lot for making me look like a clueless idiot."

"Whoa," he begins, still taking slow steps forward, the way one might approach a wounded animal. "He's going to be under my constant supervision while he's working on my property. He knows he's not to come near Fair Havens or your home. That's our agreement."

"And you're stupid enough to believe that lying jack—"

"Ruby," I cut in, appalled at how disrespectful she's being. It's one thing for her to rail at me right now, but to attack Hugo? "That's enough. We can go back to the house and talk like the adult you claim to be, but you are not allowed to speak to others that way."

"Oh, please," she declares, rolling her eyes at us. "You and your bestie here can rage like banshees at each other, but I'm not allowed to stand up for myself? You know, I think Dani's right, Mom." She says *mom* with so much derision, it actually hurts to hear it. This is worse than Dani's attack. And apparently, Ruby's been listening in almost from the moment Dani showed up. "You and your god complex, thinking you know everything, and the rest of us are just stupid minions without minds of our own. When were you going to tell me about Daddy's family?" A broken sob escapes her, and she lifts her shoulders up toward her ears. It's a telltale sign that she's getting ready to cry, like a turtle trying to retreat into the sanctuary of its shell.

"I never—I didn't—" Dani tries to speak, her words coming out broken and distraught. "Ruby, darling, oh, please, please," she pleads. I hear her footsteps on the gravel from somewhere behind me, and I turn quickly and step in front of her, blocking her from getting any closer to my daughter.

"Haven't you done enough?" I say, my throat tight. Every breath seems to require too much effort, and I just want to grab hold of my baby girl and hold her close to me. "Go home, Dani. Leave us alone."

Her expression is stricken, and in spite of all the anger and fear welling up inside me, I feel ashamed for causing her pain. But then I hear my precious daughter's distraught weeping, and I stand my ground. Dani opens her mouth to speak, but then closes it again when I just point at her car.

"Ranae," she whispers, but I shake my head.

"It's too much, Dani. This is all too much. Just go."

Dani

I WEEP THE WHOLE drive home, deep, gut-wrenching sobs, as I drag my hand, again and again, across my face to clear the tears from my eyes. I am as angry at myself as I am at the world and everyone in it. How could I have let myself, my words, my emotions get so out of control? A banshee, as Ruby put it, and I can't imagine a more apropos word for such behavior.

It's like I can feel something uncoiling inside me, and I'm not referring to my babies at all. It's in my chest, inside the cage of my ribs, clawing to get out, to be free, to be *heard*. And nothing I do, no amount of soothing chamomile tea, or extra naps, or stupid yoga stretches will still the tumultuous storm.

Temper tantrums, I have discovered, don't solve any problems, either.

By the time I pull into my driveway, my tears have only begun to subside, and I am weary beyond measure. I know it's the crash after the surge upon surge of adrenaline brought on by this catastrophic day, and I can't wait to pull the dark-out shades in my bedroom and crawl beneath the covers and close my eyes. Close out the world. Shut down.

"I'm sorry, babies," I whisper, smoothing the thick fabric of my sweater over my belly while I wait for the garage door to lift before pulling in. "Oh."

Adam's car is parked on his side of the two-car garage, and every muscle in my body tenses at the sudden burst of anxiety coursing through me. According to his phone call earlier—was that just today? It feels like this day will never end. According to his phone call this morning, he wasn't coming home until late this evening. I squeeze my eyes shut; I don't think I'm equipped to deal with another confrontation of any kind right now.

I turn off my engine, then sit there in the stillness of the large space. I take slow, cleansing breaths, methodically relaxing my muscle groups from the top of my head to the tips of my toes. I can't sit out here all evening; if I wait much longer to go inside, Adam will come to the door and ask what's wrong with me. The same question Ranae launched at me less than half an hour ago.

My response to her, pulled up out of the pit of my gut, still rings in my ears. *I'm married to a man who doesn't remember where home is.* My parents? My head understands why they did what they did, even though my heart doesn't, but honestly, I know my heart will eventually come around.

Ranae? Well, I know my friend, and even though I don't like her take charge attitude as much as I used to, I know her motives are right. The only problem now is whether or not she'll ever forgive me for the havoc I've wreaked in her life today. For what I said in front of Ruby. Sure, I didn't know the teenager was lurking around the side of the building listening to us, but then, we weren't being very clandestine, either, what with our raised voices and flailing limbs.

But Ruby. Oh, Lord, her little angel face. I know exactly how she felt—betrayed, deceived, wounded, and so much more—in that moment. How could I have done that to our precious Ruby? To Ranae?

And Hugo. I was downright vicious to that wonderful man. There he stood, caught in the crossfires, taking whatever we doled out to him, ever the gentleman, ever steady, solid, and honorable. The way he spoke to me as he held my door open for me and helped me into my car. "You and Ranae share a priceless and true friendship, Dani. Don't forget that. A little time and space will do you both some good. It'll be all right." So utterly kind.

Now there's a man who never forgets where home is. Chloe—sweet, gregarious, effervescent Chloe. Love like theirs is a pipe dream for the rest of us mere mortals, I'm beginning to think.

My husband? I grip the steering wheel with both hands and squeeze hard, all my muscle groups tightening up again in commiseration.

My husband. I smack the steering wheel with my palms way too hard and release a sharp cry at the pain that reverberates up my arm. "Enough," I say out loud. Then again. "Enough, Dani."

I am done standing down. I am finished letting things go unresolved. I'm not going to step aside and let Adam do whatever he wants while I wait for him to decide whether or not he wants to be a husband, a father, a *man*.

I shove open my door, scramble out of my car, and square my shoulders just as the door from the kitchen opens.

"I thought I heard your car pull in," Adam says, a curious look on his face. "Just getting back from your parents' place?"

"No," I respond sharply. "What are you doing home?"

His chin lifts and so do his brows. "Well, hello to you, too."

"What are you doing home, Adam?" I ask again, not moving toward him, even though he's holding the door wide for me to pass through. "You said you wouldn't be home until late tonight."

Adam's eyes narrow suspiciously. I have on no makeup—what little I did apply is surely washed away by now—I am dressed far more austerely than usual, and I saw myself in the rearview mirror before I got out of the car. With my red nose and cheeks, my swollen eyes, I look like I've been slapped repeatedly. "Where were you if you weren't at your parents?" he asks.

"Why won't you answer my question?" I shoot back.

"Why won't you answer mine?" He crosses his arms and glares at me, leaning one shoulder against the door frame. "You told me you were going to have tea with your mother today, but you didn't, did you?"

"Excuse me?" I almost laugh out loud. Like it or not, I am going to be swept up in yet another altercation on this eternal *infernal* Monday.

"That's right," Adam says with self-righteous indignation. "I was worried after I spoke with you this morning. You sounded distracted. Upset. So I called your mother an hour ago to make sure you were okay. She said you left their place long before I called, and that you were pretty upset."

"You called my mum? So you already knew I wasn't just there." I *am* smiling now, and there isn't an ounce of humor behind it. "Why call her? Why not call me?" But I already know the answer to that. Adam was checking up on me.

I'm the one who should be checking up on him.

"So, you're not going to tell me where you were?" His indignation turns to smugness. "That's what I thought." Then he turns on his heel and heads back inside, letting the door swing shut behind him.

At that moment, the automatic light of the garage door shuts off, and I'm left standing alone in the dark. I dig my cell phone out of my bag and turn on the flashlight, but I pause before following him inside. Maybe I should just leave. Go spend the night... where? I'm not ready to speak to my parents, even though I know they'd welcome me with open arms. Like Mum said, my room is always ready for me any time I need it. I won't be welcomed back at Ranae's tonight, either, that's for sure. I suppose I could go to a hotel; I have my emergency change of clothes and toiletry bag in my midwife kit. Or I could go to Breathe. The beds there for our patients are quite comfortable.

"No," I declare aloud, determination making my voice echo in the cavernous garage. "This is my home." I thrust my way through the kitchen door, half hoping Adam is standing behind it.

Adam is nowhere to be seen, but I hear noises coming from the bedroom. I straighten my spine and head down the hall, coming to a halt in our open doorway. My husband is packing what looks like far more than what he needs for an overnight. He lifts a challenging brow at me, but continues moving back and forth between the closet and the open duffel bag on the foot of our bed.

The longer I watch him, the calmer I become, and the less I feel the need to speak. I lean against the door frame and cross my arms. It occurs to me that I am mimicking his stance from only minutes ago when he stood in the doorway staring down his nose at me. It was meant to intimidate me, to make me feel inferior, powerless. I see that now, because that's how I want him to feel. He can't hurt me. Not today. I've taken all I can. He keeps darting glances at me like he's waiting for me to ask him what his plans are, where he's going, why he's packing, but honestly, I'm too weary to care.

Or maybe it's not weariness that's making me not care. Maybe it's clarity. Maybe I'm seeing things for what they are. Maybe I'm discovering that what I'm seeing is not really what I want.

Why am I fighting to make this man stay with me? He obviously wants to be somewhere else, maybe even *with* someone else. Why is it my responsibility to give him reasons to stay? He's a big boy, and he made the same vows I did. Shouldn't the promise we made to each other to love, honor, and cherish be enough reason to stay?

How long has it been since he loved, honored, and cherished me?

Maybe he left a long time ago and simply hasn't had the fortitude to take his body with him.

What's that stupid saying? If you love something, let it go? "Fly. Be free," I mutter under my breath and bring my spinning thoughts under control.

"What?" His one-word question comes out sharp as a thorn, and he glares at me over his shoulder.

"I said, 'Fly. Be free,'" I repeat, loud enough for him to hear. Loud enough for me to hear.

"What does that mean?" He's filled his bag too full, and now he's struggling to get the zipper closed, tugging and jerking the uncooperative little black tab.

I grin at his fruitless efforts, knowing it will only antagonize him, but I don't care. I don't care. *I don't care.* "I don't care."

"What are you talking about?" he snaps, raising his voice as he straightens up and turns to face me. "What is wrong with you?"

"You know, you're the second person to ask me that this afternoon," I tell him, my own voice steadier than it's been all day. "No, the third, counting myself."

He narrows his eyes at me, then starts shaking his head like he can see that I've gone off the deep end. "You were with him today, weren't you?"

The words don't even register at first. I simply wasn't expecting them, so when I realize he's accusing me of something, I frown in confusion. "I'm sorry?"

He scoffs. "You can cut the innocent act, Dani. I've seen you with him."

"What are you talking about?" I straighten a little, any trace of my malevolent grin gone. "Who is this 'him' you're referring to?" I wrack my mind for an answer that might make sense. Is he accusing me of—. "You think I'm seeing someone?"

He turns away and jerks hard on the zipper again.

"You're crazy," I retort, giving into the ridiculous urge to snicker. "Look at me. I'm exhausted, puking all the time, and preg—"

"Pregnant with twins," he finishes for me. He shoots me a withering glare. "I know, okay? I know. What I don't know is whose twins they are."

"You've gone stark raving mad."

He spins on his heel and takes a step toward me, his fists balled at his sides. "I've seen you with him." He shouts the words this time, his rage—and maybe a hint of pain?—evident in his clenched jaws and snapping words. "Did you think I wouldn't find out?"

"With whom, Adam?" I demand with an emphasis on *whom*, although I somehow remain calm and in control. He actually scares me a little when he gets like this. Fortunately, it's not often, but that doesn't mean I can put my guard down. I purposefully shift my stance so I'm standing in the open doorway in case I need to make a mad dash away from him. I rest my shoulder against the doorframe, but there is nothing casual about the way I feel. I'm tense and ready to spring into action if necessary.

"At Mancini's. We all saw you," he practically roars. "Do you know how you made me feel? How you made me look to my friends?"

I shake my head slowly, a bit mesmerized by the way he seems to be unraveling in front of my eyes. "Nope. Sorry. I've never been to Mancini's in my life. That's your hideout—I mean, hangout, remember?" I feel like a kid with a stick, poking at a wasp's nest, even though I am aware of how stupid it is to do so.

"Liar." He actually growls the word at me from between his bared teeth, then he follows it up with a series of vile names of the like I haven't heard since walking by the boys' locker room back in high school.

I raise my eyebrows in sarcastic censorship and shake my head. "My, what colorful language you have, my dear. Glad you're getting it out of your system now, because you won't be talking that way in front of my children." If he doesn't want them, I'm not going to give him the honor of crediting him for them.

His eyes narrow suspiciously at me, almost like he's sizing me up, then he clamps his mouth shut and thrusts his fist into the over-packed bag, before tugging violently on the zipper tab until it starts to move.

"You're going to break it, Adam. It's too full. There's another overnight bag under my side of the bed; you're welcome to it." The image of the angry wasp nest comes to mind, but I can't seem to stop poking and prodding. Maybe I want to get stung. Maybe I want a good reason to run for cover. "And there are suitcases out in the garage. Would you like me to fetch one for you?"

"Shut up," he mutters. Color flares up from beneath his open collar, and two bright spots form on his cheekbones. I'm certain the flush is from anger as much as anything else, but there it is again, that flash of pain in his expression. I feel like there's a big picture I'm not quite seeing, like I'm missing something.

As I predicted, the tab in Adam's pinched fingers suddenly slides forward, only for the zippered track to spring open behind it. He curses violently, and I grip my arms tighter, forcing myself not to flinch at the foul words. He storms around to the other side of the bed and yanks the bag out from underneath with so much force that it whips around and thumps against his back. I want to warn him to be careful he doesn't rip the handle off of it, but I bite back the words. He's angry enough that he might just fling the thing at me, and I don't have the reflexes Ranae does when it comes to dodging flying objects.

Ranae. I almost wish she were here with me, witnessing Adam's temper tantrum.

Suddenly, as if the rose-colored glasses have been ripped from my eyes, I see him the way she sees him. He's nothing but a child in a man's body. A beautiful man's body, yes, but a self-serving, narcissistic child, nonetheless.

I blink slowly and shake my head to clear the last lingering fingers of a fog that has kept my mind shrouded in despondent complacency.

I don't want a child for a husband. And I certainly don't want a child trying to raise my children.

I am not a runner, but it is that very sentiment that has me stumbling blindly in this murky, shadowy place where joy and peace and goodness cannot abide.

"Fly. Be free," I repeat, but I'm no longer talking to my husband. It is I who will fly. I am setting myself free. I love myself enough to let go of this toxic relationship I have been clinging to for far too long.

I straighten, uncross my arms, and say, "Goodbye, Adam," before turning and heading back down the hall. I ignore the angry retort he hurls after me.

I have more important relationships to work on right now. I call my mother.

"Danielle," she breathes into the phone after only one ring. It sounds like she's been holding her breath, and maybe she has been since I fled their home a few hours ago.

Without preamble, I ask, "Can I sleep in my old room tonight? Maybe for a few nights?" I don't even need to pack a bag. I still have a closet full of clothes there, and because my Bohemian style hasn't changed much over the years, I'm sure I won't have any trouble finding enough to wear. My bathroom, too, is stocked well enough that I don't even have to grab my toothbrush.

"The linens on your bed are fresh," Mum says. She asks no questions, demands no explanation.

"I'll be there in fifteen minutes." I hang up and make my way through the living room, scanning the room for anything I might want to take with me. Surely, there is something I can't live without from this place I've called home for the past five years. The beautiful mantle clock? The Georgia O'Keefe collection on the wall over the sofa? The stunning Tiffany dragonfly lamp on the occasional table beside my favorite Queen Anne slipper chair?

"Anything I take will weigh me down," I whisper, then I open my arms wide at my side and slowly flap them up and down as I continue through the house. *Fly. Be free.*

There is nothing here that calls to me loudly enough to halt my exodus. As I pass through the kitchen, I grab only my favorite mug from the cup hooks under the cabinet—a tall ceramic one with, "I'm a Midwife. Because Badass isn't an official job title." on it. It's from Ranae and Ruby, of course. I also pluck a magnetic photo off the refrigerator. It's of Ranae and me at our senior prom, and she has one just like it on Gran's fridge. The rest of the miscellaneous stuff on there, including the picture of Adam and me from our honeymoon, can stay right where it is.

Then I sling my purse strap over my shoulder, dig in the side pocket of it for my car keys, and pull open the door to the garage. Propping it open with my foot, I pause to thumb a quick text to my mother. "On my way."

"Where do you think you're going?" Adam is suddenly right behind me, his hand clamping roughly around my upper arm.

I go perfectly still, but I don't turn to look at him.

"Let go." My voice is icy calm. When he doesn't do so immediately, I repeat the words, louder this time, but I remain cool as a cucumber as I swipe open my phone app and hit 9-1-1. I am not afraid of this small-minded selfish child, but I'm not in any mood or condition to go toe-to-toe with him right now. Instead, I raise the phone high enough to so he can see the screen from over my shoulder, my thumb hovering over the *Send* button.

His fingers tighten momentarily—there will be bruises on the tender inside of my arm, I'm certain—then he releases me with a small shove, making me stumble forward, my toe catching on the threshold as I lurch into the dark garage. He grabs for me again, this time to keep me from falling, but my anger, so close to the surface all day long, boils up and over.

I right myself and turn on him, flinging his hand away with a sweep of my arm, wincing when our wrists crack together. I'm glad for the thick sleeve of my sweater, or it might have been worse.

"How dare you?" My voice comes out like a wild animal's, low and fierce. "How *dare* you?" I draw in a deep, shuddering breath that fills my lungs with both oxygen and long-overdue courage. "How dare you accuse me—*me!*—of cheating on you, while you are the one out there securing a whole new life for yourself. How dare you even consider the possibility of me being unfaithful, when it is *you* who can't seem to find your way home at the end of the day."

"It's your fault, you know. You pushed me to it."

"It's my fault you're not interested in being a husband to me? A father to our children?" I don't know why I'm engaging in this ridiculous conversation. I just want to go home.

"I saw you with him," he repeats, and then suddenly, I begin to laugh. It's high-pitched and percussive; I sound like a lunatic. He stares at me, fuming. "What is so funny?" he finally demands.

When I can speak, I manage to say, "Are you sure it was me you saw? Not my identical twin?" It suddenly makes perfect sense to me.

Jolene.

Jolene must live close if she's coming to Breathe for her birthing needs; maybe she lives in Mount Vernon. There are only so many restaurants in the small town. Maybe she likes to hang out at Mancini's, too.

"Your identical twin?" Adam says through clenched teeth. "You think this is a joke?"

I'm still giggling, not even bothering to try not to snort. Adam hates it when I snort. I mean, is it possible? Could our marriage be on the rocks because my husband saw Jolene Winston Sanderson with someone else—presumably her husband—at Mancini's, and assumed it was me with another man?

Of course, it's possible.

If I've learned nothing else today, it's that anything—*anything*—is possible. And if it's possible, if indeed, it is Jolene that Adam saw, why did my husband not confront me—her—then and there? Or the moment he got home that night? Was it a night he didn't come home at all? Or was Adam, perhaps, with someone else, himself?

Do I really want to know the answers to all these questions? I cover my mouth with my hand and study my husband through a whole new set of lenses.

"What?" he snarls. "Why are you staring at me like that?"

Time to poke the nest again. "You know, we do look exactly alike, come to find out, but I would have hoped that you, of all people, would be able to tell us apart, husband."

"You're a rotten liar." He adds a few other unkind remarks about the condition of my character, but I cut him off.

"Then thank goodness I'm not lying," I tell him tritely. "I'm going home."

And then it dawns on me. Of course my parents haven't cleaned out and reclaimed my old room for their own use. It seems that, like Ranae, they've known all along that this day would come. Right now, I want nothing more than to dive under my old turquoise and chocolate brown duvet comforter and drift off to sleep staring at the Notting Hill movie poster of Julia Roberts and Hugh Grant. Read the iconic words Ranae, in her flowery script, complete with hearts and daisies and bumblebee flourishes, carefully wrote in the upper corner of the poster before she gave it to me for my birthday our junior year in high school. *I'm just a girl, standing in front of a boy, asking him to love her.* I could never tell which of the characters I related to more in that film, but Anna Scott and William Thacker each spoke to my lonely heart in a way that made me feel known. They still do; both of them with that longing to belong to someone. "I'm going home," I repeat.

He opens his mouth to argue, but I cut him off with a loud hiss. My goodness, but I sound feral, and the way he snaps his jaws shut tells me he thinks the same thing.

"This house isn't a home, is it? Not to you." I fling my arm wide to encompass everything around me, then wave my hand, the one holding my mug, back and forth between us. "And this—this union between us? It's never been a marriage, either. Not to you," I repeat.

He takes a small step back as I lean forward to make certain he can see my face. The garage remains dark behind me, but the light from the kitchen is like a spotlight on me, and I want him to know without a shadow of a doubt that I am not afraid. Not anymore.

And I am not running.

I am taking.

Taking my life back. Taking my heart back. Taking my future back.

And taking my children with me. He never wanted them anyway.

"Fly." I lift my mug toward him in a mockery of a toast. "Be free. I release you."

Then I spin on my heel and fling open the door of my car, sliding in behind the steering wheel with my back ramrod straight, and my mouth set in a firm line. I practically throw my things onto the passenger seat, pull my door closed, and pray that the cab light goes off quickly so he can't see me fumbling with my keys. My hands are shaking, and it takes all my concentration to get the key into the ignition.

Adam is still standing in the open doorway, a nearly faceless silhouette backlit by the glow of all that once was... if, indeed, it ever was at all. I push the garage door opener in the console above my rearview mirror and back out into the night.

Ranae

"Ruby hasn't spoken to me for almost four days. She just goes about her business like a brooding storm cloud. If I dare look at her for more than half a second, she gets up and leaves the room or just walks away. And I'm still so mad at Dani I almost don't care if she never speaks to me again. Almost." I toss a pebble at the trunk of a beech tree across the small clearing. The *tock* it makes as it ricochets off the smooth, gray-brown bark is inexplicably satisfying. I let out a long, morose sigh. "Who am I kidding? Of course, I care. Silent treatment from two of my favorite people is almost unbearable, you know?" I shift my crossed legs so I can scour the ground around me for another rock. "Even your husband is steering clear of us these days." I pause in my assault on the tree. "And I'm sorry if this is more than you want to hear, but Chloe, I feel his absence like a hole in my heart." I throw the stone, missing the tree completely, then press my open palm hard to my chest. "It physically hurts, you know?"

Chloe doesn't respond. But then, she never does. I'm used to it by now, and I just keep talking, undeterred by her silence.

"Hugo hates that Ruby's upset with him, I'm sure, especially since he's done nothing wrong. Other than being in the wrong place at the wrong time. Poor guy." I shake my head at the memory of him standing alone in the Fair Havens parking lot, shoulders hunched, hands in his pockets, his posture one of defeat and misery as he watched each of us women go our separate ways. He held Dani's door for her, of course, but before she even turned on her ignition, Ruby spun on her heels and marched off toward the woods, ordering everyone, especially me, not to follow her. I wasn't too worried about her traversing the paths alone; she helped clear many of them, so she knows them well, at least in the light of day. And besides, she'd brought Blimey over from the farmhouse with her, and I was happy to see his rickety backside trotting along behind her as she disappeared down Wild

Rose trail. I headed downstairs to my basement workshop, and I didn't come back up until the place had gotten a thorough cleaning.

"I was worried, however, when she hadn't come back by dusk," I explain to Chloe. "But when I saw her and Blimey meandering across the back yard like they hadn't a care in the world—conveniently just in time for dinner, mind you," I added, "I was livid with relief, if that's even possible. But I kept my cool and simply told her she'd just gained two more days of work for ditching her first day." I smile now, recalling the look on her face. "She wasn't speaking to me, remember? So she couldn't offer a rebuttal. But she's come straight over after getting home from school all week."

That evening when Gran saw how bad things were between us, she insisted I tell her everything that had happened. Ironically, Ruby hasn't been at all upset with Gran this week, even though she is also guilty of keeping the knowledge of the McCray family identity a secret from Ruby for all these years. My daughter's anger toward me is all because of my decision not to tell her about Sarah's recent email.

And Gran, it turns out, doesn't blame her for being upset. In fact, she agrees with Ruby—and Dani—that my daughter is old enough to at least participate in making the decision whether or not to let her father's family into her life. Into our lives.

I stretch my legs out in front of me, not caring that my backside is getting damp beneath me. In the clearing, there is a beautifully crafted bench similar to the ones around the fire pit that Hugo made, but for some reason, I can't bring myself to sit on it today. Perhaps I feel somehow closer to Chloe sitting here on the ground.

"It's Friday, did you know? And I have to admit that I really am not looking forward to spending another blistering three hours with my cantankerous kid this afternoon." I let my gaze linger on the large unpolished chunk of gray limestone set into the foot of the mound of earth in front of me. Iron oxide impurities have tinged the marker with beautiful shades of rust and amber highlighting the hand-chiseled block letters that spell out Chloe Beckenbauer's name. Leaning forward, I brush away some of the soil that's collected in the grooves. "I can hardly stand her right now," I admit in a half-whisper. "Does that make me a bad mom?"

I close my eyes and listen to the song of the woods around me. It's so serene out here in this secret little natural clearing, tucked back off the trail away from casual viewers. Hugo and Chloe discovered the spot back when we were first mapping out the woods for the nature trails and burial plots, and Chloe fell in love with it. "This is where I want us to be buried," she declared, her eyes lit up as she looked at her husband. "What do you think? It's perfect, isn't it? Just enough room for two people resting side by side in one large grave beneath the canopy of trees."

Hugo, of course, had whole-heartedly agreed, and they'd officially become Fair Havens' first paying customers. Two years ago, Chloe was laid to rest here by herself, but not a day goes by that at least one of us—Hugo, me, even Ruby and Gran on occasion—pays her a visit.

"I feel like such a failure right now. As a mom, as a friend…" I tip my head back, and lift my face skyward, closing my eyes against the light flickering through the interlaced branches and leaves overhead. "As a woman all around. Especially where men are concerned." One man in particular, but I don't say it. There is only so much I feel comfortable sharing with Chloe. Hugo is her husband, after all. "I'm lonely, Chloe. I want someone in my life." I open my eyes and bring my knees up, crossing my arms around them.

There is evidence of Hugo everywhere I look. Virginia Creeper, one of Chloe's favorite native plants spills in gentle falls over the mound of her grave to form a lush green carpet that turns brilliant colors in early fall. It vines its way along the ground toward the closest trees at the edge of the clearing, winding its way toward the sunlight. A lush woodbine has found a place at the edge of the clearing, too, its bright coral honeysuckle flowers filling the air with an intoxicating sweetness for months at a time before producing tiny jewel-like berries that the birds go crazy for. It, too, tendrils around the trunks of trees, as it reaches for the sunlight through the canopy. Other favorite wildflowers of Chloe's come and go in every season: asters, columbine, bluebells, goldenrod. There are a myriad of wooden carvings hanging from the branches overhead, tributes to Chloe that Hugo brings. They rarely look like anything in particular, but in the curving, almost sensual lines that follow the natural pattern of the wood grain, each piece somehow captures the spirit of who Chloe was. There is one inorganic thing in the clearing; a blue gazing ball from Chloe's garden sits on a small cairn, a short stack of rough-hewn stones that form a rustic pedestal beneath it. The rules of the cemetery don't allow for anything that isn't biodegradable to be left at the grave sites, but I simply don't have the heart to ask Hugo to remove the gorgeous garden globe.

"I want what you had with Hugo, Chloe. To love and be loved like that." Tears prickle the corners of my eyes. "I want someone to talk to about all the decisions I have to make. Someone to hold me in the dark at night, someone who will tell me I'm beautiful even when I'm old and saggy. Not that you were ever old and saggy. You know what I mean. I want someone who will tell me if I'm being a good mom, a good friend, a good person. Someone who will help me become a better version of me because of him." Did that make me sound too damsel-in-distressy?

"I love Gran, my friends—well, maybe not Dani so much right now." I roll my eyes. "Just kidding. I love my friends and my family, but most of them belong to someone else. One day, even Ruby will, too. I'm tired of being alone and on my own. Is that selfish of me to want more when I have so much to be thankful for?"

A gentle wind kicks up, making me smile, imagining it's been sent from Heaven above at Chloe's request. The birds and other woodland critters go still for a moment, then pick up almost as if on cue. I lower my forehead to my knees and let the peace of the place settle around me. "Listen to me," I mutter, more to myself than to my friend. "I'm so pitiful. It's all about me, wah, wah, wah." I take a deep breath and lift my face skyward, then let out an embarrassing screech of surprise.

Hugo is standing at the edge of the clearing opposite me, the vibrant colors of the creeper vines in the trees framing his solid form. He is smiling tentatively, as if he isn't sure if he should interrupt me or not. "Mind if I join you?" he asks, not coming any closer.

"Sure. Just visiting with your wife." I try to keep my voice light, casual. What has he heard? How long has he been standing there, or just beyond the circle of trees? I can feel my cheeks burning as I try to recall everything that I have said out loud. Did I mention him by name? Did I give anything away? Other than how pitiful and lonely I am?

After a brief hesitation, he circles the grave and lowers himself to the ground beside me. I can't look at him until I know what he knows. We sit in silence for several long minutes, until I finally cave.

"It's always so peaceful here," I murmur, my tone rather reverent. "It's so perfectly Chloe. And you," I add quickly, waving a hand in a gesture that encompasses the whole clearing. "So serene."

"Sometimes I think I can actually hear her voice out here," Hugo says after a moment.

"I wish I could. I'd give anything to have some of her words of wisdom right about now."

Hugo nods but doesn't say anything. We both fall silent again.

When he starts talking, it takes me a moment to comprehend what he's saying. "I am eternally grateful to you," he begins. "For taking such good care of Chloe until I was able to be here for a service."

I smile over at him. "You have thanked me a thousand times already, Hugo. In a thousand ways," I tell him. "Every day that you keep showing up here to help me run this place, you thank me. Every time you invest in Ruby's life, you thank me. With every new grave you dig, I am reminded that it is I who should be thanking you."

Hugo just nods and falls silent again.

"I should also thank you for sticking around even with all this awful mess going on. I'm sorry you have somehow gotten stuck in the middle of it." I pluck another quarter-sized rock from the ground between us and hold it in the palm of my hand. It's flat and smooth, a perfect skipping stone. We both study it as though it might divulge some great secret before I set it down in front of me. I'm not going to throw rocks around with him here; it somehow feels disrespectful now. "Sometimes I feel like the worst human being in the world, and other times, I feel like I try so hard to be the best mom in the world, the best friend, and yet I seem to fail miserably again and again."

To my surprise, Hugo reaches over and takes my hand with his good one, lacing his fingers with mine in what feels like a very intimate act. I hold my breath for a moment, waiting to see what he'll do next. Then quickly deciding it would be a total disaster if I turn blue and pass out, I release my breath slowly and force myself to relax as I try not to stare at our clasped hands resting lightly on his thigh.

He seems unaware of my awkwardness; his focus is on his left hand. He holds it out in front of him, turning it this way and that as he studies the scars that lattice his flesh. Finally, he speaks. "I used to think of them as brands," he begins. "Marks of my failure, my weakness, my cowardice. For a long time after Chloe died, I got up every morning and stared at my scars in the mirror, twisting and turning my arm, my face, my body, to make sure I took stock of every single ridge and ripple."

I don't move a muscle, my heart breaking. He seems he's a million miles away, and yet I know he's talking to me.

"I'm the reason Chloe was driving my truck that day. Did you know she'd never driven a stick shift? I wanted her to learn. I thought it was important for everyone to know how to use a clutch and a gearshift. Why?" He chuckles deprecatingly. "In case all the car manufacturers one day decided to go back to the good old days and get rid of automatic transmissions? Or maybe if there's an apocalypse and we all end up in a real-life *Thunder Road*?"

He glances over at me, and I give him a sympathetic half smile. I don't dare speak; this almost feels like a confession, or a revelation, and I get the feeling he needs my silent companionship more than any coddling words. For whatever reason, he has chosen to open up to me in this time and place, and I don't want to do anything that will dissuade him.

"She didn't want to do it, insisted it wasn't something she'd ever need to know how to do. You know how she was; she hated driving anyway, mainly because of environmental issues, and driving my old fuel hog felt like sacrilege to her."

I nod and grin, remembering some of the conversations we'd had when we were first getting Fair Havens up and running. It was Chloe who had insisted we not use any fuel-operated machines beyond the parking lot at the front of the property. No backhoes for digging graves, no chainsaws for clearing paths, no four-wheelers on the trails. She'd finally capitulated about the golf carts because they were powered by electricity.

"I kept pushing her," Hugo continued. "I insisted that she at least learn in case there was some kind of emergency. I spouted off some bizarre scenario that would leave us with only the truck to drive, and of course, I would be incapacitated. Out in the woods camping, I think it was, and I'd accidentally chopped off my shifting hand with my ax."

"Hugo!" I stare at him aghast. "That's terrible."

He chuckles again and squeezes my hand. "I know. I can be very manipulative when I want to be."

I roll my eyes. I've never known the man to be manipulative a day in his life.

"Don't roll your eyes," he tells me, and I have the decency to blush. "I was pretty cocky before—well, before. Pretty self-important. Chloe might have been stubborn, but I had a massive head on my shoulders." He thumps his chest a few times with his closed fist. "Me big man. You little woman. Me know best."

I laugh in spite of myself. I wouldn't have called him cocky, or even big-headed back when I first met the two of them, but he has always come across as being self-possessed and confidently knowledgeable about a lot of things. So I suppose I can see how that might translate into something else in a marriage.

"Against her better judgment, she finally capitulated." He shakes his head slowly, his smile fading. "She only agreed because I wouldn't back off, not because she thought that it was a good idea." He sighs quietly, letting his breath out slowly. His brow furrows and the muscles in his jaw clench.

I want to tell him that it's okay, that he doesn't have to tell me any of this if it's too painful. I remain silent, though; still as a statue beside him.

"I should have known better than to let her behind the wheel of a beast like my old truck," he says with a small shake of his head. "Especially when she wasn't fully committed. I knew she wasn't happy with me, but I refused to acknowledge just how upset she was until about fifteen minutes into the driving lesson, she started crying. Not sniffles and sobs, mind you. Just tears." He touches the side of his face, tracing a finger from the corner of his left eye down to his jaw. "Steady streams. I asked her what was wrong, but she insisted she was fine, that she just wanted to get it over with so that I'd get off her back."

I stare at Chloe's grave marker, my eyes tracing the letters one at a time. I don't want to start crying—he doesn't need my tears right now—but I can feel the telltale tingling at the bridge of my nose.

"I told her we could stop for the day, but she refused." His words come out slower now, each one weighed down by pain and regret. "There were those endless tears, though, so I pressed her harder to at least explain what the crying was about. She finally told me she'd been in a car accident when she was a little girl, that her mother had been driving. They'd been at a stop sign on a hill, and for whatever reason, her mother had been unable to shift the car into first gear. They'd started rolling backwards, the cars behind them honking, folks yelling, and her mom started panicking and crying and then screaming as she lost control of the car."

"Oh no," I murmur softly.

"No one was hurt, but they'd backed into the car behind them, pushing his vehicle into the one behind him, and by then, her mother was inconsolable. To make matters worse, one of the drivers got out of his car yelling about how women shouldn't be allowed out of the kitchen, and a few assorted vulgarities, and ended up having to be subdued by others who'd gathered around before the police arrived."

"Nice," I interject with a flare of sympathy. I'd had the "little woman" treatment in my line of work before, and I knew how that felt.

"Long story short, Chloe's family only had the one car, and because of the accident, her father missed an important interview, they had to save up money to pay for the repairs since their insurance only covered the damage to the other drivers' vehicles, and so on. Her mother refused to drive that car again, refused to drive a stick ever again, period. Eventually, instead of fixing up the old one, they bought a new one with an automatic transmission, and her mother never had another accident again."

"Wow. I can see why that would leave a mark on Chloe."

"Yep. Even as a six-year-old child, the whole incident affected her so much that she decided she would never drive a stick shift, either. In fact, she didn't learn to drive at all until she graduated from college and discovered that public transportation didn't make stops in the middle of the woods."

"Oh, Hugo," I squeeze his hand again. Maybe this is why he took my hand like he did that night outside the bookstore after dropping Dani off. There is comfort in this kind of connection, this physical evidence that we are not alone, even in our darkest hours.

"Don't feel sorry for me," he tells me, his voice growing stern. "Had I been a better man, I would have insisted she pull over then and there. But no, I told her she was in safe hands with me, and that it was high time she overcome this mental road block about driving a stick. 'It's good for you to face down your fear,' I told her. 'It's great fun driving a stick, you'll see,' I insisted."

Part of me does not want to hear the rest of this story from Hugo's perspective. I knew Chloe had been driving, and I knew Hugo felt responsible because he wasn't the one behind the wheel, but I'd never heard any of these details before.

"She turned to me, those terrible tears streaming from her eyes, her face pale and anxious, and said, 'Does this look like great fun to you?'" He pauses to take a deep breath and closes his eyes briefly before continuing. "I teased her. Not unkindly, at least not intentionally, but I was too flippant, callous about her feelings, telling her I believed in her, and...." His sentence trails off, then he clears his throat. "I may have believed *in* her, but I didn't really believe *her*, did I? Otherwise, I would have insisted she pull over and let me drive us home."

His whole body is tense beside me, and I can practically feel the vibration of suppressed emotions in the way he's holding my hand.

"Something seemed to switch inside of her after that. She became dogged, fixated on getting it right, like she was waging a war with herself, and I was no longer in the picture. The longer she worked, the more aggressive she became. When I finally made a real effort to put a stop to the lesson, without even looking at me, she said, 'This is what you wanted, isn't it? I'm not getting out of this truck until you're happy, and then maybe you won't ever bug me about this again.'" Hugo shakes his head, a tragically wry expression on his face. "That woman. She was as stubborn as the day is long. You know how she was when she got an idea or saw an injustice. A dog with a bone, right?" He doesn't wait for my response. "So I crossed my arms and sat back in my seat, and said, 'Fine. Go ahead and kill us then.'"

I have gathered a small pile of pebbles in front of me, a miniature version of the cairn at the head of Chloe's grave. Hugo's gaze is focused on my handiwork as he speaks.

"That was the wrong thing to say. So callous. Stupid. I was angry by then, too, taking her stubbornness as a personal affront against me. She called me a little man with a big truck," he says with a rueful smile directed at Chloe's grave. "The worst insult you could think of, wasn't it?"

It breaks my heart to watch him talk to her.

Sighing, he continues. "I, in turn, said nothing, knowing how much my aloof silence goaded her. It actually took me a few seconds—it seemed like everything slowed down, like in a movie—to realize that we were going over the side of the embankment. I grabbed the wheel, trying to help her control the front end, but there were too many trees."

They'd been out on a country road that meandered in and out of patches of woods. It took the first responders almost half an hour to get to them.

"My side of the truck was wedged against a tree, so I couldn't get my door open." Hugo's posture is casual, his shoulders rounded as he slouches a little beside me. But I sense the tightly coiled core of him, the part of him he's trying to doggedly keep locked away from the world.

"For some reason, I couldn't get my seatbelt buckle to release, so I slipped out of the shoulder strap to try to help Chloe. She was unresponsive, her head resting at a strange angle on the seat back, but her eyes were closed, and I thought—" He shrugged one shoulder. "I guess I thought maybe she'd been knocked out. I got her seatbelt unbuckled, but she just slumped forward over the steering wheel—no airbags, of course."

They'd struck a tree on the driver's side, and although the front end of the vehicle didn't crumple, a low branch had snapped off and buckled the cab over Chloe's head.

"That was when I smelled the fumes, and it wasn't until that moment that it occurred to me to call for help. I managed to get my cellphone out of my back pocket, hit 911, turned it on speaker, and just started shouting. Half the time I was trying to tell them where to find us and what had happened, and half the time I was shouting at Chloe, trying to get her to wake up so she could get out of the truck."

He stops talking for several moments, almost as if the words weigh too much, and he needs a rest from hauling them out of the locked room inside him. His palm is damp against mine, but I don't loosen my grip. I sense that he's feeling a little untethered right now, and if I can somehow keep him anchored, then I will give everything in me to do so.

Finally, he takes a deep breath, and begins again. His voice trembles slightly, but he forges ahead. "There was this loud *whump* sound. Not an explosion or a boom, but like a furnace kicking on, only louder. Within moments, the flames were licking up her side of the truck, the brush beneath us caught, and then the low-hanging limbs of the branch that had broken off the tree caught fire, too." His voice cracks. He swallows hard. "Her window was open," he manages to get out.

I can't bear it any longer. I release his hand and slide my arm around his waist, pressing my body against his in a silent offer of support. When Ruby needs solace, I usually reach over and press her head to my shoulder until she relaxes into me, finding that safe place where she can fall apart and then put herself back together. But Hugo is not my daughter, and I'm not exactly sure which of us is supposed to be comforting the other, so I lay my head against his shoulder instead.

At first, he remains rigid against me, but then there is a subtle shift, a twitching in the deltoid muscles beneath my cheek. Slowly, ever so slowly, he begins to relax, almost like he's starting to thaw. He doesn't change positions, he doesn't rest his head on mine or slide his arm around me in return, but he seems to interpret and accept my invasion of his space for the comfort it's intended to be.

He holds up his left arm and shoves the sleeve up to reveal the scars that disappear up past his elbow. "I got my arm around her shoulders and tried pulling her toward me, thinking if I could get her over to my side of the truck, then she'd be safe." He shakes his head, clearly still wracked with the emotions of those terrible moments. "Her legs were trapped, though, and it was ridiculous anyway, because I was trapped, too. There was no way out on my side. Then the back window shattered, and the fire started spreading into the cab along the back of the seat."

The first responders arrived right about then and were able to put out enough of the fire to push the truck backward about a foot, just enough to clear Hugo's open window so they could reach in and cut him free.

"They had to drag me out kicking and screaming. Had to pry my fingers from Chloe's shirt. I didn't want to leave her behind." His voice breaks again, and he clears his throat tightly, but the rest of his words come out in harsh whispers. "I looked back one last time, and behind her, through her window, there was a small flareup of flames. It was like a halo of golden light surrounded her head. Her eyes looked like they were open, and I swear she was staring right at me. Smiling," he chokes out. "She was smiling at me."

Once Hugo was free, they went to work cutting Chloe's body from the wreckage. According to the report, she had died on impact, small mercy that it was.

"I felt no physical pain at first," Hugo said when he finally managed to speak again. "All I could think about was Chloe and getting her out. I could see the charred skin on my arm, my hand, and I knew at some point, it would hit me, but I remember looking at it with this singularly detached awareness. 'Yeah, that's not lookin' so good,' this little voice in my head kept saying, but I felt nothing."

My own tears fall silently, and I know I'm getting the sleeve of his shirt wet. I still don't speak, but only because of the lump in my throat of overwhelming grief and sadness for this man beside me.

"It wasn't until I was in the hushed mechanical bustle of the ambulance that it finally caught up to me. Actually, I felt my back first. When they cut away my shirt and had to peel it off in shreds." He tugs at the front of his shirt, wincing with the memory. "The moment the air hit my shoulders, it was like a jolt to my system, and suddenly, every nerve ending in my body was screaming at me." He chuckles dryly. "I just screamed back until they sedated me."

It was three and a half weeks before Hugo was well enough to attend a burial service for Chloe. I prepared her battered and burned body myself, not allowing anyone except her parents to see her until after Hugo had the chance. It was a terrible time for all of us. Chloe's mother made it no secret that she blamed Hugo for their only daughter's death, and her father was too gutted to either argue or agree. They did everything in their power to try to have Chloe's body turned over to them, but Hugo and Chloe had paperwork lined up insuring the two of them would be buried at Fair Havens. I stood by Hugo's request to hold off her internment until he was well enough to attend her services, and throughout that month-long wait, I did everything I could to offer solace to her parents. They came often, wanting to see her body, wanting assurance that she was not simply rotting away in the cold dark refrigeration chamber in my basement.

The funeral was solemn and tragic, nothing at all like Chloe would have wanted, had, indeed, requested. Her parents and their friends stood on one side of the grave, while Hugo and Chloe's peers gathered on the other side. The open grave I'd dug by myself could have been a chasm dividing them.

I knew there was no way I could perform my funereal duties, consumed as Ruby and I were in our own grief and loss, so with Hugo's permission, I asked my father to be in charge of the service.

My father. My rock. My own King of all Men.

It's how Ruby sees Hugo - a King of All Men. He's the closest thing to a father she has, never having known Solomon except by the things I've told her.

"Tim and Judy are right, Ranae," Hugo says, bringing me back to the moment. He says their names with such kindness. "I am responsible for Chloe's death."

I lift my head from his shoulder and look at him. "Oh, Hugo, no. You can't take that on," I begin, but he pats my knee to quiet me.

"I have taken it on, though, and I am finding that I can live with that knowledge. I didn't think I could, but the more time that passes, the more I realize that there are some people who are simply entrusted with a heavier burden in life. It's up to us to rise to the challenge."

I shake my head, not sure I agree with him, but I don't know quite how to respond.

"You're one of those people, too, Ranae," he says, not waiting for me to speak. Then he lifts his arm over my head and wraps it around my waist, too, pulling me back up against his side. "You have been asked to carry an enormous burden, and yet, you never complain. You never ask for it to be lifted from your shoulders."

"No, no," I start to argue, trying to pull away. But he holds me fast, and I don't fight him very hard. I return my head to his shoulder, but insist, "I have never thought of my daughter as a burden. Maybe I wish her father hadn't died, that she could have known him, but—"

"That's not what I'm talking about," Hugo says, interjecting when I pause for a breath. "It takes a strong and capable person to do the job you do, to carry the weight of all the grieving people who pass through Fair Havens' gate. A hundred thousand, maybe even more, will come here in your lifetime. How do you do it? How do you bear up under it all?"

"It's not like that for me, though," I try to explain. "I don't feel like it's a burden when I can help people go through that. Helping others isn't a burden to me."

"Exactly," he says, his tone almost forceful. "You are asked over and over to walk through the shadow lands with people, and believe me, there are some very dark places in the shadow lands. But you don't just walk with them. You sometimes carry them, like you did me. Like you do for all the folks who show up here for your Live and Let Die bonfires."

"But... it's not a burden," I reiterate weakly. I've never thought about what I do in this light before, and it's both humbling and sobering at the same time.

"Maybe not for you, Ranae, or for your parents, maybe even not for your brothers. For people like you it might not be a burden, but that's only because you have gracefully accepted the heaviest of burdens as yours to carry. I think it's in that moment of acceptance that we find our true place, that the load changes from being a burden to being a purpose. You've taught me that." He rests his cheek against the top of my head. "Don't let everything that has happened over the last few weeks make you doubt yourself. You are a fine woman, Ranae Niemeyer. An excellent mother, a true friend, and—"

I wait in hopeful anticipation for him to finish the sentence, but he falls silent. My disappointment is lessened by the strength of his arm around me, the solid comfort of his shoulder under my cheek, and the rasp of his scruffy jaw against my forehead. His soft rhythmic breathing quiets my spirit, and I find that instead of racing and fluttering at his close proximity, my heart is beating steady and sure for the first time in days.

Dani

I wish Ranae were here with me today. As I straighten the pleated fabric of my empire-waisted maxi dress over my baby bump, I find myself wanting to ask her if I look okay. If she thinks Jolene will like me. If she'll love me. Ranae would know just what to say to me right now.

"Probably something along the lines of 'Get it together, woman,'" I mutter to my reflection in the floor-to-ceiling mirror on my sliding closet door.

It's only been four days, twenty-two hours, three minutes and a few seconds since I walked away from the havoc that I'd wreaked at Fair Havens earlier this week. I haven't heard a peep from my friend—not that I can blame her—and today, Ranae released a Matters of Life and Death podcast episode without me. Granted, it was a compilation of some of our most frequently asked listener questions, but she introduced it as the first in a series. That tells me that she's not planning on me being around to record any time soon. I'm not sure if she's kicking me off the team, letting me off the hook for a while, or trying to prove to me that she will do just fine without me. None of those options sound good to me, but I'm not sure I have much say in the matter after what I did.

I wonder what she has decided to do about Sarah McCray. I wonder if Ruby has forgiven Ranae for not telling her about the email. I wonder if either of them will forgive me for the part I played in bringing this whole thing to light.

"Danielle?" I'd know my father's signature knock on my bedroom door even if he didn't say my name. It's always three back-handed knuckle raps low on the door.

"Come in," I call out, smoothing the fabric one more time before turning to face him as he pushes open my door. "How do I look?" I ask him. I know what he'll say, and although I know it will be completely honest, he's also biased. I could have mascara smeared down one side of my face, a rip in one sleeve, and be wearing mismatched shoes, and he'd still tell me I look beautiful.

But that is exactly what I need to hear from him right now. Pitiful, indeed I am.

"You look beautiful, Danielle." He crosses to me and takes my shoulders in his smooth, cool hands, then leans forward to plant a kiss on my forehead. I'm glad I've chosen ballet flats; today is not a day I want to tower over anyone, especially not my father. We are all still treading carefully around each other, but it's been so good being home under the tender care of my mother and father. I hadn't realized how much I needed some good, old-fashioned nurturing.

Jolene and her husband, Pete, are coming for dinner this evening, and we are all aflutter around here. My father looks as cool as a cucumber as usual, but he is wearing one of his light blue oxford shirts paired with a cobalt blue tie and the silver Alfred Dunhill tie bar Mum gave him our first Christmas in London when I was a baby. It's his talisman, he's said on many occasions. Whenever he wears it, he is prone to touch it, to run his finger over the smooth surface repeatedly. Not like a nervous habit, but almost a caress, as though aware that he carries my mother's heart with him wherever he goes.

Mum is down the hall in the kitchen. I can hear her singing along with the Beatles' "She Loves You," and I put a hand on Dad's arm to stop him. Touching my ear, I nod in her direction. When she croons the "Oooo!" along with John and Paul, we share equally delighted smiles, then head down the hall to join her.

When the doorbell rings, my parents are at the kitchen counter, my father having just opened a bottle of red wine to let it breathe. My mother, beside him, is murmuring something about him needing a haircut soon. I am setting a low floral arrangement in the middle of the table; I've put it together from an inexpensive, but vibrant bouquet I picked up at the grocers when we shopped for tonight's meal earlier this morning. All three of us pause in a tableau of anticipation, almost as though time has stopped for just a moment. Then, like a synchronized dance, we straighten, set our implements down, and move as a collective front toward the door.

I have had the benefit of seeing Jolene prior to this evening, even though our first encounter was less than stellar. I've also spoken with her over the phone, albeit briefly, earlier this week when I finally worked up the courage to call her.

My parents have not. Even so, it is they who manage to keep their composure enough to warmly welcome my twin sister and her husband into their home, while I stand back, gripped with something that feels like fear, as I face the woman who could be my own reflection.

Jolene, as it turns out, has no such reservations. She makes a beeline for me, both hands held out in front of her. She stops just short of touching me, but her eyes stay fixed on mine. "It's you," she says. "It really is you."

Without consciously making up my mind to do so, I reach out and take her hands in mine. There is no tingle, or electric current, nor is there a jolt of awareness that passes between us, and yet, in that moment I know her. I don't know much about her, and I don't know if I'm even going to like her, but I *know* her, and I already know that I love her. In her eyes, I see the same thing taking place.

It is only natural that we are soon embracing, and by the time we take our seats around the table, Jolene and I across from each other so we can take each other in, no one has remained dry-eyed. Not even Pete.

Pete, I soon discover, is part-owner of Mancini's in Mount Vernon. The same Mancini's where Adam insists that he saw me cavorting with my lover.

Pete, whose lovely wife does, on occasion, come into the Italian restaurant to have dinner with her husband.

If only Adam had confronted them; he'd have discovered the truth.

Except then he'd have known about Jolene before I did.

The irony of the whole situation makes me a bit sick to my stomach. I am both angry at him for not trusting me enough to approach the couple and flooded with relief that he did not.

Over the next several hours, we all compare stories, starting with the tale of our birth as told by my mother and father. Mum and Dad shed a few more tears of regret, of course, but more out of relief and joy, I believe. Their long-lost child has come back to them.

"My mother passed away several years ago," Jolene tells us, a bittersweet smile on her face as she talks about Jennilyn Winston. "She led a difficult life, choosing one wrong thing after another. By the time I was fifteen, I had become the adult in the home, working an after-school job, and babysitting on the weekends for some of the other folks in our apartment complex. Someone eventually turned us in to Child Protective Services, and two months after I turned sixteen, I was taken from her and put into foster care."

"Jolene," Mum murmurs softly, but she says nothing more. What is there to say?

My twin shakes her head slowly. "No, no. It was the best thing that could have happened to both of us. I ended up with a wonderful foster family, a couple who loved me like I was one of their own. I wasn't a bad kid, either, so I'm sure that helped." She chuckles good-naturedly. "I stayed with them until I graduated from high school. By then, I was already eighteen, so having aged out of the foster system, I moved out on my own. I already had a great waitressing job, and the restaurant was happy to have me switch to full-time, so my transition to independent adulthood was rather uneventful in the best way possible."

"What about Jennilyn?" my father asks. "You said it was best for her, too."

Jolene nods slowly. "It was. Not at first, or at least it didn't seem like it. But I think she was stuck in this outdated mentality that a single parent was a second-class citizen. That the odds were stacked against her, and there was no way she could overcome those odds while she had me to look after. It became a self-fulfilling prophecy, you know?" She shrugs, and Pete reaches over to cover her hand with his.

His large fingers curl protectively around her long slender hand that is so like mine, and I have to look away from the intimate gesture. I miss the man I thought my husband was, but not enough to miss Adam, and that knowledge breaks my heart.

"Once I was no longer her responsibility—"

"Even though in truth, she was yours," Pete cuts in, his gentle voice tinged with deep emotions I can't quite put a finger on.

"I took care of her the best I could, love," Jolene says, turning her hand over on the table so she can squeeze his. "But I was still her responsibility."

Pete's grunt is noncommittal at best, and I have to smile when my father makes a similar sound. I can't say that I disagree with their sentiments; I don't quite understand how Jolene can be so well-rounded with a childhood like the one she is describing.

"It took her awhile, but after I moved out, she finally found her footing. She somehow managed to get a decent job as a receptionist for a nonprofit organization that helps ex-cons get back into the work force. She loved it right up to the end." Jolene eyes glisten, but she smiles, a hint of pride in her expression. "Mom and I kept in touch, and when she got sick—lung cancer, because although she quit drinking, she smoked like a chimney. When she got sick, I was in a place where I was ready to be there for her again." She turns her brilliant smile on Pete, who lifts her hand and presses a kiss on her knuckles.

"Jolene applied for a job at Mancini's, and I knew within minutes of meeting her that I would not be hiring her." Pete picks up the story from there. "We have a strict non-fraternization rule between management and staff, and there was no way I was going to be able to keep that rule if she came to work for us."

Jolene smiles prettily and lowers her gaze to their clasped hands. They are so much in love it almost hurts to witness, but my heart is happy for her. Overflowing with joy for her.

"So I asked her if she'd have dinner with me so that I could explain why I couldn't hire her." Pete nudges her shoulder with his. "She didn't even hesitate to say yes, did you, Joley. We were both done for. No doubt about it."

Jolene shrugs, her expression practically glowing as they tell their love story. "He was—he *is*—perfect for me in every way. If he hadn't pursued me, I would have been Mancini's best customer."

Pete reaches over to put a hand on her baby bump and teases, "I keep telling her to slow down, but this woman loves lasagna."

We move to the living room where Jolene tells us about Jennilyn's cancer, and about the last few months she spent with her mother. With our mother. The woman is a stranger to me, but as Jolene talks about her, I find that I can accept that I will never know her, other than through the words of my twin. I will make a point to thank my parents for the wonderful life they have given me, and to never forget the sacrifice Jennilyn—and Jolene, by default—made in order for me to have this life.

"Mom never told me about you, Dani. I never knew, at least not here." She taps her temple, her eyes bright with a telltale glisten of tears, then presses her palm flat over her heart. "But—and I'm sure this sounds silly—I feel like I have always known about you." Her voice hitches a little, and I find myself holding my breath as what she says resonates in me. "I have always felt like I was living for more than just me, that there was a reason I needed to rise above my circumstances and Mom's limitations. I always felt like I knew there was more of—of—" She breaks off and shrugs, one side of her mouth hitching up in a half-smile. "I don't know. Of me. Does that make sense?"

I am nodding the whole time she's talking. "Yes," I declare. "Yes, absolutely."

"It's not silly, darling," Mum assures her. "Not at all. Of course you would know. You both had to know. You were two peas in a pod in the most literal sense of the term."

I tell Jolene about Elle, about how she looked just like me, how she was the other half of me. The me in the mirror.

I share briefly with Jolene and Pete about my rocky marriage and its looming demise, and they are both devastated and supportive. I don't tell them about Adam's case of mistaken identity. He is not their problem. Eventually, he will realize that I am telling the truth about having a twin. He will realize that his excuse to behave badly—my presumed infidelity—was just that. An excuse. A reason to justify his selfish pursuits.

Eventually he will realize that he has to grow up and accept responsibility for his own decisions, his own happiness, and his own future. Especially if he wants to be involved in the happiness and future of our children.

We talk about our pregnancies. Jolene and Pete are having a girl—one, not two—and their daughter is due about a month before my babies' full-term due date. If statistics prove accurate with me, it's quite possible that our girls could be born within days of each other.

I do not tell my sister about my best friend. I have missed her all evening. Her absence is like a rock in my shoe, or a sliver just under the skin, and every time I bump up against that spot, I feel the sharp pang of something that will fester if it's left untended. This time with Jolene and my parents, and Pete, of course, is important, and I wouldn't change anything about our time together. But the fact that I will not be ringing up Ranae the moment my twin and her husband leave this home pains me deeply.

It is nearly midnight when Jolene and Pete finally make their exit. They have not overstayed their welcome by any means, but both of us pregnant women are practically falling asleep on our feet. They have agreed to join us next week for Sunday dinner. Pete insists on bringing his signature lasagna.

"You won't be sorry," Jolene gushes as Pete wraps a supportive arm around her waist and leads her down the few steps from our front porch. "But don't ask him for his recipe. He won't even tell me what it is." She is slurring her words, and I find that I feel a little drunk myself, although neither of us have had even a sip of my father's wine.

Ranae

It has been some of the longest weeks of my life. I am weary of my daughter's silent rage, of her one-word responses to me. I miss her smile, her laughter, the way her eyes light up when something delights her. Although she was released from her grounding last weekend and spent the night with Emma so they could dress up and hand out trick or treat candy to the little kids in her friend's family-friendly suburban neighborhood, Ruby has continued this whole week like she is still being disciplined. She has come home immediately after school and shut herself up in her room until dinner. It's almost as though she is punishing herself in order to punish me. Perhaps it's like a hunger strike, but instead of starving herself until I give in to her demands, she's going to ground herself until I do.

Except that I don't know what her demands are because she won't speak to me.

Oh, I'm sure they include contacting Solomon's sister, and I'm fairly certain they also include an apology of some kind from me.

The thing is, if Ruby would talk to me, I'd tell her that I am ready to reach out to Sarah McCray. If Ruby would engage with me, I'd tell her that the only reason I haven't done so already is because I want to talk things over with Ruby first.

Maybe I'm being just as stubborn as my daughter, but I want her to make the first move toward reconciliation. She knows I am here, waiting for her, and I want her to learn the fine—although often painful—art of rebuilding bridges.

It's now Saturday again, and with no burial services on the agenda for the day, and thanks to Ruby's help last week, I don't have any pressing tasks to complete over at Fair Havens this morning. I lie in bed wishing I could call Dani and pour out my angst on her. What is she doing today? It's a day we'd usually spend at least a portion of together, and I miss her.

I miss her fiercely. I'm still angry at her, I suppose, but only because Ruby is still angry at me.

I'm so sick of everyone being angry at everyone else. I pick up my phone and stare at the screen, waiting, hoping, begging Dani to call.

Hey. Here's a thought, Niemeyer. Why don't you call Dani?

I really hate that voice of reason that speaks up now and then in my head. I shove the phone under my pillow and pull my blankets up over my face.

I finally crawl out of bed just after nine o'clock. I wanted to sleep in this morning, but I got up to use the bathroom about an hour ago, and no matter how deeply I burrow under my squishy down comforter, in spite of my chilly darkened bedroom that's usually perfect for hunkering down for the long haul, there seems to be nothing I can do to stop my mind from cycling relentlessly through all the unresolved circumstances in my life right now.

Maybe I will go find Hugo this morning. Maybe I can pour my angst out on him. I haven't seen him much since our impromptu baring of the souls at Chloe's graveside last week. I worry that he regrets telling me about that day, or even just talking about it and stirring up the memories. I worry, too, that if we don't find a way to connect on such a personal level again soon, that we will lose this new measure of intimacy between us.

It's not something I want to lose. Not ever. If I can't have Hugo's love, then I will cling to his friendship with all the fierceness of my desperate heart.

In the kitchen, Gran is starting a batch of yummy, yeasty bread. Her arthritis won't allow her to knead manually anymore, but she stands guard over her ancient Kitchenaid as the bread hook attachment works the dough for her, watching for the moment when she deems the kneading is sufficient. It's an art, bread-making is, and it's one I have not mastered.

I have, on the other hand, mastered the art of bread-*eating*, and I sidle close to breathe in the tangy sweet aroma. "What's for supper tonight?" I ask. The three of us usually fend for ourselves for lunch on Saturdays.

"Burgers if you'll man the grill, but it's supposed to be pretty cold tonight. Tuna salad sandwiches on fresh bread otherwise."

"Mmm. Burgers sound delicious, but I want some of your bread." I sniff the air and sigh dreamily. "I want to eat a whole loaf right now."

"I'm making burger buns, too," she says.

I clap gleefully. "Woo-hoo! Burgers it is, then. I'll fire up the grill around five, okay?"

Ruby hasn't stirred yet this morning, and I have to admit that it's a relief not to have her dour countenance darkening every room she's in.

Less than an hour later, Blimey and I are making our way via the back yard toward the little foot bridge that crosses over to Fair Havens. It's downright cold this early November morning, and I am bundled up in several layers, my favorite knock-off Burberry scarf wrapped around my neck and pulled up to my ears inside the fleece-lined hood of my coat. I have an insulated mug of coffee in one hand, and a paper bag with a few chocolate chip cookies leftover from a batch I made last night. They're nothing special, but I know Hugo likes them, and I feel like I can't just show up to bug him empty-handed.

Blimey is lumbering slowly along beside me, the cold making his joints stiff and uncooperative. But fortunately for him, I'm not long-legged like Dani, and I prefer to walk at a more... well, *meandering* pace. Instead of heading for the unmarked trail that leads through the woods to the Beckenbauer's place, however, I veer toward the schoolhouse where my office is. I don't need to stop there first; it's really just a ruse to put off heading to Hugo's a little longer. Just as I feared would happen, I am suddenly feeling uncertain about stopping by unannounced. Maybe I should find some work to do and wait for Hugo to come to me. Fair Havens is neutral ground, and if I go to his place, he might make assumptions that I'm making assumptions.

I shake my head at my indecision. I am not an indecisive person, not in general. I am not exactly indecisive where Hugo is concerned, either. Not really. I mean, I have no doubt about my feelings for him. I love him. I have loved him as a friend for as long as I've known him, and over the years since Chloe's death, my love has developed into so much more. I know if he loved me in return, there would be no hesitation on my part. I would give myself fully to him in every way, no holding back, no second thoughts, no cold feet.

"I'm not indecisive," I mutter as I make my way up the steps and pull my keys from my pocket. "But I am afraid." The letter from Solomon's sister has reawakened all my old self-worth struggles, and there is still a seventeen-year-old Ranae inside of me who is afraid I'm not worthy of being loved by anyone.

My gloved fingers make me fumble a little finding the right key, and the sound of raised voices coming from around the building in the parking lot catches my attention.

"You just don't get it, do you? You all think you know what's best for me, but you're wrong. You're wrong!"

Ruby.

I stiffen in surprise. I thought she was still in bed. I glance down at Blimey who slowly cocks his head, his right ear hitching up as he listens. I smooth the rough fur over the bony curve of his skull, more to settle my own spirit than anything. "Let's go see what's going on, Blimers, shall we?" Together, we head back down the steps and around the building. I jerk to a stop when I see who my daughter is speaking to.

Ruby is standing in a confrontational pose in front of Hugo. He looks the part of the quintessential woodsman grave digger, complete with scuffed industrial work boots, knit cap pulled down low to cover his ears, and a heavy military green barn coat hanging open over a quilted flannel shirt. It's one I recognize. He often leaves it hanging on one of the coat pegs inside the schoolhouse during the colder months. I may or may not have sniffed it a time or two. He has a shovel in one hand, the tip of the spade stuck into the earth beside him, and a hatchet in the other, and he's wearing the fingerless leather gloves Ruby often teases him about.

It's the look on his face that gives me pause. It's a mixture of frustration and disappointment, and yes, maybe even anger, and I've never seen him look at my daughter that way.

Ruby's back is to me, but I can tell by her stance that she is challenging him, or perhaps refusing to back down from a challenge he's given her. "You think you're all high and mighty helping out poor, fatherless kids like me and William, but you forget. I have a father. A father who wanted me. I am not William, and I don't need you to play daddy to me, Hugo Beckenbauer," she grinds out. "I've heard what you have to say, all right? Are you happy? Will you get off my back now?"

I cringe at her choice of words, an echo of Chloe's to Hugo just before their accident. I see something dark flash across Hugo's face, and without thinking, I surge forward, calling out a too-bright greeting to them.

Ruby turns on her heels toward me so quickly that she stumbles. Hugo grabs for her arm to steady her, and the shovel he was holding topples to the gravel beside him. My daughter rears back, jerking free of his grip, bringing both arms up in front of her as though she is afraid that he might strike her. "Get your hands off me," she shrieks, her face a mask of misery and rage.

Enough. This has gone on far too long.

I step between them and reach for Ruby, ignoring her angry shriek as I wrap my arms around her and pull her stiff and unrelenting body toward me. I am not much taller than she is, but I have a good fifty pounds on her. Yes, I'll manhandle her if I need to, because I know my daughter. I am hers and she is mine, and I know her like I know myself.

Sure enough, after a few moments, I feel her shudder in the first wave of capitulation. Although she is no longer trying to shove me away, her arms are still up between us, her body rigid in my embrace. But she presses her forehead hard into my shoulder, and with her hands covering her face, she releases a pent-up keening sound that just about tears my guts out. Blimey leans into my hip, whimpering in commiseration as Ruby gives into a bout of inconsolable weeping. All I can do is hold her while she comes apart.

"It's all right," I whisper over and over, doing my best to keep from keening right along with them both.

"Why?" Ruby finally manages to get out. The word is laced with pain. "Why have you told everyone about my family except me?" I can feel her stiffening again, gearing up to pull away again, but I don't loosen my hold.

"Don't be angry at Hugo," I murmur against her hair. "He doesn't know about the McCrays, sweetheart. The only people who know about them were those closest to me when your daddy died." I sigh, realizing that the moment of truth has arrived. It's time that she knows the rest of her story, and I know that also means the parts of the story that I don't know. Parts that will have to come from Solomon's family. "I haven't told anyone anything about them in more than sixteen years. I wasn't allowed to."

Ruby lifts her head and pulls back a little to peer up at me, puzzled and still clearly wary. "What does that mean?" Her voice is scratchy and raw, and she is beginning to shiver in my arms. I realize that she's not dressed warmly enough to be standing out here in the cold. Beneath her heavy down jacket, she is wearing only a pair of leggings and a long-sleeved t-shirt.

"Can we go sit inside?" I ask, and not just for her sake. My legs are a little shaky, and I think I might need to sit down.

I can tell by her stiff shoulders that she wants to resist, that she wants to have it out, here and now, but her teeth are now chattering noticeably, and she needs a tissue. She offers a begrudging nod and steps away from me. "Fine." The single word is indignant enough to let me know that she hasn't yet forgiven me, and she heads toward the front of the little white building without waiting for me.

I turn to Hugo. He stands as stiff and rigid as Ruby, his expression of misery echoing hers, as well. "I'm sorry," I begin, at a loss for words. I spread my hands in silent consternation as my eyes start to burn again. I don't want to cry. I need to present a composed front to Ruby so that she can cry if she needs to.

Hugo is before me in two long strides, and he pulls me close in a quick, almost fierce hug. "You're a good mother, Ranae. Don't forget that." He leans back enough to look at me, then smooths my hair from my face with both hands.

The gesture is so intimate and tender that I want to dive back into his arms and bury my face against his chest, absorbing some of his unshakable belief in me. I want him to hold me and to promise me everything is going to be okay. Because if Hugo says everything is going to be okay, I just might believe it. I want him to go on touching me, soothing me, and oh, how I want him to *love* me. *Why won't you love me, Hugo?* I close my eyes briefly; afraid he'll see exactly what I'm thinking.

"I'm a good mother," I repeat with a nod. I am the best mother I know how to be, but I don't know if my best is good enough.

"I'll be working right outside the door in the family graveyard for now. If you need me," he says when I open my eyes to meet his gaze again. Then he releases me and gestures for me to follow after my daughter.

I chose to have our conversation in the church rather than the schoolhouse in the hopes that the serenity of the quaint little building will help soothe the raw emotions between us. It was a holy place before I ever set foot in it, and since Fair Havens has taken it over, it's only become more so in my eyes. Lives have changed irrevocably in this room—the loss of a loved one will do that. But I have seen folks come together after years of separation, whether brought on by distance or difficult relationships, and I have seen families restored over their shared heartaches and memories. I have witnessed parents clinging to one another as they say goodbye to a child, husbands and wives pressing kisses to the foreheads of their carefully laid out spouses, siblings covering the folded hands of a sister or brother one last time in this building. And I know that mine are not the only silent prayers that have been lifted to the heavens in this country sanctuary. I know Ruby feels the hallowedness of it all; she's said as much to me before. And it is my hope that she will find the same kind of comfort inside these four walls that so many have before her.

We sit side by side while I tell her everything, starting from the first day I met Solomon, filling in any of the details I've left out of our time together. I tell her about the terrible dark days of silence that followed Solomon's visit home over the holidays, how my heart and mind feared what I thought was the worst that could ever happen, that he would have second thoughts about us, that he would choose to walk away from me and my baby.

"I was preparing myself even then for it to be just you and me, Ruby," I tell her, swallowing hard around the memory of those endless days of not knowing. "How foolish I was to think that him abandoning us was the worst that could happen."

I tell her about the day Nolan came home with the news that Solomon hadn't returned to school after winter break, that he'd died in a car accident. I describe the terrible day my own father and I spent in the law offices of Frederick and Vancour, and I give her the exact words Mr. Vancour told us about that tragic day—each syllable is stamped on my mind for eternity—about Solomon's argument with his mother, the telephone pole, his death on impact, and that he didn't suffer. And I tell her about the ultimatum I was given by the McCray family.

"Take the money and give up the baby, or take the baby and give up the money," Ruby said, the only words she'd spoken so far.

"That about sums it up, Rubes," I say, smiling dryly at her adroit turn of phrase. I've never put it quite so succinctly in my own mind.

She grunts softly, but she still sits with her arms crossed, her chin down, her eyes drilling holes in the back of the pew in front of us. There is still a good foot of space between us that she made sure to leave when I sat down.

"I chose you, baby. I still choose you, and I always will." I take a long, deep breath and let it out slowly, mentally preparing myself to broach the subject of Sarah McCray Crawley and her ill-timed email.

Ruby sighs, too, but says nothing else, so I continue.

"So when Solomon's sister wrote to me a few weeks ago and asked to meet you, I—" I break off, unsure how to explain the waves of emotions that had washed over me when I read her note. I finally reach over and touch the back of her head, sliding my palm down to cup the half-moon curve at the base of her skull. It still fits so perfectly in my hand, and I find myself aching for the days when she was a tiny baby, and I could cuddle her close against my breast, cupping her head while she nursed, our gazes locked in complete adoration of each other. "I was scared, Ruby," I finally admit, my voice shaking a little. "I *am* scared. What if I let them in, only to discover they are still toxic, vile people? What if I say yes to this sister of Solomon's only to learn that she is her mother reincarnated? What if her intentions are wrong?"

"What did she say?" Ruby asks in a small voice, still not looking at me, but she isn't pulling away from my touch, either.

"I'll let you read it," I tell her, digging in my coat pocket for my phone. Even though I told Dani to trash the email, I know it's still there. I didn't delete it from the trash file, and I know Dani hasn't either. It only takes me a moment to find it and open it up. I hand my phone over to my daughter, forcing myself to uncurl my fingers and release it. It feels like I'm handing her a grenade with the clip pulled.

I try not to watch her as she reads the few short lines, instead, focusing on the rustic décor up on the dais. An age-darkened native oak cross dominates the place, a piece of handiwork constructed by my great-great-great grandfather, from what I'm told. There's a white-washed bureau beneath it decorated with three tall urns filled with stunning seasonal floral arrangements. They are from Hettie Meadows of Meadowlark Herb and Flower Farm in the nearby town of Autumn Lake, the place where we order all our organic and biodegradable funeral arrangements and graveside flowers. On either side of the dais are tall windows draped in a pale sage chambray fabric. The curtains wash well and any fading that might happen only adds to the ambiance of the place.

"Her intentions don't sound wrong," Ruby murmurs, bringing my attention back to her. She doesn't hand me back my phone, and her eyes are still scouring the words. I understand. I have poured over those few sentences myself dozens of times since receiving it.

"I know. And it was Sarah who asked Mr. Vancour to make sure I got the ring Solomon picked out for me. For us." I purchased a beautiful gold chain last week after speaking with Sarah. I want Ruby to have the ring, and I want her to wear it around her neck as a reminder that she is deeply loved, and that she has been from the moment her father and I discovered her existence.

She nods, but doesn't say anything.

"I want to believe her, Ruby. I do." I reach over, and when she starts to hand me back my phone, I shake my head, and rest my palm on her thigh instead, letting her keep the phone. She'll likely want to reread the email at least a dozen more times, if I know my daughter. "But I'm scared. It was terrible to lose Solomon, sweetheart, but to be cast out by his family in such a cruel way was more than anyone should have to bear. I don't know if I have it in me to face that possibility again. To face *them* again. What if I'm not good enough for their high society ways? What if I'm just a country bumpkin morgue girl to them?" There's that stupid quiver in my voice again. "What if they try to come between us? What if it's you they want, and not me? I—I couldn't bear losing you, Rubes. I couldn't bear it." The last words come out in a tremulous squeak as I try in vain to swallow back my tears.

My daughter covers my hand with her own. "You wouldn't be facing them alone, Mom," she whispers. "And they could never come between us." She's crying again, too; I feel a hot teardrop land on my forearm. "Even when I hate you, I love you," she adds in all her teenage rancor. Then she snorts and groans. "Ew, nasty. I need another tissue. I just blew a snot bubble."

I burst out laughing and hold out the pastel green and blue Kleenex box. Every pew is stocked with a box of tissue. "You always did blow the best snot bubbles," I tell her, nudging her shoulder with my own.

We sit in silence after she blows her nose, then she finally lifts red-rimmed eyes to me and asks, "So what are you going to do about her?"

I purse my lips as I consider how to respond. "I think the better question is what are *we* going to do about her. What do you think we should do?" It's a brave move on my part; I already know what she wants. But I do trust her to understand my position, and to take it into consideration.

She shrugs, then relaxes her shoulders again and slides a little lower in her seat, propping her feet on the crossbar of the pew in front of her. "I don't know. I can see why you wouldn't want to meet her."

"Meet her?" I say with a large amount of alacrity. "I don't want to even acknowledge her existence, to be honest. I want to trash that email and pretend it doesn't exist, either." I tuck a strand of her curly pink hair behind ear. "I suppose that's not an option anymore, though, is it?"

In that moment, I see myself in her when I was her age. The internal battle that every teenager wages, the longing, the desire, the *need* to grow up and be taken seriously warring with the ache of wanting to stay a child forever, that being a big girl only means eating all her vegetables and brushing her teeth for two-and-a-half minutes, not visits from Aunt Flo and messy family drama and working through difficult painful relationship stuff. And I fight a fresh wave of tears as I realize that my deepest fears—and they are fears, I have to admit—are coming to pass, in spite of my efforts to hold them at bay.

My precious baby is growing up. She is becoming a young woman, her own person, and I am losing her anyway.

"I'd like to meet her," Ruby says softly. "But not by myself. I want you there." She reaches over and takes my hand, squeezing it tightly, and I sense her own fear in the gesture.

I just nod, certain my voice won't work if I try to speak.

"But..." She hesitates, then starts again. "But maybe you can meet with her first. Make sure she's on the up and up, if you know what I mean. You're a good judge of character, Mom. You'd know right away if she was full of it."

I squeeze her hand back. "That sounds like a good plan to me," I tell her. For a moment, I wonder if Dani would like to go with me. Then with a sharp pang, I remember that I sent my best friend away. The echoes of our heated words still ring loudly in my mind.

How on earth did things get so messy? I seem to be asking that question a lot these days.

As if hearing my thoughts, Ruby asks, "Are you and Dani going to be okay?" Her voice hitches a little, and I realize she might be as traumatized by our fallout as she is by the news of Sarah McCray.

I decide not to lie to her. I'm not good at lying anyway. Although I've somehow managed to keep the McCray secret and to hold onto my deep-seated grudge against Solomon's family all these years, when all is said and done, I'm really not good at secrets or grudges. Having released both—the secret and yes, even the grudge—into this sacred place with the one person I love more than any other in the world, I'm enveloped in a great sense of relief and even freedom.

No, I will not lie to my daughter. No more lies. No more secrets.

"I honestly don't know, Rubes. I believe—I *hope*—that Dani and I can patch this up. But a lot of things were said that have been left unsaid for a long time." I swallow hard, hating the truth of my words. "I think—I think it might be a little hard and sad between us for a while."

"Are you going to even try to patch things up?" she asks, reaching for another tissue. "Ow. My nose is raw," she moans softly.

"Of course I will. I promise you that. I'm going to fight for my friend, no matter what." I twist on the bench, drawing one leg up underneath me so that I'm facing her. "But Ruby, you need to know that Dani is dealing with some really big things in her life right now. She may need some time to sort through it all, and that time may not include me."

"Like, that she has a twin she never knew about? Maybe a whole family she never knew about?" Her questions are direct, but not spoken harshly. She shrugs one shoulder. "That's more like huge things, Mom. Ginormous things."

I nod. "I know. It's really huge. And the fact that her parents left out the very important detail that she was a twin when telling her about her birth is pretty huge, too. That relationship has to be top priority for her, and I want to give her the space she needs to figure things out with them."

"Why do you think they would they do that?" she asks. "I can see why she'd be upset at them."

"I don't know the answer to that," I tell her. "But I do know the good doctors Nelson and Nelson, and they are the best kind of people this world has. They must have had a very good reason for choosing to withhold that information."

"Kind of like you did," she says, lifting her gaze to me again. Her poor little nose is bright red. I lean forward and kiss the tip of it, then pull her toward me, wrapping my arms around her.

"Thank you for understanding," I whisper against her hair. "And for not hating me. Or at least for loving me even though you hate me."

"I don't hate you, Mom," she grumbles. "Even when I feel like hating you, I can't. I may not like you very much sometimes, but I don't hate you."

"Well," I say, releasing her and gently chucking her under the chin. "The feeling is mutual, you know. I love you no matter what. Even when I don't like you so much."

Ruby rolls her eyes. "Wow. Great momming, Mom. I'll just go slit my wrists right now."

"Hey." I take her chin and make her look at me. "Don't joke about stuff like that, okay? My mommy heart can't take it."

"Sorry."

"Me, too," I tell her. "About all of this. About the secrets, the lies. I should have told you sooner. When I gave you my journal would have been a good time.

I should have trusted you with my painful memories, too, and not just my happy ones, Rubes. Will you forgive me?"

"It's okay, Mom. I totally understand. I do. I kinda loathe the McCray family right now. I mean, they don't deserve us, you know? They have no clue how much awesomeness they missed out on by shutting us out of their lives." She strikes a goofy, swanky pose as best as she can while slouched in the pew, and I laugh at her antics.

"You're right. They don't deserve us. But…" I draw the word out and sigh. "Then there's grace and mercy and kindness and forgiveness, isn't there? So when do you want me to contact Sarah?"

Ruby is quiet for a few moments, her brow furrowing in consideration. Finally, she says, "I guess you should decide, Mom. I can wait until you're ready."

I turn in the pew again, planting both feet on the ground, and slide over so we're pressed up against each other. I drape an arm around her shoulders and pull her close. She rests her head against me, and we sit there in silent camaraderie.

"I'll email her back this evening, okay? Ask her if she wants to get together on Saturday morning. Do you want to be there? Or would you like me to meet with her on my own, first? You know you can hang out with Gran and her gang—she's got a bunch of girlfriends coming over to start on pies for the church's Thanksgiving outreach coming up in a couple weeks. They love it when you're around, you know. You make them feel young again."

She ponders her options a moment, then shoots me a worried look. "Are you okay to meet her first? Make sure she's not a freak? I mean, I can go with you if you'd rather, but…" She leaves her sentence unfinished.

"I'll meet with her first. Put the screws to her," I assure my daughter. "Make sure her motives are pure."

"Okay. Then I'll stay with Gran. I'll need something to keep me busy so that I don't chew my nails down to nubs while waiting to hear what you think of her. Besides, I like hanging with those grand old hootenannies, too."

"Hootenannies?" I ask, pulling back a little to try to look down at her. "Do you even know what a hootenanny is?"

Ruby lifts her head and smirks. "It's a country dance, right? But in my mind, it means nannies—or grannies—who are a hoot. Hootenannies, see?"

I laugh at her perfectly logical reasoning. "Makes sense to me. Hootenannies they are, indeed."

Ruby reaches up to sweep her curls from her face, but the moment she lowers her hands again, the pink coils spring back into their riotous disarray. She really is pretty dang cute, even with her tear-stained face, and the worried creases that still tug her brows together over her big eyes. "Gran knows everything, right? About everything, I mean? Who all knows? I mean, I'm assuming Dani does, but who else?"

I lift my hand to stop her barrage of questions. "Whoa, there," I say, sounding a little like Hugo. "Gran knows. She was the first person I came to after I found out that Solomon had died. The first person other than Sol and Dani that I talked to when I found out I was pregnant. Your grandma and grandpa know, of course, but even your uncles don't know all the details. Nolan was friends with your daddy, so I did tell him a little more than I shared with Jordan at the time. Dani's parents know the basics—I had a lot of support from them, especially from Francis, during my pregnancy."

"You said Hugo doesn't know anything." She might phrase it as a statement, but I can hear the question in her voice.

"I did tell both Hugo and Chloe that your father died before we were married, but that's about it. I'm sure they put a few puzzle pieces together over the years. It's not like we've kept our ages a secret, is it? They probably figured it out pretty quickly that I was a pregnant teenager."

"Does anyone else know about Sarah's—is she my Aunt Sarah? That's so weird. About her email? Other than Dani and Gran, I mean?"

"No," I say, shaking my head slowly. "I haven't had the guts to tell anyone about it yet. I told Gran about it because you were being such a turd last week—"

"Hey!" Ruby elbows me in the side.

I grunt and squeeze her shoulders. "Well, you were. And Dani only knows because she saw it first. Otherwise, I might have kept it from her, too."

"Right." Ruby rolls her eyes again. "Like you can keep any secrets, Mom."

"Well, I kept this one for a stinkin' long time, didn't I?" I flick her knee gently.

"Yeah, and look where that got you," she shoots back, but she's grinning, taking the edge off the words. She leans her head back on my shoulder and sighs. "Wow. I'm worn out by all of this."

"I know, baby. Me, too." Her hair tickles my cheek and I reach up to smooth it down. "Me, too" I repeat with a sigh that matches hers.

"Um, Mom?" Her tone changes, grows suddenly serious, and I hold my breath, hoping she isn't going to tell me something I don't want to hear. "I'm really sorry for going into the woods on bonfire night. I knew it was stupid, but when William wouldn't listen to me, I went in after him rather than coming to get you or Hugo. I should have come and got one of you. I know that, and I'm sorry."

I pull away and turn to take both her hands, waiting until she looks me in the eyes. "I forgive you, Ruby, and I understand. I get the dilemma you were in, and you're right, you should have come to get one of us. But I also know your intentions were good, and I want you to know that I'm proud of you. You are the best daughter a mother could ever hope for."

She gives me a half smile. "And I guess you're not a terrible mom, either."

"Get out of here, you little freak," I tell her, rising to my feet and pulling her up beside me, then hugging her hard again. "I love you; you know that?"

"I know. And I love you, too." She wraps her slender arms around me and hugs me back. A few moments later, she steps away and makes her way down the aisle. Just before she pushes open the door, she calls back, "By the way, I just wiped my nose on your coat." Then she ducks out the door.

Sure enough, there's a slime trail on my shoulder. I grab a tissue and wipe at it, trying not to gag.

I need to go tell Hugo all is well in the Niemeyer home. Then I need to talk to Gran to let her know she's in charge of keeping Ruby too occupied to stress over my meeting with Sarah.

Surprisingly, I'm not stressing about it, either. Telling Ruby about the McCrays seems to have lifted a huge dark cloud from hovering around my head and shoulders, one I didn't know existed. Or maybe I knew it did, but I hadn't realized it was so huge. Or black. It's remarkable how much the fear of the unknown can weigh us down.

I wonder again what Dani is doing. I wonder if she'd talk to me if I called her right now. I know she must be worried about Ruby, and I'm kind of surprised she hasn't at least called to see if my daughter is okay. But then I remember the devastated look on her face when I sent her away. I'm sure she's also still angry at me for all the reasons she listed and more. I will give her time, and hope that she can see that my heart is in the right place, and my intentions are good, even if my execution is often flawed.

If Ruby can forgive me, then surely Dani will, too. Someday.

Dani

"We need to talk," Adam says, his voice gentle in my ear. I hold the phone away, hating how my automatic response is to turn malleable when he uses that tone with me. He continues. "Come home, please. We can't work things out if you're not here."

"I *am* home, Adam." In spite of my efforts, there is a slight tremor behind my words. Not because I want to go back to the house Adam and I have shared our whole marriage, but because my parents' home isn't really mine anymore, either. I feel like I don't belong anywhere.

"I know you better than that, Dani." He's picked up on my uncertainty; I can hear it in the way he speaks to me. He's so good at shifting gears, at tipping the scales incrementally so that I lose my balance before I even know what's happening. "This is your home. Our home. I love you. I miss you. Your sleepy smile in the morning, your beautiful face at the end of a hard day. Come home, baby. Please."

"Adam, stop." I hold up a hand even though he can't see it. But then, the action is more for my benefit than his. I need all the tactile reminders I can get that I'm not going to fold right now. I'm not going to just go back.

I would like nothing more than for my marriage to be a good one, the right one, but in the two weeks since I've been away from Adam, it's as if my blinders have come off, the rose-colored glasses are gone, and the binding around my chest has been loosened. I feel like I can breathe freely for the first time in months, maybe years, and I can only attribute it to being out of that house. I haven't had to tiptoe around, wondering if what I say and do will offend anyone. I don't have to second guess anyone's mood so that I know how to respond. I haven't had to close my mouth and keep my expression neutral even once since being here, and my parents have done nothing to make me feel guilty for needing anything, whether it be food, sleep, a hug, or silence.

Today is the first time I've actually spoken to Adam since walking out of the house with nothing but the clothes on my back, my mug, and my shredded dignity. We've had no contact other than a few necessary texts back and forth to cover logistical stuff like schedules—I wanted to make sure he wouldn't be around on the two occasions I needed to stop by to pick up some work supplies. Other than that, I've let every one of his calls go to voicemail, and I've deleted them all without listening to them.

"Please, Dani. We can work this out."

"I didn't call you because I want to work things out," I tell him. "I called because I want to let you know what my plans are. Plans I've already made." He starts to protest, but I raise my voice to speak over him. "And the only reason I'm sharing them with you is because you are the father of the babies I am carrying. Please," I say when he tries to interrupt again. "Let me finish."

"Okay." The word is drawn out, and I can hear the challenge in it.

"Thank you," I hate that I feel obligated to be grateful to him for allowing me to talk. I clear my throat and speak firmly. "I am going to stay here with my parents through to the holidays." He makes a strangled sound over the phone, but I push on. "If you want to participate in this pregnancy, I will keep you informed of all the appointments I have. I'll be using Tracy as my midwife, and for now, I plan to give birth at Breathe. This is, as you might remember, considered a high-risk pregnancy, so it's probably best that way, anyway."

"Okay." He doesn't expound, so I don't know if that means he does want to participate or not.

"My parents are monitoring me here, and they're both home every evening, so this is also a really good place for me to be, especially in the first half of the pregnancy."

"I can be home every evening, too." He sounds petulant, but I don't take the bait.

"Daddy and I will be coming by the house this weekend to pick up a bunch of my things. I would like for you not to be there."

"Don't be ridiculous. I want to see you. Why can't I be here?" Here? What is he doing home in the middle of a Wednesday morning? "And why do you have to bring your dad?"

"Because I don't want any trouble."

"Come on, Dani. Trouble?" Petulance turns to cajoling. "You're carrying my children. I want to see you," he says again. "I want to see them, your belly. I'm missing out on watching them grow, watching you blossom into motherhood. I want to feel them kick—"

"Adam." I cut him off. The things he's saying should make my heart melt, but since my blinders have come off, it seems my ears are working better, too. There is something disingenuous in his words, his tone. The few times that he has put his hand on my stomach have been at my instigation. *They're moving a lot, Adam. Give me your hand.* He has never come up behind me and wrapped his arms around me to cup my swelling abdomen in his hands, not the way the fathers-to-be do in all the pregnancy pictures on social media. Not once has he spoken to the babies in my belly like they do in the movies, the way I did to Ruby when Ranae was carrying her—Ruby used to come to life when I'd talk to her, filling me with delight. The fact that Adam is now spouting off daddy talk makes my stomach turn.

"What?" He actually sounds hopeful, like he thinks he's changing my mind.

"Why didn't you just come talk to me at Mancini's when you saw me there?" The question surprises me almost as much as it does him. I'd had no intention of bringing up Jolene and Pete with him. Not yet, anyway.

My twin and I haven't seen each other since she and her husband came for dinner; I had to cancel the lasagna dinner because of a birth. But we have emailed back and forth several times. She did text me once, but I responded to her in email. For some reason, maybe because everything in my life seems topsy turvy right now, I feel the need to protect myself. Texting makes me feel too readily available, obligated to respond immediately, whereas emailing allows me to take my time and respond at my own leisure.

That said, I certainly am not ready to discuss her existence with my wayward husband.

It takes him several moments before he responds. When he does speak, there is a definite chill in the words. "So you're not denying it anymore? You *were* at Mancini's then?"

"Actually, no. I've never been to Mancini's. But if you did, indeed, see me as you say you did, then why didn't you just confront me?"

"And embarrass myself even more than I already was? Are you joking? Wasn't it enough of a shock for me to see my wife hanging on the arm of another man?"

He either doesn't believe my denial, or he's got selective hearing. "You really think I wanted to let everyone in my party know my wife was cheating on me?" He is getting louder with each question.

"So you chose to preserve your pride over your marriage?" And there's that kid with the stick again. I wonder if she's been here inside of me all along, just waiting for a chance to brandish her weapon. I'm not sure I like her very much, but I'm not sure I know how to give her the boot, either.

I suppose I could just repeat the fact that I wasn't there, that it wasn't me he saw... but no, he's already talking.

"Don't put words in my mouth," he snarls. "Believe me, my pride was torpedoed out of the water when I saw you there. It was all I could do to get up and walk out of there with my head held high. I couldn't trust myself to confront you. I might have done something stupid."

"Something stupid? Like buy a lake house?" I've had plenty of time in the last couple of weeks to put a few pieces of the puzzle together, especially after poring back over our finances for the last few years. I have been so naïve, trusting Adam to manage our accounts. Fortunately, I know my husband's social security number and his default passwords, so following up on credit card payments has been rather eye-opening. The lake house is only the most recent in a long string of extravagant purchases.

Ranae would accuse me of being far too kind. She'd call them *suspicious* purchases.

Or proof.

"Or plane tickets for two for a plethora of overnight work conferences—what else would all those trips be? Several new credit cards, a new car, a set of—"

He practically sputters into the phone. "You're bringing up the car again? I've told you I bought it for you."

"For me? I have a car."

"For us!" he retorts. "A family car."

"Is the lake house a family lake house, too?"

"How many times do I have to tell you, Dani? It's an investment property. For us." There is nothing gentle or cajoling in his voice now. "Why do you have to be so quick to assume the absolute worst about me?"

I let the damning words hang in the air between us, then finally repeat what he missed earlier. "I'm not the woman you saw at Mancini's, Adam. Had you not assumed the absolute worst about me—" I use his words now. "You would already know that. In fact, you would have met my twin sister before I did."

"Your what?" Adam practically shouts into the phone, disbelief giving his words broken glass edges.

"My twin," I repeat, not letting his rage get to me. "Jolene Sanderson. Who happens to be married to Pete Sanderson, co-owner of Mancini's Fine Dining in Mount Vernon. Oh, and I've heard she likes to go in and have dinner with him now and then. Give him feedback on the quality of the food and service he provides to his customers."

"You are a liar," Adam sputters. "This is some elaborate ruse you're pulling to make me look like the bad guy here. You don't have a twin."

I sigh and rub my tired eyes. "You know what floors me about this conversation, Adam? You'd rather believe the absolute worst about me—that I'm a cheating, *pregnant* wife—than that there is a fantastic and miraculous reason for you seeing what you think you saw. That I have a sister, a twin. You'd rather that I stay in the wrong so you can blame me for your selfish and self-serving behavior. I have a question for you. Who were you with at Mancini's that night? Were you, perhaps, with someone who kept you from approaching the woman you thought was me? Someone you didn't want me to see you with?"

"Oh, no. You do not get to put this on me."

I let his evasion tactic go. I don't need any names. "It doesn't matter. What really matters to me in the end, is why you didn't simply ask me about it? Why have you let this fester between us all this time?" I stand up and stretch my back a little. I think I'm finished with this conversation. "If not at Mancini's, then why not when you got home?"

"Don't be ridiculous," he begins. "I had my pride."

"No, you had your excuse." I interject before he can continue. "Your presumption that I was misbehaving justified your own bad behavior, didn't it? As long as you didn't confront me, you had all the excuses you needed to go about doing your own thing." I pull the phone from my ear and stare at it for a moment, resisting the urge to throw it across the room. Bringing it back to my ear, I say, "You are a coward, Adam. A coward, a liar, a philanderer, a cheat." *A blackguard*, I hear Gran say in my head. "We will be at the house on Saturday at ten in the morning to collect some things. I will need two hours."

"Well, I have a game to watch." For some reason, I am not nearly as shocked as I should be by his response. He seems to have forgotten that it was me he wanted to be there to see.

"Watch it at your bachelor pad."

"There isn't a large screen—"

"Take your precious telly over there before Saturday, Adam." I raise my voice, cutting him off. "I will text you when we're gone."

"We have to talk about this," he tries again.

"No, *we* don't." As I say the words, I realize how true they are. Adam has done a whole lot of talking in our marriage, telling me what he wants, how he feels, how I make him feel, and I have listened, growing quieter and quieter as time has passed. *We*—the both of us contributing—have not really talked about anything in years. Why on earth would we start now? "It's my turn to do the talking, and your turn to listen."

"Don't be ridiculous—"

"Excuse me." He has called me ridiculous three times in this conversation. I am finished. "I have to go. I will text you with my plans. I'll send a backup email," I add spitefully. "Just in case you somehow don't receive my text."

"Dani, wait—"

"Goodbye, Adam." I hang up the phone, cutting off whatever it is he's still saying on his end of the line.

I had intended to wait until after the holidays to sort through this mess of a marriage, to find an attorney who would help us undo the mess we've made. But I realize that was just fanciful thinking on my part. Adam is not a reasonable man, so believing that he will suddenly become reasonable when it comes to a divorce and custody of our children is... well, *ridiculous*.

"Whatever you do, Dani, don't be ridiculous," I tell myself, but I sound nothing like Adam when I do. "We are finished being ridiculous, aren't we, girls?" I tap my belly and grin when I get an answering nudge from the dynamic duo.

I am surprised when Adam is, indeed, out of the house on Saturday when my father and I arrive. We make short work of packing up my winter clothes, my enormous jewelry box, and the wall rack that holds my chunky pendants and bangles. I gather the few baby items I've already begun to amass, and the rest of my daily essentials I have made do without for the last few weeks. We are out of there by noon as promised. I shoot Adam a text saying as much, and although I see that he has read my message, he doesn't respond.

I do not allow myself to dwell on where he is or who he's with.

On Sunday, Jolene and Pete come for dinner once more, and then again, the following week. I wonder if it will become a tradition, these Sunday dinners. I know my parents are as interested in her life as I am, and I can see the hunger in her own eyes to belong to a family again.

We spend hours talking about our childhoods, our fears and uncertainties growing up, our struggles to belong, as well as our accomplishments and goals and dreams for the future. Jolene mourns the breakdown of my marriage with genuine sympathy and sensitivity, and her presence in my life feels like validation of who I am, who I want to be.

The more time we spend together, the more amazed I am at my sister's unflagging spirit. She doesn't seem to begrudge me even one iota for the privileged life I ended up with, while she endured a childhood of squalor and instability and uncertainty. When I acknowledge her gracious perspective of the life we've been doled out, she reaches over and grabs my hand, squeezing it so hard, it almost hurts. But I don't pull away.

"You and me, Dani," she says, her voice impassioned. "We were born with indomitable spirits. I know that's how we both endured the things we did. We may have handled our circumstances differently, but that's what makes us unique, right? I mean, look at you now. You bring life into the world. Don't tell me you don't believe in something bigger than our problems. You live every day with hope—your job depends on it."

Mum and Dad beam at us with pride in their glistening eyes, and Pete watches us with what I can only describe as part wonder, part satisfaction to see his wife so happy.

"Me?" Jolene continues, pressing a hand to her sternum. "Well, my middle name should have been Hope. I always believed there was more to life than what I knew. More to me. I didn't have an imaginary friend like you did, Dani, but there was this other *me* in the mirror. This part of me, at least, that was missing. I thought I found that missing part in Pete." She rests her head on his shoulder and nestles in a little closer to his side. All three of us are sharing the sofa in my parent's living room, Mum and Dad in chairs across from us. "But look! It's you! I love my husband to the stars and beyond—"

"And I love you even more, Joley," Pete interjects in a soft rumble that makes my heart ache for what I now realize I have never had.

"I know, my love," Jolene acknowledges, patting his thigh affectionately. Turning to me, she continues, "But you, Dani, you are the missing part of me. You and me, twin sister of mine, we complete each other."

I nod in agreement, my voice failing me around the emotions flooding through me. I lace my fingers over the bulge of my belly, hoping and praying that my girls will be the same way, that they will complete each other, no matter what the world might do to come between them.

Jolene reaches over and covers my hand with one of hers. "Isn't it amazing? How much more there is to life than just us? We don't ever have to be alone again."

After Jolene and Pete leave that night, and I am sitting by myself in the window seat of my old bedroom, I am overwhelmed by the need to call Ranae, to pour out my heart to her, to tell her all about Jolene. But I also ache to hear her pour out her heart to me. To tell me all about Gran and Ruby, to sigh over Handsome Hugo. Lord, how I miss her. I miss her strength, her decisive personality, the way she props me up and bolsters my backbone.

Phone in hand, my thumb hovers over the keypad. But in the stillness, even as I waver, I come to the realization that it isn't Ranae's strength I need.

I am strong enough on my own.

I am also strong enough to know that I need Ranae in other ways. I need her friendship. I need her joy. Her vivacious perspective on life, and her tender understanding of death. I will need her love and support as I become a mother, as I learn the ropes of raising my babies as a single parent, just as she has needed me all these years.

I am strong enough to understand that need is not weakness, not when it's symbiotic and empowering and faithful and true.

I am strong enough to acknowledge that I do not want to live my life without Ranae in it.

Ranae

Unfortunately, Sarah is out of town for the week, so we have to delay our meeting. Ruby can hardly stand the wait, but I am actually relieved. I will have time to come to terms with opening up the old wounds.

"You're a brave girl, Nae." Gran wraps her funny, flabby arms around me and hugs me tightly when I give her the update on all that's happening. I am always surprised by how strong she is. "You know what I think?"

I smile and wait for her to tell me what she thinks. Because she most certainly will.

"I think you might be surprised when you rip this bandage off. I think you're going to find that your wounds healed long ago, but you've been too afraid to look under the dressing to be sure."

Sarah is quick to agree about meeting alone first. "I want us to be able to speak candidly about the way things happened all those years ago, and I'm afraid if Ruby is present, things might get left unsaid for her sake." She sounds nothing like I thought she would. Even over the phone, she comes across as open and friendly, a contradiction of the picture I have harbored in my mind about the whole family. Other than Solomon, of course.

If circumstances had been different, I would have insisted on Dani coming with us. I considered asking Gran to come. I even thought about asking my father to join me, but I decided to face my past—or will she become part of our future?—like a big girl.

Like the full-grown adult woman I am.

We choose to meet in Mount Vernon, a nearby town where neither of us has any ties, and where it is unlikely either of us will run into anyone we know. There are a dozen pizza joints, a few busy diners and eateries, and a myriad of fast-food options in Mount Vernon, but we opt for an Italian restaurant called Mancini's. The place has stellar online reviews, and I know from Dani that Adam says the food is good, as it is a place he frequents with a few of his coworkers. I'm not worried about him being here, since he is usually glued to his sports network channels at home on Saturday mornings.

I arrive almost an hour before we are scheduled to meet. I want to have plenty of time to settle my nerves, to locate the bathroom—my bladder always gets hyperactive when I'm anxious—and I want to have plenty of time to choose the best booth where our conversation can stay private, but also one near a window so I can see her coming. I am ridiculously nervous, and it doesn't take a therapy session to recognize that even after all these years, I still want Solomon's family to accept me. To like me. I have been carrying around the wound of their rejection like a badge of honor all these years, and I am not quite sure how to take it off.

Sarah McCray is only a year older than I am, a fact I've somehow forgotten, and I'm surprised to see how young she looks. I suppose I expected some stiff-necked, nose-in-the-air old money dame, but she is nothing like that. She was Solomon's excuse to ask me out the very first time, telling me he wanted my help in buying her a birthday present because I reminded him of her. Even now, I can see why he might make the comparison. We don't really look alike. We're about the same height, but she's not curvy like I am. She's got the posture and build of an athlete with broad shoulders and long, slim legs.

Our coloring is very similar, though, and it seems we have a similar fashion sense, too. She and I wear almost the exact same shade of a scarlet coat—Sarah's is a classic double-breasted pea coat, mine is a cropped military-style one that flares out from the belted waist to accommodate my backside. We are both in blue jeans, and although I'm wearing my favorite old school Doc Martens, she, too, wears lace-up boots that give her an air of being ready for anything. She walks with a purposeful stride, though, unlike my unsophisticated amble, and not at all like the long-limbed, loose-jointed gait her brother had, but I don't get the impression she's stuffy or snobby. Just intentional. Direct. Like her emails.

"You still look exactly the same," Sarah tells me without preamble as she slides into the booth opposite me. "I would have known you in a crowded room." She unclasps her shoulder bag and pulls out a framed photo, smiles at it momentarily, and then slides it across the table toward me.

I cover my mouth and stare wordlessly at the frozen image of Solomon and I locked in time. It's a photo of us that I gave him more than sixteen years ago, and I know that if I pull it out of the sleek, black frame and turn it over, I will find the words of a besotted girl written to an equally besotted boy, complete with promises to love him forever and ever, until death do us part.

"We were so young," I finally murmur, my fingertip following the curve of Solomon's handsome, smiling face. I can see Ruby in both of us, and tears spring unbidden to my eyes.

"And so in love," Sarah says. "Both of you." She settles back in the padded seat and studies me, her expression guileless and open.

I nod and meet her gaze. "Yes. All three of us. Solomon and me were both already in love with our baby, too."

"I know." There is no excuse in her voice, no defense. She is simply acknowledging the truth in what I have said. "We all knew."

Hot anger flares up inside me, and I pick up the photo and clutch it to my chest. "I'm taking this with me. It wasn't meant for anyone but him."

"It's yours," Sarah says, gesturing with her hand that I should go ahead. She turns to her bag again, and I am momentarily afraid of what else she might pull out of it. I don't like feeling so vulnerable with this stranger. "There's more," she says.

"Good morning, ladies. I'm Matteo and I'll be serving you today." An attractive waiter in a black, knee-length apron tied around his waist approaches our table and smiles broadly as he hands us menus. "Would you like to start with something to drink?" His dark good looks aren't the only indication of his ethnicity; in a lovely Mediterranean accent, he suggests, "If you've never tried Mancini's lemonade, you should. It will make your toes curl and you will never be satisfied with any other lemonade again."

His flirtatious banter breaks the ice and I find myself grinning tentatively at Sarah across the table from me.

"Wow," she says, her large eyes—so like Ruby's—lifted to meet our waiter's. "How can we say no to an offer like that? Ranae? Lemonade that will curl your toes? My treat."

"Please," I say, and I'm about to argue about who is paying for what, then I close my mouth. *Enough, Niemeyer. Let her pay if she wants to.*

Surprisingly, though, I find that the thought isn't vindictive or in any way ugly.

Enough. That word has been on the tip of my tongue, in the forefront of my thoughts for weeks now.

Enough. Isn't that what we're doing here today? Putting an end to something that has gone on long enough? Far too long, perhaps?

When Matteo leaves with our drink orders and a promise to return with the antipasto platter we order, Sarah reaches into her bag once more. She's a bit like a modern Mary Poppins, and I have to bite back a smile at the thought of her pulling a floor lamp out next.

It's not a lighting fixture she sets on the table in front of her. It's a stack of letters. She crosses her hands over the top of them, but I have already seen the sloping cursive script in the upper left corner of the top envelope. Solomon's. I'd recognize it anywhere, even after all these years, and my heart leaps inside my chest.

"My mother died as she lived; an angry, bitter woman," Sarah says. Again, her directness is startling. "Nothing anyone did made her happy, a disease of the heart she had long, long before my brother died. But after the accident, I know she blamed herself, even though it was your name she used." She smiles sadly and adds, "I think her heart finally just got tired of beating at such a violent pace. She died a few months ago. Just went to bed and didn't wake up."

I don't know how to respond, and my focus is divided between what she is saying and what she has in front of her. My palms are damp at the thought of holding Solomon's letters in my hands, of reading his words on paper. Are they letters to me? Missives he never sent? But that hardly makes sense. "I'm sorry for your loss," I finally manage to get out.

Sarah chuckles softly and cocks her head at me. "You know, I think you actually mean that. Thank you for your kindness."

I nod in response. I do mean it. I can't imagine losing my mother; even the thought makes my heart hurt. But then I can't imagine my mother ever being described as an angry, bitter woman, either.

"When I told Daddy that I was breaching the contract they'd made with you, that I was going to reach out to you, he didn't hesitate to give me his blessing, Ranae."

Again, I don't know what to say. The situation she is describing is so different than anything I have experienced with my own family. I can't imagine my parents ever drawing such hard lines to keep people out of their lives. I can't picture Mom being so hateful to anyone, nor Dad being willing to support that kind of behavior.

"She wanted all of us to sign that terrible contract," she continues. "I turned eighteen less than a year later, and she asked me to sign it, too, since I'd become a legal adult. She was livid when I refused. She wouldn't speak to me for weeks."

I study Sarah for a long moment, then ask the question that's been plaguing me for some time. "Why didn't you reach out to me sooner, then? Why wait until now, after all this time?"

Sarah sighs deeply, a frown marring her features. It's obvious that she's choosing her words carefully, and I want to shake her. To remind her that we are meeting without Ruby for just this reason, so that we can clear the air between us without holding anything back.

"My mother was sick," she finally says. "Not physically, but emotionally. At least it was at first." She taps the side of her head. "It became a mental illness over time, something her doctors prescribed a wide assortment of medications for." Her frown deepens, and I see the muscles in her jaw tighten momentarily. "A treatment plan we are now convinced did far more damage than good."

"I'm sorry," I murmur, hating this story. I haven't allowed myself to consider what might have made Solomon's mother into such a horrible person.

Sarah nods, accepting my sympathy wordlessly. "It wasn't until I was an adult that my father told me about her past. About some terrible abuse she'd endured for much of her childhood." She puts up a hand as though to stop me from arguing. I wasn't planning to, but I get the feeling she's heard a rebuttal or two over the years. "It's not an excuse, but it is a reason, good or bad, for her inability to find any joy in life. There were times she even tried to be a good mother, like that fateful day we went Christmas shopping," she says with a rueful half-smile. "But something in her was broken, Ranae. Something that had broken long before we kids came along. Long before my father came along. He is an honorable man, you know."

I want to ask how her father, being so honorable, could have turned his back on his granddaughter, on his only son's child. How he could have cast us aside without even acknowledging us, but I press my lips together.

Apparently, this stranger can read my thoughts, too.

"He always chose her, Ranae." Sarah smiles ruefully, her expression resigned. I see pain there, too, but I think the wound has healed over and is now more of an ugly scar in her life, rather than something still raw. "Even when she was wrong, he took her side because he knew she needed someone to be on her side no matter what. He stood by her through sickness and health, through good times and bad. And believe me, there were a lot of bad times. I know it doesn't right any of the wrongs done to you, but I hope you can see why—" She falters and shrugs, like she knows she's asking too much of me.

Silence settles in the air between us, and I drop my gaze to the letters on the table in front of her. Sarah notices, but before she can speak, Matteo appears again with a large tray holding our drinks and a gorgeous appetizer platter of thinly sliced prosciutto, salami, and pepperoni, layers of provolone and Asiago fanned out next to a pile of cubed, semi-soft Parmesan, and a ramekin of bite-sized Bocconcini drenched in olive oil and fresh herbs. There are green and purple olives, fire-roasted pepper slices, quartered marinated mushrooms and artichoke hearts, another ramekin of Macadamia nuts, plus a small basket of grilled focaccia bread squares on the side. I'm not sure we'll need anything else to eat after the feast he lays before us.

"This is just the appetizer?" Sarah asks him, echoing my thoughts exactly.

Matteo explains that Italians like to linger over their meals, not just because they love each other's company, but because the longer they sit, the more they can eat. "This is the food of life, ladies. Eat. Enjoy. Live well."

By the time he takes our main course orders, Sarah and I are both grinning appreciatively over his effusive speech and gestures. It's exactly what we need to keep things from getting too serious between us.

"This place is amazing," she says, glancing around the room.

It really is a lovely restaurant, and one I think would make for a lovely date... if I were to ever date anyone. The main part of the restaurant is set up with long group-sized tables and smaller settings, too, but we are in a side section where most of the seating is in booths. It's ideal for more intimate conversations and romantic dinners. I can't help it; I imagine Hugo and I in a booth just like this one, seated across from each other so we can look deeply into each other's eyes, our feet touching under the table...

I blink rapidly and glance around the room to shake myself out of that crazy train of thought.

Adam and some woman I don't recognize are sequestered in a booth across the room from us. I would not have noticed them except that he happened to slide out of his bench at the exact moment I glance their way. He stands facing away from us and digs in his back pocket for his wallet. He counts out a stack of bills and tucks them into the black receipt folder propped on the table in front of him, then offers his hand to the woman to help her up, too.

I am frozen in place, unable to look away from the scene playing out in front of me.

As I watch, he releases her hand, but lays his palm against her low back, his fingers sliding down over the curve of her hip in a gesture far too intimate to be casual. Then without a word, he leads her out of the restaurant, both of their coats draped over his arm.

"Ranae?"

I jerk my attention back to the woman across the table from me. I can feel my cheeks burning, not from embarrassment for having gotten distracted, but in outrage for my best friend.

Sarah is studying me with a concerned expression on her face. "Are you alright? Do you know them?" She glances back in the direction Adam and his... his friend have gone.

"Um, sorry." I shake my head and try to gather my thoughts. I should call Dani immediately. I need to tell her what I've seen. I squeeze my eyes shut. No. I can't just call her out of the blue, not with the way things are between us. That will just seem vindictive and cruel. What am I going to do? "I—I'm not sure. The man reminded me of someone."

"Do you need to go after him?" Her brow is furrowed, and she leans forward, still studying me. "You seem upset."

"No, no. I'm fine," I assure her. But my pulse is racing, I press one hand over my heart against the ache there. "I was just surprised to see him, that's all. If it even was him."

"If you're sure." She's clearly not convinced that I am, but I slide my appetizer plate close to the over-flowing platter between us and prepare to dish myself up some Mediterranean goodness.

She holds up a hand and I still, my spoon hovering just above the pile of olives.

"Before you start, because I know this yummy food can get a little messy." She circles a finger in the air over the antipasto, then once again, covers the stack of envelopes on the table in front of her with both her hands. "I want you to have these. They are letters that my brother wrote to me his first semester away at school." The tragic smile she gives me makes it clear that this is quite a sacrifice on her part. "I missed him terribly, Ranae. Mother's issues made life miserable for everyone, but Solly and I were partners in crime. We were able to endure because we had each other. When he went off to school, it was his letters that helped me cope."

I shake my head. "I can't take those." I try to hide my disappointment. Not letters to me, then. "Those are obviously precious to you. As they should be."

Sarah laughs. "They are, indeed, but I want you to at least read them. They are all about this girl he met, about her amazing family, about how he knew the moment he locked eyes with her that she was the one for him."

I'm finding it hard to breathe and I have to set my spoon down on my napkin to keep it from rattling against my plate, because my hands are suddenly shaking.

Sarah slides the letters toward me, the same way she did the photo. "Take them home. Read them. I made myself copies. If you want to keep them, if you want to share them with your daughter—" Her voice cracks and her eyes glisten brightly. "They're yours, if you want them."

I reach out a hand, but for a moment, I'm hesitant to touch the letters. I'm half-certain I'll feel a current of electricity or something that might indicate Solomon's presence at this table with us, and I'm half-afraid I won't. Then I run my fingertips over Solomon's name in the return address on the top letter. What a gift this woman—Solomon's sister, Ruby's aunt, the woman who would have been a sister to me by marriage—has given me.

I finally pick the stack up, along with the framed photo, and slip them carefully into my own purse, grateful I brought the patchwork Hobo bag Dani gave me several Christmases ago. Since she couldn't be here today, I brought the bag instead. It is so much more her style than it is mine.

"Thank you." It comes out a little strangled, but I give Sarah a genuine smile. Something in me seems to be melting, a small, frozen stone of bitterness that has been wedged into the back corner of my heart. I hesitate briefly, then, before I can reconsider, I tell her, "Ruby is looking forward to meeting you. She just wanted me to check you out first to make sure you weren't a freak." I can be direct, too.

Sarah laughs out loud, drawing the attention of others in the room. A young couple smiles at us from a booth nearby, and Matteo winds his way toward us, his teeth flashing white against his dark, fashionable scruff. "You are enjoying life, I see." He presses a palm over his heart. "It makes me happy to see such beautiful ladies smile."

For the rest of the meal, Sarah and I share stories with each other. Hers are of growing up with Solomon, and although she doesn't speak ill of her mother, she doesn't pretend that things were easy. She tells me about the years that followed her brother's death, about finally meeting the man she's now married to, and of their futile attempts to have children of their own. "So far, anyway," she says with a determined smile. "We keep trying, of course. But in the meantime, we have started the process of adoption." Her expression softens as she adds, "We both want children with all our hearts."

"I'm adopted," I tell her. I think she will make a wonderful mother. I don't know her husband, but if she loves him, he must be something special. "It's one of the best things that ever happened to me, and I applaud you for exploring the option."

She reaches across the table and squeezes my hand briefly. "Thank you. I already knew that, from Solly, but I wasn't sure if you were comfortable talking about it."

"I'm rather proud of it," I assure her with a grin. "I'm happy to answer any questions you might have."

She shares the same openness that drew me to Solomon, accepting things at face value the way he did, and as I listen to her talk, I realize that she has not just mourned the loss of her brother.

She has mourned the loss of us. Of Ruby. Even of me.

"Solly told me about the pregnancy before he came home," Sarah says, her voice wistful. She points at the bench beside me where my bag sits. "It's in his second-to-last letter." She clears her throat and takes a sip of her lemonade. "This really is amazing stuff," she comments, and I think she's going to change the subject. She's clearly trying to wash down the tears that are trying to make an appearance. She doesn't though. "He was so excited to be a dad." She chuckles softly, but her voice is a little gruff as she says, "It was a little weird to hear him talk like that, but we pretty much raised each other. If anyone was equipped to take on fatherhood at a young age, it was Solly."

I tell her stories of Ruby's growing up, of how my life changed in both wonderful and difficult ways after Solomon's death. I tell her what a wonderful young lady Ruby has become, and we both marvel at the fact that she is the same age I was when Solomon and I were together. I brought pictures, of course, and not just on my phone. Gran is a staunch advocate for printed photos, and she has put together an album for every year Ruby has been alive. I culled some of my favorite photos from each album, made copies, and brought them with me on the off chance that I felt comfortable enough to share them with Sarah. After she gave me her precious letters, I am so glad I have the pictures.

"She looks so much like you and Solomon," I tell her, and for the first time, the tears that have been threatening spill from her eyes as she pours over the images that document Ruby's life.

By the time we make it through our main courses—grilled mahi mahi with artichoke caponata relish for Sarah and chicken scarpariello with lemon sauce and sweet-spicy Peppadews—neither one of us is fit to even look at the dessert menu. Matteo somehow manages to convince us to take some home with us anyway. "We make them all here in our own kitchen. How can you go wrong?"

As we stand in the foyer of Mancini's, I pass along Gran's invitation for Sarah and her husband to come for Sunday dinner the following week. "We always do a family Sunday dinner at Gran's, and we'd be happy to have you join us." When she hesitates, I stiffen, wondering if I have misread her reception of me.

She gets that deep, pondering furrow between her brows—it's the same one Ruby gets, and I suddenly want to hug my daughter until she can't breathe—but then she seems to make up her mind about what she is going to say. She takes a deep breath and lifts her chin just the slightest bit. "Thank you. I—we'd love to join you and your family, but before I accept your invitation, I'd like to ask you a huge favor."

"Of course," I tell her, but her words are careful, and I become wary of what she will ask of me.

She swallows hard and straightens the front of her coat. I think Sarah has had to keep things together for much of her life. I sense she carries an incredible amount of responsibility on her shoulders. "I'd like to bring my father. He wants to meet you, too."

I don't answer right away. I think I've been subconsciously waiting for this request since the moment she told me he'd given her his blessing to meet with us. But am I ready to meet the man who signed those papers all those years ago? If what she says is true, his signature was there, not because he didn't want to love me or Ruby, but because he loved his wife and stood by the vows that he made her on their wedding day. For richer or poorer, in sickness and health, in good times and bad, in happy times and sad.

Maybe, just maybe, the man deserves a little more happiness in his life, the kind that only a grandchild, especially one as perfect as Ruby, can bring. I already know what my daughter would say if the question were proposed to her.

I swallow any lingering reticence and nod. "Please. Bring your father."

By the time I pull onto Kirkwood Lane, I am desperate to talk to someone other than Ruby. I already pulled over on the way home and phoned her. I knew she would be dying to hear anything from me, and since the meeting went so well, I didn't see any reason to make her wait. But now, I want to talk to someone I can be vulnerable with, and since Dani is not available at the moment, I drive past the farmhouse, hoping no one notices my car go by, and head for Fair Havens in search of Hugo.

Relieved to find his truck in the parking lot, I pull in next to it, and then make my way between the little white buildings, skirting the old family graveyard. I murmur a greeting to Opa, gliding my fingers over his rough-cut tombstone.

Hugo has just emerged from Wild Rose trail with a pushcart full of deadwood, and he's heading toward the fire pit with his load; next Friday is already our monthly Live and Let Die Bonfire again. The month has passed so quickly with all that has happened, and for a moment, I feel an unfamiliar frisson of fear. I am not normally a fearful person, but I am definitely a control freak, and I don't like it when things feel so out of control.

I stop at the corner of the schoolhouse to watch the man I long for. Dani would elbow me, and in that lovely, lilting voice, tell me I'm behaving like a voyeur, but if I make my presence known, he will see everything I'm feeling splashed across my face.

Hugo has shed both his jacket and his work shirt. It's not warm out here, but the sun is shining, and he is working hard. Even from here, I can see the curls at the back of his head are damp and clinging to his neck. I am only a little surprised to see that he's wearing a short-sleeved t-shirt, and that his scarred arm is on full display. He's wearing his fingerless gloves, but I have a feeling that has more to do with the work he's doing than the temperature he's working in.

His arms are both startlingly pale, but that's no surprise since he rarely exposes them to sunlight. I can see the bulge of his biceps and the corded muscles of his forearm as he steers the cart across the clearing. When he approaches the fire pit, his back is to me, and my eyes linger on the breadth of his shoulders straining beneath the clinging knit of his shirt as he efficiently unloads the branches and other debris onto the growing burn pile.

My heart is racing and my breathing a little too shallow—*Get a grip, Niemeyer!*—and I take in a lungful of mind-clearing oxygen. Then I step out from my hiding place and make my way around the back of the outdoor chapel so he will see me coming. Besides, it gives me a little extra time to try to clear my expression.

Hugo glances up as I approach, almost as if he knew I was there all along. Maybe he did. He smiles and nods at me by way of greeting, but he keeps unloading the cart. He is waiting for me to talk first. That's his way. I still have a hard time seeing the Hugo he described to me at Chloe's grave, but I now understand why he's so slow to judge. And so easy to trust. It's the worst possible way to learn about the areas in our lives we need to work on, but Hugo has chosen to live and learn, and I know Chloe would be so proud of him.

It is a selfish thought, I'll be the first to admit, but I hope that one day soon, Hugo will also learn to live and let die. I know Chloe would want him to find happiness again. And I truly believe Hugo and I could be happy together here in this place we already both call home away from home. He—arguably—loves Ruby and Gran and Blimey as much as I do.

"They're coming for Sunday dinner next week." I say. Hugo has no need for clarification; he knows where I've been and with whom I've spent this morning. I sit on one of the tree stump benches nearby and openly watch him work. "Sarah is bringing her father."

Ruby invited Hugo over to supper earlier this week to apologize. She made him his favorite peanut butter chocolate chip cookies, and the three of us Niemeyer women told him the whole sordid tale of Ruby's beginnings, and about the upheaval caused by Sarah's surprise email. He has been so supportive of what we're doing, but he has made himself a little scarce since then. I think he's done so to give Ruby and me time to adjust to this new season we're entering, and I also know he's been busy with William over at his place when he's not here at Fair Havens. I'm still terribly curious about what he has the kid doing, but I don't want to ask in case it sounds like I'm micromanaging. *You and your god complex. You decide what's best for everyone, whether they agree or not.* Dani's words still clamor painfully in my mind.

Hugo straightens and turns to face me, one hand braced on his hip. He sweeps his hair from his forehead with the back of a hand, but it flops forward again immediately.

"You need a haircut," I tell him with a smile.

"I do. Chloe used to cut it for me at least once a month. I just forget about it until it's like this and driving me mad." He grimaces. "I go to the barber over by the old Radio Shack on the other side of town now. The old guy there doesn't seem to see my scars." He rubs the fingertips of his left hand over the mottled skin that blossoms up the side of his neck.

"I can cut it for you," I offer. When his eyes widen in surprise, I wonder if I've overstepped. "I cut and style hair all the time," I assure him, waving a hand toward the schoolhouse where my workshop is. "Granted, my clients don't usually complain much, but they also hold really still."

Hugo laughs out loud, a sound that makes my pulse race, and my body tingle. "I might just take you up on that offer," he says, still grinning.

"I don't see your scars, either," I tell him, still blushing, but it's something I want him to know.

He lowers his gaze for a moment, then meets my eyes again. "I know you don't."

I am the first to look away. From the corner of my eye, I see that Hugo hasn't moved.

Enough, Niemeyer.

There's that word again. Enough. Enough secrets. Enough lies. Enough waiting and wondering. Enough mourning. Enough. Echo Jacobson's words play on repeat in my mind, spurring me into action. *We must make the most of each time we cross paths with another soul. Never let misunderstandings turn into misgivings, because they'll inevitably become missed opportunities to love and be loved.*

I surge to my feet and start forward, pushing the words out before I lose my courage. "Hugo, there's something I need to tell you."

"Sure." He smiles encouragingly at me, and reaches for another log, but straightens in surprise when I step between him and the cart.

I take his hand, the one with the scars, and pull him over to where large chunks of limestone circle the fire pit. I step up onto one so that we are facing each other eye to eye. Hugo grins, allowing me to drag him around as I please, but I can see the questions in his eyes. At least he's not pulling away.

"Careful," he murmurs, his hand tightening around mine as I wobble a little on my perch. He is so close that I imagine I can feel the warmth of his body even through my coat.

"I'll be okay," I assure him. "You'll catch me if I fall." The words come out breathless, but certain.

"I will." His grin fades as he looks at me, studying my face. He blinks slowly, but he doesn't look away.

I don't know if we've ever stood face to face like this before. I can see every crease at the corners of his eyes, the grooves that form parentheses around his mouth, the fine lines that mark his lips, and the spiky lashes that fade to peachy blond at the tips. There are a few gray hairs in his brows that I haven't noticed before. They match those at his temples, and I wonder if he will be one of those old men with bushy, bristly brows that poke him in the eyes.

I wonder if I will be around for him to ask me to trim them for him.

It's what I want more than anything. To be around when he grows old. To hold his hand and look into his eyes for many, many years to come.

"I love you, Hugo," I tell him rather abruptly. And then, as if that were the key that opened the levy, words tumble out of my mouth. "I am in love with you. I think I have been... well, if I'm truly honest, maybe a little since the first time we met, which makes me a terrible person because you and Chloe were happily married, and Chloe was the best woman in the world, and you deserve someone far better than I'll ever be, but—" I suck in air and keep going. "I want the chance to make you happy, Hugo, and I hope that someday you'll—"

His gaze drops to my mouth, and my words suddenly evaporate. Then he is kissing me, and I am kissing him back with all the love for this man I have harbored in my heart for so long now. I try to pull my hand from his so that I can wrap my arms around his neck, but he doesn't let go. Instead, he laces his fingers with mine and drags my arm around my back, pulling me hard up against him. His other hand threads through my curls, cradling my head as he moves his mouth over mine. I comply happily, melting into him, releasing a soft sigh of submission and relief and anticipation into his kisses.

He smells like firewood and pine sap, with a hint of cologne melding with whatever shampoo he uses. There is the not-unpleasant tang of man sweat, and as I flare my nostrils to breathe him in, I wonder if it might be possible to bottle the scent of him for my own personal aphrodisiac. I am feeling rather amorous at the moment, and I'm not sure how much longer my legs are going to hold me upright under his assault.

Finally, after what could have been mere moments or a thousand days for all I know, he pulls back the smallest increment and presses his forehead to mine. His eyes are closed, and his breathing is as ragged as my own. Then he slowly releases my hand from behind my back and starts to pull away, but I grab the front of his shirt to stop him. He is trembling, and even though I'm pretty sure it's not from the cold, I unbutton my coat and hold the lapels open. "Come here," I murmur, smiling coyly at him. That kiss has made me bold beyond belief. "You're shaking. It's warm in here."

Hugo slides his arms around me beneath my coat and pulls me close again. I wrap my arms around his waist and tip my head away to let him bury his face in the curls at my neck. He takes one, then two, long, shaky breaths. Is he crying? Without even thinking about what I'm doing, I smooth my hands up both his arms, then slip them inside his short sleeves until my palms are resting over the ridged scars on his shoulder blades.

I want to help you fly again. I imagine, for a few moments, that I have a magical healing touch, that there is some ancient mystical power I wield that will help him grow back his wings.

He grows terribly still in my embrace, and I wonder how long it's been since anyone has touched him like this. Not in a sexual way, but with the desire to heal him, to tend to his hurts and wounds. But I don't want him to doubt what I said only moments—or was it days?—ago, that I don't see his scars.

"I'm so glad God created short-sleeved shirts," I murmur against his cheek, my lips close to his ear. I lace my fingers together against his heated bare skin under his t-shirt and hold on tightly while he chuckles, his warm breath sending shivers up and down my back, the sound of his laughter rumbling through me in a wave of pleasure.

Dani

I COME AWAKE WITH a gasp and a sharp cry, my heart pounding so loudly, for a few moments, it's all I can hear. My hands go immediately to my belly, relieved to find the warm, tight balloon unchanged under my touch. But I throw back the bed linens anyway, scouring the bed in the glow of the night light by my bed. I don't see any signs of blood or fluid on the sheets between my legs, and I let my head fall forward in relief as I feel a slight, disgruntled kick from one of the girls. "Hey, babies," I murmur softly, soothingly, hoping to quiet my own heart as much as theirs. "We're okay. Yes, we are."

What has awakened me? I was dreaming, I know that much, but even coming awake so suddenly, I cannot recall anything about it except for the sense of dread and overwhelming sorrow that still lingers in the air around me. I shimmy around to sit on the side of the bed; I need to use the loo anyway. I sit for a few moments, listening to the stillness of the house around me, hoping I haven't disturbed my parents' sleep.

By the time I return to my bedroom, my heart rate has returned to normal, and I am feeling the weight of sleep pulling at me again. This is the second time I've been up to use the bathroom in the last four hours, and I can't help dreading the months ahead as the babies grow larger and put even more pressure on my bladder. I know it's supposed to ease up a bit in the second trimester, but with twins, anything goes, and if the last few nights have been any indication of what I have to look forward to, then I'm in trouble. I already feel like the walking dead before the day is even half over, and more often than not, all I can think about is where I can find a soft, quiet spot to lie down for a spell.

According to my reflection in the stark light of the bathroom, I don't look much better than your friendly neighborhood zombie, either, with the dark circles under my eyes and my pale, sallow skin. But hey, at least my hair and nails are looking downright amazing. I swear my hair has grown a couple of inches in the last few months that I've been back in my parents' home, and it seems like I'm clipping and filing my fingernails every other day. Mum took me to get a pedicure a few days before Thanksgiving, so I know my toenails were overdue for attention; she wouldn't take no for an answer.

She asked if I wanted to invite Ranae to join us, but I told her no.

I had a birth to attend on Thanksgiving Day, so I didn't have much of an opportunity to miss Ranae as badly as I would have otherwise. I got home after midnight, stripped off my clothes, showered quickly, and crawled into bed. I think I was asleep before my head hit the pillow.

I certainly missed Gran's leftover turkey soup followed by a matinée movie with the girls the next day, though. It's become a sort of tradition for the women in our families, in lieu of a Black Friday shopping spree. Ranae and I, our mothers, Ruby, and Gran, and sometimes Shelly will join us, too. Somehow, we manage to choose a movie we all enjoy, and the afternoon usually ends with coffee and leftover pie back at the farmhouse before we all go back to our separate lives.

I have missed more than one Soup and a Movie Black Friday in the years since I've been married to Adam. I am so sad that this one has passed by me, too.

I am even sadder that my mother bowed out of the day, too. I heard her tell Noralee over the phone that she wanted to be home in case I needed her, that I'd had a twenty-four-hour labor and delivery the day before, and that I desperately needed some rest. But I know she stayed home with me as a show of solidarity.

Mum knows that Ranae and I have had a falling out, but I have kept the details to myself as much as possible, not because I don't trust my parents, but because I have already said too much in front of the wrong people without Ranae's permission. I owe it to her to keep my mouth shut.

Earlier this evening, right after dinner, Mum sat down on the edge of the sofa where I was sprawled out reading a book. "Why don't you call Ranae, darling. Your father and I can go sit in the study if you need some privacy."

For a moment, I considered it. Right then and there, I almost picked up my cell to ring her up. Demand that we talk. But I couldn't do it. "I hurt her terribly, Mum. I said some stupid things."

"Then go apologize to her, Danielle. This isn't like you girls, leaving things unresolved."

"I know, I know." I didn't say more, and after resting her hand on my belly long enough to get a nudge from the twins in response, Mum rose and went about her usual nightly activities. But it wasn't long before I looked up from my book to find that I was alone in the living room, the fire burning cozily, the lights around me dimmed. I finally finished the chapter I was trying to read and headed off to bed, unable to bear the pressure of the quiet room. It felt too much like it was waiting with bated breath for me to make the first move toward Ranae.

I am certain the chasm between my best friend and me is the reason for my restless sleep.

It's all I can do now to shove my legs back under my comforter and roll onto my side, my hand instinctively draping protectively over my stomach. "Goodnight, sweet babes." I mumble drowsily.

It's nearly dawn when I open my eyes again. This time, I'm instantly wide awake. I shift a little, shoving one of my pillows under the bedclothes and tucking it between my knees to ease the pull on my hips. I lie there in the early morning stillness, watching the sky begin to lighten through the openings at the edges of the curtains at my window. Tears begin to gather at the corners of my eyes, and before I really understand what's happening, I am weeping, overwhelmed by the same sense of loss that awoke me in the middle of the night.

I am grieving over the loss of my friend. It's almost as though she has died; that's how intense my emotions are right now. I miss Ranae fiercely, and yet, I've been hanging back, waiting... for what? What am I afraid of? That she won't accept my apology? Or that she won't offer one of her own? I know her better than that. The moment I open my mouth, she'll be apologizing over the top of me, claiming full responsibility for our fallout. Am I afraid that she won't trust me with her heart again? Of course not. Ranae is the most trusting person I know, in spite of all the terrible stuff the McCray family has put her through. She wears her heart on her sleeve, and she won't be able to keep her secrets from me. It's simply not in her nature to do so.

I roll onto my back and cover my face with my pillow, the cool linen soothing my flushed cheeks.

Ranae is not Adam. I have nothing to fear from my friend. Her love is not conditional, and her trust is freely given, no strings attached.

"What am I waiting for?" I mutter into the pillow before tossing the thing aside. I push up in bed and cross my legs pretzel-style in front of me, then pick up my phone.

It's barely five in the morning. I can't call her now. But I can get up and go to her. By the time I am ready, by the time I make the drive out to the farmhouse, it'll be close to six. It's a school day; surely, someone in the house will have roused from their beds by then.

Go to her. The words reverberate inside me like a call to arms.

The sky is still murky when I pull into the gravel driveway in front of the lovely, old farmhouse on Kirkwood Lane. My headlights are off so that they don't shine into Gran's downstairs bedroom. I don't want to wake her if she isn't already up; it's common knowledge that Gran isn't very hospitable before her coffee.

But even without my headlights, I see the figure huddled on the porch swing, and I am out of my Forester and up the stairs without a moment's hesitation.

Ranae is sitting in the dark, a heavy quilt draped around her shoulders and spread out to cover the dog sprawled on the cushion beside her. Blimey's head is in her lap, his mouth open, his tongue lolling. He doesn't lift his head when I approach. There isn't even an ear twitch, and the tears streaming down Ranae's cheeks tell me more than any words can.

Without saying a word, I squeeze onto the swing beside her. Ranae lifts the edge of the blanket to let me in, then she rests her head on my shoulder, and I wrap my arms around her as she shudders quietly into my thick fleece jacket.

"He started having seizures last night right after Ruby went to bed," she finally says, her voice muffled behind the tissues she's got pressed to her face. "I didn't want her to see them, Dani. They were terrible. I just had to hold him down while they wracked his body so he wouldn't damage anything or hurt himself. Then he fell asleep like—like—" She gulps back a sob, but it takes her another moment or two before she can continue.

"Oh, Ranae," I murmur against her hair. Why didn't I just shove off my pride and call her last night? My friend needed me, and I wasn't here. "I'm so sorry."

"I thought he was dead," she finally squeaks out. "But then he woke up a few minutes later and tried to get to his feet. He staggered around like he'd been drinking, eventually collapsing back to the floor, like his legs were too weak to hold him up. I was crying, he was whimpering, and I finally wrapped him in this blanket and brought him out here, hoping that a little fresh air might help revive him. He loves it out here."

I nod, my heart breaking right along with hers as she talks. Was it her pain, her sorrow and the eminent loss that woke me last night? That had me up and aching for her so early this morning?

"I didn't want him to wake up Ruby or Gran, either. I didn't think—I probably should have made them get up after all. I didn't really believe he wouldn't—that he'd—" Her words are cut off by a sob as she smooths the fur on top of Blimey's head, stroking the surprisingly soft tufts at the tips of the dog's ears. "I didn't realize how skinny he'd gotten in the last month or two," she says in barely more than a whisper. "He got his winter coat at the same time, and I didn't realize until I picked him up to put him up here. I told him we'd—we'd—we'd—" She can hardly speak past her gut-wrenching sobs. "That we'd watch the sunrise together, but then I—I went and fell asleep."

"Oh, Ranae," I say again, at a loss for any other words. I know what she's going to say even before she manages to get the words out.

"I woke up about an hour ago, and—and he was already gone."

My side is wedged uncomfortably against the porch swing arm, and Ranae is leaning heavily against me, but I don't move. I think she might be falling asleep, and I can't blame her. The trauma of what she's gone through all alone must surely have worn her out, but suddenly, she stiffens and lifts her head to look at me, then at my belly.

"I felt them," she murmurs, her nose so stuffed that her words come out sounding like *I fet dem.*

The twins are restless this morning, and I wonder if they are picking up on our distress. Either that, or they are happy to hear Ranae's voice again after going so long without. Ranae shifts a little, careful not to dislodge Blimey's head from her lap, and places her hand over my stomach. For a few moments, there is no movement, then I feel a fluttering under my ribcage where the arm of the swing is pressing in. I push against the spot, and sure enough, there is a responding bump. Even in the semi-dark, I see Ranae's eyes widen with delight as she smiles through her tears.

Gran finds us there shortly after six when she got up and couldn't find Blimey. "I thought maybe he braved the climb to yours or Ruby's rooms like he used to," she says softly, standing behind the swing and stroking Ranae's hair. "But when I found your room empty and no dog, I just knew something wasn't right. Would you like me to wake Ruby?"

Ranae sighs deeply and covers her face with her hands. But she shakes her head. "No. I need to be the one. But maybe—maybe you could call Hugo? He can help—"

Just then, another vehicle turns into the driveway. "I already called him," Gran says as Hugo climbs out of his truck and makes his way up the front steps. His eyes are still slightly puffy from sleep, and there is a crease over one cheekbone where his bed linens have left a mark, but he is here.

He has eyes for no one but Ranae, and in a flash of awareness, I know that the two of them have finally found their way to each other. Maybe because I wasn't around to get in the way of things? No. I can't think like that. Ranae's heart is big enough to love us both. To love all of us.

Hugo finally turns a warm half-smile on me. "Thank you for being here," he says to me before leaning forward and kissing Ranae on the forehead. Crouching in front of her, he covers her hand with his where it still rests on top of the dog's head. "I'll take Blimey inside now," he murmurs to her. "It's cold out here."

In a subdued procession, we move inside the house, Gran leading the way. Hugo is behind her cradling the dog high against his chest, and Ranae and I bring up the rear, our arms around each other's waists.

"I need to go see Ruby," Ranae says after Hugo has settled Blimey on his dog bed in front of the hearth. She looks around at all three of us, like she is trying to make up her mind about something. Then she sets her features and squares her shoulders. "I'm going to go up alone. We may be awhile." She turns toward the stairs, then glances forlornly back over her shoulder at us. "Or we may not. I've never had to do this before."

When Ranae has disappeared into Ruby's bedroom at the top of the landing, Hugo turns to me. He surprises me by stepping close and wrapping his arms around me in a gentle hug. It's so lovely to be enveloped by a large, warm, male body, that for a moment, I let myself lean into his strength. "It's good to see you back here, Dani," he says quietly. "Ranae has missed you. We all have missed you."

At that moment, one of the babies shifts mightily between us, and he steps back, his eyes growing wide. "Wow," he murmurs, glancing back and forth between my face and my belly.

I grin and reach for his hand. "Here," I tell him, pressing his palm flat over the same spot where Ranae's hand had rested earlier. He spreads his long, work-roughened fingers out, and I am startled at how big his hands are. I don't allow myself to compare them to Adam's. "Just wait. They're very active this morning."

Gran hurries over and nudges Hugo's hand over a little, and I can't help but giggle at their rapt attention to my baby bump. "Hello, wee moppets," Gran coos, leaning close to baby talk to the girls. "It's your Gran. I can't wait to see you."

There. A series of flutters and a solid thump directly under Hugo's palm. Gran feels it too, and she chortles in delight, but it's Hugo's face I can't stop watching. His eyes grow soft with wonder, and there's a telltale glisten as he turns his hand palm up and looks down at it like he might find a tiny footprint there.

When Ranae and Ruby descend the stairs, they are both flushed and red-eyed from crying. Hugo and Gran rise quickly, but I'm a little slower, and by the time I get to my feet, Ruby is held tightly against Gran's plump bosom, and Ranae is harbored in the sanctuary of Hugo's embrace. I stand there taking it all in, and for a moment, I once again get the gut-twisting sense that I might have forfeited my place in their lives by keeping my distance for so long. But then Gran releases Ruby and comes to stand by me as the teenager drops to the floor beside Blimey and wraps her arms around the prone animal, laying her head on his.

"Come," Gran says quietly, taking my hand. "Help me whip up some hot chocolate." She starts toward the kitchen, and I follow her the way I have done more times than I can count.

Hot chocolate in the Niemeyer home is made on the stove top with cocoa powder, cinnamon sticks, heavy cream, and whole milk, and then topped with heaps of mini marshmallows. The only healthy thing about it is the way it brings people together, which makes every calorie worth it.

An hour later, Ruby has gone back to bed, having been given permission to stay home from school for the day. Ranae has called the rest of her family, and there will be an impromptu funeral at lunch time over at Fair Havens. I sit in my usual spot on Gran's squishy, old sofa, Hugo on the other end, our precious Ranae between us. She is curled into Hugo's side, his arm draped protectively around her. Her eyes are closed, and she's resting her head on his shoulder, but I know she's not asleep, because she keeps squeezing my hand. All has been forgiven between us. We have much that we still need to say to each other, but there is time for that later. Right now, we are simply reveling in the rightness of the relationships around us.

Ruby hugged me fiercely before heading upstairs. "Don't ever leave us again," she murmured, her voice choked with grief. "My mom isn't the same without you. None of us are."

Gran is in the kitchen, having insisted she doesn't need our help. She is whipping up an enormous batch of scrambled eggs, fried potatoes, and bacon for anyone who wants food, and although my stomach is still especially rebellious during the first hours I'm up, I've managed to maintain my dignity this morning by not having to dash to the bathroom for a quick purge. Gran's scrumptious Chai tea—extra ginger, of course—and a slice of Irish soda bread she toasted for me has been a big help, and I think I might be able to at least nibble on a strip of bacon or two. It smells divine—I can't remember the last time I cooked bacon for Adam and me, and breakfast at my parents' place is often quick and on the run, as all three of us scurry off to work. But I can always count on a big country breakfast when I'm out at the farmhouse.

Hugo keeps glancing toward the kitchen, and I think if he were less of a gentleman, he'd be drooling. But I get the feeling he'd forgo even one of Gran's mighty breakfasts if Ranae does actually fall asleep against him. I can't wait to hear how this all came about, how they *finally* figured out that they should be together.

It's Ranae who finally lifts her head and smiles sadly. "I can't believe it, but I'm starving. Gran," she calls out. "It smells delicious." She avoids letting her gaze drift to Blimey's bed by the fire. Ruby tucked a blanket around the dog so only his head is uncovered, resting on the rolled edge of the dog bed. He looks like he's sleeping peacefully.

"Come and get it, kiddos," Gran calls back.

Hugo stands and turns to offer both of us women a hand up. He is such a gentleman in every way, and I am so happy for my best friend and her darling daughter. For him, too. I get the feeling there is a lot of loving left in that man, and who better to be on the receiving end of it than Ranae and Ruby?

Ranae slips upstairs to see if Ruby wants to eat, but she returns alone. "She's out cold. I didn't want to wake her."

"I can always make her breakfast later," Gran assures her. She sets a basket of warm soda biscuits covered with a red dishtowel on the table.

"Wow," Hugo groans with appreciation, holding chairs for each of us ladies. "You outdid yourself this morning, Gran."

The old woman pats Ranae's hand as she lowers into her chair at the foot of the table. "We need all the fortification we can get today, don't we, sweetie pie?"

We hold hands around the table, and Gran asks Hugo to say the blessing. A man of few words, his prayer isn't long, and for several minutes, the only sounds that follow are clinking dishes and cutlery and requests to pass things.

Finally, I sit back in my chair, sated, and surprisingly still not queasy, holding my teacup with both hands in front of my heart like a tiny shield. It's time to address at least one of the elephants in the room.

"I've left Adam," I say, avoiding Gran's gaze. I don't want to see the look of disappointment I'm afraid that I'll find on her face. Instead, I lock eyes with Ranae in a silent bid for her support and understanding. "I'm staying with my parents right now."

Ranae reaches for my hand and holds it on the table between us. I want to weep with relief—I see no judgment in her eyes, just sympathy.

I swallow the lump in my throat and continue. "Adam says he wants to try to work things out, but there is no evidence of him making any effort to do so. Words aren't enough for me anymore. There have been too many secrets, too many lies between us, and I need something more tangible than promises."

Hugo makes a sound low in his throat. I glance over at him, and he, too, is watching me with calm acceptance.

Then I turn to Gran. "I haven't filed for divorce yet, but I'm giving him the freedom to be the person he wants to be. If he wants to be my husband, then he'll have to prove it. If he wants to be a father to his children, then he'll have to prove that, too, a task that won't be easy for him. I don't believe he knows how to work hard for anything, and I've accepted that even if he loves me, even if he loves the girls, I don't think he's got it in him to work hard for us, and that's what I'm requiring of him if he wants to be a part of our lives." I'm fidgeting with my napkin, but I don't look away from the old woman's gaze. "I'm not willing to settle for anything less, Gran. Not for me or my babies."

"Good for you, Dani Girl. Good for you," she simply says.

I hesitate, then slowly add, "I'm quite certain, too, that I'm not the only woman he's been making promises to."

Ranae's brow furrows, and she and Hugo exchange glances. Then she sighs and says in a quiet voice, "I saw him with another woman at Mancini's last week, Dani." She squeezes my hand tightly. I can tell she is choosing her words carefully.

"It wasn't anything blatantly inappropriate, you should know, but there was definitely an unsettling familiarity between them."

I sit there for a few moments, staring at our clasped hands, letting the statement sink in. It really isn't a surprise, but it hurts anyway. Adam and I have had only a few conversations since that first one, but he's assured me every time we do talk that he's committed to making our marriage work.

Not promises after all, just more lies.

I nod slowly, lift my eyes to meet Ranae's, and thank her for telling me.

"And Jolene?" she asks tentatively. "Have you—"

I wait to let her finish her question, but the corner of my mouth twitches with the smile that Jolene's name brings out of me every time I hear it. Every time I think of her.

"You have!" Ranae straightens, her eyes lighting up. "Tell me everything."

So I do. Jolene and I are figuring things out between us. The more time we spend together, the more things we discover that are different and unique about us. Nothing will change the fact that we are twins, that we look and dress alike, that we have many of the same mannerisms, even. We both are self-conscious about our knobby elbows and knees, and we both cover our mouths when we feel strong emotion. But then, we both have enormous teeth, so there's that. Mine were straightened by braces long ago, and Jolene is currently in the process of aligning hers with clear retainers she wears during the day, and a hideous mouthpiece she puts in at night.

"It's a wonder I got pregnant," she chortled when she showed it to me. "But Pete insists it isn't a deterrent, and I guess here's proof!" she added, rubbing her belly.

But our upbringings have, indeed, given us different outlooks on life. The world of education I've grown up in feels foreign to her, and I can see her eyes begin to glaze over when I start talking about medical stuff. I get the feeling that she believes she's not smart enough to understand it all, and it makes me sad and angry that she was cheated out of all that I had access to. And yet, I can't help but see that I, too, have been cheated out of things in life because of the lies I've believed about myself. I look at Jolene and Pete's relationship, the deep and abiding love they have for each other. Their marriage is a year older than mine, and I realize I have settled for what I thought was the best I could get.

"I've encouraged her to listen to our podcast—we are going to keep doing it, aren't we?" I shoot Ranae an apologetic look. "I'm sorry I've been absent."

"Ha. You're not getting out of this so easy, girlie," Ranae shoots back. "The show must go on."

"Thank you," I whisper, then take a deep breath of relief. "Anyway, I've told her about the podcast, but I don't think she's listened to any of it yet. I think she's a little afraid of death. Her mother—*our* mother—died pretty tragically. Complications of a rough life." Jennilyn had a drug addiction that she couldn't conquer, no matter how hard or how often she tried. "I'm hoping that once she gets to know you, Ranae, and spends time around us and here at Fair Havens, that maybe she'll realize we're not just a couple of freaks, as you put it." I lift my mug in a salute to my friend.

"Good luck with that," Gran interjects. "I've never met any girls freakier than you two."

Hugo chuckles softly, a nice sound that reminds me once again how good it is to be back at this table with these wonderful people.

"What about this?" I say, waving a finger back and forth between Hugo and Ranae. I've talked about myself for too much of this conversation. "When—and how—did this happen?"

Ranae's cheeks go pink, and her smile is a delight to see. Her nose is still red, and her eyes are puffy from crying, but she looks beautiful in the glow of love.

"She threw herself at me, and I found myself catching her," Hugo says, smiling adoringly over at her. He reaches out to touch her cheek with the back of his knuckles, and I am so happy for them.

"That's pretty much how it went," Ranae says, shrugging nonchalantly. "The guy would have waited until we were old and gray if I hadn't." She leans forward and points at me, a mischievous sparkle lighting up her eyes. "He even thought I was in love with you; can you believe it, Dani?"

Now it's Hugo's turn to blush. "Actually," he says after clearing his throat. "I was just clearing the field. Making sure. I didn't really think it was true; I only wanted to make sure."

Ranae rolls her eyes. "Right. And that's why you didn't follow up my indignant denial with a promise of undying love."

"I hadn't planned that part out yet," Hugo defends himself. But he's smiling, taking it all in good humor. "We men aren't multi-taskers like you ladies are. We take one thing at a time. One step at a time."

"One veeeery slooooow step at a time," Ranae teases. Then she turns to me, suddenly growing serious. "After all that has gone on these last several months, Dani, after so much has been exposed and brought to light, I'm tired of secrets and lies, too. I guess I felt like hiding my feelings for Hugo was just another kind of lie. It was definitely a secret."

"Not to any of us," Gran retorts. "Your face reads like a—"

"An open book, I know," Ranae finishes for her. She affectionately bumps Hugo's shoulder with her own. "Which must mean that Hugo can't read or something."

"I'll have you know," Hugo says, turning in his seat to face Ranae fully. He takes her hand and brings it to his lips for a quick kiss. "I can read your face just fine, Ranae Niemeyer." His voice is soft and adoring, but there's a tangible ache behind his words. "I saw it there, your feelings, your love. I just had a hard time believing it was all for me."

"Aww," I say on a sigh. My hand goes to my mouth, and I think of Jolene.

"It's all for you, Hugo Beckenbauer," Ranae tells him, her voice tender in a way I don't think I've ever heard before.

Gran leans toward me, and from the side of her mouth, she says, "Getting a little awkward around here." She stands and begins clearing the dishes, and the rest of us follow suit, ignoring her insistence that she doesn't need our help.

"Seriously, though," I say to Ranae as we mill around the kitchen doing our different tasks. "Tell me what happened."

My friend launches into a play by play of the day she threw herself at Hugo, which leads to her telling me about what is happening with Sarah, and—shock above all shocks—Solomon McCray, Sr., and how they will be joining the Niemeyer Christmas Eve festivities this year. I am elated for Ranae and Ruby all over again. It seems this is the year of family reunions, and what better time to make room for more people in our hearts than over the holidays.

I have just put away the last of the dishes I was drying, and I am folding the towel in half to drape it over the oven handle. It's been like a homecoming for me, tragic though the circumstances are that have brought us here this morning.

But I am truly at home here, more than anywhere else, in this old farmhouse with these people.

"I'd like to have my babies here." The words are out before I've given them much thought. The moment the idea entered my mind, it felt so right, so serendipitous, that they charged right on through and out of my mouth. "Yes." I am nodding, like I'm agreeing with myself. "I'd like that very much." I turn around to face the others, leaning my hip against the counter and cupping my stomach with both hands. "Would you mind very much if I did?"

Ranae throws her arms around me, practically lifting me off my feet. "Yes, you crazy woman. Not yes, I would mind very much if you did, but yes, you *must* have your babies here. Right, Gran?"

Gran encircles us both with a squishy hug, her smile lighting up the room. "I can't think of a better place," she tells me.

"Did I hear what I just heard?" It's Ruby appearing around the corner. None of us heard her coming down the stairs. She makes a beeline for me, hip bumps her mother out of the way, and wraps her arms around me. "You must have them here. You can have them in my room where I was born. That would be so awesome!" She bends down and says to my stomach, "You guys want to be born in my room? You'll be cool before you even know what it means."

As if on cue, one of the twins does some kind of acrobatic maneuver, and Ruby grins up at me. "I'm going to take that as a yes."

Gran, ever the voice of reason when she isn't making some snarky comment, asks, "What about your parents, Dani Girl. Won't they want you to have them in their home?"

I'm shaking my head before she's finished speaking. "No," I assure her. "I'm not planning to still be living there by then. Although they've said and done nothing to make me feel anything but welcome, it's not *my* home anymore. My old room is great for visits, full of nostalgia and good memories. It's exactly how it was when I was in high school, but I'm not in high school anymore. Our house, mine and Adam's, hasn't been a home for a long time, so that's off the docket, too. I was just going to have them at Breathe, but if you're sure you're okay with—."

"You should move in here," Ruby declares, cutting me off. "This is your home as much as it is anyone's." She turns to Ranae, then Gran. "We have the room. We have lots of room. For Dani and the babies. We aren't even using the spare bedroom next to mine, and it even has its own bathroom."

"You should at least consider it," Gran says without hesitation.

I am overwhelmed by the way this conversation has shifted, and I suddenly feel a little weak in the knees. "I think I need to sit down," I say, and Hugo is pulling out a chair from the table for me by the time Ruby and Ranae escort me over there. I'm not sure if they are actually helping me or hindering me, but it's wonderful to be doted on like this.

Gran sits down across from me, nodding as she does. "I think Ruby and Ranae are right, Dani Girl. This is a good place to bring life into the world. Our home is one of love and family, and you belong. You're an integral part of it." She pauses, then turns to look at Hugo and Ranae. He's standing beside her, his arm encircling her waist. "And I have a feeling there might be a little more room in this house in the months to come." She leans forward to say conspiratorially, "Those two can't keep their hands off each other, and I just don't know how much more of it I can put up with."

"Gran," Ruby moans. "Gross. That's my mom you're talking about."

"Well, how do you think you came into being, little lady?"

"Gran!" It's in stereo this time, as both Ruby and Ranae react.

Gran is chortling with delight as she reaches over to cover my hand. "You don't have to make a decision today. We all have a lot on our plates right now. But I'm officially offering you this home as your own. For as long as you need it."

"Thank you, Gran. I love you," I manage to get out. I can't wait to call Jolene and tell her about all of this. She'll be so happy for me.

We all head over to Fair Havens to choose Blimey's final resting place. Hugo and Ruby ride in his truck with Blimey on the seat beside Ruby. She has wrapped the dog in a favorite blanket, one I gave her a few Christmases ago. It's made of natural fibers and colored with plant dye, so it's the perfect choice for a burial at Fair Havens.

I am in need of a nap, so while Hugo, Ranae, and Ruby stay to dig the grave and ready the site, Gran and I head back across the bridge so I can lie down for a while. Before I do, I call Gail to confirm that I'm not needed at Breathe today, then touch base with my parents. I'd left them a note this morning, so they already knew where I was, but I fill them in on what has happened. I don't tell them about Gran's offer, though. I want to talk to them about it face to face. They send their condolences, and Mum promises to send flowers to Ruby, too.

Ruby and Ranae seesaw between smiles and tears all morning, but when Carl and Noralee arrive just after noon, the girls are both smothered in waves of affection, sympathy, and support.

Nolan makes his appearance soon after his parents. He comes bearing an enormous box of chocolate truffles, both Ranae and Ruby's favorites. Jordan sends his love, but he can't get away until later in the evening. "He promises he'll come by then," Nolan assures them. "Shelly is bringing the kids over after school, though, so they can see the grave and say their goodbyes."

As I listen to everyone share stories about Blimey, it is even more evident that this is indeed, a home overflowing with love. I already know what my answer to Gran will be. I'll wait, however, until after the holidays—it will be nice to have Christmas morning with my parents again. I wonder if they'll fill my stocking this year. Or if St. Nick will, I mean.

The funeral is exactly what a beloved pet's funeral should be. With the Niemeyers, it's not possible to face death without at least a little bit of humor to ease the way, so there are both tears and laughter. After the majority of the Niemeyers head out, Hugo excuses himself, too, insisting he has things he needs to take care of back at his home. I know he wants to give Ranae and me some time to ourselves. It's so unlike the possessive way Adam always begrudged the time I spent with my friend, and I'm grateful for Hugo all over again.

Nolan, however, lingers at the farmhouse with us, and it seems he plans to stay for a while. Gran puts on coffee and pulls out her cookie jar. It's full, of course. I have a feeling I'll be putting on some weight once I move in here, pounds I won't be able to attribute to baby weight. Then again, I'm not sure that's such a bad thing, considering how gaunt I've been looking lately.

"You look amazing," Nolan says to me, as if in contradiction to my thoughts. "I don't mean to sound sexist, so please don't take it that way, but pregnancy suits you." He drapes an arm around Ranae and gives her a too-tight squeeze, making her grunt. "Not like this one. Do you remember how my little sister blew up like a puffer fish? I mean, I forgot she even had ankles—oof!" Ranae elbows him hard in the gut, and he lets her go. "Just kidding, Pippy. You were a hot, pregnant babe, too."

"Like that's not creepy at all, Uncle Nolan," Ruby says drolly, her eyes rolling. "Calling your own sister hot?"

Ranae high-fives her daughter, then with a sly grin on her face, she plops down on the sofa beside me. "Did you catch that, Dani-girl?" she asks, bumping my shoulder gently with hers. "My creepy big brother thinks you're a hot, pregnant babe."

My cheeks burn, and with my unusual pallor these days, I'm sure it's obvious to everyone in the room. I roll my eyes and wave a hand in front of my face. "Stop, please. You're making me blush." Why not call it what it is?

"Well, you are," Nolan acknowledges frankly. "Gorgeous women, all of you. Pregnancy and motherhood only enhance it." Then he turns to Ruby. "Except for you. Spoiler alert: you're getting a chastity belt from me for Christmas. Your mom told me about Gunther. Or Godfrey? Goober. That's it; Goober!"

"Gideon, you big dork." Ruby throws a cushion at him, but he ducks sideways and catches it. Instead of throwing it back, though, he holds it up to his face and pretends to passionately kiss it.

"How old are you again?" Ranae asks, but Ruby is laughing, and we all know that is Nolan's goal.

He settles into a chair opposite Ranae and me. "Has she filled you in on Sarah McCray? It's crazy how much Rubes looks like her." He winks at his niece. "Yet another beauty among the lot of you."

"Thank you," Ruby tells him, her expression softening at the mention of her new family members. Like me, she is taking her time getting to know her father's side of the family tree, and she is discovering that no one is perfect in this world, that we all make mistakes, and have regrets, but that we all have the choice to hang on to our wounds and become slaves to them, or to let those wounds heal, and be free to move on and embrace what life has in store for us. "We're actually going over there for the first time this Saturday night," she says. "The whole family. Even Grandpa."

"Dad took some convincing," Ranae explains to me. "But he's come around. He met them a few days ago when everyone was here for Sunday dinner. He says he's willing to let bygones be bygones if Ruby and I are."

"You should come with us, Dani," Ruby insists. "Since you're moving in here, and you're practically family, anyway."

Nolan looks over sharply, his brows raised in question. "Moving in? Here?"

"Yep," Ruby answers for me. "She's going to have her babies here, too. Probably in my room," she adds smugly.

"Well, I—" I start to shake my head, but Ranae reaches over and takes my hand.

"She is," Ranae cuts in. "She may not know it yet, but she is. Right after Christmas, you think?" she asks, turning to me. My dear, decisive friend.

"You read my mind," I admit with a self-conscious laugh.

Ruby lets out a whoop of delight, and Gran beams at me from where she sits in her rocker.

"Wow," Nolan says, a note of hesitant curiosity in his tone. "So... just you, then?"

Ranae crosses her arms and looks over at him, a *Shut up, Nolan,* expression on her face. He doesn't get the hint.

"No Adam, I mean?"

"Nolan!" It's Ranae's turn to throw a cushion at him. This time, he's not fast enough, and it hits him in the side of the head. "She's still a married woman. And pregnant. With twins! Stop looking at her that way."

"What way?" he demands, but he's grinning wickedly at me, and I can't help but smile back, even though I feel like my face might burst into flames at any moment.

Ranae

It's Christmas Eve and the farmhouse feels full to capacity, but in all the right ways. We have outdone ourselves this year. The rooms are over-the-top decorated in pine garlands and twinkle lights, and paper snowflakes and gingerbread people chains crisscross the ceiling. There are candles in luminaries, pretty holiday bowls of scented pinecones and antique glass ornaments, and of course, strategically hung bundles of mistletoe in every room. No one is leaving this place without a Christmas Eve kiss.

Above the chorus of a dozen conversations, Harry Connick, Jr. is singing Christmas carols in his swoony voice—Gran says he's "superdy-duperdy hot with a voice that makes my ears sizzle!" Whatever that means.

The McCrays have come bearing food; Sarah insisted on bringing their traditional Christmas Eve chicken and corn chowder, a rich, creamy soup that pairs perfectly with Gran's homemade bread, the enormous Charcuterie board Jordan and Shelly have contributed, and the array of cookies and pies and other delectable treats in a fantastic spread on the long kitchen counter.

I wonder what other traditions Sarah, her husband, Andrew Crawley, and Mr. McCray are foregoing in order to join our family here tonight. I get the feeling that Sarah and Solomon's mother was quite a hostess in her day, and that the McCray home—a mansion, from what I gather—has hosted many a holiday gala over the years. Our informal family gathering here at the farmhouse is not a gala by any account, but I see evidence that the McCrays feel welcome and right at home in our midst, nonetheless.

Ruby and I pondered long and hard over what to give the McCrays for Christmas. It was Gran who suggested we come up with something that would allow them a glimpse into Ruby's childhood, and Dani suggested we put Ruby's hemp bracelet weaving skills to good use. Weaving skills I handed down to her, the same ones that were handed down to me from my 70's era mother.

We created a large wall hanging from a walking stick I used to tromp through the woods when I was pregnant with Ruby. It's one that Nolan fashioned for me one day while we were out on a walk together, and although I've kept it all these years, I have learned—the hard way—that a walking stick in my hands can be treacherous. Instead of helping me stay steady on my feet, I tend to trip myself up with one. In fact, Hugo has all but forbidden me to use one on the trails over at Fair Haven. So I'm happy to use the slightly arched walnut branch to anchor our macramé masterpiece to, and there is enough sentimental value attached to it that it seems apropos.

We have woven into the undulating pattern of knots and braids a myriad of treasures Ruby has collected over the years. Pebbles, beads, shells, and feathers. A baby spoon—one I am willing to part with—a Velcro wrist rattle. Her favorite pink butterfly hair clip from first grade, neon pink and green shoelaces from the roller skates she loved so much in fourth grade. A bracelet made of the tiny rubber bands she had to use with her braces in junior high, and one of her favorite keys from her key collection she's been adding to since Gran gave her the original one to the farmhouse for her tenth birthday.

"These are pieces of my childhood," Ruby tells Sarah and her father when she presents it to them, holding it aloft for them to see. It's not large—not quite three feet square, although the walking stick at the top extends out a good six inches on either side. Ruby's fingers drift over the treasures, a small smile tugging on her lips as she sees the delight and joy on her aunt and grandfather's faces. Andrew rests his hand on Sarah's leg in an affectionate gesture; I can see his love for her shining in his eyes, and I truly believe he is just as thrilled as she is to have Ruby in their lives.

Ruby, her voice trembling only slightly, continues explaining the gift to them. "Each one of these trinkets has a story behind it. I'm not going to overwhelm you with all of them today, but over time, I hope to share the stories of my life with you, and I hope that you'll share your stories, and stories about my dad, with me. I want this gift to be a way for us to get to know each other."

Solomon's father nods slowly, and the muscles in his jaw jump as he works hard to hold at bay the emotions that are obviously welling up inside of him.

"Daddy, we can hang it in your study, don't you think?" Sarah asks, reaching out to touch a dark purple glass bead knotted into one of the patterns before taking the piece from Ruby. "Right next to Solly's picture."

"That would be the—the perfect place for it," Mr. McCray says, stumbling a little over the words. "Thank you, child. I couldn't have asked for a finer gift."

The words mean so much to Ruby; I know. She has been so worried that they might think her homemade gift tacky or silly.

"I also thought you might like a copy of this." Ruby hands him an envelope, and I catch my breath when I recognize it for what it is. I have to lace my fingers together in my lap to keep from reaching out and snatching it back. She turns a pleading look my way, and I know she is begging me not to be upset at her. I force a smile on my face and blow her a kiss.

To the man she has just begun to call Grandpa, she says, "This is a letter I wrote to my dad when I became a teenager. My mom told me that I would have loved him as much as he would have loved me, so this is a good letter, just so you know. But it's also a hard letter; at least, that's what my mom says." She hesitates, and I find I'm holding my breath, then she adds, "Because it's from a girl who wanted a dad more than anything in the world."

Her voice cracks, and I start to rise to go to her, but Hugo's hand around mine tightens. I wait for Ruby to turn to me, to give me a sign that she needs me, but it doesn't come, and I am equally parts crushed and proud of her.

"You don't have to read it now," my daughter says. Then she lets out a breathy self-conscious giggle. "In fact, I'd rather you wait until you get home. I was a dramatic thirteen-year-old when I wrote it, and now I'm almost eighteen and so, so, so much more mature...." She draws the words out with a roll of her eyes.

There are good-natured chuckles around the room, and several sniffles, too, not just my own. My mother is dabbing a tissue beneath her perfectly made-up eyes. Shelly is nestled close to Jordan's side, but he's the one who's tearing up, not his wife. And Gran isn't dry-eyed either, I note. But they are all good tears and what better place to shed happy tears than among loved ones?

Mr. McCray tucks the envelope into the inside pocket of his tailored dinner jacket. His suit is far too formal for this gathering, but he seems completely at home in his fancy duds. I wonder if he even owns a pair of jeans or a flannel shirt. The very thought makes me smile.

"I have something for you, child," he tells Ruby before she can return to her seat. From another pocket, he pulls out a small jewelry box. "I gave this to your grandmother when she gave birth to your father, and I'd like you to have it," he says, handing her the box.

Ruby takes it from him, hugs him awkwardly, then comes to sit at my feet, leaning one shoulder against my knee. I bask selfishly in the wave of relief that washes over me. My daughter still needs me. I am still her safe place.

Inside the box is a tennis bracelet; a very expensive one, I imagine. I'm pretty sure the sparkling stones of it are real diamonds. It's definitely not something she'll be wearing to school next semester.

"Grandpa," Ruby gasps as she gingerly lifts the bracelet from its velvet bed. "This is so beautiful." She turns to glance at me, her eyes wide with awareness and wonder. She's old enough to know what she holds in her hand; I can see it on her face. I lean forward to admire the piece as she carefully lays it over her wrist. "Mom?" she asks, holding it up for me to help her connect the clasp.

Ruby takes a few minutes to circle the room to show the others the stunning bracelet, and when she's seated on the floor in front of me again, Sarah gets up and reaches for a large, wrapped gift leaning against the wall at the back of the Christmas tree and hands me the package. "This is for both of you."

It feels like an enormous, framed photo, and for a moment, I wonder if it's a picture of Solomon. I hesitate, not wanting Hugo beside me to feel uncomfortable. But one look at him tells me he is perfectly at ease with all that is going on, and when he gently tugs on one of my curls and says, "Open it," I take a deep breath and peel back the paper.

It is, indeed, a framed image, but not of Solomon. I marvel at the work of art with its intricately-carved, highly-polished dark Cherrywood frame. The gold plaque set into the bottom of the frame is engraved with the words, *The House of McCray.* It is an exquisite painting of the McCray mansion, the place Solomon called home, and in the corner of the painting, I immediately recognize the signature. "He—Solomon painted this?" I asked unnecessarily, lifting my eyes to look back and forth between Mr. McCray and Sarah. I turn the painting so the others in the room can see it.

Solomon's father's voice is steady and sure when he says, "I think he would have wanted you to have it."

"Wow," Ruby murmurs as she gets to her knees for a closer look. We've been to the McCray's home, so it's not the mansion itself that has her awestruck. I can tell that she, too, is moved by the quality of the painting, the skill of the artist, himself. "My dad is so cool," she exclaims softly, shooting an impish grin at her father's side of the family.

"Thank you," I manage to get out, stunned by the gift. I can't imagine that it was easy for the man across from us to give up a treasure like this. I can't help but wonder, though, where I will hang the painting in our homey farmhouse. Like Ruby's diamond bracelet, it feels a little extravagant for the likes of us.

And yet, I can see how much these pieces mean to Solomon's family, and I appreciate how important it is to them that we recognize their worth.

"There's one more thing," Sarah says, pointing at the painting I'm holding. "On the back."

Carefully, so as not to drop the priceless work of art, I hand the painting to Hugo. There is a legal-sized linen envelope attached to the back of it, and in the top left-hand corner is the embossed logo of a firm I recognize with a wash of mixed emotions. The Law Offices of Frederick and Vancour. With hands that are suddenly trembling, I unwind the red silk cord from around the ornate closure and lift the flap. From within, I slide out a document, a single sheet of the finest paper I think I have ever held in my hands. I stare down at a chart of names, reading through them silently, until near the bottom, I find those that are oh, so familiar to me.

"That is our family tree," Solomon's father says, his voice gruff with pride and dignity. "You and Ruby have been officially added to it, so now it's your family tree, too." He clears his throat, opens his mouth as though he has more to say, then closes it again, apparently overcome by the circumstances.

"We would never ask you to change your name, Ruby," Sarah jumps in, leaning forward just a little in her sincerity. On the chart, my daughter's last name is written as Niemeyer, and for that, I am extremely grateful.

Mr. McCray clears his throat again and nods in agreement. "Our hope is that you will know that we proudly claim you as one of ours. Something we should have done the first moment we knew of you."

Hugo shifts the painting to his other side so that he can take my hand again. He squeezes it gently, and I can practically hear the thought he's projecting my way. *It's what you've always wanted: to love and be loved for who you are.* He knows me so well.

After everyone has gone home for the night, Hugo and I wind up out on the porch swing, cuddled together under one of Gran's many quilts. This one is threadbare in places, and the batting inside has gotten lumpy in spots, but it's made from pieces of sturdy fabric that have stood the test of time and many, many launderings, and I have no doubt it will be around long after I'm gone.

There's a cloud covering that shrouds the sky in muted shades of gray over our heads. The stars aren't visible, but every now and then, the three-quarter moon will peer through a hole in the pearly puffs and beam down on us. It's cold out here, but there is still the determined whirr and thrum of the woodland night life playing their background music to our quiet conversation. I can't imagine anywhere else I'd rather be this Christmas Eve, and I snuggle in closer against Hugo's side, if that's even possible.

Ruby has insisted she isn't ready to get another dog yet, but I believe she feels like she's betraying Blimey's memory if she entertains the thought. All three of us women are feeling the absence of a four-footed companion in our home, though, and I have been trying in vain to come up with a good way to broach the subject again. I miss Blimey terribly, but I am convinced that his memory will live on, no matter what other dog steps in to try to fill his gigantic shoes.

Earlier this evening, Hugo, king of all men, champion of champions, and hero of my heart, slipped away from the party for several minutes. He returned just as everyone was starting to ask where he'd gotten off to, carrying a large, gift-wrapped box with Ruby's name scrawled across it in large pink letters. The box had a few suspicious holes poked into the sides of it, and the pathetic little whimpers that emanated from it had me grinning from ear to ear.

Ruby, who knew immediately what the box contained, leaped up from her seat at the table where she had just finished yet another piece of pie. "Is it a puppy?" she asked, breathless with anticipation. "Is it, Hugo? Did you get me a puppy?" Not waiting for his response, she took the box, carefully set it on the floor, and began tearing away the wrapping paper.

A moment later, she withdrew a miniature Blimey, the most darling little gray and black puppy I have ever seen. At least since the day we got Blimey. "Oh, Hugo," Ruby exclaimed, her voice cracking on his name. Then she wrapped the whimpering little creature close against her chest and pressed tearful kisses all over its head.

The puppy—a male we have dubbed Blarney—returned her kisses tenfold.

Dani, my precious, pregnant, and out-of-control-emotionally best friend in all the world, actually started crying at the scene, and my opportunistic brother put his arms around her, and let her cry on his shoulder.

Ruby is upstairs in her bedroom now with her dog, which is probably the only reason Hugo and I have the porch to ourselves. When I left her room less than half an hour ago, Blarney was curled contentedly in a lambs wool puppy bed on the floor beside Ruby's bed, but I have a feeling the little guy is going to blarney his way into sleeping under his new mistress's covers before morning.

"I love you," I say, smiling at the memory of how this night has gone. I open my mouth to expound, but then, realizing there is nothing more I need to say, I simply repeat, "I love you, Hugo."

He doesn't respond right away, and for a moment, I wonder if he has drifted off. But then he takes a deep breath and lets it out slowly. "Ranae." The way he says my name with such gravity has me holding my breath. I have a childish urge to cover my ears, not sure I want to hear what he has to say.

No, Hugo loves me. I do not have to be afraid of anything he might say. The scared, rejected seventeen-year-old in me just can't seem to get the picture. "Hugo," I murmur in response, then press a kiss into the tender spot just under the curve of his jaw where his pulse throbs strong and sure against my touch.

"You have surprised me," he says, and I can tell that he is choosing his words with great care. "I never thought I could—or that I *should*—feel this kind of joy and peace in my life again."

I am holding my breath after all, but only because I don't want to distract him in any way. I am also smiling, even as I press my lips together tightly to keep from making any noise.

"Your love," he says, leaning away from me so that I'm forced to lift my head from his shoulder. I turn to look at him and he lifts one hand to smooth the wayward curls from my face. He holds my gaze as he says, "Your love, Ranae, has freed me. When I look at you, when I feel you against me like this, when I hold you in my arms..." He bends his head to kiss my lips with such tenderness that I want to weep. I smile wordlessly up at him. I will not cry; I am the happiest woman in the world right now. "When you smile at me like that, my sweet Ranae, sometimes I think I can fly."

He's growing back his wings. I swallow hard and nod. "Me, too," I whisper.

He presses another kiss to my lips, this one a bit more fervent. "I want this to be the last holiday season we spend apart," he murmurs against my mouth.

I pull back just far enough to be able to focus on both of his eyes at the same time. "What—what are you saying?"

He doesn't even hesitate. "I want to marry you, Ranae Niemeyer. Now. Tonight. Tomorrow. Next week." He's smiling, his eyes alight with mischief, but I do believe that if I were to say yes to his demands, he'd find a way to make it happen. Now.

"Next month?" he asks when I don't say anything. What he doesn't realize is that my speechlessness is not due to shock, but because my mind is scrambling for a way to make it happen. "Out there under the redbuds and dogwood trees," he says, thrusting his chin in the general direction of the outdoor chapel at Fair Havens. "Your dad can officiate for us, can't he? Are funeral directors allowed to do weddings, too?"

"I—I don't really know," I stammer, trying to tamp down my own giddiness at the lovely, but preposterous, idea. "But what about my brother? Pastor Jordan certainly can."

"Of course!" Hugo exclaims softly, hugging me tightly against his side again.

But I'm not willing to let this go. Not yet. I pry myself loose and twist in my seat until I'm facing him. I cup his face between my palms and look him in the eyes. Even in the dim glow of the light filtering through the kitchen window I can see just how beautiful his eyes are to me. "Hugo," I ask, my voice shaking ever so slightly. "Are you asking me to marry you?"

Hugo laughs, reaches up to pull my hands from his face, then plants a warm kiss into each of my palms. "I am doing this all wrong, I know." He kisses the insides of my wrists, sending shivers of delight racing up my arms and down my spine. "Yes," he says, kissing the knuckles of my right hand. "I am asking—" He kisses the knuckles of my left hand. "—you to marry me." He takes both my hands and presses my palms to his chest directly over his heart. "Ranae Niemeyer, my sweet Ranae, will you take this scarred man with my tortured soul and give me wings? Say you'll marry me." He dips his head toward me, and I am more than ready for his kiss, my heart pounding like a kettle drum inside of me.

But he waits. He just looks at me and waits.

"Yes," I manage to rasp out, and then I pull my hands free of his grasp, wrap my arms around his neck, and kiss the man I love with everything in me.

Dani

I AWAKE CHRISTMAS MORNING with a sense of wellbeing like I haven't felt in many years. How is it possible that I've been so blind to how broken things had become in the home I shared with Adam?

I lie in bed, my hands cradling my belly—it seems to grow larger by the minute these days—and consider what lies ahead for us. Adam has made himself scarce this holiday season, and for that, I am grateful. It feels like a reboot of sorts; a clean break from his toxic hold on me, and even though I am not exactly comfortable in my newly alone status, I find that I'm not lonely. This is not like the years I spent as a child, wondering where—and if—I belonged, and who I belonged to. I am surrounded by precious people I love who love me in return.

"You two sure are lucky," I tell my girls. "You have so many people in your lives already. We can't wait to meet you, my wee darlings."

I hear the tea kettle whistle from down the hall, and my bladder is telling me it's time to get out of bed, anyway. I wash my face and brush my teeth, and then pull my long, thick hair up into a messy bun on top of my head. I take an extra minute to study my reflection in the mirror. My cheeks are flushed with anticipation for what the day ahead holds, and the half-moon shadows under my eyes seem to have disappeared. In fact, in my own clinical assessment, I look healthy and vibrant, and it suddenly occurs to me that I haven't suffered from morning sickness in several days. Could it be that I'm one of the fortunate ones for whom the ailment passes after a certain point in the pregnancy? "Thank you," I say, lifting my head heavenward. "Happy birthday, Jesus."

There are an inordinate amount of wrapped presents and gift bags under our tree this morning, and I am not at all surprised to find that the majority of them are for the coming twins. There are expensive Swiss chocolates for Mum from Dad, a new set of high-quality headphones from her to him—he has become an avid audiobook listener in the last couple of years. My mother has gifted me with three sets of luxuriously soft nursing pajamas, and I open a grain and lavender-infused heating pad from my father. I give my parents a new set of gorgeous, yet sturdy, luggage for their upcoming trip to Beira in a few months, and there's the traditional box of goodies from Mum's family in England.

The three of us—and the twins, of course—spend a quiet, relaxing morning together, then Jolene and Pete join us for dinner. My mother, angel that she is, has made Toad-in-the-Hole, something I have been craving this whole pregnancy, and no one makes the dish like my mother. It's not the American version where an egg is fried into the middle of a slice of toast, but the classic English dish of crispy-skinned sausage links baked into a buttery Yorkshire pudding, and served with a rich, brown gravy.

We sit around the table and talk about Christmases past. Jolene's stories are painful to hear at times, but my twin sister is the kind of person who finds good in everyone and in every situation. She always speaks so kindly of the mother who gave birth to us, and I am overwhelmed again with gratitude that the good Lord has reunited us. I am excited for what the future has in store for us and our children as we prepare to bring our babies into the world so close together.

Finally, exhausted and sated with happiness, I head for my room as my parents settle in to watch a movie. I know I will not make it much past the opening credits in the state I'm in.

Just as I'm slipping into a set of my freshly-laundered—Mum, bless her heart, washed them for me today—new sleepwear, my phone buzzes. For a moment, I'm certain it's Adam, and I take a deep, fortifying breath. I have been expecting his call all day.

But it's not my husband, and I find that I'm not disappointed at all when I see Ranae's name on my screen. I snatch up the phone and answer it, then slide my legs under my thick blankets, and settle in for the kind of conversation that all best friends share. It's just like old times, I think to myself,

"This is just like old times," I say to Ranae a few minutes into the phone call. "You in your room out at the farmhouse on Kirkwood Lane, me in my old room here in my parents' house, and us talking for hours about boys and babies and what ifs." I am so happy for her and Hugo, and although I'm not surprised by the man's proposal, there is a bitter-sweetness to it. This will be a new season for all of us, it seems.

Ranae agrees with a chuckle, then regales me with another cute story about Ruby and her new puppy, Blarney. The name they've given him couldn't be better suited; that handsome little pup is quite the charmer.

"Nolan asked about you today," Ranae tells me, and her words jolt me back to attention. I'm drifting a little, I realize, and I push up to a sitting position and take a sip of water from the glass I keep on the table by my bed.

"Don't start that again," I tell her, rolling my eyes the way Ruby does, not caring that Ranae can't see my expression. Surely, she can hear them roll; she *is* a mother, isn't she?

"Hey, you're the one who said this was just like old times," Ranae shoots back. "And if I recall correctly, there were many late-night conversations that started with that exact same statement."

It's true what Ranae says. For the longest time, I had an all-consuming crush on poor Nolan. I'm certain he knew it, too, and he'd ask his sister about me just to get me going. The guy already knew how to string a woman along even back then.

"Fine," I capitulate in good humor. It's Christmas, after all, and a girl can dream, right? "What did he say?" I ask, dredging up my old response from days gone by, and we both giggle like the teenagers we once were.

"I love you, Dani," Ranae says a little later. She can tell I'm falling asleep, I'm certain.

"I love you, Ranae," I say in return.

"You do realize we have to do another podcast at some point, right? It's been months since our last real show."

I sigh and slip back down into bed, my head sinking into my pillow as I close my eyes. "I know. I haven't wanted to ask. Are the emails awful?" I know Ranae has been keeping the podcast afloat with reruns and bloopers and a few short newsy updates.

"It's okay," she assures me. "Folks understand, but I'm running out of back up material, and I hate doing them without you. Maybe we can do a New Year's Eve one. I might even be able to talk about Blimey and his funeral without bawling my eyes out." She sighs, and even in that sound, I can hear echoes of her grief over the loss of her beloved dog.

"I miss him, too," I tell her. "And you know if you cry, I'll cry."

"Hmm," Ranae murmurs. "Maybe we should put that topic off for a later date."

"I can talk about how soon mums and other people can feel singles, twins, and other multiples," I suggest, rubbing my stomach in slow, gentle circles in an effort to quiet the fidgeting babies inside who seem to have gotten a second wind.

Ranae chortles dryly. "Maybe you can tell our listeners how a midwife can go for a whole three months without even knowing she's pregnant."

"Maybe you can tell our listeners that you now do weddings at Fair Haven Cemetery, because that's not creepy at all." It's intended to be a comeback, but of course, Ranae doesn't take it that way.

"Heck, no," she declares. "I'm not telling anyone but our invited guests. Can you imagine the flood of requests we'd get? What kind of people want to get married in a cemetery?" she continues. "Only the freakiest of freaks, I guarantee."

"Touché."

Ranae snorts on the other end of the line. "That's right, my friend. We are the only freaks allowed to get married at my cemetery. And maybe Ruby one day. Many, many, *many* years from now. And you and Nolan, of course."

I snort at her cheekiness, but I don't bother arguing with her. She'll just tease me more about him. Even after all these years, I can admit that I still hold a flame for Ranae's handsome big brother. And the fact that he's still single isn't something I have overlooked. I'm certainly not ready to explore starting a new relationship with anyone any time soon, but Nolan wouldn't be a bad option if the day came when I was ready, and he was still available. I couldn't ask for a better family to marry into, that's for certain.

"We talked to Jordan today, and he's agreed to officiate," she tells me through a great big yawn. I, in turn, yawn, too. "Nolan wants to be ring bearer and unity candle lighter."

I snicker sleepily and ask, "Can I be the flower girl or does Ruby get that honor?"

"Nope," Ranae declares, a note of pride in her voice. "Ruby is going to be Hugo's Best Woman. And you have to be my Best Woman/Matron of Honor. I think Gran should be the flower girl, don't you?"

"I concur," I tell her, smiling at the thought of Gran leading the way down the grassy aisle of the Fair Haven outdoor chapel, tossing redbud petals on front of her from a little white wicker basket. It's so silly it might just work. Nothing about Ranae and her family is conventional, after all, and that's one of the many reasons I love them all so dearly. "When are you planning the big day, again?"

"Hugo is insisting on next week," Ranae says dryly, "but I want to wait for when the redbuds and dogwoods are in bloom. I know you're supposed to squeeze those girls out by mid-April, right?" she asks irreverently, then continues without waiting for my response. "Your folks leave the end of May, so I'm thinking somewhere in between. The first week of May, I think. By then, you'll be all model thin again, and I'll have time to lose a few pounds and shop for a real wedding dress." She sighs dramatically through the phone. "A real wedding dress, Dani. Can you believe it?

"I'm so happy for you," I tell her, stifling yet another yawn.

"And I'm sad for you, but oh, so proud of you," she says, her tone serious, but kind. "You are taking your life back, Dani, and that's a big deal. You're my hero."

"I'm able to do this because I have you," I tell her without reservation. "You, and my parents, a twin sister who I've been missing my whole life. Gran, Handsome Hugo, your parents, that Ruby girl of ours," I continue.

"Don't forget Nolan," she interjects with a smile in her voice.

"I don't have him," I say. This time, I roll my eyes behind my closed lids.

"'But you could if you wanted him."

"Good night, Ranae." My words are starting to run together.

"Think about it," Ranae replies in a sing-song voice. "That's all I'm saying."

"Merry Christmas, Ranae," I manage to get out. "I love you."

"Merry Christmas, Dani. I love you, too." The are the last words I hear before drifting off.

Ranae

JORDAN BEAMS at us from his place under the arching branches of the canopy of dogwood trees at the front of the outdoor chapel at Fair Haven. Four-petaled flowers cover every spare inch of the branches in a dazzling display of white, salmon, and pink. The rows of redbuds on either side of the little chapel have burst into color, too, the deeper raspberry hues adding to the splendor of the day. There has been a lot of rain in the last few weeks, and I worried we wouldn't be able to hold the ceremony out here, but today, the weather has cooperated, even though there is evidence of a storm building on the horizon. The weatherman insists it won't arrive until this evening, and today, I'm hoping he's right. Looking around the clearing now, ablaze in all its late spring glory, I am filled with gratitude and wonder. We couldn't have asked for a more beautiful place in which to commit the rest of our lives to each other.

We have just spoken our vows to each other, Hugo and I, and as Hugo slides a beautiful, simple band of gold onto my finger, a gentle breeze picks up, scattering a shower of blushing redbud and dogwood blossoms over all who have gathered to share this occasion with us.

"I'd call that a blessing from heaven," Jordan declares as he tucks one of the flowers between the pages of his Bible. "Hugo Beckenbauer, you may kiss your bride."

And he does. Wowza, does he ever. Hugo wraps his arms around me, bending me backward, and kisses me so thoroughly and with so much passion that folks start to whoop, catcall, and clap. Someone yells, "Get a room!" - it was Nolan, I have no doubt - and Hugo lets me come up for air.

But he's smiling like a man who just hit the jackpot of all jackpots, and I'm pretty sure the expression on my face mirrors his.

"It is my privilege and honor to present to you Mr. And Mrs. Hugo and Ranae Beckenbauer," Jordan declares, his voice raised to be heard above the rising sound of congratulations.

It suddenly occurs to me that it isn't applause, but thunder rolling across the sky. The clouds that have remained banked in the distance are now on the move, and as my husband—my *husband!*—and I make our way down the aisle, the tiniest of raindrops begin to mist down upon us.

"To the farmhouse!" Gran calls as everyone begins stirring and gathering their things. There is a mad dash of folks in all their finery trailing Gran as she leads the way over the little foot bridge and across the back yard to the house that I have called home since before Ruby was born. More than eighteen years now.

Hugo and I fall behind the group as I try to gather up my wedding dress, lest I trip over it. Hugo peels off his jacket and holds it aloft over my head, and I press my body against his and lift my face so he can kiss me again. When the rain begins in earnest, we break apart with a happy laugh and hurry, hand in hand, after our guests.

"It's about time," Dani calls out as we rush up the steps of the porch with its now-dripping wedding decorations and twinkle lights. We didn't work too hard on it—we'd seen the forecast—but we'd optimistically hung flower garlands and paper lanterns anyway. My friend is standing just inside the back door, holding it open for us, and the moment we're inside, she throws her arms around me and hugs me tightly.

"You're going to get soaked!" I tell her, making a half-hearted attempt to push away. She just hugs me tighter, so I give in and squeeze her back... and then she makes a funny little squeak of surprise and releases me abruptly.

Dani's water has just broken, and she is, indeed, suddenly soaked.

"Did I—?" I gasp, bringing my hands up to cover my mouth in shock. "Oh, Dani, I'm so sorry!"

"No, no," Dani says with a slightly hysterical chuckle. "That wasn't from your hug. I've been feeling a little off all day."

"Why didn't you say anything?" I practically wailed.

"Hush, Ranae," she chided. "It's fine. I wasn't going to ruin your wedding." Then she makes that odd laugh again. "It appears I'm going to ruin your reception, instead."

Without warning, her contractions begin hard and fast, and she is gripping my hands so fiercely, I let out my own little squeak. "Help!" I yell over my shoulder, but Hugo is already stepping into Dani's personal space. Before I can explain what's happening, she's latched her arms around his neck, pressing her forehead into his chest, and Hugo is all but holding her up.

And then, Fran is there, and I step back, relieved that someone who knows exactly what they're doing is taking over.

"As soon as the contraction lets up, we'll get you upstairs, okay, darling?" Dani's mother says, her voice calm and soothing, her touch gentle as she cups her daughter's cheek, their eyes locked in silent communication.

Hugo and a rather wide-eyed Nolan flank Dani as they help her up the stairs to her room. Either one of them could probably have swept her off her feet and carried her up, but I have a feeling Fran would have turned into a Mama Bear if they'd tried. Some things just work better in movies and romance novels

I am just about to follow after them when Fran says, "Will you call Tracy, Ranae?" I nod and hurry to the kitchen to grab my cell phone from the charger where I plugged it in this morning.

"Mom?" It's Ruby, her hand on my arm, staying me before I can get the screen unlocked. "Can I—should I—?" Her eyes are on the group making their way up the stairs, and I know what she's asking.

"Go on up, sweetie," I tell her. Dani has made it abundantly clear that Ruby is welcome at the birth. "But if Fran or Dani asks you to step out, just be ready to do so, okay?"

My daughter, looking a little pale, but determined, hurries up after them, and I am relieved to see Fran reach for her hand and give her a warm smile.

I have Dani's midwife on speed dial, but when she doesn't pick up, I call Gail, who tells me that Tracy is out on another birth. "I believe the baby has already been born, though, so she should be in touch shortly. I'll keep trying her myself," Gail promises. "She'll be there the moment she can get away." She offers to come over herself, and I agree to the suggestion. I know Dani will appreciate her favorite assistant's grounding presence. I insist that Gail doesn't need to bring anything; now that Dani is living here at the farmhouse with us, all her birthing supplies are here on hand in the storage closet in the garage.

When I race up the stairs, my damp wedding dress hoisted high, Hugo and Nolan are just exiting the bedroom, both of their expressions a little shell-shocked. I have to bite back a smile, but I kiss my new husband, thank my brother, then abandon them both and slip into Dani's room.

Fran just smiles serenely when I tell her Tracy is currently unavailable. She assures me that between all of us women, we've got matters well in hand. I know she really means that she—and her husband, if she needs him—has matters well in hand, and my heart contracts at the look of sheer relief on Dani's face when her mother tells her she is going to help Dani deliver the twins into the world.

"Oh, thank you, thank you," Dani pants as another contraction takes hold of her body. She stands at the foot of the bed, hunched forward, both hands gripping one of the posts of the footboard so tightly that her knuckles are white. These babies, it seems, are determined to come quickly.

Nolan, via text, informs me that he has taken it upon himself to call Adam, and that the man is on his way. A surge of guilt flashes quickly—and then just as quickly passes—through me for not thinking of calling Adam, myself. I thank my brother, and then grin in appreciation at his response.

Do you need me to meet him out front and explain to him how he is to behave while in this house?

I thank him again for being such a good big brother—although, part of me wonders if that's not all that is at stake here. I've seen the way he looks at Dani these days. But I assure him that Adam has been on his best behavior lately, and I don't think that will be necessary.

In the months since Dani moved into the farmhouse, she and Adam have started to work on defining their new relationship. They're no longer married; Adam filed a petition for divorce the first week of January, one that seemed remarkably fair in Dani's eyes. And because there was no reason to contest it, the divorce was final the requisite sixty days later. They're not really friends, either, but they are civil with each other, which is more than I would be if I were in Dani's shoes. Adam has insisted that he wants to participate in parenting the girls, and he has shown up for most of her prenatal visits since the beginning of the year. I know Dani is prepared for that to change, though. Her ex-husband has, indeed, moved into his little lake house with his girlfriend, a woman with whom he's apparently been having an affair for quite some time. I have not met her, but I saw her in the car with him in the Breathe parking lot after one of Dani's appointments, and she's the same woman he was with at Mancini's.

Adam, of course, never goes to Mancini's anymore, now that he's met Jolene and Pete. Nor has he questioned the twins' parentage since then, either. *The blackguard*, as Gran would say. Nolan has other, not nearly so dashing, names he uses when referencing the man.

I hurry into my bedroom and change out of my lovely sodden dress, tossing it haphazardly over the foot of my bed. I scramble into a pair of yoga pants and a t-shirt, the same kind of outfit Dani wears to one of her clients' births. I wonder if I should offer Fran something to wear, but when I slip back into Dani's room, I find her mother has already changed into a pair of colorful unicorn scrubs that I'm certain came out of Dani's closet. Fran, who is several inches shorter than her daughter, has cuffed the scrubs pant legs and is now barefoot, her shoulder-length brown hair pulled back in a low ponytail, and I smile when I see her expression, both fierce and cool as a cucumber at the same time. It's one I've seen on Dani's face more times than I can count.

I circle the bed to where Ruby stands, her back to the wall, her eyes wide as she watches the scene unfold. Dani, now dressed in nothing but a voluminous knit bathrobe that's open at the front, is pacing and panting, and her mother sits on the edge of the bed, keeping track of the length of contractions on the watch she wears on her wrist. I can read the trepidation in my daughter's eyes, but her chin is up, and her shoulders are squared; my girl is determined to stay the course and see these two little ones into the world right along with the rest of us. I put my arm around her shoulders and give her a fortifying hug. "You are witnessing a miracle today, sweet girl. There will be drama, but you can handle it."

Ruby nods, but when there's a knock on the door and Gran enters, Ruby practically sags with relief. "I'll be okay with Gran," she says, squeezing my hand quickly, then letting go. "You don't have to worry about me now. Dani might need you."

I am momentarily overcome by love for my darling, thoughtful daughter. I kiss her temple, and over her head, exchange a quick glance with Gran who is making her way to us, her arms already outstretched toward Ruby.

"Sarah kicked me out of my own kitchen," Gran declares in a gruff voice, but her eyes are lit up with excitement. "She said she'll take care of the menfolk downstairs while we manage our Dani-girl up here." She pats my cheek, then says to Ruby as she leads her away, "You come from good stock, lassie; did you know that?" To me, she says in a hushed voice, "Your mother and I got everything cleaned up at the back door, just in case Dani asks." She knows my friend well; Dani will certainly want to know that little detail at some point.

Dani's room is the largest one on the second floor. It has its own bathroom, and a lovely little alcove where there is a window seat, a comfortable armchair, and a gliding rocker with a matching footstool. The space is perfect for late night conversations and early morning contemplations. Perfect, also, for middle-of-the-night nursing, cuddles, and soothing crying babies. It comes in handy now as the bedroom fills with the women in Dani's life. Gran makes herself comfortable in the armchair, while Ruby perches on the window seat, and although they are engaged in a quiet conversation, it's obvious they are both focused on what is happening across the room with Dani.

Another soft knock on the door announces Jolene. She enters the room quietly, her own tiny baby, not yet a month old, cradled in one arm, and she stops just inside the room. Dani is now bent over her bed, her forehead resting on her forearms, her hands clasped together as if in prayer. She moans in long slow inhales and exhales, her hips rocking side to side as she powers through another intense contraction. They are coming hard and fast, with barely any reprieve between them.

As soon as this one lets up, though, Jolene hurries over to Dani, a look of love and sympathy on her face. She, of all people in this room, can grasp the most acutely what Dani is experiencing right now, having just given birth herself a few short weeks ago. Jolene doesn't hug Dani or touch her, except to hold Baby Ophelia Joy out so my friend can nuzzle the newborn's head.

"I love you, Auntie," Jolene says in a soft, baby voice. She lifts Ophelia's hand in a tightly fisted wave. "I can't wait to meet my cousins. Go, Auntie! Go, Auntie! Go!"

The silly and oh, so endearing exchange makes my heart ache the tiniest bit, but I am not threatened at all by the presence of this woman in my best friend's life. Jolene seems to have found a place of her own in our world, a spot that has apparently been kept empty and reserved all these years just for her.

Jolene hands off Ophelia to a giddy, cooing Gran, then settles into the rocker and reaches out to squeeze Ruby's knee affectionately.

My mother pokes her head in the door, but when she sees how calm everyone is—even Dani seems uncannily serene at that moment—she excuses herself to go back downstairs to keep Sarah company.

I stay close by where I can be at the ready for whatever need arises. I push my fists into Dani's back when the pressure there becomes unbearable. I sacrifice my hands when she isn't close enough to anything inanimate to grab on to. I wipe the sweat from her face with a cool cloth and send Ruby running downstairs for ice when Dani insists she wants ice water to drink. I braid her thick blonde hair when it falls free of the elegant chignon she wore to my wedding. I am just preparing to lay out all the birthing kit supplies when Gail arrives, and I am relieved to hand over the task to her so I can help Fran support Dani as she paces through yet another contraction.

Adam finally makes an appearance, and for the next two hours, it's all of us womenfolk and him, standing guard over our beloved Dani as she performs the hardest physical labor any woman will go through.

Sasha Grace arrives on the scene first, her eyes squeezed shut, red-faced and open-mouthed, ready to let loose with an enraged wail the moment her airway is clear. Not quite two minutes later, her sister, Sharon Rose joins her, silent, but big-eyed, her tiny, perfect lips already moving in a sucking motion. She latches on almost immediately after being laid at Dani's breast. Sasha, on the other hand, is apparently too angry at the world to realize that the solution to all her problems is right in front of her.

Finally, Fran picks up Sasha and turns to Adam. "Take off your shirt," she commands in a voice that is surprisingly brusque. It seems I might not be the only one reticent to forgive the man for his ongoing and unapologetic indiscretions.

Adam balks and takes a step back, then for some reason, he looks to me, desperation all over his face. "Unbutton your shirt, Adam," I tell him, ready to reach over and rip it open for him if he doesn't comply. "Skin on skin, remember? It might help calm her down if you hold her against you."

"You—I'm not sure if I—" Adam stammers, reaching for a bedpost to steady himself.

Apparently, this has all been a little much for the self-centered man, and he's looking a bit green around the gills. "You'd better sit down, Adam." I point at the floor next to the bed. "Before you fall down."

"Here," Fran says, handing the squirming Sasha to me. "I trust you know what to do." She doesn't spare Adam another glance before turning back to Dani who is still working on delivering the afterbirth.

Without a moment's hesitation, I slide Sasha up under my tank top and begin to coo softly to her in the same way I've done to Dani's belly since we discovered she was pregnant. "Hello, little angel pie," I tell her, swaying back and forth, cupping her bobbing head gently, glad I'd thrown on a comfortable, knit sports bra and not one of my armor-like underwires. "It's Auntie Nae. Hello, my sweet baby. You're okay. We're okay. Your mommy and daddy love you and so do I." It just about kills me to include Adam in the sentiment, but I have a daughter who grew up with a daddy-shaped hole in her heart, and I won't stand between these little girls and theirs.

Jolene draws close and peers over my shoulder down my neckline at the tiny baby under my shirt. "It's Auntie Joley," she says in the same voice she uses to talk to Ophelia. She pats the front of her own blouse where wet patches are beginning to show. "I've gone too long without nursing," she says with a grimace and a laugh. "You sound so much like Ophelia that my milk just let down."

Ruby and Gran come over, too, both of them wiping happy tears from their faces. Gran hands off a now fussing Ophelia to her mommy, who returns to the rocker in the alcove to feed her own baby. Sasha is beginning to settle, although her little head is now bobbing in vain against my cleavage in search of a food source. It's been a long time since I've cradled a rooting infant, so I am surprised at the way my body reacts, at the tingle of sensation in my breasts. It's only a muscle memory, I know, but it conjures up all kinds of thoughts that I haven't allowed myself to entertain... well, until today.

I glance over at Adam. He's now sitting on the edge of the bed beside Dani, who is propped against a pillow, cradling the still-nursing Sharon. "Are you ready to take her, Adam?" I ask, feeling a little guilty that I am still holding Sasha when he should be.

"I—I don't—" he starts and stops again, but Dani reaches over and puts her hand on his thigh.

Dani says, "You've got this, Adam." She's the most gracious woman I know.

Adam nods, his mouth set in a grim line, and begins to unbutton his shirt as I bring him his child. Then I duck out of the room to let those awaiting downstairs know that all is well, and to send Michael up to meet his new granddaughters.

Tracy has just appeared on the landing at the top of the stairs, looking more than a little harried, so I pause to assure her that all is well. The birth Tracy was attending was long and arduous, and, according to Gail, Tracy is going on almost twenty-four hours without sleep. She's visibly relieved, and I can hardly blame her. She'll be able to wrap things up with Fran and Gail's assistance, then call it a day, knowing her patient is in good hands.

The room has gone quiet at my appearance, and over the rail of the landing, I say, "Michael? Would you like to come meet your granddaughters?" Then I descend the stairs like the prom queen I never was, pausing briefly to congratulate and hug Michael as he passes by.

My gaze is fixed on one person the rest of the way down. My husband—will I ever get tired of calling him that?—watches me cross the room toward him, his eyes shining with love for me. I rush into his arms and he holds me close, letting me sag against him.

"This wedding day of ours has turned out a whole lot differently than we'd planned, hasn't it?" he asks after a few moments, his mouth close to my ear. "How are you holding up, my love?"

I have so much I want to tell him, but the house is too full, and really, so is my heart right now. "I'm fine," I finally acknowledge, lifting my head a little to peer over his shoulder at the array of potluck dishes our friends and family have brought to contribute to our celebration.

But Hugo knows me too well. With a quick glance around the room, he slides his arm around my waist and leads me through the kitchen toward the side door that opens into the garage. He shuts the door behind us, and we are instantly enveloped in cool darkness and quiet.

"Now, my beautiful wife," he begins, drawing me back into his arms.

"Oh, I like the way that sounds," I murmur, pressing against him, a sudden and intense ache for him thrumming through my body, making me tremble with need. "And I like the way this feels."

Hugo's soft laugh rumbles in his chest beneath my ear, and I think I will never get my fill of that sound. "Tell me true. How are you holding up?" he asks again.

I tip my head back to look up at him, and I can just barely make out his features in the dim light that's coming through the single window at the far end of the garage. He is gazing down at me, and I think perhaps they mirror the telltale heat he must surely see in mine. "I really am doing just fine," I insist. "This day has turned out even better than I could possibly have imagined." I rise up on my toes and press a soft kiss just under his smooth jaw. "But now, my handsome husband," I say, then I move to kiss the hollow at the base of his throat. Hugo lifts his chin to give me better access and makes a noise low in his throat.

"I like the way that sounds," he says with a smile in his voice, repeating my words back to me. "And the way that feels."

I pull back just enough to speak, but my breath still feathers warmly across his skin. "Now, I think I'd like to talk—"

"Talk?" Hugo interrupts, his voice turning gruff. "You want to talk?"

I smile, my lips lingering against that spot just below his ear where I can feel his pulse racing. "To talk about..." I murmur, then nip lightly at his earlobe. A shudder ripples through him, and, rather pleased with myself and the way he is responding, I whisper boldly, "About us having a baby."

Hugo goes completely still in my embrace.

We have talked about this in the months leading up to this day, but I have been hesitant to commit to the idea of starting over, especially now that Ruby is grown. She turns eighteen this year, and in only a few more months, she'll be starting college. Although I haven't said yes to more children, I haven't given a definitive no, either. I know Hugo's love for me and his desire to marry me is not contingent on whether or not I'll have his baby. But I also know that Hugo has always longed for children.

My eyes are quickly growing accustomed to the dark, and I press my fingertip into the cleft that marks Hugo's chin, tipping his face down so I can reach his lips. I shiver in response to the way his mouth moves against mine. "Think we can get started on that sometime soon?" I ask in a husky purr.

Hugo clears his throat, but he sounds a bit strangled. "Get started talking? Or..." He pauses for effect, then says, "Or get started trying?"

"Talk?" I ask, repeating his words back to him. "You want to talk?"

❧ ☙

Ranae and Dani experience some pretty big changes during this season of their lives, but their friendship proves true, and they both discover their own *hope*-fully ever afters.

Speaking of hopefully ever after, have you met Willow Goodhope in *Elderberry Croft: Seasons of the Heart*?

If you liked *Matters of Life and Death,* then I think you'll fall in love with Willow and her quirky neighbors at the Coach House Trailer Park.

~ ~ ~

On a crisp January breeze, a new girl sweeps into the neighborhood, breathing life – and perhaps a hint of magic – into the cottage she christens Elderberry Croft.

The folks at The Coach House Trailer Park can't help but fall under Willow Goodhope's spell as she charms them with her vibrant nature, her elderberry gifts, and her outrageous laughter. But there's something about her, a secret sadness that hovers at the corners of her irrepressible smile, and it has everyone talking. What brings the mysterious young woman to this dead-end place? From what—or whom—is she hiding?

Doc catches her burning letters in her fire pit, and Myra swears Willow drinks alone out in the moonlight.

Joe glimpses the whispering shadows clinging to the girl's coattails, and Patti doesn't miss the way her husband watches the young beauty.

Eddie and Donny compete to see who can make her smile first... even though both figure she prefers her men with good jobs, good homes, and good teeth.

Kathy is doing everyone a favor by keeping a close eye on the wild child next door. Through her binoculars.

And what she sees doesn't sit well with any of them.

~ ~ ~

"I meant to savor *Elderberry Croft* - I really did - but I couldn't help myself and gobbled up each installment in one sitting. Brimming with beautifully flawed characters who will make you sigh, smile, laugh, cry, and hurt over their very real struggles, *Elderberry Croft* is a must read."
Tamara Leigh, The Kitchen Novelist, USA Today Bestselling Author

Pick up **Elderberry Croft: Seasons of the Heart** today!
(Keep reading for an excerpt...)

A Note from the Author

Elderberry Croft Excerpt

JANUARY BREEZE
Chapter 1

A NEW NEIGHBOR.

Kathy expected her at any minute now. She coughed into her elbow as she peered through the narrow opening of her kitchen curtains at the empty cottage across the driveway. It wasn't much more than a shack, really. The roof needed new shingles, the ancient wooden siding was chipped and peeling where the sun beat down mercilessly upon it, and the roots of a massive eucalyptus tree slowly churned up the river-rock patio. Screens were missing from a few of the windows, and the green front door hung at an angle to accommodate the frame that had been put in with a blatant disregard for plumb lines. Its one redeeming quality, a charming little creek that danced along the edge of the patio and on through The Coach House Trailer Park, seemed slightly incongruous with the rest of the ramshackle structure.

The inside, according to Myra, wasn't in any better condition. She'd stopped by to visit the day before after doing a thorough cleaning of the place in preparation for the new tenant.

"Filthy, Kathy! Horrible! And the carpet! Aiee!" Myra often spoke in exclamation marks, bobbing her head for added emphasis, her dark, chin-length hair doing the cha-cha around her face. "It's disgusting! When I told Eddie that it needed to be replaced, he said they won't do it because it's less than five years old. But that carpet looks more like fifty-five to me! And the shower!" She went on and on until Kathy interrupted her with a glass of her favorite boxed wine, kept chilled in the refrigerator for just such visits.

"Why are you so worked up? This new one will come and go just like all the others."

Myra took a long sip. "I know, I know. But this one," she shrugged her bony shoulders. "I *want* her to like it." The sweet-tart drink puckered her lips. "I want her to like *us*."

"So? What's new? You want everyone to like us."

Myra left a few minutes later, her basket of dirty rags and cleaning supplies hoisted on one scrawny hip. "Don't let her catch you spying on her tomorrow, Kathy-la. I mean it!"

A few minutes before ten, a truck pulled in, one of those little Toyota pickups that simply refused to die, its once royal blue paint faded and oxidized by the California sunshine. The woman driving wore a pair of over-sized, blue tinted sunglasses, and her mahogany-red hair threatened to escape a clip at the crown of her head.

"Young," Kathy quickly labeled her. "Probably between boyfriends. I give her six months, tops."

Her eyebrows lifted with surprise as the woman maneuvered into the parking space in front of the ramshackle house, giving her a full view of the contents of the truck bed. Plants. No mattresses, no dressers or coffee tables, no boxes covered in packing tape and black marker. Plants in huge clay pots and delicate ceramic bowls, hanging baskets and galvanized steel buckets. Verdant bundles wrapped in twine and burlap to protect them from the brilliant January cold. She shot a guilty glance over her shoulder at the one scraggly philodendron on a plant stand in the corner of the room. Between her irregular watering schedule and the fact that the dogs couldn't resist chewing on the few brave tendrils that managed to creep over the lip of the yellow pot, it was a miracle the plant was still alive. Kathy loved plants, but she spent too much of her time and limited resources in futile efforts to add them to her life.

She turned back to the window just as the woman threw open her driver's side door and started talking, gesturing, and nodding effusively. It took a moment, but it finally dawned on Kathy that she was conversing with the plants themselves, making her way around the truck bed, cooing and smiling, fondling leaves and petals, cheering, and clapping her hands.

Kathy muttered to the old and rather obese Labrador that wandered out from under the table. "She's talking to her plants. Like they understand her or something." She twirled a finger around in circles at her temple and rolled her eyes. "I just don't get some people, Heidi." The dog responded by licking her hand and flopping its tail against her legs.

She turned away from the window and coughed deeply again. She hated the way her lungs felt, as though they were being shaken around inside her chest like a baby's toy rattle, but the cough was something she'd earned after forty years of smoking, and she'd learned to live with it. When she caught the seasonal cold, however, it always frightened her a little. Sometimes she'd cough so long and hard, she feared her insides would fly out of her mouth.

She made her way through the obstacle course of her kitchen to the sofa and dropped into one corner, strategically situating herself so she could monitor both her favorite morning soap opera and the activity outside the window. Heidi clambered up onto the cushion next to her. "That's all we need, huh, little girl? Another crazy neighbor." She sighed loudly and leaned her head back on the cushions behind her. Heidi blinked once and sighed, too.

She woke with a start, her open-mouth snoring loud inside her stuffed-up head and peered up at the clock again. She'd been asleep for over an hour! Heidi stood at the front door, scratching to get out, and fat little Trixie waddled out from the tiny bedroom to see what was going on, her stubby tail wiggling frantically. Bella Basset let out one deep woof from where she lounged on the end of Kathy's bed. Kathy sat up, massaged a crick in her neck, then turned to check on her new neighbor.

She could hardly believe the transformation that had taken place outside her window while she napped. She forgot all semblance of subterfuge and pulled the sheer panel back to see more clearly. Squinting, her eyes bleary from sleep, she struggled to comprehend what she was seeing. She turned and snatched up the set of binoculars off the end table beside the sofa. They still technically belonged to her ex-husband, but he'd never been back to claim them, so she put them to good use keeping an eye on the comings and goings in the park. It was rather convenient that the park's laundry station was practically outside her front door.

On the stoop of Space #12 sat a huge terracotta pot overflowing with fluttering yellow honeysuckle—in flower!—that stretched its tendrils up to the roof and along the low eaves. It formed a natural archway leading to the front entry of the house, and it looked like it'd been growing there for years. Delicate clusters of pink and purple flowers fire-worked out of a wire basket hanging from a decorative hook mounted on the wall below the porch light, softening the askew lines of the door frame. She thought they might be nemesia, or some kind of salvia, but she wasn't certain.

On the patio, in huge pots, red, pink, and white petals hovering over dark foliage had to be cyclamen. Kathy recognized them because they grew right outside her own picket fence, but the only time she'd seen them look so healthy and bloom so enthusiastically was on the shelf at the home improvement center where the plants were all on steroids.

Troughs of bushy geraniums were just on the brink of flowering, what looked like a huge camellia was in full bloom, and were those yellow blossoms African daisies? In January? An old-fashioned hydrangea and a spike-leafed aloe vera odd-coupled in a pedestal urn that was dark with the patina of age and countless waterings. Begonias, blue forget-me-nots, and frilly ferns were tucked into shady spots all over the patio and nestled among the roots of a mulberry tree that spread its branches over the little creek.

In the flowerbed beneath the front window, thick-leaved jades—standard issue in most rentals in Southern California—showed off the last of their winter blooms. Some quick and aggressive weed excavation had uncovered the two rose bushes that had somehow survived over the years and exposed a few saucy snapdragons and a blanket of alyssum the weeds hadn't choked out completely. The roses had been hacked back to sticks, and Kathy wondered if the woman realized it was way late in the season for trimming roses.

Wind-chimes and friar bells hung in the rafters of the porch, their various tones creating harmonies in the breeze, while sun-catchers sent rainbows of light dancing across the tiny yard. She looked over at the clock on the wall for the third time, feeling a little like Rip Van Winkle waking up from his hundred-year snooze.

"How the hula did she do that?"

Chapter 2

~ ~ ~

Heidi and Trixie were snuffling and scratching with renewed fervor, and Kathy realized she had a perfect excuse to spy on her neighbor more openly. "Oh, all right. Let's all go outside for some fresh air."

She pushed open the front door and was nearly bowled over as the dogs scampered past her and out into the yard. "Hey!" she cried out, unprepared for their exuberance.

"Are you all right?"

Kathy's eyes flew to the gate, even more unprepared for the woman who stood there. "Oh! Oh my! You scared me!" She pressed a hand to her chest and took a few deep breaths. "I have a heart condition, you know." Her words came out more gruffly than she'd intended.

"Oh dear. I did *not* know that. I didn't mean to startle you. I just came by to introduce myself; I'm your new neighbor." By now, the dogs were snuffling and pawing at the gate, trying to get out. Heidi was actually up on her two back legs, her front paws resting on the crossbar as she leaned her head into the woman's stroking hand. "Hello, pretty girl. You are a lovely old dear; yes, you are."

Kathy frowned. "Careful. They don't really do well with strangers."

"Of course, they don't. Neither do I. I mean, strangers are so strange, right?" She gave Heidi one last scratch behind the ear, reached over and ruffled Trixie's mop, then held aloft the rectangular twig basket she carried. "This is for you. And your pups, of course."

"Oh. Well. Thank you." Kathy fumbled for words. Oh dear. What would Lucy say when she saw treats for everyone but her?

"And I don't want to forget this." The woman withdrew a small drawstring pouch from her pocket and tucked it inside the basket. "This is for your kitty. She came by earlier and fell in love with it. When she wandered this way, I guessed you were her person."

Kathy made her way down the two steps and across the small yard to the gate. She thought she smelled vanilla and cinnamon, and her mouth began to water in anticipation. The image of a large kitchen, a small boy, and the floury aftermath of several batches of Christmas cookies flashed through her mind, and she smiled at the memory. She would have to call her Makani tonight. She wondered if he was eating well.

Her neighbor thrust an open hand over the gate. "I'm Willow. Willow Goodhope."

Of course, Kathy thought as she took the proffered hand. *Even her name sounds organic.*

"I'm Kathy. And welcome. I was going to come over and see if you need anything. Or any help. I mean, moving can be so much work. But… well, I…." She was flustered again, at a loss for polite excuses.

"Work? On a day like this?" Willow waved a hand dismissively. "Oh no. This is a day for doing absolutely nothing. In fact, I'm going to go put the teakettle on, curl up with a good book, and revel in my new home. I just had to make sure the plants were settled in first. But the rest? Well, moving in will take care of itself, you know?"

"How *did* you do all of that so quickly?" Kathy jutted her chin in the direction of the cottage. "It just doesn't seem possible." She didn't intend to sound rude, but she really wanted to know. She loved her little yard and put hours into it every week, but she'd lived here for over ten years now, and she couldn't remember it ever looking so lovely. Somehow, this Willow Goodhope had turned the preexisting eyesore across the way into a greeting card. In little more than an hour!

"The plants? I know! They just settled right in, as though they belong here." Willow held up her hands, palms facing Kathy. "God's incredibly creative, isn't he? And he gave me green thumbs, so I get to participate." She beamed, as if that explained everything.

The hands she held out for examination were roughened and callused, dirt under the nails. It seemed inconsistent with everything else about her, but it made perfect sense, really. The plants didn't climb into those pots on their own.

"Well, thank you again and… welcome. Again." Kathy patted the basket, then snapped her fingers at the dogs. "You girls stop sniffing the neighbor! Go on inside, now. Go!" She looked up, a little embarrassed by their exuberance. "I'm really sorry. They usually just bark at people, and then run away."

"It's fine. They're just curious. Yes, you are, aren't you?" Willow reached down, gave Heidi's ear a gentle tug, and turned to leave. "Don't hesitate to visit, Kathy. I mean it. Anytime, okay?" She fluttered her fingers in the air and headed back across the gravel drive to her own place.

Kathy stood for a few moments longer, watching the woman's long, full skirt sweeping along the ground behind her. *What an odd cookie,* she thought. Remembering the promise of cinnamon sugar cookies, she glanced down at the basket in her arms. She lifted the cloth that covered the contents and studied them, perplexed and delighted at the same time. The Christmas cookie aroma was gone.

Nestled in the folds of a currant-colored dishtowel was a set of two oriental-style mugs with no handles. Inside one was a small honey bear bottle; in the other, two old-fashioned tea balls on chains. A muslin drawstring bag was stuffed with something crinkly and lumpy, and a stitched-on label gave a description of the contents in pretty, scrolled handwriting.

Elderberries, flowers, ginger, and lemon zest,
Add a dollop of honey and you'll be sure to get some rest.
Colds, coughs, fevers, and malaise,
They'll all flee, and the flu will fly away.

The bag for Lucy held a stuffed crocheted ball on the end of an elastic string. Kathy could smell the pungent catnip, and something else earthy and pleasant, and she had no doubt Lucy would, indeed, appreciate the toy.

The basket also contained a wax-paper packet of peanut-butter cookies, the telltale crisscross pattern on top of each one. She lifted them to her nose and wondered if perhaps she'd been mistaken—maybe it was these she'd smelled earlier and not cinnamon sugar cookies after all. She tore open an end of the package, pulled a cookie out, and took a bite. Not very sweet. In fact, they were almost a little salty, but the peanut butter flavor was rich and robust, making up for any other minor defects the crunchy cookies might have. They'd probably taste better dunked in cold milk.

She lifted the edge of the towel, searching for the promised pup treats, but the basket was empty.

"Oh!" she exclaimed, realizing her mistake. "These must be for you!" Her dogs still sat pining at the gate for the neighbor who had disappeared inside her little home. Kathy, on the other hand, was greatly relieved that Willow hadn't been there to witness her *faux pas*.

"Come on, you naughty kids. Look!" She waved a cookie above their heads and laughed out loud. "I have treats for you. And I have to admit, they're the best doggy treats I've ever tasted!"

~ ~ ~

Finish reading **Elderberry Croft** today!

www.ingramcontent.com/pod-product-compliance
Lightning Source LLC
Chambersburg PA
CBHW010839190726
48286CB00012BA/2911